Whitman's Brains

a novel

by conrad cody

Walt Whitman was an actual poet who was born on the 31st of May 1819 at West Hills, Long Island, USA and apparently died on the 26th of March 1892 at Camden, New Jersey, USA.

one

"To hell with facts, we need stories"

Ken Kesey

A bus, filled with the ordinary composite of passengers was stopped for a mid-afternoon meal break where it always stopped. A variety of mumbling voices were in the air as most of the riders made their way outside to stretch their legs, use the bathroom or get a snack from the vending machines inside.

Many were commenting on what most of them had seen on the highway a few moments back. Some thought it just been discarded debris, perhaps some fruit or meat while others were more macabre in their ideas.

Nevertheless, it had caused consternation for many of the riders.

I observed how hundreds of miles and perhaps dozens of hours had left most of the passenger on the bus dazed, tired or in some sort of inner reflection. The sighting had inspired me to scan my surroundings more acutely. The sudden chattering amongst the passengers signaled that most of them had awakened from their reveries. Like me, we were all going east, myself to continue to try and write in Montréal, but first I had to find a job.

Frank Lee stepped toward the opened door of the combination bus depot and coffee shop near Kingston along the 401. He had a jazzy beat in his head from a night spent at a local motel aptly named the Roadway Inn. Once a week they had a crooner who shimmied through a songbook of Top 40 hits of the past decades without little variation or personality.

Frank had imagined the music to be that of Charlie Parker or Billie Holliday, like his father had listened to years before. But his revelry had been interrupted by a tall man in jeans and a t-shirt accounting that he wanted to go home and that the lounge was closed. Frank had gathered his sparse belongings and had headed over to the bus depot which was just a five-minute walk away to await the 3AM bus to Montreal.

Now he entered the almost empty coffee shop. Inside he saw two glassy eyed twentysomethings, looking weary but still absorbed in smartphone communication of some sort. And he saw a middle-aged woman with three suitcases at her feet, eyes closed but well dressed in an orange pant suit.

He went to the counter and ordered a coffee, double/double. He sat down at a four-seat table by himself and drifted back into a world in which people only improvised life. A world where order was the exception. For him it was not chaos, especially at 3AM where activity and responsibility seemed a universe away.

Dark rings had formed around his eyes in the last weeks of travelling from one end of the country to the other. He was reviewing his travels, not as a journey log, but as a collective of emotions and directions to the center of liberation. Liberation from the spinning swirls of several office jobs, of several agonizing restaurant jobs and unfulfilled tentative attempts at romance with women and men and even a jab at marriage. But nothing had left him with any lasting happiness. He had let go of any family years ago to find a new land without attachment, like some little silly Buddha figure.

Now his thoughts went back to a bar that he had spent two days in Calgary almost a week back, sleeping in a nearby park when it had closed. He recalled the mix of country music and loud talk that had enveloped him as his mind listened to the words of tragedy and mishap that had befell the protagonist of the tunes.

He had put himself into the stories but kept his tears inside. It had been during the Stampede and the city was in a carefree mood. He thought of his life as being without restraint. This he had pondered since he had been about 11 years old. Why had the forces of the universe imposed the need for restraint on the human species? Of course, we might have done it ourselves. But why? The answer that came seemed to be that life was just push and pull. Ebb and flow. Lightness and darkness. He had felt held up inside, like there was a dam built into his internals. He had thrown off things in his life, but still he felt an unease with the elements. Maybe he needed a new challenge, a new horizon. A new loyalty.

Frank asked himself these questions with his 33-year-old brain as he sipped his still warm coffee. The din of the lights in the coffee shop provided a harmonic bed for his routine foray into the mystic.

Now he felt like he was without direction, only contradicted by his ticket to Montreal that he had bought in Calgary. He thought of the man he had met in Calgary after the two days in The Wildrose Saloon, who had proposed a liaison with a couple local women whom he had known from his days riding in the rodeo. Frank had asked him if he thought that rodeos were a dying pursuit in the 21st century. The young dude had answered "probably" and had returned to the topic of women.

Frank had stopped listening, except when the man pulled out a stack of a dozen fifty-dollar bills and had handed them to Frank.

"Let's party" he had proposed.

Frank took the money with reluctance hoping that it would lead to some discovery. Frank had not really been interested in women that evening. At least not for what this dude was interested in doing with them. He had long ago discovered that the pursuit of "fun" always came at some price. Usually that meant losing out somewhere in the larger picture. Someone had once advised him to stop and smell the roses once and a while. Maybe a stop was in order somewhere, but he had not found that resting place yet. As he sat in the coffee shop, he thought that any noble pursuit that he may have had was to be designated for filing under Random Experience. This brought a peaceful moment to Frank's mind.

He had abandoned the cowboy, kept the leftover money, taken a cab to the local bus terminal and had headed east.

Was that cowboy intent on giving him a message to live it up or had the universe just once again made it cleat that it was nothing but an irrational series of intersections consisting of actions and non-actions to each other. Frank wished he had answers, yet he was beginning to believe that those answers were not as significant as he had once thought.

He had felt sorry for leaving the cowboy behind, but he had justified it by saying that he had never asked anything of him and had simply gone along with the cowboy's suggestions. It would be forgotten, but as Frank had learned no event or meeting ever lost its significance. Even being recruited by a cowboy in a bar.

Thinking of him made Frank feel better. He pondered where the cowboy may be now. He thought of the women. He tried not to feel regret.

When Frank had gotten on the Greyhound bus in Calgary he had only thought of the triviality of the situation, but now at 3AM in this almost barren bus depot over a thousand kilometres away it had taken on a new significance. A symbol of his fear of the unknown in human relationships. His mind was seeking what was invisible to others. He liked being in the ephemeral. His drifting around the continent had encouraged him in his aloofness.

He thought about the trip that he was on. How tired he had been from the travel not only physically but mentally. It had been an exhausting several weeks in Western Canada and Washington State. An anonymous old man on the first leg of the trip bus had told him that he was an "Old Soul" after he had asked Frank several questions about where Frank thought he was going and where he had come from.

4

This old man had looked with fixed intent at Frank, seeming to want to direct him to someplace without fixed coordinates. The old man had the face of one who had contemplated origins and exits for many years. Frank had thought that he must have had honed those skilled in the 1960s. Frank now had spinning in his consciousness a free-spirited cowboy and an old man whose mind had found some connection to purpose and meaning in the 60s and was dispensing his finding on a Greyhound bus to anyone who had a lost or searching look on their faces. "Old Soul" sounded like it had destiny and purpose to it. Frank finished his coffee and the two young twentysomethings stirred from their phones glancing furtively about the small room. The middle-aged woman seemed in her semi-slumbered state. A car horn rang out from a distance. It would be dawn soon and many things were about to happen for Frank. An "old soul" had been knocking on his brain since he had boarded the bus on the left coat over a week back.

A pock-marked face took Frank's ticket as he re-boarded the bus with the two young guys behind him and the middle-aged woman ahead of him. It was a sultry still in the wee hours of the July morning. The muted voices of the passengers whispering to one another, some in a half sleep, greeted Frank as he negotiated his way down the aisle of the crowded bus to find a seat.

He had hoped for a seat alone, but his hopes were now dashed as he surveyed the travellers in the dim light and the humid air of the Greyhound.

At last, success. Seated next to him was a nerdy looking man with a slight beard and a grey tweed jacket. His glasses had the appearance of being fogged up as he stared intently into a book illuminated by the overhead light. Frank plopped down onto the seat with his carry-on bag in his lap and immediately tried to determine the title of the book that the man was reading. He did this with a quick glance so as not to drawn attention.

He believed it reasonable that if a person exhibited behaviour in a public place, it was his right to examine the details of such behaviour without overtly sticking his nose into it. And he found that most people reading usually seemed willing to discuss their particularly choice in material.

After his furtive peering into the literary choices of his neighbour, Frank resumed his staring ahead feeling a little anxious waiting for the bus the pull out and get onto the highway. He remembered a notepad and a novel that he had in his bag. His thoughts were on what he would do once he arrived in Montreal. He would look up a friend that he hadn't seen in a year. He would find a small room. He would get a small job in an office, perhaps even in sales, and he would explore the streets of a city that he had up until now not really known that well.

Soon the driver put the bus in reverse, the beeping sound cueing the passengers to settle in for the trip. Darkness came to them. And the bus set out into the night towards the highway. A few people cleared their throats and Frank closed his eyes and wondered about things like death and how he might explain himself in the afterlife.

The grey tweed next to him stopped reading and stared out into the night now. Frank wondered if anyone else on the bus was thinking about death too. Surely others still thought about such things. Things like the destiny, the afterlife etc. Finally, the man beside him extinguished an overhead light. Sleep was in the air.

It wasn't long before Frank was awoken by a young woman's voice asking her seat mate about whether he was going to pay for her trip to Europe and Tunisia.

Was this conversation part of a dream or had this long-haired thirtyish woman really referenced it? Once he had determined that he was awake, Frank began eavesdropping in on the conversation. This was a dubious skill that he had honed since his teenager years, that he had managed to fashion over the years in such a way as not to draw any attention to himself. In this case the limited lighting in the bus helped.

"If only you had not been so rude to your mother, she would've given us the money for the trip. And it was that cult talk that put your dad down. Meg you gotta be more cool with your mom." said a male voice from the darkness.

"Dad died from a rare disease, Mike. It was his time. And that was years ago. Mom's way past that now. It's all part of the universal destiny. We'll deal with mom when I get home. You know strangely enough I feel a strong positive feeling about her now" the woman said.

"You need to be more respectful of your mother, Meg."

"It is all destiny, Mike. No worries. No worries."

Then it was silent. Frank turned his head toward them and sensed a discomfort, like he frequently did when he heard conversation abruptly stop. Something more needed to be said.

Frank asked himself what cult could they possibly be referring to? He remembered how twice in his life he had been solicited to join some group. First by the L. Ron Hubbard people and their IQ test and then in a more insidious way by a friend of a friend who had found "the light" while on vacation in Cuba at an all-inclusive resort. Apparently, some pseudo religion based in Oregon had sent some of its members to feign being vacationers and had cozied up to others on the trip and had convinced them that this world was only an experiment of a distance civilization that had the intention of only keeping only the most conscientious and intelligent of them alive to take back with them. And it just so happened that they had been picked for this purpose. And they had deemed their targets as the most qualified to join their ranks as the day approached to depart this realm.

Frank still had the books that the couple in Cuba had given him. He had their contact information if ever he had enough of this life and wanted to join them on their journey to another plane. The couple had seemed excited about their up coming astral itinerary and to some degree this had excited Frank. Yet Frank had other commitments at the time and had told them that sadly he could be apart of their elite group. That all happened during the first week of November three years ago. It had been a time of liberation for Frank, but more about that later. It was now a warmer time of the year and the Greyhound bus rolled towards Montreal.

The grey tweed next to him said "excuse me "as he got up to go to the tiny bathroom at the back of the bus. His voice was tired and whiny. Frank thought about the young woman and man next to him. Now he wanted to know something about this cult. Frank had been lost for about two years. He had roamed both Canada and the United States in search of inspiration. Working odd jobs, having short term relationships and living and leaving various cities with the intention of suddenly discovering meaning. Now maybe again opportunity knocked.

Frank switched on the light above him and found the notebook in his bag. He took a pen from his shirt pocket and began to scribble some notes about his thoughts from the last few hours. His mind whirled with the voice of some blasé crooner that he had become an earworm. He thought about the couple next to him and how he was going to engage them in conversation.

The bus hummed along now. The grey tweed returned to his seat. Frank felt some satisfaction at having a plan. Then a shout came from the back row of the bus. "Those people need to be taught a lesson!" followed by silence.

"What's going on?" Another voice out of the darkness. Someone laughed and a child's voice seemed to cry briefly. Frank switched off his light. In his notebook he had written the following:

CROONER LOST HIS INSPIRATION WHEN HIS FIRST LOVE DIED

TWO YOUNG GUYS ARE ESCAPING JUDGEMENTAL PARENTS WHO DISAPPROVE OF THEIR HOMOSEXAUL LIFESTYLE

MIDDLE AGED WOMAN WAS ABANDONED BY HER TWO CHILDREN WHO NOW LIVE IN ARUBA

TUNISIA IS WHERE THE CULT HAS THEIR COMPOUND

PRAYER IS A FORM OF SELF-HYPNOSIS

I CAN SELL YOU ANYTHING

WHO KNOWS WHO NEEDS TO BE TAUGHT LESSONS?

July 7 2020 en route to Montreal

Then Frank drifted back into his subconscious as the bus shortened the distance rapidly him and Montreal.

"Are you from Montreal?", the grey tweed asked.

It took a moment for Frank to really hear the question in his semi-slumber.

"No just visiting for a while" he finally replied.

"I noticed that you keep a notebook. You don't see a lot of those these days. Usually just Macs and laptops"

"I like to feel what it is I write, but a do have a laptop and a phone." Frank replied.

"I'm reading a book on technology and human consciousness by a guy named Ambrose J. Keel. It's called Computing The Soul. Very Interesting."

"Sounds intriguing. What did you say your name was?"

"I didn't. But since you asked, I am Ambrose J. Keel. I'm going to a conference on Sustainability and the Soul in Montreal. I'm sorry if it seems like shameless promotion of my book, but I truly believe that action is required by many if our species is to survive."

"Thanks for mentioning your book. I will make a note of it. It does sound like something that I would look at. So, you must have a Phd or something like that?"

Keel blushed and chuckled a moment.

"Yeah, something like that"

"In my travels I have always been fascinated by cults and spirituality. Never would join one, but somehow this desperate need for people to join together in common action and belonging has been fascinating to me."

"Yes" Keel looked interested.

"A friend of mine left home at eighteen. He was supposed to go to university, but instead joined The Church of the Universal Way for the Wayward in Pittsburgh. I got letters from him for awhile but over the last three years there has been nothing."

"There could be many explanations for that."

"I guess, but I'm sure that cult has something to do with it. Have you ever come across cults in your research Mr. Keel?"

"No not directly, but I know that some societies at universities are like cults with their secrecy and rules."

Keel chuckled again.

"Why that's interesting."

"I never really joined these groups. That made it harder to get work, so I ended up writing on my own. It required less dependence on the considerations of others."

"For sure."

The talk of the politics of academia nauseated Frank.

He glanced over at the couple who had been bickering about the cult earlier. They seemed fast asleep though he could not see their eyes in darkened bus. His mind searched for some thread of thought that would keep the conversation going with Keel.

"You know some people had tried to recruit me in Cuba once at a resort hotel. They told me that within five years the planet would implode and be sucked into a black hole of some sort. The ones who knew the codes for entry to the other side would have a much easier time. Like some computer vortex where passwords and encryption could save your life. Except that a person wouldn't have the time to figure out these passwords. But these people knew some people who knew some people in the CIA who knew some people who had worked in the Vatican that had the codes. It was all so ridiculous that I could only laugh at the time. But you know Mr. Keel it got me to think about whether any of this could be within the realm of possibility. Not that I believe some random guys from California or Oregon are going to have the codes that no one else has."

Keel looked bemused. He scratched his head and seemed to mumble something under his breath.

"Well, these groups just want definite answers to indefinite

questions. You have to be aware of the question more than the possible answers. It's like Socratic thinking."

"And he asked a lot of questions" Frank said sardonically.

"Well, I wouldn't dismiss his relevance in the contemporary world."

"Socrates was that old Greek man with the white beard who hung around young men all the time, wasn't he?"

The question came from across the aisle of the bus from a faceless voice. It was Mike from Meg and Mike who had earlier been arguing about getting money from her father.

"Yes, he had a beard" offered Keel.

"I always thought he was like a god with the beard and everything. Now he's just some dude with a cool name. Smart guy."

"Smart guy"

"Smart guy" repeated Frank.

"My girlfriend took some philosophy courses in Europe."

"Philosophy can sharpen the brain." offered Keel.

"Yeah, but it sure can complicate life."

"Life is complicated" chimed Frank.

"It doesn't have to be." said Mike.

Keel remained silent for a moment considering the others on the bus who may have been trying to sleep.

"I do translations and reports of various kinds. Here's my card." Mike produced a plain white card with just three lines of contact information on it and handed it to Frank. Then he pulled another one from his pocket and offered it to Keel.

They both politely took the cards and said thanks.

"I couldn't help but overhear you talking about some cult to your girlfriend before. I am interested in cults" Frank interloped.

Mike seemed a little distressed that someone had been eavesdropping on his conversation with his girlfriend and he didn't reply.

"Cults I believe are a consistent outlet for the non-conformist in history. It is where the lost and the rejected find solace."

"Or where the insane and self-deluded go." Mike said.

12

"Well, I never joined any of them, so I cannot really say. Except they seem creepy from the outside, yet they still get people to give them money, time and their lives."

"Insanity"

"Perhaps people are just looking for easy answers. Like the doctor here said."

Keel looked out of the window with feign disinterest.

Frank glanced down at the card Mike had given him, then held it up to the light to try and make out what it said. And this is what it said:

MICHAEL SCHULTZMAN

TRANSLATIONS AND GENERAL WRITING

schultzmansword@destinyweb

Mike said "Anything that you need translated to English or French just contact me."

"Well, that seems unlikely right now, but you never know."

"Insanity" repeated Mike, then laughed.

"We should be in Montreal soon"

"Yeah, my girlfriend's mother lives there"

"What's going on?" a female voice from the window seat sleepily asked.

"Nothing" Mike said "we just were talking about what I do for a living."

"Sometimes this guy works" Meg addressed this to Frank.

"We do okay" said Mike.

"Yeah that's why we have to stay at my mother's place" Meg said sarcastically.

"Meg just be quiet for now."

"It's true"

"So, it's true. So be it"

Then silence returned to the bus. Only the humming of the engine could be heard. Frank stared out blankly into the night spotting the occasional light along the highway. Someone then turned on a radio and a voice could be heard: "When the right enzymes are mixed together the sauce is irresistible, just the right formula for space travel and so compact. It comes in easily carried foil packets..." Then it went silent again. Frank thought briefly about foil packets and space travel and then drifted off to sleep.

two

I'm like a moral compass At the bus terminal of life

"

Boris Swatcupso From his poem ' On the Route, Lovely'

At the Montreal bus terminal, a man in high top sneakers and pin striped pants was observing the cluster of travellers collecting their luggage and lining up to board buses to various destinations, including Quebec City, Toronto, New York and parts of eastern Canada. Many were listening to music on ipods, some glazing off into space, others chatting amongst themselves.

The man didn't have a ticket. But he had a motive. He was looking for someone whom he thought would be arriving on the 5:50am bus from the United States of America. One of only two trips from south of the border each day. It was now 5:45am.

The man was in his late thirties had short brown hair and wore a powder blue suit jacket with his pin striped pants. His demeanor was solemn and deliberate. He had just finished a large French vanilla coffee with double cream. He was aware of the news of the day regarding the recent rash of suicides in the United States that appeared to have some connection to a hostile political climate. People seemed to be despairing. Was this divisiveness only a bump in the road or was the American mindset being permanently changed. Would the United States be divided into two or more nations?

The man's job would be to meet the leader of a paramilitary group who had been plotting to secede from the federal government in the United States and form a separate nation of people who only believed in the same things they believed in. His name was Bo Creeley. He had been in the army. He had grown up in Washington State and Oklahoma and had read books on

15

how most of the politicians in the world were in a conspiracy to get rid of people like him who didn't have positions of power.

Bo had always felt that he had less influence in the world then he thought he deserved. But now an international free lance journalist wanted to interview him for a news blog. This might mean he would get the attention he thought he deserved. The universe had been unfair to him he believed. He believed in a Supreme Director of the Universe, but suspected that most of the forces of the world had conspired against that Director and hence against him to rob him of his due respect and attention.

Bo was 45 years old and had a wife and two kids that he had avoided in the last five years to focus on developing a new nation that would unearth the devious leaders of the world and prove his side right.

Bo was coming in from New York on a bus. He felt that it would be less conspicuous than flying. He suspected that he was on some sort of list with the government and would most likely be prevented from entering Canada. By bus he could use some techniques he had learned to avoid detection. His chances were better by Greyhound.

The free lance journalist that was waiting for him was Warren Kitchholm. His stories had appeared on news blog and websites for several years. He had conducted many interviews with fringe groups and characters like Bo. Warren had started out as a sports reporter with a local newspaper in suburban Toronto. His nose had unearthed an illicit drug ring amongst a local hockey team that had turned out to be also building a survival compound in Greenland.

One thing had led to another and Kitchholm was now investigating paramilitary fringe groups.

The group of drug-using hockey players were still living somewhere in Greenland and had been exiled from the sports world. They were now being led by a rogue doctor who had made a fortune peddling vitamins on the internet at three times more than the market price. He had somehow carved out a hideout in Greenland for himself and had taken not only some of his clients with him, but a group of young women that would provide him with company in his waning years. Amongst his stable of women was a grand daughter of Idi Amin, the Ugandan dishwasher and ex-dictator. Her name was Sheila and she had been Kitchholm's source of information for his stories. Warren had no clue as to how many people currently occupied the compound. He had abandoned the story four years ago when he was making his transition from sports reporter to fringe group investigator.

Now Kitchholm was about to meet someone whom he believed would give him an exclusive angle on a fringe group who wanted to form their own nation.

Bo Creeley had amassed a contact list of 674 names of people who thought like him. Most of them owned dozens of guns and weapons. Most of them spent many hours shooting and killing live things or reading about their weapons. They believed that without weapons they would have no freedom. So, they idolized their blow-up devices as being catalysts to liberation and joie de vivre. Bo was their hero because he had written numerous articles for online magazines and blogs like "Liberty or Death", "Government Monitor: Protecting Our Heritage", "Arms of God", and "Surviving Secrecy".

One article in Arms of God was entitled: "How God came to support the Second Amendment." It was written by Creeley and contained actual quotations from the Bible to back his theory of how God really held back on giving humans killing machines until they had gotten really bad and some of His agents needed them to blow away the enemy quickly. Creeley really believed that fear was the main device that God used in humans and these killing machines were symbols of that fear. It provided the main motivation in life for Creeley.

As Creeley got off the bus in Montreal he was nervous because he had not been able to bring any guns with him. But he had contacts on the outskirts of the city where he could easily obtain some if the government forces came against him and tried to stop him from telling people about them and their secret ways. When not armed Creeley felt naked. He had little self-esteem without them. He wore a casual button-down shirt and jeans so as not to be conspicuous.

Warren Kitchholm waited patiently for Creeley. He would take him to a nearby hotel room for an interview, where he had an audio recording device ready. Little did Kitchholm know that Creeley's friend had the bus terminal staked out in case someone tried to attack Creely. In Canada they had to conceal their weapons because it was illegal to carry guns without a special permit in the city. Seven men were camped out around the bus terminal to keep an eye out for any plots by the enemy to apprehend their hero.

Kitchholm recognized Creeley when he got off the bus. Kitchholm had a collection of photos of Creeley. He signalled with his hand to get Creeley's attention.

"Warren Kitchholm?" said Creeley as he nervously put Kitchholm's right hand in a vice.

"Yes, Mr.Creeley I presume" said Kitchholm, thinking that the hand shake had been a bit too firm to be sincere. Creeley had wanted to make sure that Kitchholm knew that he was a real man.

"We'll grab a cab to the hotel room"

"Ok" said Creely furtively.

Soon they were on their way to a small hotel room just four blocks from the terminal. In tow were a couple of vehicles containing not only Creeley pals but several firearms.

Creeley felt much more at ease when he noticed the faces of the men who had nodded their heads at him from a distance before he had boarded the cab with Kitchholm.

"We get right to the interview and have breakfast in the room because I know that you are on a tight schedule Mr.Creeley"

18

What Kitchholm didn't know was that Creeley intended to stay in Canada because he had become convinced that the American government was about to arrest him. He would hide out here. He had entered the country under a false name with false identification. After giving Kitchholm a whitewashed interview Creeley's plan was go with his supporters to a cabin in the Laurentians.

Kitchholm's first question for Creeley was "What was your father like?"

The question put Creeley on the defensive, but this was not uncommon for him. Before Creeley could answer Kitchholm ordered breakfast. A Jumbo meat lovers breakfast for Creeley with coffee and orange juice and a muffin and coffee for himself. Creeley was hungry and ate with gusto, grateful for opportunity to reflect on the answer he was to give about his father, whom he had not thought of in years.

Creeley didn't know that his father was still alive in a senior's residence in Boise, Idaho.

As Creeley was beginning the interview his dad was having his diaper changed and telling a black nurse on the fourth floor of a government subsidized home to "fuck off". The doctors told him that his father had dementia. The Creeley patriarch thought that the world had been taken over by apes who had captured him and stolen his family from him.

"So, what about dad?" Kitchholm asked again.

Frank's arrival was at a different terminal, a sub-bus terminal near the major sports and entertainment arena in Montreal called The Graham Centre. Frank had been to Montreal many times before.

19

Now he got off the bus with the others and thought madly about where to get a drink at 7AM. This was his tonic to ward off regular attacks of nausea and dizziness. This had been a constant with him going back to his early twenties, but the attacks had seemed to come more frequently lately. Doctors attributed them to lack of sleep and anxiety, he suspected that something much more complex had a grip on him, but he was not certain of its origins.

He knew that the bars and dépanneurs didn't open until eight. He had taken note of the professor's conference on Sustainability and The Soul. Professor Ambrose J. Keel had told him that it was on all weekend at Orbital Hall. He pictured himself having a few drinks and heading over to Leacock University later in the day to hear some lectures. The young couple, who were sustained by the irregular income of Micheal Schultzman's translations and his girlfriend's mother's generosity, had said goodbye to Frank quickly and begun to walk away briskly toward the Métro station.

Since the prominence of the internet, people had become less talkative and friendly with each other because of all the lying and misinformation that had been stuffed into their brains and sub conscious. Lots of people were suspicious of each other and Meg had been one of those, but not so much Micheal.

People didn't care if their whole lives and identity were exposed on the internet, but in person many people would not give each other the time of day. The internet had many apps and devices that kept people at a safe distance from each other. These devices provided a way of making smart and not so smart comments to authenticate one's existence, but not have to take responsibility for it. Some people were developing neurosis and paranoia because of this. Others were no longer interested in human affairs and considered the human body gross. The word "soul" referred only to music for some. And Frank pondered this as he watched people around him in various cities staring at screens instead of each other. They studied their screens for signs of life and information that would validate their existence.

Groups and clusters of people online organized under banners such as The Acid Balloon Society, Gary and Karl Marx's Pep Show, NapeVolume, GrapeCutters, Twits and Twisters, Barry Bingo's Blog Out, Gods Gunnery, YouCanBAStarToo, Spaceformypigideas, and Creeley's gang OneBigLie Ltd with a link to one of the leading gun manufacturers in the world.

Frank watched an African family getting their luggage organized on the sidewalk. They talked loudly and spiritedly in French which despite Frank's fairly good knowledge of he failed to comprehend what they were saying. The teenage children tried to pull the wheeled trunks and stare at their smartphones at the same time.

Smartphones were what the devices that most people carried with themselves were called. People stayed in touch with the world, did business and sent out smart and witty symbols to the universe hoping for an answer. Any answer. They had a screen that when you touch it with your fingertips it would go to places in space where you could communicate with total strangers who were called friends and you could give them your thoughts on things or reveal truths about yourself. Some people lied on these devices. Many people were sceptical of what they read but trusted their existence to the devices anyhow. Now they were really part of the universe. They called this interacting. They were inventing their own languages as they went along. Soon what many had seen as the mystery of life's origin would be recreated by the creatures. Frank had some of his own creations but had not yet exposed them to the universe. They were in virtual lockdown. They were shadows on the wall of his personal cave. And now he needed a drink. It had been over twelve hours since his last.

Frank found a bank machine and checked his accounts. He had several because he had several incomes from various sources including a company in San Francisco who paid him to provide cute little tagline for their website. That company was called Toffee and Bed Inc. They provided an app so that people could prearrange meals from various restaurants to be delivered to their hotel rooms. Sometimes meals would come from halfway around the world and show up at people's hotel room still hot. A young couple on a cool trip in Kathmandu could if they were not impressed with the local food could order a Philly Cheese Steak from The United States of America online and have it there in less than a day for under $2000.00, not including the tip which could be added separately. In fact, Toffee and Bed president Jay Jay Curlman Jr. had just tweeted out that beginning the following week Toffee and Bed would have the ability to send food to anyone anywhere, even if they had no physical address. So technically a homeless woman in Kamchatsky, Russia who had lost her job as a chemist because of political differences could order a Kale Salad online and have it delivered to her at an abandoned mental hospital where she slept most nights for just under $1500.00.

Frank found a machine, got some cash and began roaming the downtown area scouting out which bar he would commence to drink in. Frank didn't take pills or recreational drugs very often but would on occasion indulge if the mood struck him or if he found the company interesting. Frank had only a small shoulder bag with him. He had a smartphone which he used only when necessary. He still used payphones sometimes and the internet in public places. It was now close to seven-thirty and Frank was thirsty and feeling the busy energy of the city closing in on him.

The air was still warm. It was mid July and Keel was in a cab to the St. Thomas Hotel. Mike and Meg were in a crowded subway train to Montreal West and Frank was heading for what he thought was another down period in one of his favourite cities.

three

"Fascism needs Baptism coast to coast"

Ken Kesey

Bo Creeley was counting the number of tile-like windows which surrounded the door of the small hotel room that Warren Kitchholm had brought him to while Kitchholm waited for an answer from him. It had begun to rain outside and Creeley was thinking of his buddies who had been close behind him in case Kitchholm was part of the worldwide plot to stop them from exposing the conspiracy to keep arms out of the hands of people like them who hadn't read books with small printing and big words.

Creeley really didn't want to talk about his father. It really had been a lazy question to start the interview by Kitchholm.

And Kitchholm knew it.

"Why don't we start again?"

"Ok. I wanna finish my meat first anyhow."

"You probably are hungry after that long bus ride anyway."

"Sure am. Y'a got some really good meat up here too"

"Yeah, we do"

"Now is it ok if I make a call to a buddy?"

"Sure, go ahead"

Creeley scarfed a large piece of meat with his fingers and wiped them on his pants. Then he took a smartphone from his pocket and touched a couple of icons on the screen and put the phone to his ear. It was easy now to call people up with the smartphone. All you had to do was tap the screen and buddy was being summoned.

The meat that was now in Creeley's stomach had been part of the body of a pig just a couple of months before. The pig had spent the last days of its existence on a farm in Illinois with 2389 other pigs. The piece that was now being attacked by Creeley's digestive enzymes had been part of a group of 27 pigs that had been terminated just a couple of weeks earlier.

Creeley spoke into the smartphone.

"Hey Shep. Got me covered?"

Then there was a pause. The bar fridge in the room hummed. Kitchholm sat in a soft chair near the bed and waited patiently.

"No, he's ok. Yeah just put it in the back of the truck. I can't talk now Shep. Sure, grab some liquor. Byyyye"

Creeley tapped the phone and said, "Ok Kitchholm I'm yours for an hour. Shoot what do you want to know?""Well first what to do think of Canada so far?"

"Friendly people up here."

"We have been told that a lot. Is this you're first time here?"

"My first mom brought me to Vancouver when I was seven. We went on a ferry boat and I had a triple scoop ice cream in Stanley Park. I petted a pony and then we ate in a fancy restaurant. I hated that restaurant because the waiter gave me a dirty look."

"That's some memory you have there Mr. Creeley."

"Just call me Bo."

"Ok Bo. So, what was the first time you felt that the government was against you?"

24

"Well, it's pretty obvious isn't it? When you start to listen to teachers who are trying to ram all kindof shit into your head about the world and ya can't say anything against it. I never believed them. All myteachers were like talking heads, except for Mr.Ripper, my grade 10 history teacher who owned a firing rangein town. He took us there one day and we blew things into oblivion all day. My buddy Ches killed a squirrel. Ifound my future wife at Ripper's Gun Bonanza. That's what it was called, Ripper'sGun Bonanza. And I fucked Gwen behind the targets on our second date. Do you like whiskey, Mr.Kitchholm?"

With that Creeley produced a flask from his inside jacket pocket and after offering some to Kitchholm took a swig.

"They can't stop me from drinking and shooting."

"Why would they Mr.Creeley?"

"Because they don't like it when we enjoy our freedoms. They want to control everything we do."

"Do you feel that you are being controlled now?"

"No, because I choose not to be. Let someone try and I'll blow their heads off."

Creeley looked to be troubled by the question.

"You really are naïve aren't ya Mr. Kitchholm?"

"Let's get back to you Mr. Creeley."

"Ok"

"So, you knew that you had an uphill battle right from high school?"

"Of course. If you want to keep your right to fuck and kill you have to see that. The IRS came and got my daddy when I was fifteen. They took his car away and put him in jail. Then I never saw him again for a few years."

"Your dad is in a home now, isn't he?"

"Yeah, they got him under surveillance somewhere. Last time I saw him was three years ago."

"Does your father believe that the government is out to kill him?"

"Well, they could knock him off anytime they wanted to. Don't ya think? I mean they got himunder their thumbs. They need him for experiments, like a CIA did here in Montreal with LSD. You guysshould know about that stuff."

"Oh yes at the Allied Hospital with Dr. Boethius."

"Yeah, that's the guy. He was being paid big bucks by the CIA to perform mind control on youpeople. Those were really the first robots in America. They were sent all across America to turn kids on to drugs, but they never got me."

"So, you think that the whole counter culture was a plot by the CIA?"

"Of course, William Sam Bilderbourough was an agent of The Firm. Creeley winked when he said The Firm.

"What was the The Firm?"

"Well, if you don't know that I can't discuss it here. You just have to do your own research."

"Maybe we'll get back to that. Did you read Bilderbourough when you were a kid?"

"No, but my daddy did. He told me that Bilderbourough had been programmed with drugs to corrupt the purity of the America, mostly white people and that his writing had really been done by the CIA. I read a bit of the book Jack's Junk, it was filth, naked boys and kids sticking needles in their arms."

"A classic."

"Well, if you're into going to hell and all that stuff."

"Sure" said Kitchholm.

"So, update me to the point where you knew that you would start your own counter revolutionary group."

"Well, I was born in 68. Six and eight are fourteen. There were thirteen colonies, but a lot of people didn't realize that there was a fourteenth one called Ozarkia. That's where I came in. I was born Torevive, Ozarkia. At the age of fourteen in 82. Eight and two are ten like the ten nations of the Anti-Christ in Revelations They wanted me to be an anti-Christ, but I fooled them. I learned their tricks and armedmyself so they could never capture me. I got married and me and Gwen lived in the Kalispell Mountains for ten years."

"Where is Gwen now?"

"She died in a car crash in 99"

"I'm sorry for your lost."

"Thanks"

As he said this Creeley stared blankly at Kitchholm with no emotion. Then he took another swig of whiskey and belched.

"So ya see how it all fits"

Kitchholm was beginning to see how it all fit

four

"I'd rather have a bottle in front of me then a frontal lobotomy."

Tom Waits

It was now eight o'clock and Frank had assembled his consciousness at a bar called the DregStore. He was at the heavy wooden door when a short young guy from Costa Rica opened the place from the inside.

Frank said thanks and good morning. He trudged up to the bar with a slight impatience. The young guy from Costa Rica asked Frank to wait a moment and went into the back. Frank sat at the bar which was without acoustic accompaniment or any other human form. He dug into his bag and pulled out a copy of a book by Richard Maurice Burke M.D. Burke had been a nineteenth century psychiatrist who graduated from Leacock University and had written amongst others papers, a visionary work called Cosmic Consciousness: A Study of the Human Mind.

Many of the Leacock fraternity considered this work to be of dubious academic merit but could not deny that he his magnum opus was a noble work that deserved full attention. Burke had been friends with many poets and mystical thinkers including Walt Whitman and had had his own mystical experience before writing his major work. Burke had died by slipping on an ice patch and busting his skull. His lost of consciousness was quite sudden, like his original leap into the realm of cosmic consciousness had been.Frank opened the book to the first page and scanned over the description of precept, recept and concept, which Burke claimed led to intuitive thinking or cosmic consciousness. Frank still wanted a large draft beer. This meant that Frank had to go back to the precept stage and initialize the recept stage to obtain a glass vessel of the golden alcoholic substance. He was curious about the cosmic consciousness and laughed to himself that he somehow knew that he would reach that stage at some point in the near future.

Tito, the Costa Rican bartender, then appeared from around the corner and cheerful said, "What will it be?"

28

"Just a draft, any old draft, a large one"

"Coming up."

The DregStore was somewhat of a dive bar, which at night attracted a geeky crowd, who like to loosen up a bit, to slum it. Frank had been here before, years before, but was not familiar with the staff or the clientele at present. So what, he thought, I just want to feel a familiar environment.

"Is it busy here in the day?"

"No, only after five. Sometimes we have some people that come in around lunchtime."

"My ex-wife and I came here a few years back. And I drank in here with a friend for awhile a couple of years ago."

"Oh, so you know this place. I only started working here last summer. A year ago. Nice boss."

The beer arrived and Frank took a generous gulp. He sensed his dizziness subsiding. He looked around the bar and said,

"Not much has changed here. Same table and chairs. Same place where the DJ is. The furniture is a little worn down."

"Yeah" said Tito faintly as he stared blankly passed Frank.

"I guess the poker machines bring in a lot of money."

"Yeah, a lot of people come here in the daytime just to play poker."

"I'm just back in Montreal. Been working around the country. Do you just work here or do you go to school too?"

"I go to school part time. University courses."

"Leacock?"

"No, Camden."

"Reputation is overblown when it comes to universities. You can learn anywhere is my motto."

"Yeah."

"I never finished university anyhow. Too much of the world to see. Too restrictive for me."

"That's why I just go part time. I can do more things this way."

Another gulp of beer for Frank. Then he glanced at his book which now rested on the bar.

It was a large volume with a red binding and wide margins. It had been rebound but still held the original type and page designations. Frank wanted to work this book into the conversation, but feared that Tito might be lost and skeptical of Frank's intention if he began to talk of cosmic consciousness.

So instead, he talked about baseball.

"Do you follow baseball?"

"A little. We have it on here sometimes. In the afternoon"

"The Blue Jays have a great team this year."

"That's what they say."

And the conversation paused there as Tito had to go to back to get some lemons and limes. As the alcohol slowly seeped into Frank's brain and reorganized his consciousness, he began to wonder about Walt Whitman and how he had arrived at peace of mind. Frank suspected that his heavy drinking was not going to in perception be the easiest route to tranquility, but yet he felt this detour provided him with the sudden change that he required to be at ease with his surroundings. Some people had become an annoyance. But he could shut them off when he wanted to. At other times he could see the world as a zoo and just watch and not participate. But that would soon be changing for Frank.It began to rain outside as Bo Creeley left his interview with Warren Kitchholm. He had on a black pair of soft cotton pants with deep baggy pockets and a grey t-shirt. He wore a camouflage baseball cap and was slightly overweight. He walked out of the hotel and down the sidewalk a bit before turning left on St. Amos St. Then he entered a quaint and cool little place called Le Café Fritz and ordered a coffee with difficulty. He sat at a small table uncomfortably and watched for signs of his friends outside. The instructions had been to wait at least thirty minutes at some coffee shop after the interview before making contact. The rain came down harder now and Creeley became frightened. He saw some red and was not comforted by the young and hip staff of the café. A young man with shoulder length hair eyed him occasionally between glances at a thick hard cover book of poetry. Others were on lap top computers doing various tasks. They seemed oblivious to Creeley. The young man smiled at Creeley.This did not comfort him. Creeley worried about his friends. Creeley worried that the young man with the book might have sexual desire for him.

He was assuaged when a young woman entered the café and sat across from the young man. She knew him. The two began a conversation. Creeley could not make out the gist of the talk, but from the smiles on the young people's faces he knew that it was friendly.Yet he was uneasy and feeling out of his element.

A crazed-looking fiftyish gentlemen then entered the café and began to poetical address the clientele.

"Come black boxers of the northern sky, Close one's mouth forever to the political speech, only to find the women, men to be so high, And the ever-wanting love beyond reach."

Then the recent arrival plopped himself into a chair at the back of the room and laughed.

Creeley was alarmed. Not at the quality of the poetry, but at the fearless and disrespectful attitude of the man.

Also, he sensed that he wasn't liked here.

He waited for his friends with anxiety.

The young man and woman now laughed loudly.

"Quite a speech. Do you know him?" asked the young man of the young woman.

"No, but I've seen him here before. He is harmless."

The meeting of cups and saucers could be heard. Murmurs seeped out into the air of the café and into Creeley's consciousness. His brain balanced the anxiety of potentially being arrested, with the detached meaningless poetic words that had been uttered in the café and also the quiet friendliness of the clientele. The anxiety was winning. Creeley was reddening. He looked with tension out of the place for a sign of his friend's truck. It seemed like it was not coming. And it wouldn't come for at least an hour.

The rain had stopped by then and the young couple had left.

The man of words at the back of the café had apparently dozed off with half a cup of coffee unfinished in front of him.

This man of words was an old drinking acquaintance of Frank. The man's name was Boris Swatcupso. He had been in Canada twelve years and had come from eastern Europe. Boris knew poetry and sculpture. He was also a line cook and had worked at many of the local diners and restaurants in downtown Montreal. In his revelry, he was reuniting with a girlfriend that had recently left him. She had been angered by Boris' adamant refusal to buy her a small home in the country and with Boris' occasional spirited attention to other women, especially when he had been drinking. In his dream world his girl had come back apologetically begging Boris to forgive her. Her name was Patricia Gorman. She was 41 years old and had a birthmark on her left cheek which she felt self- conscious about most of the time. Boris really loved her, but he could not understand why she would not accept his romantic excursions with other women.Boris lay in his chair mumbling in a state of semi-sleep. This made Creeley nervous.Boris' state of attire included a purplish t-shirt that had been crumpled, soiled and machine- washed beyond recognition. He clasped a shoulder bag tightly which contained pages of emotionally charged poetic notations, focused a lot around Patricia Gorman. He did not know.what she signified in his life as of now. But he still wanted her. He was still in an emotional upheaval about her leaving him and he was wondering where she might be. This was why he had come to Le Café Fritz today. He now stared at the movie posters of Fritz Lang which hung on the café walls. He had seen most of those films, especially the earlier ones.

Creeley's eyes focused mostly on the one with the word "Metropolis" across its bottom.

The face of the figure looked like an alien to him. He used it as a distraction as he nervously looked for his buddies.

Creeley's theory was that everyone would soon be turned into robots soon by the government so that we could work for them.

He had not seen the movie but he suspected that this was

Swatcupso now roused himself from his fantasy. He thought that he had been really fair to Patricia telling her in advance of his sojourns with other women. He was not a machine. He was not from Hell. And he really loved her. This is what he would say when he encountered her. He knew that she would come to Le Café Fritz sooner or later. He thought that he would wait for her even if it meant missing a couple of days work at The Bovine Eatery where he worked at least forty hours a week.An hour had passed since Creeley had entered the café and impatience was settling in. He worried that he had no gun or weapon nearby if some weirdo like Swatcupso took a notion to attack him for some obscure reason. The rain came down outside hard and this troubled Creeley. Such a meteorological drama might ruin everything. He wondered if his pals had been delayed by the rain. Creeley needed them to get to the rendez-vous point where someone would drive them to a remote location north of the city.

By this time Swatcupso was coming into full consciousness from his slumber and was mumbling poetry again. The air seemed to suddenly increase in humidity.

"...man seems to delight me not, nor women, Though, by your smiling you seem to say so."

Swatcupso continued:

"All breath is ugly breath when wasted on such beings, As come from human copulation, love made, love wasted."

Creeley, who was losing patience, thought that he would love to have wasted Swatcupso, who seemed like an easy target for Creeley's frustration. But he restrained himself. Creeley was not so much becoming enraged by the Shakespeare-like orations of Swatcupso as he was of the irreverence that Swatcupso seemed to have for Creeley and the others in the café. Creeley wanted quiet so that he could ponder his next move.Swatcupso then noticed Creeley's agitation and smiled at him. He then got up and walked over to where Creeley sat and said,

"Hello, my friend where do you come from? You don't seem to be at ease here."

Creeley looked up at him with some fear in his eyes.

"Pal, I'm just waiting for someone."

"So am I. A woman creature, maybe not so much a woman as a being in search of womanhood. A body with mixed longings. Are you pining for these things?"

Creeley looked truly puzzled. Inside he was beginning to feel his fear turn to anger.

"No."

"I can point you in the direction of some unrepentant group of beings who will soothe your troubled soul and satisfy longings pent up in your repressed mind."

"No thanks pal"

"Oh, come that is what a trip to this city is for, my wandering friend."

Creeley thought that Swatcupso had perhaps been separated from his group day trip from the local mental hospital. He felt a nausea pass through his body. Then he farted as Swatcupso pronounced.

"What time is it, big man of passion? Are you about to embark onto conquests of human territory or is your heart so black, like mine, a well of indecision..."

"Please stop buddy I don't need this."

"Oh, but you do. Like me I sense that you have been disappointed in love."

"Not really pal, I'm on Partner Search dot com"

"Such trivial pursuits will not satisfy the heart."

"It does. Ok buddy. Now would you mind leaving me alone?"

"Oh, such hostility. Ok fine. solitude for the restless heart and mind."

Swatcupso slowly walked away, still in consternation trying to find another soul with which to share in his troubles. He thought of Partner Search dot com.Partner Search dot com was a website where one posted all kinds of information about oneself, both true and false in order to attract a suitable mate for both romantic and sexual purposes. It was a "respectable" way of meeting people without the icky feeling of looking directly at them and coming up with things to say on the spot. It reduced the chance of misjudging someone else by not catching them at a bad moment. One could prepare a summary of the qualities that one wanted to promote about oneself without revealing the ones that one did not want to reveal. Not right away anyhow. So, this was how people could meet with less complications and more conveniently. No work or labor involved. No mystery. It was great. But Swatcupso was a skeptic and not impressed by websites like Partner Search dot com.

His friends had tried to convince him to use it, but he saw it as inhuman and sad. But now he too was sad. Where was his Patricia? He heard some weird sounds come from Creeley's direction and chuckled to himself.Swatcupso felt unstable, erratic, in danger. But he was not. He just needed someone to vent on. He remembered Frank. He remembered that he had said that he would be returning to Montreal.

It was approaching noon and Frank was in a semi-intoxicated state at the DregStore slumped over a large draft beer at the bar.

"It's raining out now, Frank." said Tito, the friendly bartender.

"Rain is good." said Frank.

Over the course of a couple of hours the two of them had begun talking to each other on a first name basis.

Frank continued,

"In a couple of days, I will be going to a conference on the soul of humankind. Has it been forgotten, Tito?"

"Probably. Do you want another draft, Frank?"

"Yes, my man. That will help my soul."

"My wife takes courses at Leacock too. In History. She likes History."

"What about Herstory." Frank joked without effect.

"Where are you staying in Montreal?"

"Nowhere in particular. You know, around."

"Just drifting around?"

"Yeah, but I making some money."

"Oh yeah doing what?"

"I write taglines for websites. Easy."

"So why don't you get a small apartment or room here?"

"I am an anarchist Tito. I don't want to be tied down to anything."

Frank was not truly an anarchist in the political sense, but the word seemed to cover both his feelings and philosophical outlook on the world, especially in recent months.

"It's not good for your health to be just wondering around like this."

"I'll be okay, Tito. Thanks for your concern."

Frank thought of the coming night and knew that Tito had a point. He must find shelter Frank had money but was reluctant to commit to any particular abode. Some sense of wanderlust made him hesitate in this matter. He liked being between a perpetual state of dizziness and semi-intoxication. Maybe he would slow down the drinking soon and find a bed to sleep in for the night.

Tito wiped the counter and watched the rain come down outside the window.

In a park, just a mile or so from Frank and his erratic musings were a group of young people in dialogue with a bearded lean man whose mind and soul had manifested itself from some yet undiscovered genetic mutation which crumbled the boundaries of time and space, taking full advantage of the full range of possibilities in the universe. Few people noticed this assembled motley crew. They had the appearance of some group of artists, which fit right into the tapestry of the city. And more specifically the district of St. Amos. The bearded man would talk in sweet cadence but within rhyme, he explained and accepted everything, but still expounded that more mysteries were perpetually being created and that it was insanity to try and capture or control them. Wildlife and plants were metaphors for his little diatribes. The group would then discuss and ask questions with him. This had been a recent happening.

Frank was deliberating his own philosophical dilemmas back at the bar.

Frank was of medium height but slightly underweight. He got around easily and quickly when he needed. As it became late afternoon Frank had decided, despite his semi-drunken state to walk the almost two miles to his favourite hotel.

The St.Viateur Hotel was not only familiar to Frank in terms of comfort and sociability but also cheap. He wanted to walk to not only get some fresh air, but to see people along the way, to get a barometer on the city.

It was the same hotel where Warren Kitchholm had earlier that day concluded his interview with Bo Creeley and was now working on his story for the news website Newsguts.com. Kitchholm had entitled his article, Manufacturing Secrecy: The Creation of a Paranoid State. Creeley was a part of the article, but not the featured personage, yet Kitcholm's brain focused its power on Creeley and how such a man could be so dismissive of any evidence that contradicted his theories.

Frank said goodbye to Tito at the DregStore and began his pedestrian journey towards Kitchholm and the St.Viateur. He thought freely as a fresh early evening air sobered him a bit.

He remembered the conference on the soul that he had learned of from Professor Ambrose J. Keel on the bus. It certainly would be a worth attending he thought. What was the name of the conference again? He couldn't remember.

The Soul and the System? Something like that.

As the sky darkened Frank felt at ease with the people moving about on the sidewalks of Montreal. He sensed the joie de vivre of most of the souls. He observed the diversity of the fashion on display. He sensed the poverty and power, both going places and looking for things. He felt a restlessness that he was familiar with in Montreal. What would be a good tagline for the city?

Vibrant Island? Franco, Festive Frolic and Fun? He couldn't think of it now.

He recognized some of the faces of the street people who hung out around the Palais des Arts looking sometimes pensive, sometimes depressed. Many of them panhandled for money or shuffled aimlessly along the streets of the city in search of some lost family connection or meaning to their lives. Others were focused on their own souls. Many had abandoned life to only consume alcohol and drugs and forget as much as possible about anything.

This didn't concern Frank so much on this trip as on previous ones where he would worry on how such issues as poverty, economic imbalances and the like would be addressed in the future. Tonight, he was just going to forget the problems on his mind and get some sleep. Then in the morning he would get his head back in shape and perhaps attend that conference on, what was it? Saving the Soul? No, it wasn't so religious sounding.

Kitchholm was at the St.Viateur and just adding some of Creeley's quote into the body of his story.

Before him was his meal consisting of a spinach salad, melba toast and an organic fruit smoothie. Kitchholm felt good about his new eating habits. He was trying to not only lose weight but also to make his brain work better. He really valued his brain. Good food equalled good brains, which meant good writing according to him.

Kitchholm's article would end with these words:

And so, as we head toward a world sustained by robotic technology and computerized social networks the old mystique of conspiracy theories and hidden agendas still are with us to give the world impetus to not be satisfied with the answers put forth by high tech engineers and contemporary visionaries who claim that no information can be remain hidden from the public eyed any longer. Wikileaks may be trying to capture the star position of disseminating hidden plots, but new ones are being hatched more quickly then ever. Voices whether they come from scenarios imagined or real will not be quelled so easily by pure science.

A spirit of the unknown is still with us.

Kitchholm liked his conclusion but was still working on putting more evidence into his article to back up his argument. As he finished his spinach salad Creeley was getting into a lime green pick up truck outside The Fritz Café and being driven to a remote cabin in the Laurentians where seven heavily armed men, who were the real flesh and blood evidence of Kitchholm's thesis, were housed. They were plotting to blow things up in the future in order to draw attention to not only secret plots in the world, but also to themselves and their weeping hearts. Hearts represented and protected by an arsenal large enough to raise eyebrows, especially in Canada.

five

"gonna find myself a city to live in"

David Byrne

Boris Swatcupso was left by himself at the café. He returned to his armchair with a certain disappointment, but a bit more relaxed. His brain, which had been filled with desperate thoughts moments before now settled a bit and he began to think with more precision of the options before him. He questioned whether his search for Patricia was of any value to either her of himself. Certainly, he would like this relationship of just over six months to continue but was that just narrow-minded of him. He suspected that this came from his parental influences, some of which he had not been fully successful at disposing from his behavior patterns. At least not the ones that did not work in his life in North America.

Swatcupso sat for a time thinking of past relationships with woman. He had had at least four of what he called full relationships. Each had its own peculiar characteristics.

Two months with Jenny a part time teacher and yoga instructor had been mostly mystery and lust with almost no conversation involved. It was doomed from the beginning, even though there had been sincere jesters of forming mutual understanding it really came down to two people who needed to vent an animal lust and had found the platform for it. Boris had been grateful for Jenny, but he saw his willingness to continue the relationship leave him by the fourth week. Jenny perhaps had more long-term plans

Yet how could he know, since Boris craftily began to cut off conversations and detract from the subject of love at every opportunity.

Then there was Michelle, a French girl who was somewhat lost in the world. She was 27 and Boris had been 35 at the time. He cherished his role as a guide and mentor to her. But that was the limit of that hookup. There had been some sex of course, but Boris always had a feeling that he was taking advantage of her and that she was not a full willing participant in the love acts or even in the places they would go to on nights out. Boris always felt like an instructor and by the end of six months he was becoming exhausted. So, he told her this and suggested that she look for a younger man with which she could participate more fully in love acts. Boris felt he had been fair with her. She had gotten upset at him. He had had to finally concede to remain friends with her, which perhaps had been just what she had been looking for all along.

Rachelle was an American living in Montreal part of the year. Boris was with her on and off for a year. He really did not want to think of her now. It had been a tumultuous affair with many scenes of public humiliation and agony. She had been sleeping with girls and women during her time with Boris, including some of co-workers at the coffee shop she worked at while in Montreal. And that was not only causing tension between them, but the fact that she was working illegally in Canada and would have put her status here in jeopardy if by chance one of females she was bedding happened to want avenge herself by revealing things that she wanted concealed. So, Boris had walked away from this scenario even though he still lusted after her sometimes. Yet he now realized that he may have had some feelings for her, but after Jenny he wasn't not in the mood for another work project.

And now Patricia had left him after just over six months. And he had begun to snap. His head pounded now as he thought of her. Perhaps he should call a friend and just talk it out and then forget about it. Or maybe he could do that on his own. How to get emotions to leave? Not so easy without a certain level of dishonest thinking or denial. He would read Hamlet and Romeo and Juliet again. Shakespeare had been one of his literary staples as a child and he still sometimes relied on the plays for solace. Patricia would be a more complex thought process and it seemed that it had only begun. Begun with an insane tirade at Le Café Fritz.

Frank walked rather briskly through the pedestrian traffic as he headed towards The St.Viateur. He had a radiant look on his face as if his mind had become roused by the atmosphere of the city's viral talk and colourful street people. The consequences of his encounter with alcohol began to fade into a backdrop against which Frank drew a firm illustration of what he wanted to do while in his favourite city. He reviewed his recent travels through the country in which he had witnessed a heroin overdose on the desperate and frenzied streets of Vancouver's East side, had dinner with the president of an oil company in Calgary quite inadvertently, climbed a mountain near Lake Louise with seven twentysomethings who were intent on talking of nothing but American politics and who counteracted its effect with eastern meditation techniques, worked as a mascot in the Calgary Stampede parade, was given a brief course survey course in astrology by a slightly rotund woman from Saskatchewan who appeared to be under the effects of a myriad of legal and illegal drugs not to mention 50% Wild Turkey whiskey, and been propositioned by a gay army officer in a parking lot in Winnipeg amongst other adventures.

He envisioned these personages and more in his mind as he strode towards the hotel. They were all souls that had bumped into him for some reason or perhaps for no reason. Frank, though, was determined to search his own mind and soul for any indications of meaning to these convergences. How and in what way could this seeming randomness be placed in line with his life path.

Frank had grown up with a single sibling. A younger brother who was born four years after him. His parents had been both born on Prince Edward Island. His father had been a been a graduate of an aeronautics course and had worked as an instructor at a local training base for pilots. His mother was a free lance artist who had never gotten much recognition for her charcoal drawings and water colors, but nevertheless felt inspired to pursue her creativity as well as raise two boys in the process. When Frank was sixteen and his brother Jesse was twelve his father mysteriously began to not come home for days. This period stretched out for two months before the boys after much pestering of their mother found out that their father had started

44

a serious extra marital affair with one of his female students and that he was thinking of permanently moving out of house and asking her for a divorce.

It had upset Jesse more than Frank. Frank had become quite independently minded and was absorbed in school work and books. Jesse on the other hand had been struggling with school and had little interest in much at all. His father worried about him and had been planning to take him with him when he moved away. This he had been trying to sell to his mother over a period of weeks. She had been quiet on the subject thinking that the affair would heat up and peter out eventually, like a couple that he had had before. But this one seemed to be of a more permanent nature.

After a couple months more of tension and some verbal arguments it was agreed upon that Jesse would go live with his father and that Frank would stay with his mother. Frank and Jesse would still get to see one another on certain occasions. Frank and Jesse really were not that close, especially since Frank had began distancing himself from the family after he had entered high school. Frank read a lot and Jesse just dreamed. Jesse had been closer to his mother, but did not object much to the move, having a rather passive nature. But underneath he was troubled by many things concerning life. Deep inside he was developing the soul of a poet or musician who needed to let his consternations pour out into words and sounds in order to make sense of things. The normal vehicles of communication seemed blocked to him. Frank had seemed to understand this and to some degree respected his little brother's space.

Jesse didn't really know if his father understood this. What the elder paternal Lee revealed to his family about his personal feelings were always vague notions and ideas unconvincing. Though he could certainly talk about politics and sports. And of course, airplanes.

So, Frank had known that he would have a somewhat checkered existence but took comfort in his strong interest in knowledge and observing people. He had rarely turned back to visit his father or mother but had written several times a year to his brother, trying to be sensitive and strongly suggesting what Jesse should be doing with his life. He had never gotten any replies, so had had stopped trying to communicate with him three years ago when Jesse would have been 26 and Frank would have been 30.

Frank's mother lived alone and worried about him a lot. He rarely called her. And since he had been astray from Jesse for a few years he didn't know if his younger brother had any contact with her either.

six

"I live now, and die later, But blood always gets my attention"

Boris SwatcupsoFrom his poem 'Big Bloody Weekend'

Boris Swatcupso was 42 years old. He sat at Le Fritz Café thinking of his interlocutions with women. He still had a hope that he and Patricia would somehow reunite and that he could go back to being a line cook/poet and not some heart broken manic beast whose life had been derailed by a series of unfulfilling relationship with females.

He thought back to his childhood and the hardship that he and his parents had endured. His memories were fuzzy concerning his older sister and how his parents managed to obtain money and resources, but he had clear images in his mind of the girls that had made his heart leap and his groin move. Girls had been the soft part of his adolescence. He had worked hard in trade schools and factory jobs into his thirties when opportunity came to leave home and go to the United Kingdom. Never having been close to his family and craving adventure and romance a friend's connection in Montreal was the eureka moment of his life. He had been inspired by the poetry of his native land as well as the classic English literature. He had developed an interest in sculpture when a girl he was seeing while in trade school took him to gallery and exhibitions. He had tried his hand at pottery and ceramics to impress the girl and he had remained at it after she had lost interest in him.

Boris thought about the first women he met in Montreal at the age 40, within the first week of his arrival in Canada. He had never married and still considered himself to be carrying on the bohemian tradition of keeping a free spirit. Somehow Hélène caused a stir in him that brought out a hidden desire to perhaps have children and a home. She was a 32-year-old bureaucrat who had an artistic side to her. She worked in a government department that promoted and funded Canadian artist and writers. She was attractive and vibrant and believed that an authentic life was a balance of work, play and rest. She attended many cultural events and was honest and earnest in her day job. She had few hang ups, but liked a clean and organized household. Boris was convinced that he had had met stability and fun in one human form. They had met quite by chance at a non-descript coffee shop near Hélène's office. Boris taking the first initiative to ask her about how to get to the Service Canada office, a catch all government office. And from there they discussed immigration, arts funding and how poetry had become an underappreciated art form in the world.

Boris' speech revealed his Eastern European origins, but yet his English was remarkable. It was something that he had consciously devoted himself to over a period of twenty years. He had obtained a plethora of English books after the fall of the Soviet Union, including many with poems by a man named Madison J. Butterworth who had recently turned 72 and had once resided in a cabin like house filled with books in some remote northern part of Ontario. Butterworth had been a Russian émigré who had spent most of his years in London, England trying to figure out how to be a respected literary man. He had read his way into Cambridge and had been impressive in poetry circles for many years in England, appearing on such radio shows as Wits and Words and Arts Roundup.

Butterworth and Shakespeare now occupied Swatcupso's mind along with the women he had seen since arriving in Canada. His heart had become able to ride the emotional wave by keeping a steady hand on the tiller. He used his memory bank to recall experiences of his early feats survival and his intimate times with literary works to adjust himself to new life scenarios. Sometimes he knew that he appeared erratic in his assessment of others, but this bothered him only marginally. The real Boris Swatcupso had emerged from these confrontations with life. At least this is what he told himself. And he also told himself that Shakespeare was still relevant in the contemporary world. He was doing all of this thinking in Le Fritz Café below the poster for 'The Blue Gardenia', a film in which Raymond Burr plays a nasty sexual predator who is killed in self defense by one of his victims. In the film, the female victim had to stay away from the cops or she would have been charged with murder. Swatcupso had seen the film twice.

The first time he had empathy for the Burr character thinking that the woman had asked for it by going with him. Two years later he watched it again and saw it completely differently. What a nasty man the Burr character was. He noticed all the lies that he told. Not lies that were retractable or forgivable, but outright mischaracterisation of himself and his motives.

Swatcupso thought back to his own lies. They were not so bad. He didn't really remember them as being game changers. Maybe he had told some of his woman friends that he was in one place and not another to avoid them becoming suspicious of him flirting with another. Or he had fabricated and embellished an experience from his youth to make himself look more heroic or intellectually correct. But nothing that got anyone into trouble. He was just protecting the woman from the harm of their own suspecting minds.

This was how he had thought.

Now he had to handle Patricia. Or not handle Patricia.

Maybe he could just write poetry or make a sculpture in his loft apartment slash studio.

He could take a long walk in The Old Port by the river and watch the old men with their poles fishing for aquatic life that they will not be able to eat.

Or he could go by The Joint and block the whole thing out with a dozen drinks and witty conversation.

Boris had to work the next day, so he didn't really want to get drunk. Eliminating that from consideration he returned to the possibility of tracking her down through her friends at the Friends Centre where she volunteered or even in the frippèrie where she worked 30 hours a week. But he was apprehensive about these options. They perhaps would involve lengthy explanations (and some lies) to people who may have a prejudice against him already. He questioned his own relevance in this world. Was he avoiding, denying, hiding in old notions that had been grafted in his psyche?

At the same moment, Warren Kitchholm, who had come to a somewhat satisfying arrangement with his Creeley article entered Le Fritz Café intent on relaxing but still was pondering tweaking his piece. He went to the counter and ordered a regular coffee then sat down at a small table for two near Swatcupso. He placed his laptop on the table, briefly glancing at the troubled man and thinking of him as an overwrought soul. Kitchholm went back to the counter to pick up his coffee, paid the young woman behind the counter and returned to his seat. He plugged in his computer and took a sip of black coffee.

Swatcupso now was on the verge of deciding whether to forgo his next day's shift at work and get drunk at a place called The Joint. Kitchholm was sitting down going over his expose on Creeley's gang and conspiring governments when the sounds of a scuffle came from outside the café.

The words were inaudible and it was not clear whether they were in French or English but it was clear that someone had been attacked. A voice was then heard to shout "It's him. Chase the fuckin bastard".

Heads in the café went up, but no one moved. Why would they? Why get involved in what could be a personal matter of no concern to them. So, they were not concerned.

But Swatcupso noticed from his seat that the man, now lying on the sidewalk on St. Amos St. in a heap was someone that he knew.

His heart quickly shifted from a mix of self-pity and consternation to a leaping joy at seeing an old acquaintance. Then concern came and Swatcupso bolted up from his chair and went out to see the man and the blood

50

seven

A small crowd had gathered around Frank as he held the back of his head where the blood was seeping through his hair. He said that he was ok. The dazed semi-drunken state that he was in seemed to have cushioned most of the physical and emotional impact of the blow.

"Ya want an ambulance?"

"Hospital?"

"Tu veux qu'on appele un ambulance?"

"I'm ok, I'm ok"

"Frank!!" shouted Swatcupso.

He broke through the thin crowd and knelt down beside the man that he had not seen in over a year but had instant recognition for. Swatcupso's head was now reeling with some excitement and dismay at the scene before him. He had quickly replaced all of his agony over Patricia with a sense of bewilderment at what his mind was witnessing before him. He had thought that he would run into Frank again but not under these circumstances.

Frank squinted a bit at Swatcupso, then he was quietly puzzled at the face before him.

A moment later he managed, "Boris?"

"The one and only. Song of myself. The unique Whitmanesque womanizer of the West."

Swatcupso still had a poetic sensibility about himself that acted as a circuit breaker in highly charged emotional situations. Like this one.

"So, Boris you just happen to be here… now…wonderful."

"A figment of your mind no more."

Frank chuckled for a moment, then remembered his head.

Boris helped Frank up and took him into the café.

He found him a cushioned seat near the door.

"You might need help with that thing"

There was no more bleeding. A couple of drops had gotten onto Frank's shirt. Frank looked around the room to get his bearings. Boris was now smiling, but with a streak of concern in his eyes.

"How have you been, Frank?"

"Great. On the endless road. I just keep trying to climb that mountain. You know"

A belated rush of alcoholic inspiration came to him. He saw before him a man with whom he had accompanied on at least a dozen remarkable binges. Most of them had left the pair with good memories, but a few that would be horrifying to recount to the moderate user of alcohol or recreational drugs.

"Some guy just hit me over the head with a blunt object, Boris" Frank managed.

"I see that. The jerk got away. No one chased him. Looked like some hyped-up guy. Probably on crystal meth."

"I don't know Boris, but I need a drink."

"Sure. I was just going to a bar. You sure you shouldn't get that head checked out first?"

"I'll be ok. It's just a bruise."

"But it's on your skull, Frank."

"I shall bash on, Boris."

Frank had regained his composure. He was putting the events of the day into perspective now. He had arrived at dawn after meeting a professor on a Greyhound bus which had stimulated some intellectual curiosity in him. The chance meeting of a man of such calibre had set up a certain mind frame for Frank. It had peeked a philosophical thread of thought regarding his future. This had both disturbed him with questions of self-doubt and provoked a desire to seek answers. At least temporary ones that would act as stepping stones to a passion or occupation, that he saw this professor had.

He had also met two seemingly normal young people who were having quite a normal conversation about the merits of being a part of a cult.

And then there was the conference, being held at one of the English universities in Montreal, called Sustainability and the Soul.

The guy from the couple obsessed with cults had been apparently a professional translator and had given him a card. He had gone from the bus terminal in search of a bar to get sloshed in before deciding on going up to St. Amos St. to a small hotel he knew when he was for no obvious reason bashed on the head by what his friend, whom he had not seen in over a year, but happen to be on the scene, had speculated was probably some dude on crystal meth.

That friend now sat before him as much in amazement as he was.

53

Boris was sitting in front of Frank with a surreal look that contained both concern and elation at having ran into a old friend. He was hesitating taking him to a bar in this condition. Boris recalled a similar scenario when he had spent a few weeks in London with a transgender person with whom he had been sharing a pint when they had been promptly attacked while going to the loo suffering a bash on the head as a result. They had insisted on continuing to drink at the bar only to have dropped dead 20 minutes later right at Boris' side. Boris had shortly afterward decided that he had been starting to have feelings for them, perhaps love and had wept privately over the tragedy. He had even attempted to pursue the perpetrators and enact some sort of revenge but to no avail. He had attended their funeral dressed in pink, not a colour that he had been accustomed to draping himself in. Boris recalled him (the pronoun he sometimes preferred) as he stared at Frank trying to determine what to say or do.

He did not want this to happen to Frank. Frank looked a little better as the moments passed. Still Frank's eyes were glazed and Boris could not decide whether they were that way from the blow to the head or because Frank was drunk.

"How much have you been drinking Frank?"

"Enough. Do I look drunk?"

"I don't know. Maybe you should go to the emergency."

"Naw. I'll be good. You know Boris my divorce with Katrina is final."

"You never really loved her. She took you into her prison of lust and labour."

"Stop with the Shakespearean allusions Boris. Don't you think that the Bard is a little archaic?"

"Ok, but it does ring true, doesn't it? And you must be glad that it's over."

"I am, but I did like her."

"Sure, like you like people on the street, but she wrecked an illusion for you Frank. All people are not so selfless as you wanted them to be. They have a personal agenda that very often negates compassion and understanding. Frank, even though you fell for this ruse, you were smart enough to fight against it and file for divorce and get it with no strings attached. Now stay unattached my friend."

"Yeah, you are probably right. I never ever enjoyed the sex much. And that when I think about it is very... odd... or... I dunno, Boris."

Frank shook his head slightly.

Boris sat back and contemplated his friend for a few moments considering what they should do. But he had no doubt that he would stay with him.

eight

Bo Creeley was in a SUV going north on the 15 heading out of Montreal. He was in the back seat and his three of his cohorts were around him, two in the front seat and one more beside him in back. They were silent as Creeley contemplated what the wording of their next press release would be. It required tact and some self-discipline on their part, considering that Creeley was in self-imposed exile from the United States of America. His interview with Kitchholm had brought in $5000.00 for the group and he had been assured that his whereabouts would be kept confidential by Kitchholm.

OneBigLie Ltd ran a website from various locations in the United States. Articles would be submitted by private courier from Creeley to these locations. It wasn't foolproof, according to Creeley, but they could always create new locations as they went along. Creeley truly believed that he was under constant surveillance. He listened to a talk show host from Texas named Big Andy Jones whose bigness extended to people like Creeley around the world, but particularly in America.

Jones himself said that he was under surveillance and that anyone who possessed knowledge of the truth about America would be under the eyes of government. Jones' videos and audio disc were in Creeley's luggage. He had corresponded extensively with Jones, but strangely Creeley considered those communications, covert and beyond the radars of the conspirators.

Creeley had been living in New Hampshire at the time, occupying a small cabin about a mile from a place called Santa's Village off of highway 2 in the middle of the state, when he had heard Jones begin the second hour of

56

his show with the news that a group of government officials had been tracking the rise of paramilitary groups in the northeast. Jones had gone on to say that the identities of these people were known and that this proved the fact that all of America was rising up against government corruption in Washington, even in the "liberal" northeast, where Jones alleged the wheels of the Illuminati turned most effectively.

Later after informing his audience that their identities were more than likely being stolen and misused right at that moment, and that they needed to send all of their banking and personal information via the internet or by mail to something he called "The Vault" in care of his radio network, in order to be ensured of protection against government hackers and their affiliated co-conspirators. Jones shouted into the microphone that they were coming for people's guns. This had sparked a signal in Creeley to prepare for an evacuation of the premises where he was. Canada had always been in his contingency plans and after a couple of days of deliberations with his closest buddies a plan had been hatched to cross the border.

Jones had also informed his loyal listeners that $19.99 per month would be billed to their credit card or taken from their bank accounts by "The Vault" and that he personally did not fiscally benefit from any of this. "The Vault" being unaffiliated with Jones or his subsidiaries including Jones' Cheesecake Factory, Jones' Homemade Energy Biscuits or Jones' Toiletries.

Creeley had packed up quickly, contacted friends north of the border informing them that he was on his way and arranging for a rendez-vous. No guns were to be brought over the border. This was part of their plan to avoid suspicion. They already had fraudulent ids made up. The Kitchholm interview which had been scheduled for three days prior to Jones' verbal radio warnings in New York State were switched to Montreal. Creeley could not afford to cancel out on $5000.00.

As the One Big Lie contingent were rolling north into the wilderness Creeley was settling in his brain how the blurb on his website should go. He would tell his followers that they were to remain in preparation for a full assault on any of their lands by the government. Especially where natural resources were to be found. They were to take a defensive stand only until the next election and then further information would be provided. Many amongst his readers did not like or believe Creeley fully. They considered themselves "sovereign citizens" or according to Creeley rogue factors. But according to him these individuals could be helpful when the chips were down. He did not want to generate only clue as to his location or destinations.

"Turn on the radio, Clive." Creeley barked in the car.

"Sure, what station?" Clive replied.

"570AM. Big Andy's on."

"Oh yeah. Almost forgot"

Clive was a stocky middle-aged man who normally wore camouflage but for this rueful occasion had opted for a navy-blue t-shirt and jeans. On the t-shirt was a slogan for a hot spiritual yoga centre just off of St. Amos St. in Montreal. It read: "Get right with yourself, get right with the world, be cool, get hot"

And below was a website and phone number.

"...so once we have the necessary support to oppose these shameless cretins and purveyors of lies we will be able to return the powers of government back to the people. For years now these, mostly men, have been operating under one assumption and that is that they are too big to fail. Well, my friends, we the people are too big to fail this time...Sirs, I am now challenging you to a showdown at the Washington Hilton Ballroom next Friday morning. I will be armed with the facts and audio and video equipment ready for your answers."

And Jones' voice continued on as Bo Creeley and his cohort's emotions soared with their hero. They didn't see the three RCMP unmarked cars hidden up ahead by the side of the road. Or notice the one behind them.

The group was arrested for illegal entry into Canada plus some minor violations and taken into custody at a local station near Mirabel Airport. They would be questioned for days by both Canadian and American Intelligence then driven back to the border and released back into the United States of America.

After his arrest Creeley decided to take the position that this had all been a charade on his part. He tried to appear as relishing in all of it knowing that it would get the group some publicity. Unfortunately for them the authorities went to lengths to keep it all under wraps. Creeley would have to wait until he could update his website and get word to Big Andy in order to garner any attention for himself.

Really Creeley was planning to blow something up, but the authorities would not find the evidence to detain him for long.

As Creeley was being arrested Creeley's father had just finished listening to Big Andy Jones' radio show in his old age home in Idaho and had thrown the radio across the room and said "Fuck you, Jones!" A nurse had stuck a big needle in Creeley's father's arm and he had drifted into unconsciousness after babbling something about his son not understanding common decency and the American constitution.

"That should keep him for awhile" the nurse had said.

nine

"Of the terrible doubt of appearances, of the uncertainty after all, That we may be deluded"

Walt Whitman

Many people have thought about the future, the afterlife and life beyond our planet. Humanity has taken major steps to explain in physical three-dimensional terms what may have occurred before us and what we can expect in the future. Some have satisfied a certain curiosity by naming things in the sky and labelling the various properties of the element found here and there. They have studied the behavior of light and how it carries information from place to place. Most of these people are called scientist. Some have more specific and fancy titles. Some of them wear t-shirts and jeans and live life like regular people. Many become pop celebrities and go on television programs and the internet and exchange curt and derisive statements with other people who have been sold on certain fixed ideas about the nature of the universe and its inhabitants. Some of those ideas have come from a compilation of books commonly referred to as The Holy Bible or perhaps from another collection of statements and stories called The Koran. They were other ones too with even more ancient references. Most people referred to some of these as myths. They detailed wars, sexual activities and laws, both worldly and other worldly. It kept people in line and explained the dilemmas of the days and nights that people had. Many people also got their ideas about the nature of life and death from horror or science fiction movies, which personified in a more contemporary manner some of the same frightening facts about the universe. Well, maybe some were comforting too.

The ones who argued for fixed ideas and definite conclusion were usually called religious people or ministers. Many were accepting of the scientific theories and findings, adapting to their own notions of the past and future but still arguing that there had to be a home base for it all and that they knew what that home base was and who lived there. Sometimes they called the lifeform that lived there, God.

That would get the scientists angry and they would shout at the religious people and call them stupid. The religious people would laugh and say that the scientists had no faith. Usually, the two sides would shake hands at the end of the discussion and agree to disagree. These sessions had been going on for thousands of years even before what was now called science existed. Many people would take vehement positions based on their personal issues.

The leader of The Church of the Universal Way was a woman named Frida S. Wharton and she had been the point of convergence for a massive dissemination of information from an anonymous source in the universe which had outlined how the scientific and the religious communities had both been correct. This was detailed in a small booklet entitled Why the Arguments? And it assured its readers that there would no longer be any conflicts because Frida had had the answers transmitted to her in 1979 in her bathroom where she lived near Pittsburgh when she was 27 years old. This great, transcendent and unrivaled dispensation which would affect the entire universal frame, came shortly after she had been dumped by her boyfriend whose homophobia demanded that Frida denounce her younger brother for sleeping with Andy Warhol.

This rejection had bruised her ego and fostered her need for attention. This coupled with a misfiring brain had led her to the conclusion that maybe if she possessed something no one else had. But she also needed money. From these circumstances The Church of the Universal Way was brought into existence.

She combined these desires with her teenage experiences in church, which had mostly been negative, and her knowledge of cosmetics and fashion. Over the period of two years she laid the foundations of her new

61

church. She lived with her parents at this time and this kept her living costs low. They were always busy travelling and doing business around the world so they hadn't a clue as to what their little Frida was up to.

Frida had also obtained the title of Reverend for herself by completing a 17- week internet course in biblical studies. She had read some of the pamphlet they had sent her and had underlined passages in the bible and they had given her a mark of ninety out of a hundred. She had spent the money that an aunt in Cleveland had left her to get her diploma. It amounted to over $27,000.00, but Frida knew that it would pay off one day and she was right.

In her second year, she had recruited 12 people, including a cute new boyfriend whom she quickly got married with, to be part of her Church.

Over two years her misfiring brain had slowly revealed what the nature of the universe was to her followers.

The Church of the Universal Way today had about 3000 members, including Michael Schultzman and his girlfriend Meg Barton. Michael had joined very reluctantly and now wanted to completely disassociate himself from the group. Meg, who had had a strong faith from her youth that there was some form of czar of the universe was not so convinced that Frida and her bunch were not on the level. Michael was born in Oxnard, California and Meg only two miles from Frida's childhood home outside Pittsburgh. Meg had remembered Frida's recruitment rallies at the Summit Mall parking lot when lived there in her early teen years. Frida's new cutie pie husband Jack Bowers had done most of the talking using a megaphone to shout out promises of peace and riches to all who listened. Most of those who listened had had troubled lives with many failures. They had a diverse dilemmas and difficulties in coping with their existence on the planet and were in hope that a better world lay somewhere else. At least a better explanation than they had been given by their leaders and family.

Frida and Jack could whip up people's emotional state with ease and then get them to recruit others who perhaps would have more resources to

62

donate to the cause. They also used the postal system to mail out letters promising riches to people who had given them personal information on four by five inch cards that had been filled out at various rallies. Some were promised thousands of dollars in heavenly money and gold or lots of success in personal relationships if they showed faith in Frida by sending her money. Frida had decided on the powder blue as being the most alluring color for the cards. To Frida it would signify that heaven was getting closer as more money was sent back with the enclosed Business Reply Envelope.

And Michael and Meg were now on their way to Mary Barton's home in Montreal. Meg's mother lived in the city's west end and she was quite pleased to have her daughter come stay with her for a while to meet her boyfriend. She lived alone and really wanted the company. Montreal was the city of her birth. She had met an American man at a music festival, they had dated for three weeks when Mary was impregnated by him and they had decided to move to his hometown of Pittsburgh, get married and raise the kid. It was the only child she had. Her husband had died after having a seizure at the Summit Mall shortly after witnessing one of Frida S. Wharton's rallies.

What precipitated his ceasing to inhabit the planet was a rare liver disease called Reye Syndrome. The doctors had not been able to reverse the illness, despite the fact that no adult in dozens of years had died from the it. It had been a shock to Mary, but her husband had only been sick for a few weeks and been diagnosed only days before he kicked the bucket. She could not tolerate living alone in Pittsburgh what with Meg already living on her own and travelling, so she took the insurance money and moved back to Montreal. It was shortly after Meg's father died that Meg and Michael had ran into each other at an ice skating rink in downtown Pittsburgh. Michael was taking time away from a Translators Conference at the local university by indulging in one of his favorite pastimes when he and Meg had met began talking and began seeing each other. They kept in touch by Skype and after six months moved to California to be with him. It seemed like real love to both of them. But as she became more involved with The Church of the

Wayward her commitment to Michael waned and her fixation on Frida S. Wharton rose.

Frida's gang had been prompting her to find more recruits in the fertile land of cults so that they could start a branch in California. And they did soon after Meg had established herself there.

All of this was just an aside in Michael's mind when he first met Meg, but as time went on it was becoming slightly disturbing because of her insistence that he attend the church services. Michael was fairly broad-minded when it came to things like churches and faith but could not deny that some of inaccuracies and feeble conclusions that were being spouted from the podium of The Church of the Wayward were deeply troubling and that because of his love for Meg he was determined to get her out of Frida S. Wharton's grasp. He was an intelligent man, with a warm heart. They had been together just under two years and the tension over the Church was still mounting as the couple settled in for their brief stay at Mary Barton's humble two-bedroom apartment. But Michael did not want to bring up the subject in front of Meg's mother.

They arrived at the apartment, had a nice dinner, nice conversation and retired to their room to rest up from their travels. Michael bit his tongue all evening and Meg plotted in her head how she would convert her mother to seeing that the path to freedom from care and worry and to financial success were contained in the brain and aura of Frida S. Wharton.

She had brought three booklets and a few pamphlets with her that she would leave on her mother's coffee table for her inspection.

The first one was orange and red colored and written across the front page in bold black lettering was:

HOW MEDIA LIES TO STOP YOU FROM FINDING PEACE

Inside it said that the mainstream media was a shell to keep people in ignorance and pain so that big business could sell the people relief. It proposed that ancients from thousands of years ago were whirling about in space and waiting to rescue a portion of the world's population at the appropriate time. It also related to how Frida S, Wharton had been telepathically given the task of rounding up these chosen few. The pamphlet concluded that those reading the message in this pamphlet were so fortunate and special. Then it went on the give some assorted details of the coming rapture and a bunch of biblical quotations.

At the end of the pamphlet was a small head shot of Frida, herself, a mailing address and website that people could go to to fulfill their "birthright destiny to escape the falsity of human existence" and "the pain and sorrows of the lies being perpetrated by humanity." It was suggested that the checks be made out to Frida personally.

Another pamphlet announced that a diet spawned from ancient formulas unknown for over 3000 years was now in the hands of the members of The Church of the Wayward. This diet would prevent all diseases and illness and add years of physical and sexually vitality to all who practiced it. But it could not be revealed to just anyone but the privileged and if you were reading this information you were amongst the privileged.

By sending ten dollars one could get the menu for the first stage of the perfect interplanetary diet that had been in existence for over 100,000 years and one could be on their way to perfect health and vitality. In the pamphlet, which was colored burgundy and green, was a half page sized photo of Frida and her husband Jack holding a yummy looking casserole dish of food in their kitchen. And they were smiling and looking pretty healthy.

The pamphlet was entitled:

FOOD, SEX AND ETERNAL LIFE: SECRETS UNKNOWN NOW KNOWN

Mary Barton picked this one up from her coffee table after Meg and Michael had gone to bed and read it.

She had been lonely for some time.

ten

It was evening before they knew it. Frank had survived the attack on his skull and was now in philosophical thought about what road to take. Boris was glad to have ran into Frank even if it had been under less than desirable circumstances. Such is fortune, thought Boris.

Both of them now contemplated the evening before them as they sat behind the window of Le Café Fritz looking out into night. Despite Boris' sometimes erratic manners he had been always supportive of Frank when Frank had been in dire straits. He had been there to support him through his divorce and a subsequent hospitalization. When Frank was contemplating departing from the planet Boris had convinced him that better days were ahead.

Now anyone could have done that, but it was Boris whom the universe had deemed to be the soul necessary to properly transmit a message of patience and persistence when walking through the firestorms. Frank reflected on this as he sat in the café sucking up an Italian soft drink through a straw.

Boris was wide-eyed, but very much in control. He felt empathy returning to him, after thinking so intensely on his errant girlfriend-at-large all afternoon. He examined Frank's face for signs of direction. He was not sure of Frank's state of mind.

"How do you feel, Frank?"

"A bit tired, but good. I think we should get out of here. I need to find a hotel room. The St.Viateur is what I had in mind. But maybe I'll stay at *L'Hotel* Fish Pond on St. Hippo Street."

"You can stay at my place. There are currently no women there. You won't be in the way. Let me rephrase that. You are never in the way, even if a bed mate may drop by."

"I have the funds to stay at a hotel, Boris. And I think that would suit us both better."

Frank needed to put up a pretense of independent. At least for a while. He had to determine a definite path for himself and not cling to anyone too much even if he had been bopped on the head and it was his old friend Boris who was making the offer.

"On our way we'll get a bottle of something"

"Sure, Frank. For old-time sake."

Boris got up from his seat and went and paid the bill to the pleasant young woman behind the counter.

Frank looked around the room for the first time. He wanted to get some sense of being in reality after the attack. He spotted Warren Kitchholm, who at that moment was staring intently at his laptop screen. He observed two young gentlemen giggling over some nonsense that they seemed to be mutually listening to on their smartphones.

There was a young woman alone, who seemed to be a student studying away in the corner of the place. Frank could just make out the title of the book that she was reading, even in the limited lighting of the place. It was Modern Man in Search of a Soul. Frank knew this to a collection of essays by Carl Jung, the Swiss psychologist. Frank was reminded of the conference at Leacock University that he wanted to attend.

He would have to find an internet connection to look up the times and locations.

Boris was chatting with the young woman behind the counter. Kitchholm looked up from his computer. Kitchholm seemed satisfied with his work.

In fact, Kitchholm was more than satisfied and felt that his article was ready to be sent in for publication. He hit send and closed his laptop. He gazed over at Boris who had become somewhat animated in his flirting with the coffee woman. Boris was certainly quickly forgetting about Patricia. He had that ability to overcome emotion but assertive action.

Kitchholm was unaware of Boris' situation as he got up to leave, but he did notice Frank on the way out. He did notice that it was him that had been attacked on the streets, moments before. He felt compelled to ask him if he was alright.

"Excuse me, sir. I couldn't help but notice what happened. Must have been drugs. Don't know what kind of person in his right mind would do something like that."

"Yeah, probably." Frank managed.

"I'm Warren Kitchhom. I am a free-lance journalist, so my curiosity always gets the better of me and I feel compelled sometimes to stick myself into situations. Did you know the guy that did this to you?"

"No, it just happened so fast. Never got to see him really"

"I caught a glimpse of him through the window. He looked to be in his early twenties, maybe mid-twenties and had shoulder length hair. He had a black t-shirt on and I think black jeans. He might have had some make-up on, his face looked pale and powdery. Maybe eyeshadow too."

"Your pretty observant."

"Part of what I do."

69

"I just got back to Montreal and this is what happens. Still, it's great to be in town. I don't know how long I'll be here for. I do a little writing myself for websites. Taglines. Slogans. Advertising. You know. My name's Frank Lee."

"It's good that you have a friend with you"

"Oh, Boris. We go back a long way. Old drinking pals. Just happened to be here. What luck"

"I don't know if anything is really just luck."

"Well to me luck is just an expression when someone's uncertain."

"Yeah, the uncertainty principle." Kitchholm laughed.

At the counter Boris seemed to be in full conversation with the young woman.

"Your friend seems to be quite interested in that girl."

"Oh, Boris. He does not appear to have changed. He's always been a bit of a sexist."

"Oh."

Warren Kitchholm had been a bit caught off guard by the label sexist. But since he knew nothing of the relationship between the two men, he said nothing.

"Well maybe I'm being a little harsh on him, but he can be stuck in tunnel vision sometimes."

There was a silence for a moment. Kitchholm was hovering near Frank seemingly waiting for a conversation to open up. Frank obliged.

"So, you write. Anything in particular that you are working on now?"

"Yes, an article on conspiracies and paranoia. Can't really tell you anymore. It will be on NewsLink probably by tomorrow."

"I'll have to look for it."

"Do you mind if I sit down here, I'd like to interview you about what just happened. Maybe there's a story here."

"Not much of a story in my mind. Just some drugged up kid."

"Yes, but your reaction to it might be interesting. And the fact that you just got into town. Are you originally from Montreal?"

"No, but I lived here quite a bit over the years."

The conversation continued like this for a while.

Meanwhile Boris had signaled over to Frank that he would be just a couple of minutes. No doubt he was trying to get the woman's phone number.

Here I have to remind the reader that Frank could be induced very easily into conversation with almost anyone. This was due to an acute condition of loneliness. Frank had felt cut off from his father and younger brother and did not desire to be close to his mother and he had a very sterile relationship with his ex-wife. One where there had been very little in the way of emotional osmosis. Frank had always been convinced that he had to be heterosexual in order to be a functional in society. But recently he had wondered if he really was functional at all. After all he had been drifting around the continent and parts of Europe for a number of years without any desire to be in a relationship. It must be noted that Frank was feeling more like he was more comfortable being asexual than anything else. It was my opinion at this time that Frank was merely stranded on an island in the high seas of life and love and not a confirmed asexual person but a lost soul who needed to find a purpose in the universe again. He was indeed, still somewhat of an adolescent

71

in a big bad world. Then again so was Boris. But Boris knew that he liked
women. And poetry.

And Boris was now strolling back to where Frank and Warren Kitchholm sat talking of about theories regarding the assault. Boris seemed to have been satisfied by his progress with the woman behind the counter. He turned his attention towards Kitchholm.

"Hi"

"Oh, excuse me, I was just asking your friend about the incident. Warren Kitchholm. I'm a free-lance journalist."

Kitchholm reached out to shake Boris's hand.

"I'm Boris Swatcupso. Poet, bon vivant and line cook."

"Interesting. Well, I don't want to keep you from your friend. So maybe I can do this later."

Kitchholm turned to Frank as he said this.

"You know" said Frank, "I don't really understand why I am so 'interesting' to you."

"I'm just looking for another story. Maybe there isn't one here. But I would like to find out."

"Well, I'll leave you my email address and you can contact me."

"Fine"

Boris was getting anxious. Frank was thinking about a drink. And the young woman behind the counter was keeping an eye on the trio, especially Boris, who seemed charming to her, but also a little extreme in his poetic and observational ramblings.

72

In his conversation with her he had touched on climate change, cloth diapers, Ibsen, the Trans-Siberian Express, the 1970s underground New York music scene and he had quoted from a least three of William Shakespeare's plays, a 1970s television commercial for facial cream, made reference to hippie singer Tim Buckley and the current band Thee Oh Sees and he had offer her a sample of his word manipulations. She also had observed that beads of sweat had formed around his neck.

Her name, by the way, was Amelia Pettibone. She was 23 years old and a student at Leacock University. She was currently unattached but not interested in men, especially men as old as Boris. Her interest in him was purely out of curiosity. She was always friendly and liked to keep things platonic. But Boris amused her. And Boris was assuaged for the moment.

Now she watched as Frank, Boris and Kitchholm got up and exited as a group from Le Café Fritz.

eleven

"The clear truth no man has seen nor will anyone know concerning the gods."

Xenophanes 525 B.C

Michael Schulzman awoke from a fitful sleep on a bed of rabid dreams which featured Frida S. Wharton and her lovely husband Jack singing and dancing on a vaudeville stage. They moved about with canes and tipped straw hats to an audience of one. Behind them were a cast of chorus girls on pink and black clouds out of which the face of some godly figure seemed to emerge. Was it crying or was that simply the moisture of the skies in the god's eye? Schulzman was a bit concerned about this trip into the sub regions of his brain and decided it might be wise to make a note of the date and details of the encounter. He leaned over and saw that Meg was sound asleep. He finished his notations and got out of bed trying to focus on what he needed to do that day. He had to reply to emails concerning work to be done. And Meg wanted to go sightseeing in old Montreal.

Schulzman was having doubts about Meg especially because of the pamphlets that he had read the previous evening and the dream which seemed to him like some self-regulatory system in his brain giving him a warning sign not to pursue this relationship. But he loved her. He did not want to see her harm herself. He was hoping that she would disavow Wharton's assemblage of All-Knowing Truth bearers. He had hoped that by meeting Meg's mother he could find a way to convince her that she was throwing her life away.

Mary Barton was in kitchen preparing breakfast. She was scrambling eggs and cutting fruit while humming an indistinct tune based on chords and notes

74

from 1950s movie musicals. Her cheery mood hid some of her apprehension towards the pamphlets that her daughter had brought into the apartment. She had said to Meg the previous night, on the sofa that she thought that the pamphlets were nice and very informative being careful not to reveal any skepticism. Over the years she had become very good at this kind of deception, though she had in recent years been waiting for a moment where she could just blurt out what she really felt. She had tried it with a tiresome trio of fellow card players down at the senior's center and it had felt remarkably liberating. Yet this morning she was deliberately blocking anything to do with the Wharton crusaders.

After breakfast had been prepared, she walked over to the bedroom where Meg and Michael slept and lightly tapped on the door.

"Are you people up?"

"Yes" came Michael's voice.

Then the door opened and Michael stood there with a crooked smile. He said good morning quickly and gently skirted past Mary Barton to the bathroom.

"Gotta go"

"That's nice" Mary managed.

Then she peered in and saw her daughter crawling sleepily out of the double bed, rubbing her eyes.

"Mornin' mom"

"I have breakfast made for the two of you."

"That's nice. But I'm on a diet, mom"

"Michael must be hungry."

"Yeah, probably. But he really doesn't eat much breakfast."

75

"That's a shame."

"Well, that's the way he is."

Here the thought came to Mary Barton to say something regarding how she felt about Frida S. Wharton and her diets from the far reaches of the universe, but she stopped herself. She had heard the toilet flush in the background.

Michael finished with his affairs in the bathroom and shuffled back to the bedroom. He came into the bedroom checked his smartphone for messages, looked at the three that were there. Only one was important. It concerned work. He turned to Meg.

"What are you doing today, Meg?"

"Well after eating we'll go down to the Old Port"

Michael's mind was not particularly enthusiastic about this point. He would have rather confirmed the work that he needed to do, and spent the day talking Meg out staying in that cult that she was in. But right now, he did not want to start an argument in front of her mother. Maybe her mother could help him. He would find a private time to confide to her how he really felt.

In Pittsburgh, the Wharton office was abuzz with staff reading mail, both by computer and snail mail and printers going at full capacity. Frida was in her office in full make up and jewelry opening envelopes with checks of various denominations inside. On her desk was a white fluffy cat and her oversized Holy Bible. Also, on her desk was a phone with a bank of lines. A computer screen to her left depicted a screen saver with a high-definition photo of a mostly clear sky acting as a background for an ominous mountain range. A card on the frame of the computer had a slogan said:

She was in a moneyed trance now. She believed that the universe had given her privilege and insight that no one else had. She believed that a certain alignment of magnetic fields in space had provide her with the powers to decide with whom she would share this information. This was of prime importance and she needed to have the financial security to be able to deliver the goods. It was Lords of Lords in her mind that had blessed her. In her brain the chemicals had formed a wall of indifference to other paths of salvation to protect against deception. She could not be wrong.

Amongst the incoming mail was an envelope containing a check for $50.00 from Meg Barton. Accompanying the check was a note with questions of a broad philosophical and spiritual nature that would send any post-graduate student of the liberal arts whirling and headed for the stacks. Meg had been sincere in her devotion to the church, but her naivety lay in her need to experience instant resolve to her dilemmas both of the mind and practical. In her seven months as an official member of The Church of the Wayward her belief that the Wharton heavenly vessel would answer all her questions became more and more entrenched into her consciousness. She had read and reread the 27 booklets published by the church and the source links that they had provided. She had been attempting slow conversion of her friends and relatives and foresaw in her mind leaving them out of her life if they did not eventually conform to the church doctrine. In this particular letter one of the questions that she had for Wharton was:

Why do people feel pain at the death of others sometimes?

It was a basic question.

Meg had always been fascinated by people crying at funerals or their depiction in movies. She frequently had tears herself when others cried. Her heart broke quite often over the pain of others and now that her mind had expanded a bit, she had begun to ask herself these types of questions.

After Meg and Michael had finished eating and Michael was conceding to the idea of going sightseeing. Mary Barton fussed over them a while and then when Meg was in the bathroom whispered to Michael that she really was worried about her daughter and this cult that she had joined.

"I'm really worried that she will get herself into a heap of trouble with this stuff. I was reading the pamphlets and booklets that she had given me and it looks bad Michael. I saw a documentary on TV about cults and the brain-washing that happens to people. I don't want to lose my only daughter to this stuff. You seem like a smart guy Michael. What would you do?"

"I'm seeing the same thing. When I first met her nine months ago, she seemed quite well adjusted, maybe she needed some guidance, but I really thought that I could provide that. This church at first just seemed like a normal church, but lately it has been different. She can't seem to see anything in the world that is not related to something from the Wharton lady. I'm happy that you see this Mrs. Barton."

"I'm not sure that I do, Michael, but something must be done, I think. My husband, when he was alive always would have answers and solutions for Meg and me to these questions. Now I feel helpless. I almost feel like I should join this thing."

"I don't think that's the answer. We should maybe team up and have an intervention with her."

"I don't know. I've never done anything like that before."

"Well, I read some articles about how it's done on a couple of websites. I'll print out some stuff later for you"

Meg entered the room. She knew that she had been discussed quickly repressed this thought.

"So, what's up?" she said.

"Let's go see the sights"

"Have a fun day, guys" said Mary as she turned awkwardly back towards the kitchen.

As Meg and Michael walked out of the apartment, Michael thoughts were focused on stringing Meg along until he could get together with her mother and perhaps one other person to plan an intervention. He had read where it was suggested that at least three people be present when doing one of these things. Meg and Michael would be using a bus and the metro to get downtown. It was a beautiful July day.

twelve

"We marched in step to Stravinsky's muse."

Boris SwatcupsoFrom his poem 'Evolution Vomit'

A bit later that same morning, Boris Swatcupso was just pulling himself off an undersized couch at Frank's hotel room at L'Hotel Fish Pond, which was a considerable downgrade from the St.Viateur, where Warren Kitchholm was staying. He had a terrific headache and his body was stiff all over. His inner organs felt like slowly hardening cement and his eyes saw sparkles and black spots. As he hoisted himself up into a seated position, he spotted his remedy on the little coffee table not five feet from him. It was a third of a 26-ounce bottle of Wild Turkey whiskey. He knew that if he could mix this somehow with some soda and get it down, he would instantly feel better. He tried to think of work and the time of the day. He searched for his smartphone.

Frank lay like he had been shot dead on a single bed in the corner of the room. The television was on at low volume across from the couch and beside the bed. On TV was an old movie with James Stewart and Hedy Lamarr. Lamarr was trying to get Stewart to agree to a platonic marriage and Stewart was contorting himself trying to say that love and marriage are integral and that it is a man's responsibility to be self-sufficient.

Boris stared in catatonic state at the television for several minutes, then suddenly broke his trance and began looking for his smartphone. Stravinsky's "The Rites of Spring" streaming from just underneath the bed where Frank lay had broken his mental coma. He found the source of music. He reached down and grabbed the phone. Looking at the screen he saw that it was his work calling. He also noticed that he was thirty minutes late for his shift. He took a breath of courage and answered the call.

"Hello"

"Yeah, Boris. Where are you? It's 11:30."

"Had a family emergency, Patrice."

"OK, well get your ass down here as soon as you can. It's gonna be busy today."

"I don't think I can make it today."

"You should have called me earlier, Boris. I would have gotten Steve to come in. Are you gonna be in tomorrow?"

"I don't know"

"I need to know before tonight or I'm gonna to have to let you go, Boris."

"Right, I know. I just really got caught up with some stuff here."

"That's fine I don't want to know. Just let me know if you still want to work here or not."

"I'll call you later."

Boris then terminated the call. He turned and reached for the bottle of whiskey but thought better of it and went to the cramped bathroom and picked up the cloudy looking water glass from sink and filled it up with tap water. He gulped it down and filled it again, drinking the second glass with equal gusto. He looked at his tired face in the mirror. Maybe Patricia, not Patrice, had a good reason to leave him. His eyes had little life in them, except that they gave the appearance that they were about to explode.

A faint odour of vanilla tinged with sweat and inexpensive alcohol played in the air. Old memories seemed to inhabit the yellowed walls and well-trodden carpet that gave the room its seasoned look. Was that a type of flower in the wallpaper or a horse's head? Boris stood on warped pinkish and green tiles

81

that provided contours for his bare feet. Boris thought about how he and Frank were just two more dying souls providing another layer of visceral experience to the aura of the room. He knew that he had to re-create himself one more time if he wasn't going to sink any further into these smells, these infusions of despair, these nasty mental places where time and space have no conscious meaning.

Then he felt a little jolt of life in him as he remembered that they had bought a third of the bottle of whiskey and it must be in the room somewhere. He wasn't sure that he could keep it down. Then he thought a beer would be better. James Stewart was now getting upset at Hedy Lamarr's inability to conform to basic American family values. Frank stirred a bit in his tiny bed and cars honked outside in the streets.

"Pain pays the income of each precious thing" Boris offered to the air. With this he consoled himself and looked for his shoes.

Frank then came to life.

"Pain is knowledge, Boris."

"An audience speaks."

"Be quiet for a while, Boris."

"I'm going to the store. I'll be back."

"Not going to work?"

"I'm quitting. I'm going back to the assembly line of bad poets."

Frank looked up at Boris.

"Don't crucify yourself Boris. What are you going to get at the store?"

"Beer and meat."

"Wow what a way to support the North American economy."

"Please some semblance of reality here Frank. That's just what we need today."

"Fine, Boris, fine."

Frank's brain was under strain and refused to pursue the matter any further. He got up and looked for his duffel bag which contained his computer, spare clothing, notebooks and his copy of M. Richard Burke's Cosmic Consciousness: A Study in the Evolution of the Human Mind. When he found it, he pulled out the computer and opened in on the mini-sized coffee table carefully removing the third of a bottle of whiskey first and placing it on the floor.

"Be back." Boris left.

Frank had to focus for at least three minutes before he recalled how to get to his page of taglines. He wanted on this particular morning to reinforce the fact that he was technically employed. It had at times seemed like a lark this slogan writing gig, but it had turned out to be pretty lucrative for a single guy randomly navigating existence in survival mode. Frank still was not sold on the notion of this form of income, feeling that it was only a matter of time before it all came crumbling down on his poor head and then he would become destitute and begin to write despairing verses for desperate souls like Boris.

But this morning he would need to confirm to himself that his work meant something. Later he would have to find somewhere with an internet connection to check his financial situation. He did not yet employ a smartphone.

It was my opinion that Frank had always had a slight paranoid streak about him. Though not debilitating, it kept him in the shadows sometimes. On the other hand, this caused his thought process to be more meticulous. He would consider a matter longer than most people, being scrupulous with decisions. It seemed like Frank would only adopt new technology after he had seen the affects it had on others and more positively on how others handled it. I was not quite ready to make a judgement on whether Frank was approving of cyberspace or not. But regardless of my opinion, Frank knew that he had to step into the reality of it.

Frank then picked up his paper notebook and entered the following:

RANDOM YOUTH HITTING RANDOM PEOPLE RANDOMLY

BORIS' DESPAIR HAS A NEW EDGE TO IT

FISH POND NEEDS A RESIDENT UNEMPLOYED ARTIST

BORIS' OPTIMISM IS SHAPING A NEW WORLD

SUSTAINIBILITY IS NOT LIVING? BARE EXISTANCE?

NO SPIRIT? NO VISION?

After perusing his notebook and laptop for ten minutes he saw that it was past noontime. He poured himself two fingers of whiskey and turned up the volume on Stewart and Lamarr.

thirteen

"I say that the created universe is itself the maker and creator of itself"

Heraclitus 510 B.C.

Warren Kitchholm was at his hotel room awaiting a reply from an editor on his article Manufacturing Secrecy: The Creation of a Paranoid State. He had emailed his girlfriend in Toronto and gotten caught up on world affairs. In his brain a certain picture formed of dying planet, a certain doomsday scenario had gotten a hold of Kitchholm. Perhaps this had been from watching too many news programs over the years. He had inadvertently created distance from his girlfriend and ergo had been losing a meaning and purpose to his life. And he had begun to ruminate on the idea that he would soon become tired of interviewing people. These thoughts would only creep into his psychology when he had no good story on the horizon. He had just finished one and was waiting for his piece to be published. He still felt uneasy even though the acceptance of his article was only a formality at this point. He had been solicited for the idea weeks earlier. It was expected that they might make a few minor editorial changes. Still Kitchholm was nervous.

Kitchholm was 29 years old and had been writing since his early adolescent days. He had dropped out of university at 22 while working on an arts degree. He was nevertheless well read and had worked for some small publications as a staff writer, been a courier, worked as a bartender all the while continuing to write and submit articles and short stories to publications around the world. When he faced the threat of poverty he would return to his parent's home in the west end of Toronto. But in the last two years he had been fortunate enough to have had his work accepted with some regularity and had been able to have his expenses paid for travel by several media sources. He was becoming a reliable free-lancer with his pulse on the times. He had been with the same girl for a couple of years. She worked as a financial services manager in a bank.

Now he ate a bowl of Frosted Flakes and stared at his laptop screen reading news items. He did this for several minutes before deciding to check his notebook to jog his memory on any ideas that he may have noted but forgotten. It was here that he recalled the curious pair of men that he had met the previous evening in the coffee shop.

Kitchholm was not a particularly religiously inclined person. Nor did he have a great sense of things metaphysical or philosophical. His parents had not been church goers, in fact if pressed he was likely to say that he was an agnostic. His parents had been quite mundane in their daily business and social affairs and had never really been inclined to discuss esthetics or subjects of that ilk with their only son.

Kitchholm himself, had never been inclined to try and explore anything that may or may not have been transcendent about the universe. With Boris and Frank, his brain was being provoked in an area that had to this point been almost left barren of consciousness since his brief stint at university. A natural curiosity had been awoken in Kitchholm in the idle time that he now faced. He began to think that a good tale lay behind the lives of these two.

It is my opinion that the difference between the brain and the mind was one of developmental level of the consciousness of a person. Kitchholm's brain had been churning away, as most brains will, on stimuli regarding Boris and Frank ever since the assault on the previous day. The process had gained access to other parts of the brain and had built momentum until the moment that Kitchholm's mind was available for its conscious discovery. Now Kitchholm had a choice to make. Would he encourage this line of thinking or search for other angles of pursuit?

Kitchholm made a note of the hotel address that the pair had given him via email the previous night. L'Hotel Fish Pond was only four short blocks from where he was staying. He decided that he would spend the rest of the afternoon deciding if he had a story there. He had a scheduled flight just after midnight which he could cancel if necessary. He was only going back to Toronto after all and he had nothing else on his itinerary.

He used the hotel phone to call the L'Hotel Fish Pond.

"L'Hotel Fish Pond", a gruff French voice answered.

"Yes... Oui... My name is Warren Kitchholm and I was inquiring about a client of mine that may be staying at your establishment."

"On ne peut pas parler de nos résidents au téléphone. Il faut que tu viennes ici¨

And with that the man at the St.Viateur abruptly hung up the phone.

Ok figured Kitchholm, he would have to go to the L'Hotel Fish Pond in person to see if Boris and Frank were still there.

It was fairly warm summer day outside and Kitchholm enjoyed the four-block walk to the hotel. There was very little pedestrian traffic. Only the occasional panhandler or lost tourist interrupted his thought process. He observed the faces of the people and the behaviour of the drivers on the street. He took in the sense of fun that seemed to be in the atmosphere of the city.

As he approached the Fish Pond a young guy, strangely resembling the one with whom Frank had had the encounter the previous day rushed up to him with a wild look on his face and said,

"I know you. You were at Le Fritz yesterday. I know you. You don't fool us. You are a puppet of the system. You need to read our zine "Conspiremouth". Are you aware of the changes coming down around here? Are you?"

The young man seemed about 20. He was wearing a ripped t-shirt and ripped up jeans and had pink and gold hair. His face had handsome qualities and he did not demonstrate any quirky mannerisms, outside of his impromptu confrontation of Kitchholm. His eyes looked eagerly at Kitchholm for some sort of response. There was a sweetness about him.

"'Conspiremouth.' Never heard of it. Do you have a copy?"

"Yeah, sure right here in my bag. And it's just 'Conspiremouth', no 'The'. We don't like 'Thes'. Usually it's five dollars a copy, but I'll make a special deal for you."

"By the way... how is it that you know me, again.?"

Kitchholm was fishing for more information about why this young supporter of the journalistic arts had chosen him as a target for his ideas.

"I saw you at the café, yesterday."

"Was that a friend of yours that attacked that man on the sidewalk?"

"Not really a friend. He's just some freaked out guy that hangs around this area. Sometimes he has some cool things to say."

As the young guy was saying this he reached into his bag and pulled out a photocopied issue of 'Conspiremouth.'

It was on 81/2 X 10 white paper and contained five two sided pages stapled together in the upper left-hand corner. Across the top of the front page, it read:

CONSPIREMOUTH

'all of us are people ... what you identify as is your choice'

88

Below that was the month, a volume and issue number. Then came a headline of sorts:

HOW FUCKED UP IS THE POET NOW THAT

THE MALE MYTH HAS BEEN EXPOSED!!!

And below that was a grainy photo of some gender-neutral person seemingly taking their clothes off on a tiny stage. Kitchholm quickly scanned the rest of the page and took more interest in a shorter article that he had in the main piece. This article was announced with the headline:

IT'S A RIGHT TO LIVE IN A DWELLING, COPS PROTECT LANDLORDS.

Kitchholm had done a recent piece on homelessness. He scanned it quickly and looked up at the young guy.

"How many people put this together?"

"As many as we need. Anyone who has something to say that the media won't let us say."

"I'll read this later. Thanks. My name is Kitchholm. Warren Kitchholm. WarrenK1222.com. And you are?"

"Binky" the darkly dressed young guy said, so quickly that Kitchholm had to ask him to repeat it.

"And why do you assume that I'm a puppet of any system?"

"I overheard you talking with those guys yesterday. You thought that you could just get yourself some story, some publicity for yourself by exploiting some fucked up kid who jumped someone."

"I don't think that I was exploiting anyone."

"All journalists exploit people."

"Now that's a false generalization. Do you know what I mean, Binky?"

"Sure. You mean that I have no right to my opinion."

"No, I didn't say that."

"That's what you meant. Listen I gotta go. Read the zine."

And in an instance, he was gone down the sidewalk. It almost seemed to Kitchholm that he was running away. Kitchholm looked up at the dilapidated neon sign over his head that read 'L'Hotel Fish Pond Vacancy'.

It was above a single door behind which was a staircase leading up to a front desk where a dark-haired middle-aged man shuffled some papers around absent-mindedly on a desk. Behind him was a wall of slots with room numbers written in some type of florescent marker below them. On the wall was a poster for Art Film Fest. It was in orange and black and had a photo of a woman about to leap off a bridge into a river in what looked to be rural area.

Instead of the river being filled with water, it looked as if a flow of screaming people were moving downstream and calling up to the sky and to the woman for help. At the bottom of the poster it read Dominique Where is your Heart? A Film About Saving the World by Harry Parks.

Kitchholm approached the desk and said hello.

"Comment je peux vous aider?" the clerk asked roughly.

"English first, sorry"

"That's ok, sir." said the man transitioning into English without hesitation and no hint of a French accent.

"My name is Warren Kitchholm. I called earlier. I was looking for two gentlemen who are supposedly staying here. One was kind of thin and about thirty and the other middle-aged."

"Ah, yes. And what are their names?"

"Well, I only got one gentleman's full name. Boris Swatcupso. I think the other guy's name was Frank."

"Swatcupso, um, let's see."

The man behind the desk checked on his computer.

"Kind of an odd name Swatcupso." said the deskman.

"Yes, could be African, but he isn't black."

"Well, I have nothing here under that name."

The deskman looked at Kitchholm with some anxiety and impatience now.

"Perhaps if I described them to you?" Kitchholm suggested.

"Look, I really don't try and remember what people look like."

"Yes, I can understand that."

"Sorry I can't help you anymore than that."

"Do you have a lounge or waiting area here?"

"Well, you can sit over there for a while if you like."

The man indicated a three colored leather looking upholstered chairs that sat next to a couple of vending machines. They were an off red rusty colour and had metal arm rests. Kitchholm said thanks and wandered over to the chairs and sat down. He felt some trepidation at his coming here. He also was not looking forward to waiting too long for the pair considering that any thread of hope of a good story behind these two was quite flimsy.

He sat down and observed the deskman for a while. Then he looked at the meager selection of sandwiches behind the plastic compartments in the vending machine. The other vending machine contained chips and assorted healthier snacks. He glanced at his watch. It was now 12:45. He would wait fifteen minutes and think of his next move.

Down the hall in room 115, Frank was sipping whiskey and watching James Stewart work his fumbling love magic on Hedy Lamarr.

Most people today don't know anything about these films thought Frank. What do people know anyhow? Is anyone engaged with any thread of reality today? Is love worth discussing? Was love a real thing or only a fantasy of Hollywood or some philosophers and poets? Frank pondered in this fashion for a while. Then the film ended with Stewart and Lamarr embracing. Frank checked the television for something else. Nothing. He shut it off. He went over to the window and wondered where Boris might be. He was sure taking his time. Frank hoped that Boris hadn't gotten enthralled with another woman. That would mean that he might not come back today.

Frank then decided that he needed some mix for the whiskey and that he wanted to check his bank account just a couple of blocks away. Frank had not adapted to internet banking yet. He thought that it would leave a mental cloud over him if he had to worry about fraud all the time.

He would leave a message at the desk for Boris and the key. He would return from the bank and pay for another night at the hotel.

It was getting warm in the room anyhow and some fresh air would help.

Frank left the room, locked the door and walked briskly down the hall towards the front desk. Before he turned the corner near the lobby a door opened in front of him and a young man of about 25 exited. He wore a light blue bomber jacket and brown pants. He was thin and had shaggy long hair. He looked anxious and determined not to be noticed. But Frank noticed him. He gave Frank a furtive look and quickly scrambled ahead of him towards the lobby, almost running past the front desk and down the stairs.

Frank felt a strange attraction toward this young man. He thought of his last couple of years of wandering around and sure felt that perhaps he was lonely.

Frank's mind quickly changed course as he turned the corner to enter the lobby.

Kitchholm spotted him.

"Frank."

Frank stopped, a little stunned but managed a half-smile.

"I didn't think I'd see you again."

Kitchholm stood up.

"Well, I had the afternoon off, so I thought I'd see how you were getting on after your little incident with that guy."

"I'm ok. Just slugging back a few anesthetics for the pain."

"Yes, well I thought I'd would check on you guys. Where's you friend Boris?"

"Just out on business."

Frank didn't really want to talk with Kitchholm much. He was beginning to feel a little trapped by Kitchholm manners. But he did remember that he had a positive feeling about Kitchholm when they had first met.

"Look I have to go down the street to the bank and the grocery store. Do you want to tag along?"

Frank was not inclined to curtly dismiss people. He had a polite streak sometimes even to the point of apparent passivity. But he could always get out of situations when he wanted to. He hadn't made up his mind yet on Kitchholm.

The two made their way down the stairs and out onto the sunny street.

When they had walked about 50 feet down the street Frank was inspired to ask Kitchholm a question.

"Do you believe in the human soul Mr. Kitchholm?"

"Well, that's quite a complex question. It depends on what you mean by the soul."

"Well, let me put it to you another way. What does 'human soul' mean to you?"

"Well, I'd have to think about that one. You caught me off guard."

"Sure, it's not an easy one. But I'm sure you have thought about it before, after all you do write for a living."

"Well, yes but not exactly about things... um ... metaphysical."

"I'll tell you why I ask it. I'm considering going to a conference this week at the university. It's called Sustainability and the Soul and I was just wondering exactly what a soul is myself. I have my own idea but I wanted to get someone else's thoughts."

"Well, I'm afraid you may have asked the wrong person. I don't really have a theological or philosophical background. In fact, I'm probably what you may call an agnostic when it comes to this sort of stuff."

"I'd like an impression from you anyhow."

"Well, really I wouldn't know where to start."

"Start with the here and now. How do you feel?"

"I don't know. Pretty good I guess."

"You feel good. That's good. Is it you that feels, or just a part of you?"

"Now you are making things difficult."

At this point Frank stopped his gait and lifted his index finger indicating that he had spotted Boris just ahead of them. A few people hurried past them on foot and bikes. A skateboarder whizzed by startling them. A chain of blue air seemed to flow between Boris and Frank as they spotted each other. Boris was in seemingly jovial mood. He shouted out.

"Frank."

He walked quickly towards Frank and Kitchholm.

"Hey, where are you going?" he asked.

"Bank and grocery store. This is Warren Kitchholm, the writer, from last night."

"Yes, I remember. So, you decided that this guy was worth the time of day."

"I had the afternoon free, so I just thought I'd see how you two were getting along" said Kitchholm

"Well, we've managed to almost kill a couple bottles of bourbon and some beer. But you know Frank here does a bit of writing. Advertising man he is."

"Not real writing. I keep a notebook." Frank chimed in.

95

"Well, words put together in a coherent fashion is writing no matter how many of them that there are" said Kitchholm.

"I guess. Listen I have to get to the bank and the store. Why don't you guys meet me back at my hotel in about thirty minutes."

"Ok"

"And, by the way, I think you make your own soul up as you go along."

Frank walked away without waiting for a response.

"What was that about the soul?" asked Boris.

"He was asking about what a soul was. I guess he answered himself."

"Well, Kitchholm, I think someone named Goethe had something to say about the soul. That's where I first read about it."

Another skateboarder raced by them just missing Boris. A taxi driver yelled loudly out of his car window at some woman who appeared to be struggling with some luggage. A young woman in sunglasses carried a bouquet of flowers down the street. A young man walked down the street with his head buried in a small volume of what appeared to be poetry. Many others wore earbuds and headphones from which they listened to various interpretations and manipulations of the air. A couple of punkish looking dudes walked with fierce determination. A man in a beret watched with dancing eyes through a coffee shop window as a barista prepared an elaborate cup of coffee. And Boris seemed blinded and deafened for a moment as he tried to remember what Goethe had written almost 200 years ago.

"Goethe, eh?" Kitchholm finally said, "Faust."

"Faust, yes. Ah fuck, I can't remember."

"I'll look it up for you later."

And, St. Amos Street continued its vibrancy. Boris suggested that they go for a beer around the corner.

Kitchholm didn't want a drink,but agreed to go anyhow.

"You know I think I quit my job today." Boris announced before leading Kitchholm into a darken establishment one door down from St. Amos. It was called 'Bar Nun.'

Boris found them a table near the opened terrace.

"Well, you seem like the type of soul that just improvises his life."

"You may be right. But there is one thing I don't improvise with and that is woman. I know them too well. Need to be prepared for them, Kitchholm."

"Really now. Don't you think that you need to be prepared for any person that you want to have a relationship with."

"Perhaps but I've learned that not all, let me say, genders are the same."

"Maybe you're right."

"Beauty is in the eye of the beholder. Something like that." Boris intoned.

"Goethe didn't say that did he?"

"Something like that. Beauty is made by man in his mind."

"That seems a little closer."

"I had a beautiful day. Where has my beauty gone? She has run away with another."

"Lost a woman recently, Boris?"

"Yes. At least temporarily. She cannot appreciate my wide-ranging outpourings of love."

"You mean cheating."

"I don't cheat. I spread myself more evenly about."

"Well, that's another way of putting it."

Boris laughed and signalled for the short brown-haired woman serving drinks to come over.

Kitchholm ordered a ginger ale and Boris a large draft beer.

"The creation of beauty is the ongoing occupation of humanity. Its destruction is only a pastime."

"Who said that?" asked Kitchholm.

"Don't know. Maybe I just made it up. Could be Goethe, but I doubt that. He wouldn't have used the word humanity."

Kitchholm just chuckled. A breeze came over them from the street.

fourteen

Bo Creeley was under the gun now at RCMP headquarters in Montreal. He sat in a small windowless room with a metal table and three metal chairs. He occupied one chair. Seated in the other two chairs were detective Bob Bird of the police and William Sloan of the Canadian Border Police.

They were both firing questions at Creeley about his reasons and contacts in Canada. They both knew that they needed to have more evidence in order to hold him much longer.

He had demanded a lawyer. He had demanded that he either be charged or released. Now they had found that he had entered the country illegally, but that only required that they deport him promptly or release him under his own recognizance. He would have to file papers with immigration in that case.

But Creeley was not happy. Neither were his cohorts who were undergoing a similar grilling just a few doors down from Creeley.

"It's all bullshit. All bullshit, sir. None of that information that ya guys have is worth the paper that it's written on."

"So, you expect us to believe that you are not the Creeley that is behind the website OneBigLie?" asked Bird, the bigger of the two officers.

"Listen a man has a right to freedom of expression."

"But not entering the country illegally."

"Well, send me back then. That's what ya guys want isn't it. Send me back to my doom. Ya can send me back but it won't shut me up."

Both Bird and Sloan had quickly realized that this method of extracting any more information about locations and contact was not working. They really were getting more and more frustrated and were becoming further inclined to turn this all over to the American authorities.

Creeley now tapped his foot and asked for a cigarette.

After another twenty minutes Bird came in.

"We're going to drive you to the border. You have over two thousand dollars. We'll let you go there."

He didn't tell Creeley that they also were arranging for a reception on the American side. The FBI and other department of the government were all interested in Creeley. But they really had no case against him, they just wanted to keep an eye on him. He was an angry man with an elaborate arsenal and many opinions which pointed at the government as the source of all problems in society, mostly the ones that Creeley and his father had experienced.

As Creeley and company were being chauffeured back to America, Creeley's daddy was defecating in his bed and cursing the president of the United States of America for working in league with Arabs and the Catholic Church to poison the drinking water of children so that they would either become suicidal or turn 'homersexual'. That was how Creeley Sr. pronounced it. And he could spot the 'homos' from at least twenty yards away and within ten seconds.

Creeley Sr. had just days before called a male nurse 'a sodomite' as his diaper was being changed. Later he demanded that the nurse be tested for AIDS. Most of the staff at the nursing home secretly wished that the old fart would die soon. They failed to see any reason that this man should keep on living just to be a nuisance to everyone.

But inside Creeley Sr. was a heart and a soul. They were buried deep down under years of unresolved anger. Occasionally the old guy would say thanks to a nurse for giving him an extra blanket or moving the television set closer.

Now Creeley Sr. shouted for someone to come and clean up the mess he had made in his bed. It was a sad state for him. A nurse came and with a kind and patient attitude finished the job despite Creeley's protests and admonishments Then he demanded that the television be turned on for the four o'clock news. He needed more things to yell about.

Within moments the story of Creeley Sr. son being deported back to the United States from Canada came on.

Creeley Sr. was suddenly silent. He did not want to betrayed any feelings to the nurses and staff around him that might be in on the plot. But in his heart, he was proud of the 'arrest'. And angry at the authorities.

This time, though, he held it in and waited patiently for his dinner to be served. It was one of the quietest evenings experienced on old man Creeley's ward ever since he had been admitted.

fifteen

"I don't want to go to heaven, none of my friends are there."

Oscar Wilde

Warren Kitchholm and Boris Swatcupso were just finishing their drinks as the two o'clock hour past on the sunny summer afternoon just off of the St. Amos street strip. Boris was sleepily suggesting that perhaps they should be going back to the hotel to see Frank as he probably had returned by then. Kitchholm agreed.

It was getting hot out. It was sticky and people's faces demonstrated more frustration and impatience as the level of humidity increased. A paralysis was developing in the city. Kitchholm and Boris slowly moved through the laboring sidewalk traffic as they made their way back to the hotel. Boris' mind had gone into a place of fantastic imagery featuring woman of all of types and situations where he could rescue them from peril. This revelry was being aided by remembrances of the poetry of Madison J. Butterworth, the Russian born literary man and poet now residing in London. One of his poems to the restless sex as he referred to woman many times on his radio show rantings was entitled, "She behind the tender tearing Face".

Boris thought of this one as he approached the Fish Pond. He was jolted out his fantasy by Kitchholm.

"We are here, Boris." Kitchholm grabbed Boris lightly by the right arm.

"Yeah, I was just thinking about someone."

They went swiftly upstairs and Boris opened room 115 without knocking.

They both entered.

"Here we are Frank."

Frank was looking at something on his laptop. Kitchholm checked his smartphone and saw that Creeley had been arrested or detained more accurately. He would have to add a couple of paragraphs to his story or perhaps revise it entirely.

He called up his editor.

After some discussion, it was decided that they would just add an extra paragraph at the end of the story as a teaser for future developments in the Creeley affair.

Kitchholm apologized for the distraction but within five minutes had composed and added the necessary information to the article.

Frank sat on the couch looking out on the street. He hadn't opened the fresh bottle of whiskey yet. Boris was on the phone still trying to locate Patricia.

Kitchholm would soon speak up. He was still curious about why someone would have hit Frank over the head, seemingly without provocation. Kitchholm wanted a little background on Frank and then he would combine that information with the zine that he had in his bag and keep it on file for further investigation.

Or perhaps the story would go nowhere. But he had looked into homelessness and street youth in previous stories and this could perhaps be a good follow up. He watched Frank who seemed to be sinking into a depressed state. Maybe it had been the booze. Maybe Frank was suffering a concussion and needed the attention of a doctor.

"Are you feeling ok Frank?"

"Yeah, sure. Why?"

"You look catatonic."

"I'm thinking of my brother, Jesse. I haven't seen him in three years. I don't know where he is."

"Do you want to see him?"

"I don't know. Somehow, I think that I would have a bad influence on him. He is such a dreamer. In his own world. I prefer not to interfere with that. But I could probably find him if I wanted to."

"Frank, how do you feel about being attacked at random like you were last night?"

"I think it was absolutely random. I don't feel any fear. Some kid on drugs probably."

"You don't think that you were targeted, then?"

"Naw."

In reality Frank was holding on to a paranoid feeling about the incident. He had been careful not to show this to anyone. The drinking had helped but he had to slow down on the booze at some point and this was concerning him now. He began to detest Kitchholm's presence. His thoughts were growing into a mystic combination of how his life had become so haphazard and yet it was somehow desirable. He enjoyed the meandering path that he had been on the last couple of years since his divorce. Deep in his recesses was a fear that he would be blamed for choosing this path. Why he didn't know. He sometimes thought that his quiet brother would have an answer. All the times that they had spent together Jesse had been observing him and maybe he could come up with an answer to why Frank felt guilty. Now with the lump on his head he felt that his guilt was justified. But he would never reveal this to anyone, including Boris and especially Kitchholm.

Boris was now sitting quietly in an armchair sipping whiskey and water.

Kitchholm spoke.

"So maybe I should be going?"

Frank reacted to this statement with two impulses. One was with a sense of fear at losing a new friend in Kitchholm, and the other was with a sense of relief that any potential inquisition was over.

"Maybe" he finally said.

"You know you should get that thing on your head looked at by a doctor."

"Yeah, thanks."

"Go to the hospital, Frank." Boris chimed in.

"Your friend is right."

With this Kitchholm picked up his things and motioned to leave.

"Well, I need to leave. I have to finish up at the hotel and get ready to catch my flight back to T.O"

"Thanks for your concern Mr.Kitchholm. I'll be ok"

Frank managed a smile. Boris was now sullen, the alcohol taking effect.

After Kitchholm was gone Frank felt relief. He turned to Boris and said.

"You know that guy was strange."

"Writers are strange, sometimes." Boris looked up at Frank.

"I'm not feeling so well, Boris. Maybe you'd better go home. Take the bottle with you. I don't need it. I have to think awhile."

"Are you sure?"

"I'm sure, Boris. A day or two of rest and reflection is what I need."

"Ok, Frank. May your wishes be granted. I will exit from your life for a couple of days, but I will be back. And Frank, take care of that bump on the head."

"Sure."

But Frank wasn't much concerned with his head in the manner that Boris was thinking of.

Boris got up and put the bottle of whiskey in a bag. He walked toward the door.

"Well, Frank see you soon"

"Later"

And Frank was left alone with the stale odours and ancient décor. He tidied up the room and poured himself a glass of club soda from the mini-fridge.

He climbed into bed and stared at the ceiling for a few minutes trying to induce sleep. His mind drifted into a state semi-consciousness where ideas were forming from an unknown region of his brain. His memories of the previous evening now were becoming haunting. He no longer had an anesthetic to ward off the fears. But he considered himself to be well. He considered that he only needed to reset his priorities for the day, the week, the month. The slug on the head perhaps had awoken a desire for order in his days. That need to facilitate order had long ago disappeared just after he had married. His wife had provided the order in the home, arranging appointments, preparing budgets, doing tax returns, planning trips and nights out at concerts and arts events. He had seemed satisfied with this arrangement for quite awhile. He enjoyed just having to focus on his work. At first, he enjoyed the romance and the sex with his wife, but by the second year of the marriage he had become restless. He took her preoccupation with making certain everything flowed in their lives for granted. Her activities became background to his life. He seemed to be seeking a more spirited and random route, something with less predictability and more chaos. Her voice was sounding to him more and more mechanical and so was the sex. He began frequenting porn sites and reading novels that evoked less established lifestyles. He would frequently demean regularity as being uninspired. His wife was saw that he was changing and that it worried her. He began to stop arguing with her or even defending himself, but instead made excuses to go out at night or be away from the house. They had lived in a suburb of Toronto and many times he would visit gay bars in the city's core and just sit there watching people (mostly males) and eavesdropping on their conversations. Other times he would drive around the city without a destination and end up at one of the east end beaches just looking out onto the lake.

One day he just came home around eight at night and told his wife that he was leaving her. It was a something that she had intuitively felt, but that she had never thought he would execute so abruptly. He put some things into a bag and told her that she could have the car and that he would take half of the money that they had in their savings accounts, which wasn't a lot, and that he would send her a portion of his income periodically by check. She had began firing questions at him when she saw that he was serious. Her ordered plans were now in disarray. She had never been a yeller, but she tried yelling. He was stoic. This brought on more yelling and then finally she just asked why. It now seemed that she had never known her husband.

And Frank had never known her. He really hadn't known himself. His stone-faced attitude reflected bewilderment at his current life situation and a hidden desire for a new one. Or perhaps a hidden one.

So, Frank left their rented house on foot walking towards the nearest bus stop as his wife sat in astonishment and anger in the living room. She probably called some friends. She probably called her family, but more than that she probably questioned the sanity of her husband. Her intuition had told her that he had been losing interest in their life together, but she had felt that because of her life management skills he would always need her and would not leave. She probably now wondered if she had ever loved him. Probably not. Such were the probabilities of their marriage. The odds had been shifting for some time.

Frank had caught a bus into the city and gotten on a Greyhound for Vancouver. He had contemplated this road trip many times in his mind but had not systemized an itinerary. He had a vague desire to have sexual relations with a male for years, but had not made any plans to put those thoughts into action. Now that he had executed his departure from his wife, he felt that he could make more decision for himself. On the bus he thought of his wife and decided that he would phone her frequently and send her money, after all she was not an evil person and did deserve that much consideration. Yet, he felt no sorrow for his decision. No second thoughts came into his head. It was as if he had known that this move was going to happen for years, but he could not have anticipated when it was going to happen until just hours before he did it. The time spent only thinking of embarking on a new life had always seem unrealistic to Frank. He had not thought that he would have the courage to make the move when the time came. He was becoming increasingly unhappy and staying with her seemed unjustifiable. He had really believed that it had been a wrong choice for him to marry. And as far as he was concerned, she had been totally blind and unwilling to listen.

He found that he could not tell her his thoughts and frustrations in a manner that would cause her to really hear him. So, he gave up what he thought was a futile cause and embarked on an adventure that now found him supine in bed at a low-end hotel in Montreal. Had he ran out of courage? Maybe he should call her now? He still cared for her and it had been a while. He wasn't ready yet to contemplate his life here on earth being in demise. So, what if he had no fixed address or was incommunicado with his family. They could all go screw themselves, he was going to be happy. He felt some anger toward his childhood, then began to count slowly to a hundred as he drifted away.

Maybe the bump on his head had done its magic.

sixteen

"I see myself as an intelligent, sensitive human with the soul of a clown, which forces me to blow it at the most important moments."

Jim Morrison

Jesse had been living with in Montreal for two years. He had a part time girlfriend and a small 21/2 room apartment in the west end. He worked as a barista at a Coffee Express near Leacock university. He listened to music a lot and played some guitar. His girlfriend considered herself an anarchist and read books by obscure authors who talked of politics and social ideals which she preached to Jesse constantly. Jesse was a sensitive, caring young man who felt like a woman inside. He had the ability to absorb the world and its diverse ideas and people without it disturbing his peace of mind. He had just accepted what surrounded him as a youth and had gone with the flow. But he had some disturbances coming from within.

Because of his boyishness and easygoing nature, many young woman and girls who had things to say about the world were attracted to him. He had soft hair and a clear face that featured high cheekbones. He was mostly soft spoken but could be exuberant at times. His current girlfriend's name was Cassandra and she was a motivated woman who worked at the university radio station as a program coordinator. She talked a lot and had varied opinion on how many communities in Montreal were underrepresented in places where decisions were made. Jesse and Cassandra were for the most part monogamist. They saw each other twice a week and usually had sex after they had gone out to some concert or political event. Cassandra worked at the radio station during the day and would sometimes flirt with guys but never with the intentions of leaving Jesse behind. She was experimenting. And really so was Jesse, though he only vaguely would be attracted to other women. At work he would sometimes have women come on to him, but he never took these women's attention to him as anything but peccadillos. Yet he often wondered if an older woman could meet his needs better. But Cassandra was pretty good at that and he did really like her, besides she was teaching him so much about the world. In fact, she had suggested that they attend The Sustainability and the Soul conference featuring Dr. Ambrose J. Keel, but Jesse had been working that day.

Dr. Ambrose J. Keel was a man with an open mind, not only as an academic, but as a human being. He considered what others had to say seriously and was rarely dismissive of diverse opinion, even when he knew them to be wrong. He tolerated it but would be certain to make his own views equally known.

Though he had developed debating skills, he rarely used them anymore, finding that arguing against something seemed only a futile exercise and that action only came about through positive ideas. This was his considered and developed philosophy.

Little did his colleagues and friends know that Keel's even handedness was not some personally developed quality, but came from many sources that his peers had dismissed or chose to ignore. He had read and believed in the intuitive writings of M. Richard Burke and what he saw in the further development of these ideas in people like Carl G. Jung. He believed that he had tapped into a source of Cosmic Consciousness. A level of seeing through the immediate and practical use of material things and realizing a much more expansive meaning and purpose to the mundane. He never believed in magical heavenly beings or the supernatural and still didn't, but he saw the mind as something barely understood or comprehended. Capable of so much more than what it had been used for to date. In fact, he believed that much of the mind's qualities in contemporary society were being squandered on repetition and inane tasks that produced no quality of life or peace of mind. Yet, he acknowledged that there was a lot of hope in the young people as they strove to better understand the planet. He thought that at least some were doing that. Others still drove the old bus of profit and practicality, a vehicle that valued immediate gratification and social status as two of the most important qualities in life.

Burke's book had chapters on prominent figures who had reached Cosmic Consciousness in the past, including, Buddha, Jesus, Mohammed, Dante, Francis Bacon, Bartolomé Las Casas, William Blake and quite remarkably, Walt Whitman. Burke's book was regarded by most as unscientific but it struck Keel as realistic insight into how inspiration worked in the human mind and not necessarily just the brain.

Keel had created this formula to explain his idea:

Brain/Experience/Instinct + Willingness/Faith/Persistence = Inspiration

He had it written in many of his notebooks. To him it gave his students and others an idea, in basic terms what life was about. To him it was a point of clarity no matter what field of study one chose or how elaborate and complex was the process of one's life and work, it applied.

Also, in Keel's notes was this equation:

Brain+Soul+Spirit+Body = Mind

To Keel the brain was both the factory and warehouse where raw material was taken to, developed and made into ideas and thoughts through a complex chemical process. When an idea seemed worthwhile to an individual's brain it could be submitted to the Soul and Body for consideration as a possible action. This process, which according to Keel, happened most of the time was unconscious or involuntary. The Spirit added the unknown or mysterious and Keel had not attempted an explanation of Spirit but saw it as sort of a random factor not yet known and perhaps unknowable by the Brain alone. It was Keel's view that all these areas were subject to bad information, bad faith and bad intention. Sometimes Keel called these diseases and illnesses of various sorts. These dysfunctions could be physical, mental or more mysteriously spiritual. Now Keel had a pretty big brain and lots of experience using it so he had many answers but had recognized how little he knew. He had reached this conclusion not only because of his big brain but as a result of acting on inspiration. As he went further in his research, he developed a sense that all of this work he had been doing had no ending and perhaps no beginning, except if one arbitrarily set some sort of artificial start and finish line.

To Boris Swatcupso all that mattered was the present time. His mind was not concerned with beginnings and endings but with immediate words and actions. Sometimes that worked brilliantly and sometimes it ended in catastrophe. After leaving Frank, Boris had spent the night cruising women in bars up and down St. Amos street. He had finally ended up with 37-year-old Polish violinist who had been having trouble finding work in her profession in Canada. She was working in a daycare centre and going out at night looking for a man and Boris had impressed her with poetry and charm and they had ended up sleeping together. In the morning, she quickly made up some excuse and left without leaving Boris any number.

Boris was not too perturbed by this. In his heart he still was hoping that Patricia would return.

He had a cup of coffee at his loft and phoned Frank.

"Hey" said Frank sheepishly.

"Frank, how are you feeling? How the head?"

"Ok"

"You should really go to the hospital."

"I'm fine, Boris."

"Ok, if you say so."

113

"Hey the conference that I was talking about the night before last starts today. I think I'm going, just to see what this Keel guy has to say."

"Right Frank, always the curious one."

"Want to come?"

"Why not. I don't have anything else on the burner."

"Just behave yourself Boris."

"So, in other words, no fun."

"Whatever. Come over here and we'll walk down to the university. Keel's first talk is at 2 P.M"

"On my way."

Boris put his smartphone down and decided that he needed a shower and a shave. This was not routine for him. His hygienic practices were quite unscheduled and many times left out all together. But when it counted, he made a point of washing up. This usually involved a woman or a public event. Boris switched on the radio to an all-news station to get some worldly information.

The announcer went through the same old stories of wars, political schemes, crimes and terrorist threats but then hit upon a story that captured Boris' attention.

"In arts news, the ex-Russian, now British poet Madison J. Butterworth will be arriving in Montreal as a last-minute addition to the Sustainability and Soul Conference at Leacock University tomorrow. Butterworth will be not only reading his poems on the environment and politics but will taking questions from the audience. Butterworth is known for his activism on radio and

114

websites regarding ecology and the future. The session has been added in for tomorrow at 6 PM in Orillia Hall."

Well, now thought Boris, it will be really worth going to the conference. Madison J. Butterworth had always inspired Boris, not just has a wordsmith, but as a charmer of woman. Boris still had a mindset that embraced the classic seduction and the Butterworth poetic caravan enabled him to continue in this vane despite the increasing resistance of many of the female persuasion to cooperate. But Boris was unaware that the caravan had been parking in a transgendered spot for the last three years and Madison J. Butterworth's infatuation with a seemingly female Olivia, had become a more deeply felt love for a male named Brandon.

These facts had not been reported in the media because Butterworth had made sure that Olivia turned Brandon was well hidden from publicity until his partner would be completely comfortable with the transformation.

It is my opinion that Butterworth had known of the inclination of his partner to become a male when he had first met "her". But Butterworth had given no overt hints of just how fluid his sexuality had become. Butterworth had the reputation of being a classic traditional "ladies man". He had married three times and had quickly divorced three times. Then he became satisfied with not having a wife and just "seeing" woman, and now it appeared just "seeing" people.

Having read all of Butterworth's poetry I believed that he years before what he was going to be up to. But the final piece of evidence for me was in a poem that had appeared both online and had been orated over the radio not more three months after the rumors had circulated that Butterworth was keeping a lover hidden away somewhere. He was always appearing in public alone. That had not been his style before. The poem was entitled "Brave To Love A Soul Changing". It addressed a sexless "soul" and a heavenly meeting where all sexuality and love came together. Butterworth had never written words of this sort before. I didn't have proof but I had an intuitive sense of where he would be directing affections.

115

Butterworth was releasing via internet and on CD a recording of his poems put to music and sung by some noted vocalists. He, himself, also would be appearing on the CD. Therefore, it appeared that Butterworth was in a state of fully recreated himself and carrying a box of his new endeavors with him across the Atlantic to Montreal. The old codger had become inspired again. Who was the new muse?

Boris arrived at the Fish Pond around noon. He and Frank both decided to have lunch at an outdoor bistro before going to the conference. Boris was in a spirited mood. He ordered salmon, shrimp, bruschetta and ice cream

"What's up with all the fancy food?"

"Frank, wait until you hear who is going to be at that conference tomorrow night."

"Who, Boris, Lady GaGa?"

"Get serious my friend."

"Well let's see Margaret Atwood?"

"No, not that serious"

"Ok the ghost of Michel Foucault in drag fighting climate change but not sex change."

Boris chuckled.

"Good one, but way off base."

"Well, who?"

"Madison J. Butterworth"

"That's right, I remember you talking about him many times on our little drinking excursions. You even read his stuff to me in a bar once. What's he up to these days?"

"Still at it. Last I checked he was keeping a hidden lover somewhere north of London. But he still does his radio shows and podcasts. He just published a volume of short stories and poems called 'Where Have all The Women Gone?'"

"Well, he might answer that question tomorrow night."

"Maybe, Frank."

The waiter came with the bill. They paid and walked out of the bistro and toward the conference. Boris decided that he needed a small bottle of hard stuff to sustain him. Frank disagreed, thinking it better to hold off on the drinking until evening, but he couldn't convince Boris.

By the time, Boris and Frank had arrived at the conference hall it was close to 2 P.M. The hall was only a third full and Boris was feeling buoyant having consumed half a mickey of whiskey. He was in a type of excited state by the time Keel was being introduced. He whistled and hollered when Keel came on even though he knew nothing of Keel's view, politics, opinion or favorite sports teams. Boris, the poet provocateur, was coming out and Frank was not comfortable. Frank had become truly interested in Keel ever since they had met on the bus into Montreal. He had done a cursory investigation of his work on the internet and really wanted to listen to him and ask questions. Boris it seemed might sabotage the whole thing. He refused Frank's suggestion that he sit on the opposite side of the room from Frank so that if Boris was eventually removed Frank would not be linked with him and he could get his questions. Most of the time Frank would not be uncomfortable around Boris, especially when they were both drinking. But now Frank was sober and really wanted to hear Keel.

117

"Thanks to the conference Sustainability and Soul for inviting me. I'm not one to make preliminary remarks so I will go right into my subject matter...". Keel began.

Suddenly Boris stood up and exclaimed fairly loudly.

"When are you going to keel over?"

Frank moved away from Boris looking for a seat near front.

A couple of young men laughed a little. Most of the people just turned to look at who had said such an impertinent thing. Most of the people were in a serious mind set. Boris was obviously slightly impaired. The moderator quickly made a move towards the back of the room to quietly address Boris.

"This is the end, my friend, the end..." warbled Boris.

The audience murmured. Keel stopped his speech and was staring quietly with concern at Boris who was nearly a hundred feet away.

The moderator, who had a distinguished look about him and wore heavy rimmed glasses, approached Boris from the side and whispered into his left ear.

"You see, I was right it is the end, my friends..."

He then turned to the distinguished moderator and whispered something in his right ear.

"Sorry, people I will give you back your most excellent guest. You are now back on an even keel."

Boris blurted this out emphatically before smiling with acquiescence at the distinguished looking moderator and wobbling towards the back doors. But he had not finished.

"My friends, do not miss the orations and literary dispensations of Madison J. Butterworth tomorrow night in this very hall at 6 P.M. You have been forewarned and have no excuse."

He then paused for about three seconds and shouted with even more resolution.

"And Frank, I'll see you at the bar across the street in an hour."

He then aggressively pushed open one of the doors with his right arm and left the space free for Keel to resume his address much to the relief of the audience. But it was especially consoling to Frank. Keel held the reins for the next sixty minutes.

seventeen

"Whatever satisfies the soul is truth"

Walt Whitman

"Do you think love lasts forever, Michael?" Meg Barton asked her boyfriend as they wandered around the city, looking in stores and visiting a couple of museums. It was their second day of sightseeing. Michael had been bringing up questions about religion, the soul and immortality in an effort to get Meg to see that she was being foolish in supporting the fraud that was Frida S. Wharton and her Church of the Wayward.

Michael Schultzman did not think of himself as a non-believer in some higher being or the concept of perpetual life. He was not comfortable with the word atheist. It had too much of a ring of cynicism and negativity for him to use it as a label for the way he saw purpose and meaning in the world. But he surely could spot a fraud when he recognized one. And what he had seen Meg fall for was just that.

They were both sitting on a park bench near the university and Meg was beginning to cry when she asked Michael about love. She had been thinking about Michael's questions. She had been waiting for an intuitive response that would satisfy her soul. She did not want to answer Michael dishonestly, believing that his questions did not have verifiable answers. With her tears she was coming out of her fantasies of achieving instantaneous enlightenment in this life. She cried lightly when she asked Michael about love being forever. She didn't expect an answer from him. She really was asking herself the question. She began to question the series of events that had led her to joining the church. Her desperation and lack of confidence in herself. Her perpetual doubt as to love being a real thing in life and her cynicism towards making the world a better place. All this had slowly been swirling in her mind over the last days.

Now she sat opposite a man that she believed loved her. He had proven this over a considerable period of time. She had really been down on human love for quite awhile, but before her sat a man who had been proving her wrong. Why had she been so full of denial? Was she that naïve to have been taken in by the Wharton gang of soul robbers and fraudsters? How could she explain this to her friends now? Her pride was hurt, her heart ached, but she felt a sense of gratitude for the existence of Michael who now sat next her comforting her and talking in sweet tones and soft questions. She had been lost in some desperate attempt to escape a deep pain and sorrow regarding suffering in the world. So now she really felt that it was important to her to establish whether love would triumph in the end, like a lot of songs that she had listened to said. Love always won out in those songs.

"Sure, love, it lasts forever. Whatever forever means Meg. I think that it's important to know that. Just to maybe believe in it." Michael answered.

Meg looked down at the ground.

"I'm sorry for being such a fool, look I'm crying, what an idiot I am."

"You're not an idiot, Meg. Come on it's ok. You just got sidetracked. Your too sensitive to things and wanted easy answers. There are no easy answers to those questions. We just have to live with what we have. Or love the one you're with, like the song goes. Can't remember what song that's from."

He laughed.

Meg smiled and pulled out a couple of booklets from the Wharton church from her bag.

One was entitled:

WHERE ARE YOU GOING TO END UP IN LIFE?

Another had a photo of a star-filled night sky with a young man and woman looking up in awe. The heading stated:

YOUR SEARCH FOR PEACE COULD BE OVER.

And in smaller print below the photo it said:

DETAILS INSIDE.

"These are really silly, but you know Michael they are really important questions."

"I don't know if they are. Maybe all that is important is what satisfies your soul today. I think we really need answers. Not the ones in those books anyhow. But Meg I want to try and understand what it is that you need."

"That's sweet, Michael. I love you."

"I love you too. So why not give up this nonsense. It's a waste of time."

"Maybe your right, Michael."

"I think I am."

The roar of cars and buses in the city swelled and Meg and Michael embraced. Michael wanted Meg just to be the woman that he had first met. He saw all that had gone around the church as just twist that he had to tolerate if he truly loved her.

At that moment, the two of them were feeling released from the tension that had grown between them. Biology won out.

They went to a more secluded part of the park up on the mountain and made love.

On their way down from the mountain they noticed a poster announcing the Sustainability and the Soul conference.

"Look Meg, remember that professor we met on the bus. Here's that conference he was talking about. Wanna check it out?"

"Sure Michael, may as well. But if they start preaching and lecturing, we'll get out. Don't need that, today."

They both laughed.

"Yeah, if it's boring, we'll do something else."

And they headed toward Orillia Hall where Ambrose J. Keel was just getting to the crux of his views on how developing a consciousness of the soul was the engine for perpetual life. Keel smiled a lot and seemed at ease with himself. But many in the audience had doubts as to the existence of anything called the soul. They had some questions for him. They thought only the brain had to be satisfied with the answers. And the questions they had for Keel were ones that would get the chemicals in their brains saying to themselves they were right all along and other peoples brain chemicals were usually wrong. This ego battle of neurosciences versus the humanities was about to unfold when Meg and Michael entered the hall and quietly sat near the back.

eighteen

"I acknowledge the duplicates of myself the weakest and the shallowest is deathless with me, what I do and say the same waits for the, every thought that flounders in me flounders in them."

-
                                                                    Walt Whitman

Boris Swatcupso was sitting at the bar across the street from Orillia Hall pondering nothing in particular. He sat hunched over a large pint of beer thinking of how he had been shortchanged in life. Where was the audience he needed for his works of art – his poetry, his paintings, his sculptures. No one appreciated him. Would he feel sorry for himself? No, he thought. He would use Butterworth for inspiration tomorrow. Then he would launch on a major reformation of his life. A new start. He had to stop this drinking nonsense. It was taking its toll on him. He hadn't spoken to anyone in the arts community in months. He hadn't produced anything that he felt good about in over a year. He had become more clown than artist and he had felt disheartened with himself. Would seeing Butterworth help? Probably, he thought. He could not go on with occasional public rants and outbursts. He felt himself being eaten away from the insides, he was even striking out with women most of the time, which he was not used to. He had to get himself in line or he would end up in complete poverty. He knew this today. He felt life slipping away from him, but what could he do? He saw no way to stop it. It was moving away from him and as he reached out to bring it back it would shift again just out of his grasp. All he saw now was an empty space. The only light at the end of the dreamlike view from his ledge was Butterworth's upcoming appearance. And the fact that he could keep drinking to hide from the despair.

And Boris sat there mulling over these things and tried to laugh about it all.

He pushed the drama of his life from his mind and focused on the comedy of errors his life had become in the last year. For the moment that assuaged him.

At the conference hall Keel's speech was just winding down with what he considered quite a closing argument.

"With our systems and functions so integrated and becoming more so each and every day, an omega point of interdependence will be reached at which time an all-encompassing collective brain of information will have been achieved. Yet this assemblage of knowledge, though seemingly all that can be known, will still fall short of understanding the origins and meanings of life. So, under the domination of knowledge life would most likely again begin a downward spiral mostly due to lack of inspiration and mystery and from which recovery may not occur for many centuries. So, find what inspires, find what adds more mystery and questions to your life and stop the onslaught of answers. And I will take a few questions."

A few young students lined up behind a microphone that had been set up for the occasion. Frank got up and moved to a seat closer to the microphone.

Keel answered two questions, then it was Frank's turn.

"Can believing in something make it happen?"

It was the shortest question that Keel had ever been asked. Many academics and students in the audience smirked at the question. It seemed to lack depth or analysis.

Keel recognized Frank from the bus. This made him smile a bit.

"I see some of you are amused by the question. Rather short, considering the first two questions were at least four paragraphs long. I will say that the gentleman asking this pithy query is a recent acquaintance of mine. We shared are thoughts on bus ride two days ago and I am glad that you are here, Frank."

Some heads turned to observe Frank and see his reaction.

"It's good to be here, Professor Keel."

Keel smiled. Some of the academics were uncomfortable at the ease of the conversation with someone whom they did not know. But they were curious to see how Keel would respond.

"So in regards to your question, and it is a brilliant question, believing is like trusting. Only what I can develop trust in can I honestly believe in. Otherwise, we are mired in false belief, lies and self-deception. Basic knowledge that has been proven true through repetition and verification can be said to be trusted. But this only takes us to what we can see, touch, smell, taste and hear. Your question goes to the heart of much of what I am saying about how we are going to sustain life in the future and what are the factors and elements that will be required to do that. I maintain that what is needed is visualization of the future. A picture, if you will, of what is to come in the mind, which incorporates not only what is considered trusted and proven knowledge but also imagined realities. It is how ones uses these faculties that is crucial and not what the faculties are themselves that will be vital in sustaining life. Not techniques and technology but the ability to foreshadow, hope and wrestle with what we want life to be. So, the simple answer to your question is yes. But the rider to that answer is to be careful what you believe, because though it may be considered true or untrue by others at the moment, it could become true or untrue if enough souls believe it to be one or the other. And you may have created a world that you did not want with spiraling consequences and an infinite number of factors that no amount of data or algorithms could foresee. We hope that what you choose to believe as an individual is what is best for us all, free of self-deception and dishonesty. And thanks for your questions. I will be at tonight's seminar listed on the schedule. Thank you."

And with that, he walked off the stage, but not before nodding to the distinguished looking moderator.

At the back of the room Michael and Meg left.

"I want to get that guy's book. He must have one." Michael said to Meg.

"I didn't quite get his mumbo jumbo. Maybe I'm just dumb."

"Why do you say that, Meg? I don't get it all either, that's why I want to get the book. It just seems exactly what I need to read right now."

As Michael exited the hall, he felt a blunt blow to his head. Meg let out a yelp and a darkly dressed figure ran away from them, down the hall. A few people in the hallway turned and gasped. Two young men rushed over to Michael who had now fallen to the ground. Meg had dropped her bag to the floor and was asking Michael if he was alright.

"What was that?" he said.

Someone had chased the attacker. Some yelling could be heard outside, but the perpetrator had quickly disappeared.

Meg was speechless.

"I think he had black hoodie on that said RANDOM GUY" said one of the young men.

"Good eyes" said Michael with some exasperation.

"Are you alright?"

"I'll be ok. I'm just wondering what the point of that was."

"We'll call the police if you want."

"I dunno."

The two young men and Meg took him over to a nearby couch.

"I just need to sit awhile."

At that moment Frank exited from the hall and noticed the consternation and the group that had gathered around the couch.

"What happened?" he asked someone.

"Some guy just came up and hit him on the head for no reason" a voice said.

Frank was taken aback.

The memory of two nights ago shone brightly in his brain. Suddenly the pain, which had subsided on his skull came back. He had a sudden chill, but not a real fear. He had begun to dismiss the incident outside Le Café Fritz as being just the actions of a frustrated kid, perhaps on drugs, but now he suddenly had reservation about that conclusion.

"The guy came through here like a ghost. A dark ghost" said a young guy who had broken away from the crowd.

"A ghost?" said Frank.

"He was in and out and no one saw him once he disappeared through that door."

"I don't believe in ghosts."

"Just a figure of speech."

Frank walked over to where Michael and Meg were remembering them from the bus. He wanted to say something to him right away, but decided to just wait around until the commotion had died out.

"I'm ok. I don't think calling the cops would help?" asked Michael.

"Maybe we should" said Meg.

"Look, Meg these things happen. It's nothing."

"You're not even interested in why this guy picked you?"

"I don't think he picked me. I think he was just on some trip."

"A trip, eh?"

"Yeah, we'll just forgot it."

"How can you just forget it, Michael?"

Frank then inserted himself into the conversation.

"Sorry, but I couldn't help but notice what happened."

"Yeah, some guy just streaked through here and then disappeared. Hey, I remember you from the bus a couple of days ago. Meg, you remember this guy. What was your name again?"

"Frank. Frank Lee."

"He had a black hoodie on and he looked about 20, maybe 25" said a voice from the small group.

"It's weird, that just happened to me two days ago on St. Amos, in front of the Le Café Fritz" injected Frank.

"I think I gave you, my card. Michael Schultzmann. This is my girlfriend Meg."

He offered a fist pump to Frank. Frank met Michael's hand with his.

"Hi again. We get to Montreal and this is what happens" Frank said with some light-heartedness.

"What did your guy look like?" said Michael.

"No one got a good look at him. He had no hoodie but was dressed kinda punkish. Young guy. Dark clothing. Black jeans."

"Could be the same guy."

A young girl, about 19 or 20, then came up to Michael holding some papers.

"Hey guys, he dropped these I think."

Another girl held out an iphone.

"I got his picture from the back."

Then another voice said.

"We'll catch him on the security cameras."

But Frank was only interested in the papers that the perpetrator had dropped.

He asked the girl for them. Michael nodded his approval and Frank began to scan them

At the top of the page, it read:

SONG OF MYSELF FROM THE OTHER SIDE

And then the rest was filled with scribbling of what seemed to be poetry.

The second page contained a map of what looked to be New Jersey and Manhattan.

The third page had a listing of name and numbers indicating either files or coordinates of some kind.

Frank did not get a chance to examine the last two pages before he noticed campus security approaching.

He quickly hid the papers in his bag.

nineteen

"I am so glad to be still amongst the living, though my body and soul have moved to another place. And you, my little duplicates of me, my lesser attributes, I will let you roam free, but do not go where I am not conscious of you." The white bearded man spoke with a soft smile and a tender voice to the young people dressed in black, one in a leather jacket with spiked hair, another wearing a hoodie and smoking a cigarette. Some were tall, short, some skinny, some more muscular and plump. The one in the hoodie wore black jeans and was sitting on a large stone. He was thin and had long flowing hair, large eyes and looked straight at the white bearded man.

One member of the group, rose pronounced,

"I will not be tamed by boundaries of humankind, nor the chapters of history, I will dance in the streets knocking sense and consciousness into those whose faith is without it. I cannot forget the mockers and those that insulted me, but corpses rise and gashes heal."

Another person said

"Wherever there is imbalance I go to lift up the other side. I bring them all Osiris, Brahma, Buddha, Jesus, Krishna, Balzac, Allah, Nietzsche, Gibran and a thousand more souls to join in complicit harmony singing the song of myself."

Yet another sat and meditated in silence looking at up the stars counting the souls that were reflecting there.

They all sat assembling visions of the earth and sky, not knowing their origin or destination but sure of life, sure of purpose.

And the bearded man smoked a pipe and smiled gently happy to be together with themselves

twenty

"He (my other self), nor that affable, familiar ghost (The Cosmic Self) which nightly gulls him with intelligence."

William Blake

Frank lay face up not fully awake but vacantly staring at the piss-coloured stained ceiling of his hotel room contemplating his next move regarding the pursuit of the illusive character or characters involved in the rash of head banging that had taken place in the last couple of days.

Later that afternoon, after Michael Schultman had been knocked on the cranium, Boris Swatcupso had taken a fall coming out of the bar across from Orillia Hall and sensing that he may have like been bopped on the head by some blunt object. He had managed to get to Frank's hotel room.

Frank had suggested at first that Boris' fall perhaps was due more to his brain's relationship with alcohol than with an ellusive street punk that had been aiming high. Nevertheless, Boris was not convinced that he hadn't suffered the same fate as Frank. Then Frank briefly informed him what had transpired at Orillia Hall that afternoon.

Boris was in no frame of mind to rationally contemplate the situation. He decided to go back to the comfort of his loft and sleep whatever was ailing him off.

After Boris had left felt a rush of mental energy and was inspired to go over the evidence that he before him and what he had witnessed. The punkish hair, the dark clothing, a blunt object, the silence of the perpetrator, the youth of the perpetrator, the quick in and out, the lack of facial recognition, a seemingly impossible ghostlike escape, and most tellingly the

134

five sheets of paper left at the scene containing poetry, a map, names and numbers, and a manifesto which covered the last two pages.

The poem, in its entirety, was as follows:

Are You the New Person Drawn Towards Me?

Are you the new person drawn towards me?

To begin taking warning, I am surely far different from

what you suppose;

Do you suppose you will find me in your ideal?

Do you think it so easy to have me become your lover?

Do you think friendship of me would be unalloy'd

satisfaction?

Do you think I am trusty and faithful?

Do you see no further than this façade, this smooth and

tolerant manner of me?

Do you suppose yourself advancing on real ground

toward a real heroic man?

Have you no thought O dreamer that it might be all maya,

illusion?

Frank decided to go back to sleep for an hour or so. He rationalized that it would clear his mind. But he awoke just twenty minutes from a dream in which all the pertinent parts of the recent events had manifested themselves into a mental stew that sat ready to be digested as he awoke. On the rickety hotel room table before him was the physical evidence. The five pages that he had procured at the scene.

He looked at his watch and realized that he hadn't slept very long. He checked his phone. Boris had left a message that he was ok and would be down for the night. That was not surprising. Frank then moved to an armchair and re-examined the words of the poem. He then thought of who the author could be? He would begin with trying to match the poem with a name.

His mind then went to the second item on the trail, the map. It looked to be a non-descript outline of New Jersey and New York City containing some of the outlying areas.

Looking more closely at it, he noticed the two places had small check marks beside their names. One was in green ink and the other in red. West Hills, NY on Long Island was indicated in green and Camden, NJ was accompanied with a red checkmark. Red was 'stop' and green was for 'go' thought Frank. He mulled this over for a few minutes before it occurred to him that the colours might indicate a beginning and an ending. Or birth and death. Born in West Hills, NY, died in Camden, NJ. He inspected the rest of the map for more evidence.

He heard yelling from the next room. It annoyed him momentarily but he was determined to make progress. People fighting over drugs, sex or money he thought. It was nothing. Despite his fatigue and irritation, he forged on. In his mind, rested not only a need for clarification and truth, but also a duty to his friend Boris and a curiosity about what motivation lay behind these seemingly connected acts. And after all he was a party to all three. He recalled some of Professor Keel's lecture about the yearning of the soul for continued meaning and purpose, because it was the part of life that never ceased to be. This motivated him.

On the next page were the names and numbers, nine of them. They made no sense to Frank. They were not phone numbers, not map coordinates, maybe serial numbers of some sort. Army numbers. He had to go to the internet to see how many numbers were in a military serial number. He checked both Canadian and American military serial numbers. But they didn't match the current system of assigning numbers to soldiers. He spent most of the night looking for military serial numbers that matched the sequencing of the numbers on the page. In the wee hours of the morning, with the seeping in of occasional cries of revelry from the street, he found that the numbering of the American Civil War personal matched the ones on the page. And the name that stood out amongst the nine for Frank was George S. Whitman. Attached to the name was the number G-53 I 2-123.

Whitman had been a poet, thought Frank. But that was Walt Whitman not George S. Whitman. He looked back at the poem, he didn't know Whitman that well and '*Are You the New Person Drawn Towards Me?*' didn't ring any bells. But he soon found a listing of the poet's titles and indeed it was one of Walt Whitman's.

He was on to something. A relative perhaps who fought in the war. Did Whitman have a brother? Yes, he found out. Did he fight in a war? Yes, the civil war. Was Walt in the war? Well partially. He worked in the army's paymaster's office in Washington and he volunteered as a nurse. Curious, a male nurse in the 1860s? Frank read more and discovered that Whitman had been a mysterious literary figure at the time. Not having formal education or being connected to society his writings generated speculation about his true identity. Rumors had spread in the1850s as to whether he was a fictional creation of the more spiritually inspired thinkers of the time. A disembodied muse who had haunted publishers of poetry and prose. And he discovered that Whitman was probably gay.

After doing some more reading, Frank turned to the manifesto. His reading was now being aided by the natural light of the morning. He switched off the room lights and settled down to go over the two-page declaration of sorts. It began:

To whom it may concern,

I have lived forever in some form or dimension. I still live now among you.

I have many duplicates who exhibit the attributes of my soul.

I return here today to show the lost and deluded that they need not worry.

I declare that I live forever, therefore you live forever.

I tell you here that no body is without a soul, and no soul without a body.

I show you that all knowledge is infinite and that nothing is original.

I say to you that how you put together the pieces of life is where originality resides.

I declare that proof of anything, is in its permanent value.

I say things without proof need none except that they are there.

I am silent and soft, I am loud and harsh, I practice restraint and attack.

I know all interconnections to be the basic ingredient of the soul.

I declare a resurgence of the spirit of liberation from physical laws.

I declare a new emergence that will demote contrived rule to footnotes.

I come in love and resistance, with a warm embrace for all souls, saying it's ok.

I come with empathy for the wants and needs of all who are anxious.

I bring not only words, but actions of both the body and soul.

I love a male soul with a male body, I love a female soul with a female body.

I love a female soul with a male body, I love a male soul with a female body.

I have expressed desires and I have hidden my wants from many.

I know everyone who has been declared dead and whose minds still live.

I know the illusion of death and the reality of life.

I stand away from the chattering brains whose words fill space.

I see all words on the paths that lead to a common point.

I have found nothing that is not accessible, but the workings are secret.

I lived in the politics of the world, and seen selfishness and good intention.

I come now to bring great news again that game does not end.

I want it known that where it begins is the moment that you read this.

I will be here to comfort you and sleep by your side.

I am the laborer and the homeless soul, a worker of change and calm sage.

I am a fool and a master, silly and well thought out, laughing and crying.

I see the futility of your efforts and the results of your good will.

I will satisfy your hungers, for food, spirit, sex, security, and peace of mind.

I will bring light and darkness, color and shade to your mind.

I will become you somewhere in space and time.

And sorry about the knock on the head.

Signed, ME.

Frank was trying to make sense of the pages. It certainly seemed to him to be a well thought out manifesto that exhibited not only philosophical and spiritual ideas but also a common thread. The declaration was the most difficult to place in context, but Frank recalled some of what he knew of the poetry and philosophy of Walt Whitman and it did fit.

Frank had always been a person who believed himself to be rational, even if he had succumbed to a somewhat drifting dreamlike lifestyle, following his decision to leave his wife. He knew that he needed to cling to rationality in order to get anywhere with his investigation. Yet, there was a side to this that appeared to have been inspired by motives unstirred by simple brain arithmetic and mathematics.

Why had he decided to attend Keel's lecture? Why had he talked with Keel on the bus? Why had he met Keel at all? Why had Michael Schultzman come to the conference? Both he and Frank had been on the same bus and both had bumps on their heads? But what about Boris? He too apparently had been a victim of physical violence, but he hadn't been on the bus. Yet, he had been at the lecture too, albeit in the role of a clown. But Frank was certain that the three incidents thus far were related. Was randomness not so random after all?

He suddenly felt a pang in his stomach. He needed to eat something. A sandwich. A bowl of chilli. A bowl of cereal. Some fruit juice. No alcohol today. No DregStore. No Tito. Oh, yeah there was that guy that had aroused his interest in the next hotel room. What was happening to him? Would he never fall for a woman again? Had he ever really wanted a female?

Now was not the time to ponder these questions, he quickly concluded and set out on the more practical tasks before him.

twenty-one

"A childlike merriment was in his aspect; here was a soul at play; he had dropped his pen to be happy among friends, and it was impossible not to be joyous where he was."

Lamartine (describing Honoré de Balzac

Boris Swatcupso awoke surprisingly refreshed from what had started out as fitful sleep and had developed into a slumber that was saturated with pleasant dreams which he did not want to awake from. In previous days, he had gone from anger at losing Patricia, to bouts of toying with madness, to being diverted by a friend that he hadn't seen in ages, to a plunge into the bottle and to finally being bopped over the head by some phantom figure.

Now, suddenly he was in a good mood.

He wanted to start on some new project. Would it be looking for a job? That seemed the most rational thing to do, considering that he had just let his last one go the day before. Or would he find a new woman to occupy his mind? Maybe he could write poetry or work on that sculpture that he had abandoned weeks ago? No, he would call Frank and see what he had planned, besides they now shared a common misfortune.

"Hey, Frank What's up?"

"Boris, I was about to phone you. What time is it? I lost track. I was getting lost in something."

"It's almost noon. What do you have on tap, Frank?"

"I think I'm turning into an amateur detective, Boris. That, guy Michael, Michael Schultzman, that got hammered on the head last night at the conference, you remember I told you about him?"

"Yeah."

"Yeah, well what I didn't tell you was what I salvaged from the scene."

"What is it?"

"You'll have to come over to see it. Can't describe it, besides I'm a little paranoid about discussing sensitive details on the phone."

"Oh, I see Sherlock. Send it by email."

"Won't do. Too important. You need to see it. I want your input on this."

"Ok. Be right over. Still at the lavish L'Hotel Fish Pond?"

"Same place, Boris."

"Be there in 30 minutes."

Boris put the phone down, quickly showered, didn't shave, got dressed and grabbed a couple of energy bars on his way out of his loft. He also took with him a large bottle of water. He had a fierce thirst.

Boris lived in a second-floor loft which contained a separate kitchen area and a bathroom. It was modest as far as lofts went. He had gotten a deal from an artist-friendly owner six years ago and the rent had only been modestly increased since then. He was happy here.

He walked out on to the street with a curiosity regarding Frank's tone. He did not remember Frank being so direct and serious about anything in such a long time. What could Frank have that had inspired him to this extent? It must have had something to do with the rash of assaults in the last

143

two days. Frank was always seemingly looking for some crisis or catalytic event in his life. To Boris, Frank had seemed unhappy many times with the present and was always looking to a future event to spark an affinity with life. As Boris approached the Fish Pond he began to understand Frank's sudden need to play detective. It was clues to his own life that Frank was looking for.

I was just having breakfast across the street from L'Hotel Fish Pond when Boris was going in to see his friend Frank. I was certainly wondering where Frank had hoped this would all lead, but after considering everything that went on it was now my opinion that Frank had never been comfortable in the role of husband. He had more of an affinity for his lost brother Jesse and was supressing a desire to reunite with him. Really his sudden eagerness to engage in detecting activities had been prompted by his lost brother, Jesse. The trio of head attacks had only brought this to the surface for Frank. That day I finished my breakfast of yogurt, juice and coffee and watched Boris enter the hotel. I also was thumbing through a copy of Boris' first volume of poems at the time. Even Boris had forgotten about them. Boris had been quite deeply moved by the female sex in his initial stab at verse.

Frank let Boris into room 115.

"Well, Frank what's the big mystery? Have you figured out who got the sudden need to be pounding people on the head?"

"Not exactly, Boris, but I believe I detect a motive."

"Well, the sleuth bug has really got a hold on you. Motive, eh?"

"Listen, Boris I really think that we have a deep psychological motive here. It's not one of the overt ones that we thought of before. Look at these pages that were left behind at the conference when that Michael, uh, Schultzmann was bopped."

He handed Boris the five pages. Boris read them.

"Wow, and who do you think wrote this? Those punks running the streets?"

"Not exactly. If you noticed, Boris the poem is from Walt Whitman, the American poet. I researched all night and it all fit together."

"Walt Whitman, now there was a man who believed in immortality without religion, love without the romanticism, and the soul. I studied him for a while when I was in London."

"Yes, well there is no question that somehow the reason for the attacks must lie hidden in someone's mind. They were not just some random drug induced outbursts. I am convinced of that."

"Well, you are probably right. But what are we suppose to do about it. Why don't you just call the police and give them all this evidence. You know you could be charged for holding on to that stuff."

"Boris, haven't you ever wanted to do something just on your own, without having it sanctioned by some authority?"

"Sure, Frank, but really these are assaults. Everyone's involved. Society's involved. The authority is society, don't you think?"

"Boris, I really feel that these attacks were personal. Not in the sense of revenge for something that happened in this world, but for something that happened in perhaps another, maybe metaphysical world."

"Now you're fucking with me Frank. Really, a metaphysical world."

"No, I'm not fucking with you Boris. A world outside the one that we call mundane or mechanical. A level of existence like the one Walt Whitman had created in Leaves of Grass. A poetic universe, where he could reveal hidden dilemmas and issues of the soul that he could not be otherwise be expressed."

"Now that I understand. How do you tell someone what you feel and not just what you think? It is the ancient conflict between these two. The answer is action, that is how it gets resolved, Frank."

"Sure, Boris that's nice. But listen. You write poetry. You must know that there exists more than one level of consciousness."

"Sure, but who are these young guys in black?"

"Surrogates, Boris."

"Surrogates? For whom?"

"Well. if you look at the pages, the theme seems to be Walt Whitman. The poem, the map indicating West Hill, New York and Camden, New Jersey – where he was born and where he died. The numbers indicate his brother's service in the Civil War and the manifesto is in Whitman's style, but I'm not certain that he wrote that manifesto."

"Who did?"

"We are going to find out, Boris?"

"We? You haven't asked me if I want to be involved with your little unofficial private investigation yet?"

"Boris, I think you not only want to do this, but it is also exactly what you need. Something to dig your teeth into besides women."

"Are you implying that I'm some sort of vampire, Frank?"

"No, Boris. The metaphor just goes so well with your name."

"Ha, ha. Very funny. Droll, Frank. Do you have a drink somewhere? I know that you do."

"Hey, no heavy drinking today, Boris. We've got to be sober for this."

"Just a couple short ones, Frank. I'll keep it clean."

"I don't want an outburst like yesterday at the conference."

"Naw, not now that we have this 'case' to solve."

Boris really put some sarcasm into 'case'.

"Frank, don't forget Madison Butterworth is at the conference tonight. He's speaking at six."

"I'm not forgetting and we are going to be there and you have to promise me that you are not going to act like some 19-year-old fanboy. And that you will be sober."

"Yeah, sure of course, Frank. How's your head?"

Boris was beginning to think that the blow had had more of a mental than a physical effect on Frank.

"Fine, Boris, fine."

Boris found the whiskey, poured himself a belt and smiled at a skeptical looking Frank.

"Let's go"

"Where are we going?"

"You'll see. It will be fun, Boris."

"Ok."

As they were leaving, they passed the young man next door in the hallway. Frank noticed him and they exchanged smiles.

Meanwhile, Michael Schultzmann was lying in his girlfriend's mother bed, ambiguous about the attack, but definitely feeling better about Meg's sudden realization that perhaps the Wharton angelic caravan didn't have accurate galactic directions for her soul after all. And who did, thought Schultzmann. He was thinking that it was curious that he would get attacked just after something had been resolved with Meg, yet he stopped himself from overthinking it. He had taken Frank's contact information and Frank had his. But that didn't mean that what happened to Frank had anything to do with him. He got up and tried to focus on a translation job that he had received a couple of weeks back and had neglected because of his growing concern for Meg. Now maybe he could get some work done.

Then his phone rang. It was Frank.

"Hi, it's Frank from yesterday. I need to talk with you."

"Well, I'm kinda busy right now."

"Listen, I have something to show you that I found on the floor of the conference yesterday. It could explain the attack."

"I'm not sure I want to get involved with this."

"Look, you don't have to get involved. You don't have to do anything. All I want you to do is read something and tell me if it relates to anything in your life. Just an intellectual exercise, no police, no revenge, no spying on people. What do you say?"

"Well, I dunno."

"Look, what part of the city do you live in?"

"Well, I'm not actually living here, just visiting."

"Fine, where can I meet you?"

"Ok, there's coffee shop two blocks from the conference hall where we were yesterday. I'm going downtown to pick up a book later today. I can meet you there. It's called The Coffee Express on University Avenue."

"Great, I'll find it. Let's say three o'clock."

"Ah, yeah, sure three o'clock is fine."

Michael Schultzmann put down his phone still uncertain as to whether he was doing the right thing, but he had been feeling a desire lately to get things resolved. He had the beginnings of success with Meg and now he felt that maybe he shouldn't let this assault on him go without some effort on his part to clear it up. He was showing some courage he thought. It felt good.

At the Coffee Express Jesse was just beginning a 1 P.M to 9 P.M shift.

twenty-two

"If I had known it was harmless, I would have killed it myself."

Philip K. Dick

Bo Creeley was sitting in a greasy spoon near the Canadian border on the American side eating steak and eggs with his two friends. They were waiting for someone to pick them up and take them to a compound in Washington State. That had been the plan. Now Creeley was sure that he would be followed and perhaps arrested. He would have to devise a way to lose them on the way out west. Creeley was anxious. He dared not acquire too many weapons so soon after being thrown out of Canada. But he would need them soon. And the plan was to have them covertly placed into a vehicle that Creeley would pick up near Gary, Indiana in two days. For now, he had what he needed.

The Frida S. Wharton cavalcade, made up of three diesel busses and a Winnebago was making its way at that moment to Gary, Indiana for what they hoped would be a gathering of desperate souls willing to part with their earthly attachments for a shot at eternal bliss. A small arena had been leased for the occasion and publicity had been sent out to all the neighbouring communities.

Living just over two miles from the arena in Gary, were two adherents of Creeley. They had amassed an arsenal of killing devices, some of which they were planning to slip to Creeley as he made his way west.

Creeley's phone rang in the greasy spoon.

"Yeah."

"It's Kirk. This Robert?"

That was code for Creeley.

"Yeah."

"The ship is waiting for its captain."

That was code too.

"Gonna wash out the critters."

More code.

"Ok Big Guy. You gave them the slip?"

"Could've blown away those pinkos?"

That was code for, "If I had been fuckin armed, I would've blown those Canucks into kingdom come."

"Wait for Gary, wait for Gary."

That was code for, "Don't worry, your gonna be fuckin armed to the tits after you pass through Gary."

Creeley hung up and prayed for his soul.

Wharton was in her bus praying that she would have a good pay day.

Near to the arena were three young guys, in their early twenties sitting in a burger joint. They were dressed in black and were carrying copies of The Soul Manifesto, subtitled A Creed for the Acceptance and Liberty of All. Part of that manifesto was the page that Frank had found on the floor at Orillia Hall. Apparently, a bop on the head was coming to the Wharton charade in Gary, Indiana.

I had just finished my breakfast in Montreal and was been keeping an eye on the Bo Creeley story via my phone and also listening to snippets of the 'Big Andy Jones' radio show. In my briefcase I had pamphlets and booklets authored by Frida S. Wharton herself. I worried a little about Frank and Boris and sat contemplating how things would unfold when I received a phone call. It was Binky from 'Conspiremouth'. They needed an article on living on rooftops in Montreal.

twenty-three

"I followed the trail out of the room, invigorated by the possibility of reinventing my own body. The meaning was mine, as long as I was with those who had the vision and vocabulary to understand my creation."

Nick Krieger

There was a buzz of lively conversation in Coffee Express at mid afternoon. Words were being used with liberty and without restraint by some, while others were being careful with their utterances dancing around meaning and inference. Present were mostly students, but also a smattering of office workers.

Jesse was busy preparing café lattes, frappes and other mostly hot beverages. His demeanour was friendly and cooperative. Cassandra, his girlfriend would be stopping by at the end of his shift to take him out to see a film. He smiled a lot and was nice with the clientele. Everyone liked Jesse at the Coffee Express. He felt accepted and that was why he had kept working there despite the unusual hours and the stressful and hurried pace of the job.

Being well received was important to Jesse because he was not quite fully accepting of himself as a her. He was still ok with being called a male, but really knew that it was not honest for him. But he hadn't told anyone at work, though some of his colleagues had notions to ask, but did not want to offend. Jesse was getting close to the day of asking them to call him Jessica. And also, to refer to 'him' as 'her'. Though he didn't show it this was causing him quite a lot of internal stress. He would let Cassandra direct his thinking and actions at times in order just to not have to make decisions, but he, becoming she, knew that this had to change.

Cassandra knew somewhat of Jesse proclivities to be feminine but did not quite comprehend to what extent they went. And neither had Jesse until he had begun to work with the public and began to feel his femaleness as he interacted with the clientele. He was close to telling all.

He had read up on the subject and had heard friends and people talk about it, so he felt that he was not a complete freak for wanting to bring the woman inside him to life.

And today he would run into his older brother, whom he had not heard from in over three years.

Michael Scultzmann arrived first at the coffee shop. He was curious about what Frank had only hinted at on the phone. He ordered an herbal tea and sat at a small table that had just been vacated near the plate glass window that faced University Avenue. He glanced at his phone. It was 2:50. He had told Meg all about what Frank had said and that they were going to meet. She had not insisted on coming with him. She thought that nothing really important would come of it and besides she wanted to spent time with her mother, talking about how misguided she had been about the Church of the Wayward and Frida S. Wharton.

Schultzmann sat and looked out the window on the streets filled with students and office workers, street people and couriers, people shopping and tourists wandering around looking lost and pointing at things. He for a moment, admired Montreal, but knew that his heart was in America. His soul would return and continue to carve out a life with Meg there, now that she was being separated from her obsessions with that cult. But it had been a long process that he imagined would continue. As he checked his phone for messages Jesse came by to clean a table next to his. Jesse's feminine mannerisms caught Schultzmann's attention and he felt something flip in his gut. Jesse smiled at him and walked back quickly to his counter.

"Hey, Michael."

The voice came from just over his shoulder. Michael turned.

"Hi, I just got here. Nice city, Montreal. I've been walking around it the last couple of days."

"Yeah, it is." said Frank acerbically.

"Well, I guess you have something for me." Michael said seeing that Frank wanted to get right down to business.

"Yes, here look at this." Frank said as he handed Michael the five pages that had been left behind by the young guy in black.

As Michael was scanning the pages Frank looked up towards the counter thinking of what he might have to drink. His heart leap at who he saw. Could it be Jesse? His hair was longer, but yes there was no mistaking it. It was him. His brother. What would he say or do? Should he even say hi or maybe Jesse had some sort of secret life that he would only be interfering with? He felt an awkwardness. Michael was consumed in reading the manifesto. Frank thought, ok I will just say hello and smile and acknowledge him. Though the two brothers had never held deep resentments, there was a coldness between them that had begun when Jesse was near puberty and had gone to live with his father. Frank had withdrawn from family affairs and had begun only focusing on reading books and seeing a few friends from school. Frank had conceded Jesse to his father. Jesse had always seemed to be in some dreamlike world and Frank had thought that maybe his father would bring some reality to him. But over time the two had done nothing but drift apart. Frank had been concerned about Jesse at times but his father had insisted that he was okay. And besides Jesse never returned any of his calls.

Frank got up and walked over to the counter. He deliberately stalled awhile so that Jesse would be at the counter when it was his turn and not the young woman who was also working behind the counter.

"Coffee, please Jesse." Frank said attempting a lighthearted approach.

Jesse looked stunned. He then managed a smile which was his default expression.

"Frank, your live here, in Montreal?"

"Just got here. How ya been?"

"Good. I'm good. So, what do you do?"

"Well right now I'm a detective."

"Detective? You mean a cop?"

"No, far from a cop. I'm really an internet writer. Just trying out some private sleuthing on the side. Seeing you here is a real surprise. Why did you never answer me when I tried to contact you?"

"That's a long story. But I'm doing good. How about you?"

"Good. Good. Listen can we get together and talk sometime? I'll give you, my number."

"Well, maybe, I dunno."

Jesse did not want to further complicate his current life. Yet he also felt an attachment to his brother, even though they had not been deep. He wanted to talk with him and explain everything, yet he felt that he wouldn't know where to start and how long it would take. Would Frank understand the woman that he was bringing to life inside himself? Would Frank only hamper her creativity? These questions shot through Jesse mind as he stood before his brother.

Frank looked at him with empathy and simply handed him a small card that had all of his contact information on it.

Jesse nervously took the card, shoved it in his pocket and asked his brother what he wanted.

"Do you have iced tea?"

"Yeah, raspberry, lemon or regular?"

156

"Regular."

Jesse went off the get the order.

Frank stood there still somewhat stunned by the chance encounter.

When Jesse returned with the iced tea, he said nothing, but managed a quick smile.

"Jesse, I don't believe it. You gotta call me."

Jesse felt a warmth inside.

"I will."

And he would. But not as Jesse, but as Jessica.

Boris Swatcupso was being administered alcohol three doors down by a heavy-set woman who was tending bar at a place called Marty's. The place was almost empty, except for a few regulars who had assembled at a wooden table in a darkened corner. The place had photos of Montreal history on its walls along with beer logos. Boris did not like the atmosphere and had only stopped here because Frank had insisted on meeting Schultzmann alone. And, well Boris needed refuelling.

He stared glumly at the television which hung from the wall to the right of bar which was tuned to CNN. He tried to supress the nausea that he felt at the news. Another terrorist bombing, another virus attack, another political corruption scandal and a series of assaults across America on people by young men dressed in black. Well, now Boris took notice.

"The attacks were first reported in West Hill, New York and were not considered significant until several other similar incidents were reported in places like Camden, New Jersey and Framingham, Massachusetts. Authorities

are attempting to traces any links that may appear on social media where discussion of the attacks is taking place, but no one has taken credit for them. The attacks are all marked by the same modus operandi, a blow to the head with a blunt object. Nine such incidents have taken place in the last three days. CNN will keep you up to date if any such assaults occur in the near future" the anchor on the screen said

"Frank's gotta hear about this." Boris thought to himself.

He slowly finished his beer and shut out any sound from the television or the regulars in the corner. He was formulating a theory about these young guys in black, the immortality of the soul and Walt Whitman. As Boris' brain was firing signals in the bar Michael Schultzmann was attempting to make sense of what Frank had put before him.

twenty-four

"Life is a succession of lessons which must be lived to be understood. All is riddle, and the key to a riddle is another riddle."

Ralph Waldo Emerson

He sat looking out at the sea, barefoot in the sand, around him were souls, male, female or both, wild-eyed, dark and soft in the heart. They looked into the starry night above the water and saw a bluish tableau. A rushing wind was felt by all thoughts that covered their dreams. They loved the contradictions of the man that was returning again to his tiresome life, that he had infused with word and deep consideration for its integrity. They were but dispatches of that wholeness that had yet to be revealed to anyone.

"I have together with myself included you all in my returning to the world a soul mission, to bring news that all discovered realities hold another undiscovered secret. I bring souls together, to uncover, discover and discard. Souls must always unburden themselves of childhood fears and desires, then let go of adult delusions of power and effectiveness. I never had any control of space, time and cosmic energies. Words were just a feeble attempt at redemption for me. Now I tap people on the head so that they may remember who they are and what they can do. They can make decisions, that shape their gods and their heavens. To idle trying to explain and control is the path to a hell of pain and suffering. I share a secret with myself, now with a warm touch and caress, I am that which I seek."

Male, female and those creating new bodies for themselves listened to the calming voice over the gentle roaring of the sea. All of them knew to which soul they all belonged. One soul, which could appear in many places at once. This is, what the bearded man had discovered in his poetry. One soul imagined many souls appeared.

twenty-five

"A man is what he thinks about all day long."

Ralph Waldo Emerson

"It certainly bares some thought" said Michael Schultzmann as placed the five pages on the small table at the Coffee Express.

"I've taken the liberty to make copies and filed copies on my laptop," said Frank.

"You've got me intrigued. What do you think it all means? It seems to me to be something written by a guy who had a lot figured out. Some lonely guy who maybe who had nothing better to do with his time. Maybe, a little ... mixed up?"

"No, I don't think so. At least I don't think he had anything figured out, maybe he wanted us to figure something out. Like a Zen koan. You know what a Zen koan is?"

"Isn't that like some simple sentence that answers a complicated problem?"

"Well, sort of. It's a little story or some words that gets you to question the logic of words altogether. It makes it dubious whether words can bring you to any logical point at all. Of course, words do have significance they just don't lead anywhere on their own. They are just as impermanent as anything else in the universe. They are self-contradictory in themselves."

"That's like saying I don't know anything, isn't it?"

"Not at all. It is saying that the words themselves are not the journey. I need to continue the journey regardless of whether I think I know anything at all, because I could find a whole new set of answers in the next moment. So, I suppose that is what they mean, by living in the moment."

"So, what do you think this guy is a Buddhist monk or something?"

"It would be worth exploring that path. The guy was probably around 25."

"Well, good luck on finding all the 25-year-old Buddhists in Montreal."

"Maybe we don't need to do that. We need to narrow down the odds by looking more closely at the clues."

"I really can't spend a lot of time on this. I'm just visiting my girlfriend's mother in town. I'll only be here a couple more days."

"Well maybe that's all we need."

Frank had found a deeply buried confidence in the last couple of days. He was almost certain that the reasons behind the assaults could be found quite quickly. In fact, he felt compelled to find the answers. It had become crucial to him. He had felt a surge of energy at having this somewhat bizarre but thought-provoking task serendipitously dropped into his life. He saw it as good fortune. Much of his life, since he had decided that conforming to a married life with a woman was not going to be his destiny, had been a wandering crooked path that only kept leading back to the same spot. And that spot seemed devoid of inspiration only yielding certain material benefits, but not giving Frank any clues as to who he was. Now, Frank knew this. He was a seeker. He was stubborn. And he was someone who wanted love on his own terms. He wasn't satisfied with explanations that he had been given of life from his parents or school teachers and professors. He truly felt that he would one day have his own ideas about the universe, gods, spirituality and the secrets of life. He read what he felt was a reasonable number of books, but he felt less than knowledgeable about many subjects. At times really knew that given sufficient time and space he could garner enough information on a subject to make an objective assessment. He prided himself on his aloofness at times, but was unfulfilled in his ambiguous attitude towards love, sex, emotions and deeply rooted feelings in general. He had avoided these things, even in marriage, where he had let his ex-wife steer his life for years. He had not been able to form any sense of what he valued in these areas of life in childhood. His mother and father had been mostly self-consumed and offered little direction, except material support and practical advice. So now, he sat here in the Coffee Express where his long-lost brother, Jesse just happened to be working, in a city that he had disappeared from for quite a while, returning only on a whim and out of misdirection and about to launch out on an investigation of bizarre happenings, which could turn out to be dangerous. For what reason had he suddenly jumped on this path of playing the sleuth? Even he didn't know that but he did know that he needed to care about something or someone.

"You know," Frank said to Michael across the table "all the attacks have been on people who were connected by chance meetings. I didn't look for Boris when I got here. I just ran into him. I went to the conference, not to meet anyone in particular and you were there. Boris, you and me we all got the dinged on the head. Maybe if we just prepare for the next attack, we can follow this guy and see where he lives."

"How do you know that he will attack again? Maybe he's finished."

"I don't think so. Read those pages again. This is someone who is on a mission of some sort. This person, or persons, will not stop until there is some sort of reaction. I've read about these types in psychology books. They are determined to have some of sort of major effect. Just read that manifesto and that poem over again. No, Michael he or they or she will not just stop. Somebody has a message to deliver."

"You have piqued my interest, Frank."

"No police, no professionals, they would only waste our time and get nowhere."

"Wouldn't the police be able to help us locate the guy? We have a description."

"Yes, but why would they want to share any information with us?"

Michael was silent. He looked closely at Frank and began to see the resolve of the man.

"You know, that's my brother working behind the counter. I hadn't seen him in over three years. I come here and I just run into him, just like that."

Michael looked over at Jesse.

"Looks like a nice guy."

Frank had been wanting to see Jesse for a long while, but when his emails, letters and phone calls to his mother and father had failed to get any results he had lost hope. He loved his brother, who was becoming his sister, deeply, but he had been disconnected from his family. And he really liked it that way sometimes, but now that he had run into his brother, he realized that perhaps Jesse needed him. He felt a chill. He sensed that Jesse had never been at ease with being a boy or becoming a man. What did Jesse think about in his day? This is what Frank had asked himself the past few years. What was he making of his life? Jesse had always been so mysterious and private and so had Frank and therefore they never got to know each other very well. They only knew that their father had a fascination with western outlaws, hence Frank and Jesse, but this certainly had no effect on the boys. Neither had aspired to a rebellious lifestyle let alone a criminal one. Frank was thinking about playing a detective and solving a crime, not creating one. His brain was full of ideas about who the perpetrators could be and what the motive was. Frank thought that the person or persons involved must be somewhat educated or well read, have a definite goal in mind, and be a defiant in nature. He theorized that the person or persons may have a utopian philosophy, probably did not have a regular steady job or jobs, resided in either rooming houses or with a group of similar thinkers in large apartments. Maybe they were vegetarian or vegan, had severe problems with relationships. Maybe they had joined religious groups or cults, were in financial distress, had great belief in human integrity, had certain definite values and maybe were rejected by their family or families. These, it should be noted were ideas that he did not want to voice yet. They could wait. They could be wrong. They needed verification. He did not want to box them into a corner quite yet. He wanted them to make the next move.

"So, what do we do Frank? Just sit here?" asked Michael.

"Yes, I believe we are being watched."

"Nice, Frank, very nice."

twenty-six

"The supreme art of war is to subdue the enemy without fighting."

Sun Tzu

-

Warren Kitchholm had arrived at Pearson International Airport on the same afternoon as Frank had met his brother. He had stopped at a kiosk to buy a magazine and a beverage. He was lookingforward to going home and relaxing for a couple of days. He looked forward to time with his girlfriend, Christina. She was a good match for him because she was quite comfortable spending time alone with her photography business and doing household chores when her husband was away and that had been fairly often of late.

Kitchholm appreciated her much more after not seeing her for a few days and the reverse was true as well. They had decided against children, at least until Kitchholm could settle on taking a job that didn't require that he had be out of town so often. Christina did not want to be the sole person responsible for a child, though she did cherish the notion of having one.

Now Kitchholm had dismissed the idea of pursuing any story having to do with Frank and Boris. He had mulled it over on the plane but had dropped the idea and instead just thought about putting his feet up at home, watching movies and spending some intimate time with Christina. Kitchholm had a fact based practical approach to the writing process but on occasions he could find a creative streak. He had few eccentricities, but admired people who did. He had a curious streak, which was required in his field, but did not feel the need to adopt any peculiarities himself. He had few apprehensions about his soul and the afterlife. He rarely thought about those things. Never in his youth had he questioned his sexuality or his wondered what the purpose of his life was. He always had a simple answer to those questions. He liked woman and wanted to feel like he lived a normal life in a sometimes

166

somewhat crazy world. But he did like to watch the world and was fascinated by how people did weird things and got themselves in and out of trouble. When things troubled him, he could easily dismiss those thoughts with more positive ones. But he did have a skeptical side, which he only applied in his job. Some would say he lived his life in air tight compartments.

Kitchholm walked through the airport and out onto the loading zone, where taxis and limousines waited for potential passengers. He only had one rolling suitcase and a shoulder strap bag. He found an available cab and got in.

"Where to?"

"6154 Markham Avenue. It's a condo. Just drop me off out front."

"Ok"

The cab driver checked his navigator screen, imputed the info and pulled away towards the 401collector lanes. He asked Kitchholm if he minded the feminine voice on the navigator. Kitchholm said that he preferred it if it was turned off. The driver turned it off.

The driver had been in Canada for 23 years. He was born in Uganda and had been a doctor there before leaving for political reasons. His wife and two children had been butchered by very mean and greedy people who thought that the poor doctor was asking too many questions and not cooperating with them. So, they threatened him several times before ending his family's life while he was at work in a local hospital in Kampala. He had been angry for quite a few months about it and had demanded action from the local authorities, but when he had realized that no action was forthcoming he knew that fear had consumed the country. He mourned and then thought of the best plan of action. He believed that his family was in heaven, because he believed in a Christian God and both his wife and two children had been confirmed Christians. He knew that he had to find a way to forgive the nasty brutish bastards that had put a halt on his reason for living or he would not be able to carry on himself. He couldn't bare to live in the same place where the tragic events had taken place after a while, so he planned his escape to Canada even though he knew that it would be almost impossible to be a doctor there unless he went back to school for many years. He had very little money, but he borrowed from friends and made the journey. Now he was a Canadian citizen, had a girlfriend here, drove a cab and had a small online business. He felt that he was doing ok.

"You coming from Montreal?" the cabbie asked.

"Yeah"

"What's happening up there?"

"Oh, just the usual festivals. It's quite a party town. Lots of tourists."

"What do you do, if you don't mind me asking?"

"I'm a writer for a newsmagazine, but I free lance mostly."

"Ah, a writer. So, what are you writing about now?"

"Well, I don't talk about that before it's out there. It should be on NewsMax on the internet early tomorrow."

"Yeah, that makes sense."

"So, anything going on with the cabbies these days?"

"Not much. Just that Uber thing. Everything is online now. I think we should all just go that way and the problem is solved."

"Yeah, that makes sense."

And the conversation continued on like this until they had reached Kitchholm's condo. Kitchholm had texted Christina to let her know that he was at the airport and on his way home. The cab driver pulled up in front of the condo. Kitchholm paid him and driver popped the trunk. He went to the back of the cab to get his suitcase and the next thing that his consciousness experienced was himself lying in bed and having a doctor's hands feeling around his scalp. And it wasn't a Ugandan doctor's hands.

The Ugandan doctor/Canadian cab driver was at that moment talking to a police detective at the local detachment about how he had gotten the assailant to talk to the police. The detective told the cabbie that he had at first suspected that he had delivered Kitchholm to the land of the stars in kahoots with another guy, but after an hour of asking the two of them questions the detective became convinced otherwise. Through friendly persuasion the assailant had agreed that he had better explain himself to the authorities, because not only had the good doctor recorded the incident on his phone, but he had been informed that the victim was a journalist who would probably investigate the story to death. This was how he had been persuaded to admit to the crime. And he was made of real flesh and blood. He wore a black button-down shirt, dark pants and had green hair. He was thin and bony and looked about twenty. He seemed calm and didn't run like the others assailants had. And he had something to say.

He sat in a small barren room at the police detachment as another police detective questioned him. He had no identification, so the police had to take him at his word when he said that he was Jake White and was a physical manifestation of the immortal soul of Walt Whitman.

The psychiatric arm of the department had been notified. Mr. White had also said that he represented a posthumous development of Mr. Whitman's attempts to become a whole person by the adoption of knowledge gleaned from the collective consciousness of humanity.

"Listen Mr.White, if you don't give us straight answers we going to have to turn you over to psychiatry where they could keep you indefinitely without a lawyer or us charging you with anything" the detective warned sternly.

"I'm telling you the only thing I know. I'm a manifestation of the mind of Walt Whitman."

169

"I looked up your friend Mr. Whitman on Wikipedia and he's been dead for over 100 years."

"His soul still roams the upper American east coast and parts of Canada."

The detective chuckled.

"Ok, we're done here, we're moving you over to the hospital where a nice doctor will examine you."

Jake White said nothing.

In another room down the hall the Ugandan doctor/Canadian cab driver was being released.

A couple of miles away at North Markham Hospital on the edges of Toronto, Warren Kitchholm was recovering well from a pretty nasty blow to the head. His girlfriend had been informed and was on her way over. He had managed to get his phone and was making audio notes of the incident. The police had questioned him as to any possible motive for the attack. He did not tell them of the incident that he had witnessed in Montreal just days earlier. He wanted to connect the dots for himself, sensing a possible story. But he would tell them the full story in time, if he could make a definite connection in his mind.

A nurse attended to Mr.Kitchholm after the doctor had left.

"We're just waiting until the tests come back to see if you've suffered a concussion or not Mr. Kitchholm. That was quite a blow you took."

"Well, these things happen."

Kitchholm was deliberately downplaying the incident for the staff.

When the nurse had left, he got out his phone and called Montreal.

170

In Gary, Indiana Frida S. Wharton was preparing for her revival by studying prayer request cards that had been sent in from the northwestern portion of Indiana. Her entourage, who exhibited glassy eyed loyalty, were scrambling about getting the hall ready for the expected crowd of about 3,000 people. The Church had hoped many of them would join up and eventually commit to living on the church's compound in Washington State. To do that all they had to do was to legally turn over all of their assets to Mrs. Wharton and give her power of attorney. Easy Peesy.

Amongst the crowd this night would be other parts of the posthumous manifestation of "America's poet", Walt Whitman and a late arrival by the Bo Creeley's conspiracy convoy. Creeley was motoring along interstate 90 at that moment just a mile outside of Gary.

"Should be in Washington State by tomorrow night Bo" one of his cohorts, Larry, said.

"You know Larry I can't wait to get out there. I know that they're on our tail right now. We're gonna shake em' in Chicago like we planned, then switch cars in Minneapolis and Helena. No cellphones, Larry, no cellphones."

Larry was playing with a handgun in the passenger seat beside Creeley. He was mockingly pointing it at traffic signs as they passed them on the interstate. He was doing sound effects like "kaboom" and "pow" while Creeley tried to maintain the speed limit.

"Hey, Larry keep that thing down, there are lots of cops along here. Remember we're wanted."

"Can't take my gun, away, Bo."

"Yeah, but they can take us away."

Larry laughed, and then not realizing the safety was off accidently shot Creeley in the right thigh.

They both jumped.

"What the fuck?" Creeley shrieked.

Managing to hit the brakes and steer the car to the shoulder, Creeley could not avoid a traffic sign and the ditch behind it. They both smacked they heads on the windshield in front of them.

"Fuck"

"Shit, man"

"What you do that for?"

"I didn't know the safety was off."

And they kept saying 'fuck' and 'shit' for a few more minutes as the nature of their situation began to sink in. Larry even managed a few other choice expressions of extreme disappointment and intense frustration.

Creeley had blood coming out of his leg.

"Larry, get the mini-hospital medical survival kit out of the back seat. Gotta get this fixed up quick before the cops get here."

Larry complied.

They decided that they wouldn't get the bullet out before someone noticed and the cops came so they dressed the wound quickly. Then they realized that the car was stuck. It wouldn't start. Bo punched the steering wheel. Larry said 'fuck' and 'shit' and few more times.

"Come on Larry grab a couple of guns we gotta get out of here, before the cops come."

"We gonna walk?"

"   No, we're gonna carjack someone. What do you think? We're already in Gary, Larry."

Of course, Creeley was being sarcastic about the carjacking, but Larry almost believed him.

Just off the interstate they could see the cars driving into the arena where Wharton's instant pathway to heaven was twenty minutes away from accepting them into the fold.

Creeley was in pain and limping, but he did not want to be picked by the authority. What he wanted was a 40-ounce bottle of hard liquor or some other suitable anesthetic and a private place to remove the bullet that Larry's insatiable fetish for firearms had left in his thigh.

"There must be some motel around here somewhere" thought Creeley aloud.

"There's some sort of hall right there, Bo. Maybe they got a toilet in there?"

"Yeah, maybe they do, Larry."

Again, Creeley was being sarcastic. But he was in so much pain that he didn't dismiss the idea. He recognized it as some sort of church meeting because people looked dressed up and there was a makeshift billboard by the side of the road that said:

TONIGHT: COME AND FIND OUT HOW YOU CAN BOOK YOUR PLACE ON THE SPACE SHUTTLE TO HEAVEN FREE ADMISSION – DON'T BE LEFT BEHIND – DR. FRIDA S. WHARTON CAN FIX YOUR SOUL AND POINT YOU IN THE RIGHT DIRECTION >>>>>>>>>>>>>>>>>>>>>>>>>>>>>>>>>>>>>>>

7 P.M ALL ARE WELCOMED.

And in smaller print it said The Church of the Universal Way. All major credit cards and cash are accepted.

173

"Come on, Larry. Hide those guns in your jacket. Any blood showing?" Creeley said.

"Your good, Bo."

They tried to inconspicuously blend in with the people entering the hall. Creeley managed a hearty smile that was masking a grimace caused by searing pain. Larry kept his head down and tried to not be noticed. They got in but were looked at with suspicion by Wharton's muscle at the door. One of the muscle men decided that he would keep a close eye on the pair. In fact, he radioed to the head security guy to watch for the couple. Creeley had managed to find a washroom and installed himself on one of the toilets. Larry stood outside the door keeping an eye out. Moments later short squeals could be heard coming from the washroom. Security moved in.

"Your friend, ok in there?" one of the men asked Larry.

"Sure, just had food poisoning, I think."

"Well, maybe he should go to a hospital."

"Naw, the Lord will fix him. He's just praying in there."

Another squeal came from inside.

"Just his own private way of gettin' the Lord's attention."

The security men looked beyond Larry and at the door of the washroom. A young man came out looking uncomfortable.

"I think we better go in and check on your friend" one of the men said.

"He'll be ok." Larry insisted.

Then a gasp came from inside.

"Got it, Larry" came with the gasp.

"I think he's ok now guys", said Larry.

"We'll just hang around and make sure your friend doesn't need to go the hospital."

"Sure" said Larry covering his panic.

"I forgot that I had a flask of Wild Turkey in my jacket pocket, Larry" came Creeley's voice again.

"You guys haven't been drinking, have ya?" one of the security men asked.

"No, just for medicinal purposes," said Larry.

The two men smiled, but one of them said,

"I think you would be better not to go inside. We don't want Frida's service to be interrupted."

"No, we wouldn't want to interrupt Frida" Larry said wryly.

Creeley then emerged from the washroom.

He had a look of concern on his face when he saw the two strapping males in a discussion with Larry.

"See, he's fine", said Larry.

"I'm good" said Creeley working up a smile.

"Let's go, Larry"

"Thanks" Larry said the two.

Creeley tipped his hat and quickly gestured to Larry that they should make for an exit. Loud organ music streamed from inside the hall as the two defenders of freedom made their way toward the doors. As they stood outside trying to decide which way to walk they were approached by a couple of men dressed in black jackets.

"You are to come with us" one of them said.

"   Who says" Larry retorted.

"Larry, be quiet" Creeley injected.

Then he added, "Is there some reason we should go with you?"

"Yes, we can save you from a horrible ending to your horrible little lives." Creeley and Larry chuckled.

Larry was reaching for one of the guns in his jacket pocket.

"Wait, Larry"said Creeley. "Are you guys working for Big Andy Jones?"

The two darkly dressed men looked at each other with some puzzlement.

But one of them said, "sure, Big Andy Jones."

"You guys are just in time, I'm hurtin' here"

"Just come with us we have a car just over here."

Creeley and Larry went with them.

"How'd Andy know where we was?'

Everyone was silent as the four men left the parking lot in an SUV.

twenty-seven

"When hatred kicks you in the face, lovingly beat the crap out of it"
Boris Swatcupso From his 'Poem for the Blameless'

Frank had left Jesse his contact information before leaving the Coffee Express. They had exchanged smiles and Frank and Michael Schultzmann had walked out onto University Avenue still with the five pages of clues on their brains, when Boris Swatcupso voice came from just a few feet behind them.

"Frank."

"Frank and Michael turned around.

"Frank, I've been looking for you all over."

"We were right here, Boris."

"Must've missed you."

"Must be drunk, Boris."

"Not quite, Frank. I have to tell you something, did you see the news. It's happening all over the place."

"What's happening."

"The bops on the head, Frank. The bops on the head. Camden, New Jersey, Chicago, Boston, everywhere."

"Really and where did you hear that?"

"On CNN."

Frank and Michael looked at each other.

"This is getting big", said Michael.

"We have to keep it small here though, guys. I think the larger this gets the harder it will be the find out who or what is behind it."

"What you gonna do, Frank?" asked Boris.

"First we have to get a list of all the victims. Names. Occupations. Relatives. Birthdates. Education."

"Real detective work, eh, Frank?" said Boris.

"Sure, why not?"

"You guys are really getting into this", said Michael.

"I hope you're with us" said Frank looking at Michael.

Michael hesitated, then said "I have to call my girlfriend."

"Yeah, sure", said Frank.

"Let us plough through the files of those whose blocks have been bruised, my dear Franklin" Boris intoned.

"Sure, Boris, let's."

"To the bar for a quick research session."

"You need to slow down, Boris."

"What was that place you used to drink at Frank, The DregStore. That's it.

Let's go there."

Now Boris was attempting to entice Frank into a drink. But Frank needed a clear head, at least for the next few hours, in order to go through the list of victims and their information.

It was now just past 4 P.M.

"Why don't we go to The DregStore for a couple of drinks and you can do your research there and then we'll hit the conference. Don't forget, Madison Butterworth, 6 P.M, Orillia Hall."

"You mustn't miss that, Boris. Very important for your soul as a poet."

Michael Schultzmann stood by listening and wondering if he had gotten into some sort of runaway train wreck that he would need to extricate himself from. He was not nearly as free spirited as Boris and really wondered about this guy, Frank's, motive in pursuing this affair independent of the authorities.

But something gripped him. He had read Whitman in university and had done some poetry translation in his time, so maybe this could work out to his credit in the long run. Experience for sure.

"Ok, Boris" said Frank "let's go to The DregStore, but just for two drinks. Maybe Tito might have some ideas about this."

"Yes, Tito, the former Yugoslavian dictator who now works as a bartender in a gay bar in Canada. Or is that his grandson" declared Boris with cheery impertinence.

And the three of them hailed a cab, though Schultzmann was still just towingthe line and trying to contact his girlfriend on the phone. When they had installed themselves into the cab, with him and Boris in the back seat and Frank in the front, he texted her saying that he had been delayed by a potential translation job.

And the cab weaved its way through traffic toward The DregStore where Tito would probably just be finishing his dayshift.

Meanwhile Madison J. Butterworth was in his hotel room planning a surprise as part of his address to The Sustainability and the Soul conference. He had brought his new lover along and was going to spring him on the audience that night. The former she, now a he, had almost completed the transformation in the last three years, since he had met Butterworth and Butterworth had fully supported it, both financially and emotionally. Olivia Jones had now become Brandon Petrie and Butterworth was going to use his own personal life as evidence of that the world had to be more accepting and understanding of times that we lived in if humanity was to not only to survive but be happy with life.

Respect and compassion were the watch words for Butterworth. Respect for the environment and compassion for all life forms. He had a short paper prepared for this and several poems and of course the CD of music and not to forget Brandon himself, who had his hair trimmed short and wore baggy jeans and a button-down shirt for the occasion. His look was intelligent but streetwise. Butterworth was not one to get stuck in some academic time warp of respectability.

Frank had managed to get his iphone to work so that he could track down the information on eight of the nine victims. He hadn't heard the details about the incident in Toronto and that would put a different twist on the case, but right now, he had more than enough clues to start putting together patterns.

He was sitting in a booth at the DregStore consumed by the some of the info he was digesting on his iphone as Boris was laughing at his own poetic conundrums and making Michael more uncomfortable.

"Please, Boris control yourself. We need you for inspiration, not perspiration."

"I will promise to emit only the finest bouquet of the celebrated domestic beers of North America, to not only spirit the occasion, but also to inspire us to pursue the source of these troubling attacks which have been terrifying, but obviously of some metaphysical importance to all souls."

Michael was trying to relax with a glass of white wine, but felt as though he might be losing his grip on reality. Why did these two people draw him in like he was in some sort of magnetic field?

"What do we know about the victims, Frank?" asked Boris.

"They all have a connection to poetry or prose of some sort, except one in Chicago. He was a radio host on a local talk radio station, but he may have written something in the past. Grant Dimietro is his name. He was hit harder than the others. He's still in the hospital according to the station he works at. Been there over a day."

"Grant Dimietro Sounds familiar. Used to do film reviews. I haven't heard him in years" Boris added.

"I heard him before" piped up Michael. "I lived in Chicago for a year when I was 23, doing a masters, and he did late night movie reviews. Pretty good."

"Well, that's good to know. It means that he could have written some things", said Frank.

Boris was now looking at the television screen up on the wall above where Tito was standing slicing lemon and lime wedges. The sound was muted, but by the crawl at the bottom of the screen and the pictures he could make out that a seemingly random attack to the cranium of a guy in Toronto involved a darkly dressed young man. Then the name appeared in the crawl – Warren Kitchholm.

"Frank, check out CityTV news in Toronto on your phone."

"Why?"

"I just saw something on TV, another attack. It looks like the writer that was in your room the other day. Warren Kit... something."

"Warren Kitchholm" said Frank as he searched his phone for a Canadian news app.

Boris signalled Tito for another round as he finished off the one in front of him. After a few minutes Tito came over with the drinks. Boris took Frank's beer. Michael had another wine.

"Here it is guys. I think we may have something. It says here that the police have a suspect in custody, but they haven't made the connection with the other attacks yet. That will be our job."

"What do we do Frank?"

"We go to Toronto."

"Not me, Frank."

"Fine, Boris you can stay here and go fawn over your Madison J. Butterworth. Michael and I will go."

"Listen, I can't go. I've got my girlfriend."

182

"Well, I guess it will be a solo job. You guys can keep me up to date on any developments here."

"Sure thing, Frank", said Boris.

"Cut down on that boozing Boris before you pass out somewhere. You don't want to miss out on Butterworth, do you?"

"I'm leaving for the university after this one."

Frank checked his watch. It was 5:15 P.M.

"You better step on it, he's on in 45 minutes. I'm heading for the airport. Just gotta check to see if my credit card's okay."

"Maybe I should go back to see Meg. She's probably worried."

"Maybe you should, Michael."

Soon Frank and Michael got up to leave. Frank smiled at Tito and waved. Boris was slower, but he managed to tear himself away from the booth moments later.

"Let's split a cab, the university is on the way to the airport" Boris blurted out as they were walking out the door.

Boris arrived at Orillia Hall just moments before six o'clock. Outside the hall he noticed a group of well-built young guys in their early twenties who seemed to be laughing at something.

To be more accurate they were mocking the two guys who were in a preliminary state of lovemaking on the lawn in front of the hall. The two young male students were lounged out on the lawn kissing and whispering intimacies while twenty feet away four jock types chuckled and make indistinctive remarks.

Boris Swatcupso would not have been prone to interfere in a situation like this, even though he had a great sensitivity to people being mocked or embarrassed unnecessarily, especially by those who seemingly should know better. But his consumption of an abundant amount of alcohol had lowered his ability to censor his behaviour and had caused a disruption in his cranial functions. As a result, his honest thoughts and feelings were being processed with less editorializing by the part of his brain that regulated decision making. Thoughts and feelings were raw. As might have been the case also for the juvenile display being put on by quartet of jocks.

"Find anything funny about two guys making love, my friends?" Boris asked in the most intrusive manner that he could muster.

The four turned toward Boris continuing to laugh and with an air of superiority one of them said "And how is this any of your business?"

"Whenever love is challenged by hate it is my business as a purveyor of the love craft to defend its manifestation."

The four went silent. Then one of them blurted out "Queers shouldn't do that in public."

Boris could see that he was dealing with people who had not had much exposure to the wide spectrum of possible couplings. But the urge to convince them that they must change their perspective on the matter, greatly consumed Boris. He felt feisty and combative.

"So, you think that what they are doing is unfit for display, while you stand here and are perfectly ok in having your display of ignorance go unchallenged."

"Come on, we have the right to say and think what we want."

184

"As long as it does not infringe on others right to do likewise."

Boris felt like prolonging the conversation but the quartet were suddenly having a change in brain activity which had them considering the wider scope of the situation. Boris would have to curtail both his intellectual and possibly pugilistic urges for the time being.

"Why don't you come to the lecture at Orillia Hall, you may have your consciousness expanded by a man whose has had considerable experience in both writing about and participating in love making."

The young jocks exchanged awkward glances. Then they decided to follow what they thought was probably a professor into the hall. Boris was right behind them being vigilant, looking dishevelled and a bit erratic which made the muscular quartet nervous. Outside, the two male lovebirds were moving on to a more intimate setting for their pursuits.

Boris found a seat near the front on the aisle noticing that one of the four had found himself a seat alone off to one side.

The first person to appear on the stage was the distinguished looking moderator, who outlined the agenda for the evening, gave a few comments on the theme of the conference, and made it known that Madison J. Butterworth was a pleasant though unexpected addition to the conference lineup and would be participating in a debate afterwards with Ambrose L. Keel.

Then Butterworth came on. After some preliminary remarks, he read a poem that chased away the glum outlook for the future of the planet that had prevailed at the conference and injected a political plea for the resurrection of the soul into public initiatives. His words reverberated in the room creating a theatre like atmosphere. Butterworth had arraigned for sound effects and mood music to accompany his wordy cry to the invisible side. Boris was even moved by it.

Butterworth spoke poetically of freeing the mind from the dictatorship of crooked logic and authoritarian reason, that only pushed young people into incestuous relationships with the accepted scholarship of the times.

"…when the air is thick with facts and test tube words, strip the beast
Of its self-indulgent shell woven together by stifled souls and deaden Minds,
Repeating results, repeating tests, repeating, repeating until all the boxes have been counted, all the dots have been connected,
nothing left to spark the flames of love and life, all that is left is to explain to those ignorant souls who cling to hope,
mystery and vague loves and beliefs.
That they are stupid to say that more is to be revealed, don't they know
That we know all, we know better, we know what is good for you, so
sssh
Little children.
Listen to us, all the data will be programmed into your Minds.
All the facts that you need we already know.
Just build on our love…"

And Butterworth went on to a crescendo. Then he introduced his love, his breaker of reason and logic in love and romance, his Brandon. A masculine figure appeared from the side of the stage. Butterworth beamed and he embraced Brandon and gave him a big kiss. They raised their arms and Butterworth said,

"Brandon, whom I met as Olivia, has been all the evidence that I need today to leap into the arms of spirits unseen. It has been there that I have found what was so elusive to me as a young person struggling with the

186

facts. I could never understand why I had to incessantly explain myself and my work to others. Why my life had to be justified to the world. I indulged in wordy and winded arguments to impress others but I failed to make a mark or to be honest with the one that I needed to be true to the most, myself. It has now been shown to me that my journey is only beginning again, just when a few short months ago I thought it was ending. I declare that I have not known, in my soul, anything like a beginning or an end and I wish upon every soul here today that you seize each moment to work, inspire and play with life and love. There you will find the truth about yourselves. Not a truth that is etched in stone forever, but a truth that is forever changing, becoming and evolving. A transformative truth, of creative forces unbounded by any logic which would leave the whole self outside of consideration. This is a truth worth going after, a truth relative but convincing. I will now take questions."

Brandon had stepped aside and sat just off stage while the questions came. When he had been a female he was enamoured by Butterworth, feeling an openness and freedom in his poetry and prose as a university student in England. They had met at a seminar, through her own persistence, and had the mutual attraction blossom over time until the moment where Olivia had become comfortable as Brandon. It had been a difficult at times for Brandon to communicate with Butterworth truly where he was on the journey. Butterworth had to really make sustained efforts to find where Olivia's voice ended and Brandon's began, but he truly knew that he was pursuing something worthwhile. It was confirmed to him each time they had conquered a hurdle.

Brandon was now 36. Butterworth was 72. This fact created issues concerning public perception for many in academia and with a more salacious twist amongst the general press and gossip websites, to whom this story was a positive. But really the two didn't care and just answered questions about age without any seriousness or reverence.

Butterworth of course could do this with more polish and authenticity than Brandon, so he would generally issue commentary that went something like this:

"One is always amazed at the opportunity that comes from being thrust into the public eye. It presents one with a chance to sell the public all kinds of products that otherwise would be just taking up space in one's basement. My lover and I do wish to express our sincerest thanks to the press and the public for clearing out our warehouse of fictional tales, misinterpreted allegory and moralizing plotlines that were only blocking us from enjoying each other's company. Now, if one is curious about the state of our souls, I encourage the insecure to not be afraid to follow one's conscious, to pursue self-honesty and read my poems. Thank you for living your lives."

I was also present at the lecture. My opinion of the presentation was that it was much too irreverent concerning logic and the scientific method considering that Butterworth had almost no qualifications in the applied sciences. How can one poo-poo reason and then embrace with fervor a universe about which most of the facts are not in. Now if I were grading the lecture, I would have given Butterworth points for inspiring thought and displaying the need to rely on a muse when working in the creative arts. Though I wish he had spoken more about the Soul and Sustainability.

Boris was inspired by the first part of the presentation. In fact, he was taking notes. Later, someone asked a question about the scientific method. Butterworth answered by saying that any exact way of thinking about something was not necessarily a one hundred percent check on reality but was definitely an encouragement and a support. Another had to do with raising the standard of living for all inhabitants of the world. Some discussion followed about individual dignity and respect. But by the end of the session Boris was tiring of the questions as it became quite transparent that the questioners were much more interested in having their own opinions and statements heard then in hearing anything that Butterworth had to say. He slipped out. He would pick up a copy of the book later.

But Butterworth's sudden attraction to a transgendered person fascinated Boris. He knew of many examples in the literary world where the gender of the beloved was in dispute, but now it was before the world as a cold hard fact and not theoretical. He laughed to himself. He thought of Patricia. His mind wondered about all those people who worked in construction, in the oil fields, in factories, in labor intensive occupations who did not have the opportunity or time to reflect on their own gender preference and had to keep it under wraps.

Those who misunderstood and confused gender with sexual preference etc. Boris had been both a cook and an artist. He did know that the demands of mundane work left one little time to think about such things. Boris had a sudden wave of melancholy pass through him as he loitered outside the hall. He felt a tear in his eye. He sat down on a bench for half an hour and scribbled down some lines. He knew that he could not go back to working in a kitchen and experience the desperation and dishonesty of the lives that he saw on display there. He wanted to help, but how.

Maybe this little detective game that Frank had initiated would be a path for Boris. What would Frank discover in Toronto? Boris was now truly engaged in helping solve a mystery. He had kicked many people in the face in his younger days when it came time to defend what he believed in, now he recognized that he needed to try and have empathy for the blameless and not look for more people to blame. And it would have been easier for him to just blame people for the bumps on the head rather than try to understand the threads leading to them.

Boris called Frank to see if Frank had gotten a flight yet. Frank said that he would have to wait until 10:20 P.M to get out of Montreal. Boris walked slowly back to his apartment not really wanting to drink anymore, but just to sleep, maybe he could dream. He watched through the windows as people worked in the small restaurants and cafés along the St. Amos and the other side streets leading to his apartment. He got home, undressed, showered and crawled into bed letting go of Frank, Michael, Butterworth and

Brandon and particularly Patricia from his thought process. He turned off his phone. He looked forward to awakening refreshed.

twenty-eight

"If I kidnapped my soul, then no one could hurt me."
Boris Swatcupso From his poem 'Painless Poem'

About the same time in a large open warehouse space somewhere west of Chicago sat a bearded man with soft eyes and a gentle demeanor. He looked with a compassionate eye on Bo Creeley and his friend Larry as they sat mystified about the nature of their being taken from a hall parking lot in Gary, Indiana, and then suddenly waking up in this large space. A substantial amount of time seemed to be missing. Had this been a rescue or a kidnapping? It had the qualities of both. Creeley was unnerved about the whole thing. He suspected that the people who had largely remained silent during the process were somehow affiliated with the government. Larry was just quiet, taking his cue from Creeley. Both of them had lumps on their heads.

Then both of them were taken into separate rooms where a doctor treated their wounds. Creeley's questions were answered with "you will know in due time." Creeley and Larry were then given a lunch and told to sit on a couch near one of the walls of the warehouse space. The bearded man paced back and forth in front or them smiling periodically with a look of friendliness on his face.

"Now what the fuck is going on here?" Creeley finally blurted out in frustration.

"I appreciate that you are insecure and do not trust us, Mr. Creeley. I cannot answer all your questions to your satisfaction. I can tell you that you are safe and well protected as long as you remain with us. No harm will come to you here. You can only harm yourself if you choose to go it alone. It is you

191

who must decide Mr.Creeley and your friend as well. I can assure you that all of the forces in the universe will be with you if you let them be. Do not resist tears, or laughter, my good friend. Relax. Disarm."

This last word shook Creeley. He felt his two guns still with him. They had not disarmed him. He could easily just pull one of them out a threaten his way out of here. He could kill these people, who probably didn't have any guns. Larry had a couple of guns too. Creeley still could not see this affair as a kidnapping and he was right. Why had he not used his guns? And there was a lump on his skull too.

"Mr. Creeley feel free to leave if you wish" said the soft voice of the wise old man figure who now had stopping pacing and was seated before them in armchair.

"I just want to know why you knocked us out and brought us here. Where the fuck are we? What is it that you guys want from us?"

"Only your honesty, Mr. Creeley. We wish only authenticity. We have no agenda but to document that life is eternal and death but a moment in life. And conversely that death can be eternal and life but a fleeting moment in that death. It is your choice. So, what is it that you want is the question you should be asking yourselves? No one wants anything from you here."

"Are you guys for real?"

"Mr. Creeley just move on from here. You will begin to comprehend in your own time."

"Listen, you guys must have a few screws loose upstairs. Larry, I think we have some shit to do. We gotta go guys. Nice knowing your little cult here and thanks for the help, but it's time to blow."

Creeley suspected the government was behind this but did not want to tip his hat. He noticed that his wounds had been carefully treated and the pain seem to be subsiding in last ten minutes. He would recover. Larry was just in stunned silence ready to follow Creeley's lead.

The two young men in black who had originally insisted that Creeley and Larry get into the SUV outside of the Wharton rally, now appeared from a side room. They had shown no intention of blocking the way out. They smiled at Creeley and Larry and one of them said,

"Be well, men."

The situation was getting more and more incomprehensible to Creeley. His feeble brain could not imagine the motivation of this group. He had some fear of ghosts and now these events were playing on that fear. He went to shake hands with the two young men, to touch them to see if they were made of real flesh and bones. And they were.

"Who are you guys really?" he asked one of them.

"We are manifestations of the lost souls, the blameless, the misunderstood, the forgotten innocence of life. Beauty, my friend, beauty."

"Sure, ok, let's get the fuck out of here, Lar. This is too freaky even for Big Andy. And I thought you guys were from Big Andy."

The bearded man voice then came from across the expansive room.

"Big Andy Jones has laryngitis today. He will be back tomorrow. Tune in tomorrow gentlemen."

Creeley and Larry looked at each other and the old man in silence and walked out.

"See ya" Creeley managed as he left. He was puzzled and in disbelief. With Larry in tow, they walked briskly through a warehouse district that they had never seen before, looking for signs of humanity. They heard an engine in the distance, they saw a figure get out of the back of a vehicle a block ahead of them. The figure appeared to be male and was waving at them from the back window to join him. With some trepidation they approached the car. As they got within 50 feet of the car, they realized that it was a taxi.

"Hey, guys it's all right. I know where you guys came from."

He was a short chubby man, looked to be in his late forties and had shoulder length dark hair and had a strong voice that projected well.

"Who are you?" asked Creeley.

"I am Grant Dimietro from WNG Radio 920. Get in, I just met the old guy too. Got bopped on the head three days ago."

Creeley and Larry both hesitated.

"Come on, we'll go for a beer and I'll tell you all about it. WNG Radio 920? Or maybe you guys are not from the Chicagoland area."

Creeley was still in stunned disbelief, not just from this seemingly random invitation to share a cab ride with a semi-obscure radio personality, but from the entire series of events. Creeley saw that it was nearly sundown, he looked around and saw no other sign of life. He glanced in at the cab driver, who looked straight ahead with indifference. He looked at his loyal companion's face. Meanwhile, Larry just shrugged his shoulders.

The trio were soon squeezed into the backseat of the cab.

"To Nap's Tavern, driver" ordered Dimietro, then he continued.

"Ok, guys don't panic. I was in the other room when they brought you in. They call themselves a cell from infinity. They claim to be old souls whose existence, may be only in our imaginations, but nevertheless are real on some level or dimension. Just stay calm, I don't even have it figured out, one minute I was in a coma in the hospital and the next I'm having a beer with Walt Whitman in a warehouse. He's telling me about how he used to go swimming naked but couldn't find any body of water that isn't polluted in America these days."

The cab driver glanced at them with the benefit of his rear-view mirror.

"You boys sure you want to go to a bar?"

"Yeah, don't worry, I'm telling my lost friends here about a movie script I'm working on."

Dimietro was being coy.

The group remained silent for the rest of the trip until they had reached Nap's bar which was located just off of Irving Parkway just west of downtown Chicago and near the university.

Dimietro paid the cab with a credit card and found a quiet corner in the nearly empty bar. It was not a busy bar, but it was Dimietro's favorite neighbourhood drinking establishment, just three blocks from his apartment and very discreet and friendly.

"Beer, guys?"

"Sure" said Creeley looking vacantly at his sidekick.

"Do you guys believe in an afterlife, because I certain don't. I think that these guys are part of some terrorist cell, or cult. Maybe it's prank or political group like Anonymous. I've been checking online."

Creeley sat somewhat dumbfounded for a moment. Then he managed a question.

195

"Who's this Walt Whittier guy?"

"Whitman, Walt Whitman. He was an American poet in the 1800s. A kind of gentle soul, who was considered by many as one of the great American poets. Kind of a free thinker."

"1800s?"

"Yeah, so this bearded guy that you guys met, looks like him, talks like him, acts like him, but can't be him. He's an imposter."

"Fuckin weirdos if you ask me."

"Yeah, but for real. They really are doing it."

The beers came and the trio drank in silence for a minute.

"So, Dimietro are you gonna call the cops?"

"The cops know, but they don't know, if you know what I mean. They know that I was assaulted, but they don't know that I was kidnapped and that these guys tried to brainwash me. I haven't told them that part yet. They wrote it down as a simple assault and probably won't investigate it any further unless I press them. I gave them some bullshit story. That's how things are in this city."

Creeley and Larry looked at each other.

"We really don't want the cops involved" said Creeley.

Creeley had a very selfish motive for not involving the authorities, but he was not inclined to discuss it with a radio personality from Chicago.

"Do you guys think that you may want to come on my show and talk about what just happen?"

"Not really."

Dimietro envisioned turning his experience into a series of program that would captivate an audience for days, perhaps weeks. He wanted to break the stories himself and he saw Creeley and his sidekick as being instrumental in authenticating his experience.

"Look I have a show tonight at midnight. I called my producer earlier. She's the only one that knows where I am. The hospital must think that I just jumped ship. I can guarantee your anonymity. You can disguise your voices if you want, as long as you are believable when you're on the air. Just tell the truth guys. There might be some money in it. What do you say?"

"How much money?"

"Well, I don't know, but we may get a sponsor and sell t-shirts, caps stuff like that. It's hard to say right now. You know the abducted by alien stuff. A lot of people go for that stuff. Especially my late-night audience."

"I believe in aliens."

"That's great then it will sound all the more real."

"You know this Whitfield guy he could be a real alien. His pals they didn't say much, like they were in some sort of trance."

"Right, so we'll play that angle up. Listen I don't know who these people are, but I'm not going to let this pass without capitalizing on it. What do you say, guys?"

"Sure, all right. But we wanna get paid."

"I'll talk to my producer. Remember we're just a local show, we're not national."

The trio finished their drinks and headed downtown to the WNG studios.

twenty-nine

"Exact science and its practical movements are no check on the greatest poet but always his encouragement and support…scientists are the lawgivers of poets… in the beauty of poems are the tuft and final applause of science."

Walt Whitman

Madison J. Butterworth was awake in his hotel room bed reading a very serious scholarly work with Brandon Petrie sleeping soundly by his side when he received a phone call.Butterworth's ring tone was an excerpt of a Dmitri Shostakovitch concerto. It didn't awaken Brandon at all.

"Yes" whispered Butterworth very quietly turning his head away from Brandon.

"Mr. Butterworth, this a voice from the past. Do not be alarmed. It's Walt Whitman the poet. I'm only an echo for you, but an infinite soul for the universe. You are not crazy Butterworth. I am alive and working as a part time instructor in creative writing in Vancouver, British Columbia. It's a lot of fun and I get to be near the ocean. I always loved the water. I know you probably think that I am a fake, an imposter, but that is not so. Some of us old poets have found a dimension where we can extend reality and inhabit new bodies and continue living on in the worldly plane."

Butterworth was taken aback by the suddenness of all the information that was dispensed and not believing any of it. But he remained calm and accepting of whoever was at the other end.

He suspected one of his literary buddies from London was playing a prank.

"Ah yes, Mr. Whitman how are things in your realm? Do you have friends and family where you are?"

"I wept for my friends and family for many years, they are gone to some other ledge of time and space, but I've been able to compose reams of verse about it. In fact, I can send you pictures and words of what I have been up to. I have a new love interest here, a young handsome angel who has taken the form of one of my creative writing students. He is what keeps me shining inside so that I do not slip onto a lower plane. I sit with him in the evenings and watch the sunset over the Pacific Ocean. He's a bit of a rebellious free thinker Butterworth, too volatile for the normal everyday gay lifestyle. He needs an alternate realm to do his loving in."

Butterworth was becoming more and more impressed by the ruse. He smiled to himself.

"Well, Mr. Whitman you certainly have gone boldly into the starry night."

"You know Butterworth, people need to be rudely awakened from the slumber that science is all about the material plane, you know, see, touch, smell, taste, feel, those sorts of things. They are a few of us here doing what we can to affect a change. We are filling in the gaps, hooking up the loose ends, Butterworth. But, you know, ever time I think that I have reached solid ground the poem is asking me to be revised. I have to change the tune all the time Butterworth. You know how that is?"

"Sure, Mr. Whitman. I wish that I could go back and re-edit my books all the time. Say, Mr. Whitman is there any chance that I could arrange to meet you, in person. I would love to see what you are working on now."

"Certainly, but mostly now I just do revisions and pay some souls personal visits."

"Well, I must consider myself lucky then. Where can I reach you?"

"Listen, I will be at a small underground magazine in Montreal tomorrow. It's called the Conspiremouth. My friends work there. They run it out of a small apartment near the university. Go to 3628 St. Martin Avenue and ring apartment #14. Ask for Binky. Tell him you want to see Walt."

200

Butterworth was getting a little scared. This was creepy, but he made note of the information and would consider going to the place, with some support of course.

"Mr. Whitman it has been a pleasure. I do hope to see you again."

"Mr. Butterworth, the pleasure has been all mine. I do hope that you overcome your disbelief in the infinite endurance of the poetic muse and come and see me. You have been a champion professor. But I must go now my friends await. Good night."

And with that the call was terminated.

Butterworth put his phone down onto the night table. He glanced at Brandon sweetly sleeping away. How would he tell him? Should he tell him? Should he call a colleague in London?

He turned off the night light in the hotel room and stayed awake in the darkness thinking. He thought to himself that if this were truly a spirit or soul from another realm, that would be something that he would keep to himself. Any self-respecting poet would keep the intimacies with his muse private.

But what was he thinking? This whole experience had been totally unscientific, had no basis in reality. Had he dreamt it up? He could check his phone and see where the call had come from, if there was any call at all. He quickly snatched the phone from the night table after grappling in the dark. He found the call log. Yep, it was there a call from a British Columbia area code. He remembered the prefix from last year when he had been in Victoria. What did this mean? It had to be a prank. Who had his private number? He had no brothers or sisters. No family to speak of. Maybe it was someone from the BBC?

He laid up and pondered the many books that he had penned. He tried to remember the critical reviews. Was there someone that had it in for him? Had he offended someone on an academic or personal level? No, he could not think of anything that would warrant such an elaborate and

201

mischievous set up. Who would go to such an extent to deceive him? He certainly had given people the impression over the years that he was up for a good joke, but not such a seemingly sinister subterfuge. It brought to mind the plot lines of many Russian novels and short stories, but they always ended with some valid scientific explanation. The trickery and so-called magic were always exposed in the end. Would he have to play this out to get a satisfactory answer? It seemed that way to Butterworth at the moment. How could he explain this to Brandon or his colleagues? He would have to devise a ruse himself.

Butterworth lay awake for awhile deliberating on his options. He also ruminated on his career. Eventually he fell asleep. He dreamed of the American Civil War and Walt Whitman's time. He dreamed of colorfully dressed soldiers and of his mother serving him hearty meals. He was a young man again. The dream was pleasant.

It wasn't so pleasant for Frida S. Wharton and her associates in Gary, Indiana. About sunrise, as Butterworth was slumbering with one of America's poetic giants, Wharton was being busted for mail fraud at her hotel room. Three of her partners were also being carted off by the F.B.I. They had seized many of the documents that she had with her and were simultaneously busting into her Pittsburgh office and home and appropriating massive amounts of paper files and several computers. The arrests had been the culmination of a seven-month investigation and hundreds of complaints going back five years.

The investigators knew that Wharton would employee some hot shot lawyers and probably avoid jail, but they wanted at the very least to shut her down and perhaps return some of the people's assets. This bust could result in many people seeing Wharton for the fraud she was and they could also fully reveal her plans to operate what could have become a full scale and dangerous cult.

About sunrise Grant Dimietro was just finishing up his all-night radio show at WNG. It had been difficult for him to explain to his audience the assault and his subsequently leaving the hospital, but he had done it without sounding like he was making shit up. Creeley and Larry had been installed in anteroom in the building where they napped and listened to Dimietro's show. Creeley was listening to Dimietro sign off and turn the station over to the morning host, when he heard the lead story about the Wharton arrest. He remembered the washroom at the arena where he had in fact only attempted to remove the bullet that Larry had so carelessly arranged to be embedded into his thigh. Now, he suddenly realized that it must have been the people at the warehouse that had actually gotten the piece of metal out his leg. This and the Wharton bust made him smile. He truly thought that she was a fraud. Dimietro then appeared at the door.

"We're going to the cops, guys."

"The cops? Listen we got a lot of things to do and people to meet. We don't have time to got stuck here with all this weird shit going on."

Dimietro was sympathetic with Bo and Larry.

"Ok, whatever you guys want, but I want to stay in touch with you. I'd like to see where this story goes."

"You know, we just want to go home."

"Where's home guys?"

"Ah, Washington State."

"What were you guys doing here in Chicago?"

"Well, like we told ya. We we're just passing through when we had, um, a little accident. We had to ditch our car and when we tried to get help at this arena near Gary these two guys sort of kidnapped us."

"And brought you to Chicago?"

"Yeah."

"You know guys since I was snatched from the hospital and after waking up from that blow to the head, I've had this strange sensation that I'm never going to really die. I had it last night. This feeling that death would be only a moment. Tonight, I just breezed through my show. I don't remember what I said, but it felt wonderful. I still think that the police should know the full story. They may be looking for me now, even though it was written up as a minor assault with no charges being laid at the time."

"I think the cops always mess things."

"Well sometimes they are not needed, boys."

Here Dimietro paused, reflected for a moment while looking out of westward from the fourteenth floor of the office building and then declared.

"You know what I'm going to leave the cops out of this. I don't know why exactly but I'm going to give you guys a break. I'm feeling pretty good since that blow on the head. Maybe there is something mystical happening here."

"I dunno know, but we got the blow to the head and there ain't nothing happening with us."

"Well, all I know is that these guys are strange and I don't intend to let it go. But I will hold off on the cops. I feel so good. I feel like a new man guys and I don't want to blow that. Can I drop you guys off somewhere? I'm taking a cab north."

"No thanks we can take care of ourselves. We like it better that way."

"Yeah, I can understand that, now. Here's my card. Keep in touch. It's been weird, guys."

And with that he disappeared. Creeley and Larry left shortly after that. It was a pleasantly cool summer morning in Chicago. The traffic was still light. Creeley found his wallet and decided that it might be best to take a

Greyhound bus the rest of the way to Washington State. But first he had to check on something in Gary, Indiana.

thirty

"Be careful about reading health books. You may die of a misprint."

Mark Twain

In Toronto, Frank was sitting in a Coffee Express near the hospital before visiting hours pouring over the texts that he had received from Warren Kitchholm looking for hidden clues in them. Frank had felt a dizziness coming on shortly after getting off the plane. His ill feelings came and went mysteriously, though he had noticed that an attack was frequently a portent of some shift in the affairs of his life. He needed to sit for awhile alone when they came on. This was one reason why he had refused to move into Boris' loft when Boris had offered to let him stay there indefinitely. He needed to have some control of his environment and Boris was at times capricious. He had enough money to sustain himself for awhile. At least until he had come to a resolution on this affair. He would wait until his dizzy spell passed, then he could refocus on the matter.

Kitchholm had been informed by the police that his assailant may have had misguided motivations for assaulting him. Kitchholm had already felt like a link in some strange narrative being directed by an unknown source and was anxious to reunite with Frank. The messages gave Frank further determination to stay the course and find the source of the string of attacks. Kitchholm had not sensed that anything more than bad chemicals had to led these incidents. Before being bopped on the noggin he didn't suspect that there was a recycling of anything metaphysical going on. To him the world was simply a big ball of dirt mixed with water and chemicals that pursued a random course of activity causing things to happen. To him any patterns that developed were only explainable by immediately exercised free will on the part of the chemicals and their compounds.

206

Kitchholm believed that his brain operated like this and he could not see how anyone else's could function differently. Anything alive that had any other notion than a pleasant survival for as long as possible was a victim of delusion according to Kitchholm's view of things. This was before. Now as he lay in the hospital bed he began to question those ideas. Frank's little theories also contributed to Kitchholm reconsidering his previous outlook. Somehow Kitchholm was beginning to seek a spot in his imagination where all that was about him became of less importance. He felt lighter and less tied to what he had viewed before as a big ball of dirt, water and chemicals.

Frank sat with his coffee thinking of possible motivations for the attacks. He seemed to have found a new energy within himself in the last few days. He was looking back on his time in Toronto, with his ex-wife and the mundane jobs that he had held. He recognized that he had been trying to eliminate any thoughts of those times from his consciousness for the last three years by continuously moving to different places and pursuing new adventures. The years had slipped past quickly and to him it seemed that not much had happened. It had been just one day after another. No relationships or friends of any kind had been developed. No projects had been worked. He had only worked for a pay check. Which wasn't so bad, he thought, until this moment at the Coffee Express within view of the North Markham Hospital, where he was having some deep moments of reflection on his life. He felt now that he had been given a task that would provide his mind with some consistent purpose. If only his dizzy spells would stay under control. Like the attacks on people's cranium, his periodic feelings of nausea and loss of equilibrium seemed so random and unattached to any practical motivation that they had tapped into Frank's curiosity. But the blows to the head had also restored an even deeper wonder about life, one that was similar to what he had had as a child. Something in Frank was in a period of restoration. And Frank knew that he wanted to take advantage of this time. He thought about how he had stopped defining himself in the teenage years and had begun just accepting a dull existence. He smiled now. Was this some sort of awakening that he had heard and read about people having? He didn't know. He would probably not know this, at least not for a long while, but he did know that for the first time in many moons he had a sense that he would be okay in the long run. He looked out of the Coffee Express window at the hospital and thought that in there was another link in the mystery. And for the first time in his over 30 years on the planet he realized that it was not the answers that motivated him but the wonder of the mystery. Even if he found nothing, he would be happy with that. He got up from his table at the Coffee Express and walked toward the hospital and Warren Kitchholm, whose mind was also whirling in the metaphysical realm.

As Frank approached the hospital his phone rang. Boris was calling. He was upbeat.

"Frank, I've been touched by the muse of Butterworth. My molecular structure has been altered, the sun is shining, it's cool outside, the starlings are whispering the genius of love into my ears, Frank. I need nothing more than ever, Frank. I need nothing, Frank."

"Um, I see you've crawled back into your adolescence and tapped into the fanboy innocence that you were looking for in those women you dated."

"Frank don't destroy a rare uplifting moment in my life with an amateur attempt at instant pop psychology. Save your detective work for what is happening in the conscious world, the scientific world, not what may be buried below. I want to surf above the water, not drown below the waves."

"Oh, that's nice, Boris, very nice. Your metaphors have really developed since our days of drinking in cemeteries and hospitals."

"Yeah, not to mention, public parks, dive bars, airports, and movie theatres."

"So, besides corresponding your exuberance is there anything regarding the case that you would like to tell me?"

"Ah, I see it's a case, now, is it Colombo?"

"Yes, so why not call it what it is?"

"And who's going to pay us for our time?"

"In other words, Boris why are we doing this?"

"Yes, why indeed."

"The answer to that question is not important, Boris. There probably is no satisfactory answer to such a question. Any possible answer is probably irrelevant at any rate. All that is important is that we jump into the mystery with a vigorous determination. With that we cannot go wrong, my friend."

"Do you have to call me a friend? I know that already. But alas I will not dispute your redundant semantics."

"Friends are not easy to come by. I learned that early in life. I never trusted people easily Boris, and I certainly don't trust what gets passed off as friendship in some circles."

"Well said for a man who is not yet forty. Are you being critical of social media?"

"Yes, I am, Boris, but not philosophically just in practice."

"I'm going to leave that one, Frank. Now about Kitchholm did you see him yet?"

"I'm just going into the hospital now. We will soon find out if there is a definite connection here."

"Frank, do you believe our lives survive death?"

"No evidence of that Boris, but I am sure something must go on. But I don't think it has anything to do with our personalities. You are thinking of our old friend Mr. Whitman, Boris. Glad that you are working on the case."

"But ideas survive, they get passed on."

"Boris, that is just where the evidence here is leading us. But how do ideas get transmitted without personalities mistaking them for their own?"

"Frank, I'll get back to you on that one."

"We will stay on the trail, Boris. I'll call you tonight."

With that, Boris and his muse terminated the phone call and proceeded to the local used bookstore to find a copy of the Complete Works of Walt Whitman. He needed verification. And he suspected that Butterworth would be next in line for a blow to the head.

thirty-one

'Conspiremouth' had very little presence online. Butterworth had gotten Brandon to do some research but almost nothing came out of it. It was a print publication with a two-page website stating its mission as being a forum for stories and poem written by marginalized people. But it did publish articles and pieces relevant to issues around sustainability and current political dilemmas particularly to do with the city of Montreal. Butterworth was not concerned with all of this. His main reason for deciding to visit the little publication had been the mystery that the late-night phone call had created in his mind. Not only had the voice claiming to be Walt Whitman been bold and assertive, but it had tickled Butterworth's fancy for surprise and practical jokes. He was certain that somebody had arranged this for his and their own amusement.

There was a part of his mind that wanted to believe that at least the spirit of the poet was still alive somewhere on the planet even though the actual poet had become almost irrelevant. And he also wanted to believe that the dozens of poets and scribes that he had read and studied over his fifty plus year career still lingered perhaps as spirits or inhabited souls in the present.

Butterworth had a practical mind when it came to religion, but he still had a deep respect for the what many labelled the 'unknown'. For him it was enshrined in the irony and hidden psychological motivations of characters in the Russian literature he had read as an adolescent and young man before he had opened his mind to more academic books and theories.

At his core, he thought of himself as an atheist in his values, believing that the human species simply made it up as it went along. Yet, when he reflected on humanity's potential or future, he honestly had to admit that very little was knowable. In his appreciation of literature, he had uncovered a tremendous amount of chance encounters of personages and sub conscious meanings and as a result he had developed a sense for reading them into the 'real' world. So, this phone call had precipitated a thought process that he found could not be resolved by simple deduction or a phone call to his joke prone friends in England. He had to see for himself. Besides Brandon had inspired a youthful sense of adventure in him that he had not had in years.

He had decided to bring Brandon along. He might make friends, thought Butterworth. The two of them sat ensconced in silence, but with a certain excited anticipation. Butterworth was thinking slightly dark thoughts that revolved around how sinister it was to resurrect the ghost of a long dead genius. Let him rest and let his words speak for themselves, thought Butterworth. Brandon was hoping to not be seen as only Butterworth's lover, but as having a voice of his own. This dominated a lot of Brandon private thoughts. He prepared himself to be assertive and to disagree with Butterworth whenever he could, not to embarrass him, but to overcome his long-suffering problem with self-condemnation. This stemmed from not being accepted by his peers in adolescence and having an awkward life in school. But he had survived thanks to a few good friends and now had gotten through some of the most difficult parts of transitioning into a male.

His relationship with Butterworth was also a most important catalyst to his becoming well with himself, so he did not challenge his lover on a personal level but made sure not to let himself off the hook if he saw things differently. He sometimes looked dreamy and stared off into space when he had conversations with people. He was not a disciplined thinker and this sometimes irritated Butterworth, but it also endeared him to Brandon, because it would get Butterworth to try a find out what hidden gems were on Brandon's mind. Part of Brandon's motive for keeping a low profile during his transition was not only for his lover's sake, but to help him develop his confidence slowly as a male. He would go out on his own to public places, including social clubs and sporting events as a male just to get the hang of it. More importantly though was his work with his therapist and transgender group. Butterworth made sure not to hang out with Brandon during these times. He felt that Brandon should just experience some things for himself and not need some pseudo-public figure like himself to provide validation. Besides Butterworth wanted to spring his lover on his friends and the world only when Brandon had at least some comfort level of confidence in himself.

The two of them disembarked from the cab at 3628 St. Martin Avenue. The address had an entrance with a single door that was covered in puncture marks, had powder blue paint peeling off it and was ajar. Brandon went ahead holding Butterworth by the arm. Butterworth was still quite spry but Brandon knew that he enjoyed Brandon's aid.

"Oh, my Brandon. This looks promising."

Brandon laughed. He pushed the door so that it was fully opened and he heard the sound of clinking bottles falling behind it.

"Well, I'm sure those aren't milk bottles?", asked Butterworth.

Again, Brandon laughed.

"Would you like your milk in bottles, Maddi?" said Brandon.

Brandon had gotten used to calling him Maddi lately and Butterworth enjoyed it. Butterworth had no delusion that it made him any younger, but it tickled his heart when he heard it.

"Now Brandon where are you going to get milk in bottles today?"

"I'm sure I could find somewhere in the world where they still sell it in bottles."

"Yes, Brandon I'm sure that what is politically correct changes so fast nowadays that bottles could be a 'good' thing today and be 'bad' tomorrow. I hope you and I are a good thing for a little while anyhow."

213

They both smiled. They had an understanding, that when the time came Brandon could choose to spend more time away from his lover, but not abandon him completely. Butterworth had his academic and artistic work that would never leave him lonely and besides he loved Brandon and would never want to feel like he had restricted him from anything that would expand his life.

Inside the doorway was a narrow staircase that had been marked up with black streaks both on the steps and on the handrails. There was a slight smell of alcohol, marijuana and room deodorizer in the air. They climbed the stairs carefully with Brandon supporting Butterworth. At the top there was no indication of where number 14 was located.

"Wait here. I'll just check the numbers", said Brandon.

He went to the right a way and then yelled out "down here. Maddi."

On the door in magic marker was written the number 14 and below that pinned to the wooden door a piece of paper which appeared to be ripped from an issue of 'Conspiremouth.' It read:

CONSPIREMOUTH – GOOD READS FOR ALL – HOME OFFICE HERE

"   Well, that's cute" said Brandon.

Butterworth remained silent. Now he was a little more concerned, thinking that perhaps this had not been a practical joke at all, but some sinister plot to discredit him. Or maybe some psychotic student of Walt Whitman had set this all up. He was getting closer to the truth. Brandon was just hoping for the best choosing to remain naïve in his thinking. Brandon knocked.

The door opened and the strained face of a young man with shoulder length hair wearing a black t-shirt appeared.

214

"Yeah?" he said.

Brandon spoke first.

"We're here to meet Walt Whitman. This is Professor Madison Butterworth. We were asked here yesterday."

"Yeah, well I don't know anything about that. But you can come in Binky will be here soon. He just went down to the store."

"Binky, that's the name I was given" Butterworth mumbled to Brandon.

Inside were three chesterfields, a large table covered in papers, two laptops, an old fridge, a gas stove, several paintings, two deformed futons, four large bookcases filled with books and small boxes, some plants and a big orange cat that sat on a windowsill staring intently down onto a side alley. All of this was in a one big room with what appeared to be a washroom at the back next to a rear exit.

"Sit down" said the young guy assertively.

The two visitors sat down unsteadily.

"You want something to drink. Ginger tea, wine, beer, tap water?"

"Not for me. You want something, Brandon?"

"No, thanks."

"Casey", the young guy stuck out his hand to Brandon.

"Brandon"

"Are you a student?"

"Well, kind of. I'm actually Mr. Butterworth's partner and student sometimes."

"Brandon is my link to real world, he is my medium to love, heartache and conversations that don't involve theses, esthetic, metre, stanzas, plots, themes, zeitgeist and all that literary nonsense that I must say did me quite good for most of my life but has become a bore talking about anymore. Excuse the rhyme ... bore, anymore."

Brandon managed a smile.

"I'm having a beer" said Casey. He went to the fridge.

Butterworth was looking a little worried. Brandon was concerned.

"So, Binky will be here soon?" asked Butterworth.

"Yeah."

"So, you guys put out a paper here?" asked Brandon.

"Yeah, here."

Casey handed Brandon an 81/2 X 11 stapled copy of 'Conspiremouth.'

Brandon scanned the pages. Articles about housing, homelessness, indigenous peoples, poems and photos of some art work, paintings, jewellery etc.

"Can we keep this?"

"Sure."

Butterworth then said quietly to Brandon.

"We'll stay another five minutes and then..."

At that moment the door burst open and in walked a short young guy with a dishevelled look.

"Who's this?" he asked.

"Some professor and his student", said Casey.

"Good he came. You came. I came. We all came. We're all here. I'm Binky and you must be Professor Butterworth."

"Yes. And I'm here to meet Walt Whitman" said Butterworth half seriously.

"Walt is just down the street in the park feeding the pigeons. He'll be here in a moment. If he takes too long, I'll go get him. He doesn't go for cellphones I'm afraid."

Binky's nonchalance disarmed Butterworth for a moment.

"So, this must be some descendant of his family then, because he didn't have any offspring, did he?" Brandon said half-askingly.

"No, it's him. The actual soul of Whitman, not his body of course."

Now Butterworth was thinking that they should probably leave. He sensed some form of delusion and he was getting tired.

Brandon was thinking the same thing. These were characters from some dark psychological place. He looked at Maddi for confirmation. Maddi was stoic. In his mind he was staying, but part of his brain was telling him that there could be trouble here, especially for a man of 72.

"We'll wait" he finally said. Butterworth was overcome with the idea that he was being overly fearful of the situation.

"We'll wait five minutes" Brandon then said.

At that moment in walked a bearded man with poignant reflexive green eyes, dressed in baggy clothing and wearing a worn-out fedora. He nodded at Maddi and Brandon like he had known them for years and expected them to be there when he arrived. He went over to the corner of the room and from behind one of the chesterfields pulled out a folded lawn chair that had a rocking function. He set it up and very deliberately sat down

217

in it. Then he pulled out a pouch of tobacco and rolling papers and began rolling himself a cigarette.

"What's up Walt?" said Binky.

"The sun has damaged my eyesight. I will need sunglasses soon, Binky. Be a dear and bring me a hot coffee. Have you offered our friend anything?"

"Yes" answered Casey quickly.

"And did they want anything?"

"No"

"We are okay." interjected Brandon.

Walt Whitman displayed a warm smile to the room. He looked at Maddi and Brandon with soft eyes that seemed on the brink of tearful explosion.

"You are Madison Butterworth?"

"Yes, and you are?"

"Just call me Walt. I have no regard for formality as you may know. I am just an ordinary newspaperman who stumbled upon the English language by sheer necessity of survival in a hellishly vicious and stupid world, where beauty has been ignored and banished to the scrap heap of practicality and convenience."

Butterworth was still deliberating what the real nature and identity was of the man before him was.

Brandon was thinking that perhaps the authorities may need to be called, yet he felt a strange attraction to this 'Walt'.

Casey and Binky sat down on the chesterfield near Walt and drank some generic beer from large cans. They stared at some space anon in front of them.

"I'm very curious, Mr...er...Whitman" began Butterworth, "what precisely was your purpose in bring us here? At first, I thought that this might have been some practical joke concocted by one of my mischievous colleagues. But I considered other options as well, which I will not mention. It just seemed so unusual though that I could not resist coming. So, you have us here, Brandon and myself, what is it exactly that you want?"

Whitman looked at Maddi and Brandon quietly and with empathic eyes.

"I'm sorry gentlemen if I caused you consternation. I did not wish to worry you, but I did want to see how curious you may be. As you may or may not be aware, there have been a series of designed little assaults that have been occurring across the continent recently. These were done not to engender hatred or anger but to awaken thought in slumbering individuals whose minds were being wasted on impotency. Any regard for beauty and love was being flushed away by these precious beings on misguided mediocrity and deluded ideas that all hopes in life were lost causes and that immersion into a creeping cynicism was preferable. I fear that if left unchecked this would grow to render a whole generation dead to the spirit of life."

"Well, that is formidable Mr. Whitman. I would concur with much of what you have just stated with a few annotations of course and plenty of questions regarding your being alive in the 21st century. First, how old do you claim to be?"

Whitman chuckled.

"That is an unanswerable question from where I live now. You see gentlemen I have found serenity and rest from the trouble and ignorance that the world hurled at people who sought love and beauty. It has the added features of a suspension of time and space as you are now experiencing it.

219

And trust me my friends, I have not radically altered my brain chemistry to achieve this state. It occurred as I embraced death and finality. With the acceptance of an end I have discovered a new beginning. And a new task and that is what I am going about doing, with the help of my darlings here, Binky and Casey."

Butterworth had to ponder this a moment.

"What is it that you need us for?"

"I need you to help us awaken souls from delusion. Delusions of living in a bubble, delusions of attachments and dependencies that kill them, that kill their souls and minds, that make them stupid and you know Professor of what I speak."

"I think so."

Something in Butterworth wanted to trust this man, though he was still convinced that he was some sort of mentality ill being, who had just hit upon some worthy ideas by chance.

"So, I am going to disappear soon, but you will be given an occasional inspiration or even perhaps precise direction as to what you can do to further this work. Binky and Casey amongst others will be there for you along the way. They are my surrogates and they will make themselves known to you in various creative ways, so do not despair my fellow travellers you will not be alone, ever again."

Brandon looked quite perturbed and even frighten by what had just transpired here. He was worried about Maddi.

"So, Mr. Whitman that is it. And what precisely is it that we get out of this?" Butterworth asked.

"A natural question. You will begin to experience the peace of mind that I have. And Brandon you will be inspired to create, you will never be without intellectual or emotional curiosity again. You both will see a whole new light, but I cannot tell you anything more precisely. That as you may have guessed is for you to experience not for me to tell you about. So, Professor I certainly don't need to be lecturing you on all of this. I trust that you have the knowledge and you do understand what I am saying. I have just been a catalyst for the soul and spirit already embedded in you. So, boys do you have any questions?"

"Just two questions Mr. Whitman. First, why the elaborate ruse and secondly how do I get published in 'Conspiremouth?'

"Ah, you are being droll Professor Butterworth. I like that. I do not see our efforts as a ruse, but simply a laying out of options to be experienced or not experienced, that is all it is. The freedom to accept that one can decide what and how much they will be dependent on anything or anyone in life. That's why we have a soul to make independent choice, not with just our brains which vary in the amount of information they contain, but with a wider field of data spanning back millions of years. The spirit is the willingness to make those decisions and the soul is what we make them with, so far as I learned to date anyhow. Have fun with that, boys. And don't worry. You don't need to know everything. I'm out of here guys."

With that he got up with a large grin on his face and stridently exited the room winking at his two surrogates as he closed the door.

Manni and Brandon looked uncomfortably at one another and then with even more unease at Casey and Binky.

They then both got up, gestured good bye and left the room.

Now down the street a bit I was pursuing the selections in a used bookstore. I was particularly interested in books about how soul and spirit got to become actually things in the mind of humans. I suspected that this extension of the poet Walt Whitman may be simply someone whose brain had been soaking in a 'song of itself' for quite awhile and had been carrying on as if he had some evangelical mission to perform. I was not yet clear on whether

221

Professor Butterworth's mind had bought the idea of transcendent souls and spirits or was still clinging to the more tradition logic of deductive reasoning, that being that human behaviour can be self-justified or appear to be random, but behind it lies some objective explanation. I was getting concerned that the young surrogates of 'Whitman' might get ideas of their own and that would completely upset Whitman's agenda. Or maybe there had been no set agenda at all. I knew at the time that I had to dig deeper. I purchased a few volumes and went to a Coffee Express to do further research. Frank's brother Jesse, feeling more and more like Jessica, was happy to serve him.

thirty-two

"A functioning police state needs no police."

William S. Burroughs

Frank asked the front desk for Warren Kitchholm's room, he found it without trouble. Frank had exchanged emails with Kitchholm briefly before his flight but had asked him to save the details about the assailant for when he got there. Any words that had been said preceding, during or after the incident he wanted to heard directly from Kitchholm. He had analysed the non-verbal evidence quite well but had not gotten much further along in forming a clearer picture. He found Kitchholm sleeping.

"Hey, Warren" said Frank while shaking Kitchholm's arm firmly.

After a few seconds Kitchholm opened his eyes.

"Frank, yeah glad you made it. No more blows to the old noggin?"

"No, Warren. How are you, feeling any better?"

"I'm ok Frank, just needed a few moments here to get my head straightened around. I feel like sleeping a lot. The doctors told me that there's no evidence of a concussion. I have to believe them, I'm just very tired Frank."

"You don't look too bad. Just do what the doctors tell you to do."

"Sure."

"Listen, Warren have you ever heard of a Professor Madison Butterworth? He's on BBC Radio a lot. He's written a few books."

"No. Why?"

"Well, Boris, you remember Boris?"

"Yeah."

"Well, Boris seems to think that Butterworth is positioned to get it next. And from what I can see it fits. All of the victims except one have been tied to the written word and each other in some way, except for one, some radio host in Chicago. And I found a show on the station's website that told the story of another victim in that area. He wouldn't name the guy, saying that it would unfair to put the spotlight on them. We have a real thread of evidence happening, but Warren I need to know about this guy that the cops have in custody."

"Well, really there's not much more than what I texted to you. Apparently, they have him under psychiatric observation. They asked me if I knew anyone named Jack White, so I would assume that that is his name and from what I recall he was a young guy, in his twenties."

Frank sat down in an armchair beside Kitchholm. He pondered for a moment.

"Did the police ask you anything about money, bank accounts, insurance anything like that?"

"No."

"Did they ask about a revenge motive?"

"No, not really, well they wanted to know if I knew the name."

"That doesn't help us."

"Did they ask you anything about schools, universities or courses that you took?"

"Ah, yes they did. They wanted me to try and remember anyone I might have gone to university with, especially courses to do with literature. They wanted me to try and recall anyone that I had met or had any link to that had a literary disposition, though they didn't use those words."

"Very good, Warren. So, the cops have clues very similar to ours. This Jack White must have told them something that put them on to that line of questioning. Maybe Walt Whitman was mentioned?"

"Ah yeah, you mentioned that you had all this stuff left behind that talked about Whitman. I can't say that I know much about him, but it really sounds like a bizarre motive."

"Well, Warren we are without a clear motive, so any possible lead is relevant. I won't dismiss anything yet as a motive, even a poet who has been dead for over 120 years."

"You've got me interested Frank. I'm beginning to wake up."

Kitchholm scrambled for his notebook and made a few jottings regarding what had been said.

He was now particularly interested in the academic angle. That would make for a very intriguing approach to what seemed so far to be a fantastic tale.

"I'm out of here, Warren. Catch up with you later."

And with that Frank was gone. He had to go find Jack White. He wondered how he would get by any doctors, nurses and particularly police that surely surrounded him. Perhaps he could send him a written letter or note of some kind.

Boris Swatcupso was comfortably seated in an armchair in the university lobby. Boris was being enthralled by the soul penetrating words of Walt Whitman. His brain was vibrating with mental waves that incorporated messages that seemed to come from places which he had never been introduced to before. All these words were taking on a new significance. He read that 'all truths wait in all things' and pondered that order of words waiting for a new meaning to reveal itself. 'They neither hasten their own delivery nor resist it' told him that he had no control over the evidence and that it would come to him, if he just could place himself in the right place, at the right time.

And Boris was enjoying this literary exercise. The afternoon had passed rapidly. Him and the large volume of poetry before his eyes. It was a 'song of myself' for Boris, where he was able to block out any movements or audible sounds taking place around him. He could not remember the last time that he had been able to do that. He had begun to mentally superimpose the soul of Whitman over top of the body of Madison J. Butterworth. Now he had to figure out how Whitman would attempt to interact with a guy like Butterworth. Maybe the professor would be difficult to convince, considering that Butterworth was a world-renowned figure, not only for his works of fiction and poetry but also for his political stance and his daring forays into the sexual politics of the times. He had said that he would always remain a rabid devotee of the logical methods of science, so Whitman's ghost or some spirit inhabiting another body would not win Butterworth over. Boris then read the following lines:

"Logic and sermon never convince,

The damp of the night drives deeper into my soul."

Now that could be it thought Boris. The damp of the night, the elements, the circumstances. Boris had been going through a unique emotional experience of late. His perception on events and circumstances had revealed uncharted territory. It seemed to him like he possessed a bright shiny light beaming into the night. Soul and night were juxtaposed by Boris. He stopped reading and remembered something that his literary inspiration

226

had said last night at the lecture. "When I begin a story or a poem, I broker my own thoughts with that of my environment. We must therefore be perpetually cognizant of our relationship with the all that surrounds us. What we contribute and what comes back."

These words Butterworth had uttered near the end of his talk. Now Boris knew about weather and people's obsessions with climate and its effects on their daily lives. To him he had always been a person to function regardless of the forecasts or lack of forecasts. He was proud that he could get done what needed doing irrespective of the conditions that presented themselves. His relations with women had been turbulent at times, sometimes downright violent, but he had a firm trust in his ability to locate the love in himself to keep the chemicals flowing with his partners. When things didn't work out, he would either attribute it to lack of willingness on his partner part or that the chemistry had been upset to such an extent that it would require a whole new set of formulas to produce anything soluble.

Where would Whitman start? With a confrontation no doubt. He had employed that method so far.

Next would be where at. Something perhaps related to a newspaper or publication, this having been Whitman's primary means of employment. Or maybe a weather situation of some sort. Or perhaps the creation of some catastrophic situation. What type of publication would involve a guy like Whitman?

He got up, stretched his legs and called Frank to get 'Sherlock's' opinion.

Frank had just scribbled a handwritten note for Jack White not more than 50 feet away from the police detachment in North Markham where White had been held earlier as the prime suspect in the Kitchholm bopping. Frank was not aware that White had been transported three hours earlier to a big psychiatric facility in downtown Toronto to be observed by doctors for a couple of days. The police wanted to know how much of the verbiage that

227

White was spewing at them they could trust to be relevant in the case. They really wanted to be sure that White had a logical motive for the attack and was not being guided by forces that were the result of bad chemistry in his brain.

Frank's plan involved sealing his note in an envelope addressed to White. He hoped that the police would not make too much of it. He purposely wrote it with some poetic subterfuge so that the cops would not easily figure that they had competition in solving the case. Once he had sealed the envelope he went to the front desk of the detachment and handed it to the young female officer at the desk who looked at it with puzzlement.

"Who's Jack White?"

"He's being held here, I believe."

"Any message for a detainee has to go through the officers in charge."

"I realize that. All I want is that he gets this. I don't care who sees it first."

"Well, I can't confirm that we have anyone with that name here."

"The City newsblog says that you do."

"Well, that may be true, but I cannot confirm it. I can keep your letter here or return it to you. What do you want to do?"

Frank tried to be patient. He had dealt with the protocols of bureaucracy many times before, so he had half expected snags.

"Is there no way that I could perhaps find out his lawyer's name and get the letter to him in that manner?"

"I can't give you any information regarding lawyers."

228

"Can you tell me if he is here at all?"

"Just a moment."

The female officer coyly hadn't answered the question as to whether she could give him any information but instead had moved with what seemed like deliberate sluggishness toward a computer screen way off in back corner of the office. She was behind a glass partition so that Frank could not overhear anything that she or any other officers were saying. She mulled over the screen for over five minutes. Frank felt his phone vibrate. He checked it. It was Boris. He would not answer it here. He didn't want to tip off anyone here about what he was up to. Then he saw that it was a text.

The text read:

Frank, Whitman was a newspaperman He will contact Butterworth Read 'Song of Myself', Whitman liked weather and the soul. He liked males, body and soul. I'm ok, cheers Boris. Call me. how's it going?

Frank sat down and absorbed the text for a few moments. He scanned a news website to see if there was anything new. He read about a group of armed men were in a standoff with police in Gary, Indiana.

The story related how two subversives had been tracked to a cache of weapons in a Gary, Indiana house where a dispute had arisen and police had been called in. Some of the men had now barricaded themselves in the house and had actually fired shots at police. Frank recalled the name Bo Creeley that appeared in the story and he also saw a picture of radio host Big Andy Jones attached to the story.

In Boise, Idaho Creeley's father had moved into a state of boisterous jubilation at his son's appearance on the news seeing it as a culmination of his efforts at drawing attention to the destruction of liberties.

The senior Creeley was vocalizing his joy much to the consternation of the staff at the Boise Oldtimers Farm.

"Go, boy, go. Ya show em' who's boss in these here United States" he said amongst invectives that he had for the federal authorities.

Creeley Sr. was close to death. He would be dead by the time the American federal officials became involved in the Gary, Indiana incident. His son would also be increasing his chances of an intimate encounter with the soul of Walt Whitman soon after as well. His sidekick Larry would survive to tell tales and send letters to Big Andy Jones. Jones would in the future feature some of Larry's scribbling from prison on his enlightening and profitable radio show.

Creeley Sr. would be in a between life and death for awhile, where he would meet Whitman and a few other people who had no worldly meaning to him but would provide a transition to a state where his mind would encounter logical thought sequences that had to this point been foreign to him.

As Frank awaited a confirmation on the whereabouts of Jack White, he jotted in his paper notebook:

COPS ARE PEOPLE LIKE ANY OF US, BUT THEY

MUST BE HARD TO WORK WITH IF YOU'RE AN OUTSIDER

WHITE – THE NAME STARTS WITH WHIT – LIKE WHITMAN

NO SO WITTY – BORIS HAS SHARPENED UP SINCE THE ATTACK

CALL JESSE – STRANGE THAT WE SHOULD MEET – WHAT ABOUT

230

THE GUY DOWN THE HALL AT THE FISH POND – WHO GETS

DRESSED IN ALL BLACK? - MUST KEEP OFF THE BOOZE

And then he tried to nonchalantly stare out of the window of police station. He noticed a blackbird in a tree and watched it to assuage his impatience.

thirty-three

"The modern, cheap and fertile press, with all its translations, has done little to bring us nearer to the heroic writers of antiquity."

Henry David Thoreau

Maddi and Brandon were installed in the back of a taxicab snaking its way through the city. It was nearly 4 P.M and the Professor had scheduled an interview with a local community radio station that would be aired a few days later.

"Brandon, my dear, I don't think that we should be too emotionally invested in this Whitman stand-in. Yet, I do believe that it was a worthy visit and it certainly makes for fertile story material. It would seem to me to be nothing more than a group of attention seekers who have gathered forces under some pseudo intellectual banner, vital though the cause may be, it is a ruse that has no legs, Brandon. Any idea that demands the incorporation of an afterlife template will not fly in our current literary climate. If fact any climate which involves logical thought cannot presume a post earthly existence without being classified under the heading of fantasy. But I do admire inspired efforts that draw attention to forgotten figures and metaphors. Therefore, I say to Whitman, Binky, Casey and whomever else is on their ship of poetic enlightenment, BRAVO!"

Now to some, Butterworth's backseat summary of his opinion on the afternoon's events did seem quite cold, aloof and maybe even pompous But, it they did betray a real underlining faith that Butterworth had in the unseen. Despite his pronouncement to the contrary, Butterworth exercised severe doubt on most matters concerning the continuation of life after physical death. He just could not defend those opinions based on any logic that he had been taught after fleeing Mother Russia more that forty years ago.

Butterworth had plotted to leave in the 1970s when he was 22 years old after he written several poems critical of the cap put on freedom of expression in his country of birth and for which he had been brought before a committee and admonished. There was also the fact that many who had written stories which uncovered embarrassing truths about the government had gone missing and he did not fancy being next in line for lengthy imprisonment or worse. He had managed to make contact with others like himself and had escaped to England, where he furthered his education, worked at many jobs and was able to see his talent flourish. His workmanlike habits in academia soon became appreciated. He had developed a hybrid voice that incorporated both Russian and British cultures.

"You know, Maddi I think we should write some encouraging words for the publishers of 'Conspiremouth.' They seem so earnest and I think that they need reassurance. Maddi, I really believe that it's just wonderful what they are doing" Brandon said to his partner.

"Brandon, remember this, one does not want to encourage self-delusion or worse still collective mental illness."

"Maddi, I think you are being much too judgemental. I don't see this as doing any harm. To invent an alternate reality may only the veneer of a plausible vision of the future. It is like putting something out there for people to consider."

"Brandon, there are plenty of things 'out there' to consider, much of which is already bullshit. We don't need more. I believe in the spirit but I cannot support the propagation of such nonsense as being anything authentic. End of discussion. And I love you dearly, Brandon."

With that he kissed his partner and they rode back to their hotel in silence.

A few miles away at the home of Meg Barton's mother, Michael Schultzmann, had received an email with an attached text of some poems by Walt Whitman to be translated from English to French. This had been a very rapid reply to inquiries he had put online in the last few days about the poet as recent events had sparked his curiosity. He needed the work so he sent back an affirmative reply and said that it would take him at least two weeks to complete, considering that it was poetry and that he had very little familiarity with the works of the celebrated American poet. The poems in question were celebrations of self-discovery and love. Schultzmann immediately began to delve further into his work. By late evening after becoming familiar more than a dozen pieces by the author he had become convinced that his receiving a blow on the head and receiving the Whitman job were no coincidence.

"I celebrate myself,

And what I assume you shall assume,

For every atom belonging to me as good belongs to you."

Schultzmann pondered these lines as he embarked on the new job. he began to understand Whitman's desire to be one with those he loved and with that which he loved. 'Then if we die, we die together (yes, we'll remain one)' Whitman had scribed.

Schultzmann had been puzzled by the ease with which Frank and Boris had accepted the theory that at the heart of the motivation for the attacks were some of the themes of Mr. Whitman. But now this hypothesis did not seem so far fetched for Schultzmann. He was now reading with gusto. He could not explain this to Meg or Mary except to say that he had a big job to do. He knew that his work could help Frank and Boris.

By the time Maddi and Brandon had reached their hotel it was pouring rain. They quickly made their way to the room, ordered a small meal via room service and relaxed in with some reading. It continued to rain steadily outside, the sounds of the water making contact with the surface of the window and the side of the building provided an atmosphere which was cozy in the minds of Maddi and Brandon. To the two this condition had given them a glimpse of some what eternity could be like if it were to be given any plausibility. As the time passed the two were each more absorbed in what they were reading and the clacking of the rain muffled the sound coming from above them.

Dripping from their bathroom ceiling were goblets of blood which had been in the body of one of Whitman's cohorts up until sixty minutes after the arrival of Maddi and Brandon at their hotel room. The cohort's consciousness had ceased to be in the hotel room above them. At the time of his death, he had been wearing a black cotton jacket and black jeans and had shoulder length hair and was about 25 years old. This had not been a mere tap on the skull but a bludgeoning. The weapon used had been a sculptured piece by one of Boris Swatcupco's favorite artists. The perpetrator had worn a brown leisure suit and yellow high-top sneakers while terminating the young man's physical vitality. He had not been noticed entering or leaving the hotel but evidence of his presence would be recorded on CCTV and that would become a key exhibit in the eventual trial for the murder of this member of the Whitman clan and one other important crime.

As this crime was taking place, I was sitting at the Coffee Express where I had witnessed Jesse/Jessica being verbally assaulted by some guy whose latte had been prepared exactly to his satisfaction. This had resulted in a totally inappropriate and insensitive remark being hurled at Jesse/Jessica. I felt badly about it and wanted to straighten out the source of the artless and base verbiage that had come from the connoisseur of latte's mouth but I remembered that my role in all of this was as an observer and not a main character in the narrative. I sat there and only glared at him, like others had in the coffee shop, hoping that he would leave quickly. And he did.

Jesse/Jessica recovered from her wounds with the help of the staff and some customers, including my modest contributions and in fact grew stronger as a direct result of the incident. By the way, if you are ever in the Coffee Express on University Avenue the bold continental coffee blend is the best in the city and Jessica service is also of superior calibre.

thirty-four

I saw all those drunken Shakespeares appear at my door, and then I knew that we were all actors in a B-Movie."

Boris Swatcupso. From his poem 'Noir Hamlet'

As Frank waited at the police detachment for information on the whereabouts of Jack White, he decided to pull up a movie on his phone. He not only loved jazz, but old movies, especially film noir. He found a little gem that he enjoyed with Lucille Ball and Mark Stevens entitled 'The Dark Corner'. It featured Ball, who was better known for the situation comedy 'I Love Lucy', as secretary to a low end private eye who suspected that he was being targeted by his shady ex-partner. Frank watched a couple of scenes from the film and wondered if he needed to hire a secretary. But he had Boris of course. And he didn't have to pay him anything. Not yet anyhow.

About 20 minutes had passed and then Frank heard a muffled knock on the glass partition between the waiting area and the office space of the detachment.

The female officer waved Frank over to the opening in the partition.

"Your friend was here but was taken to a hospital for observation."

"Do you know which one?"

"We can't tell you that. You will have to contact his lawyer."

Frank was beginning to get a little frustrated. He now understood why private dicks in movies were always manipulating people in order to elicit information. He was learning on the job and not even getting paid for the training. But he didn't care about the money right now.

"We'll his lawyer just recently changed offices and has a new number. Unfortunately, he hasn't given me his recent contact info yet. Do you, by any chance, happen to have his phone number or address?"

Now Frank was a little nervous about overtly lying to the police like this. He hadn't had a lot of contact with the law in his life and didn't know what he could get away with and what would get him into serious difficulties. But this officer seemed to be buying what he had said. He must have sounded unaffected by the fact that what he had said was a complete fabrication.

Moments later the officer handed him a small slip of yellow paper with a phone number on it without uttering a word. Frank nodded his head in gratitude and promptly got out of there.

Now he knew that it would take further subterfuge to garner more clues from a lawyer's office, so he first looked up a list of all the major hospital in the city, including all the psychiatric facilities. He would call them all asking for Jack White. After getting nowhere with the first half dozen calls he tried the first one that was exclusively for the mentally afflicted and soon realized that one could not get anything from these places over the phone without permission of the patient or doctors in charge. Another hurdle to jump. It was now dark outside. Frank had not even thought about where he was going to sleep that night. He now understood why in the future he would have to charge people money to do this job. He figured that he had enough money to last him a week or so at the rate that he was going through it and then he would have to find some alternate means of garnering revenue.

Looking at his phone he saw that he had another text from Boris.

'Frank, I'm at Butterworth's hotel having a drink, he isn't taking   messages. I'm looking for clues – watching the news – saw a guy on Tv in the Indiana stand off that I just saw in Montreal. Brandon, Butterworth's beau just came into bar. later – Boris'

238

Frank was pleased to hear from Boris. It warmed his heart that Boris was being earnest in pursuing answers to this mystery. Now Frank understood that perhaps many of the questions surrounding these attacks would not be answered by attaching oneself to a 'metaphysical' motive. but by being driven personally with a desire to inject some level of danger into his life.

With this juice in his blood and his brain operating on full steam he set to first find a cheap motel and continue making phone calls. He needed to talk to this Jack White directly.

Meanwhile Boris was sitting in the Parisienne Lounge of Marriott Hotel sipping his third bourbon and switching his attention between CNN on the muted television and Butterworth's paramour, Brandon. Brandon seemed to be engaging the bartender in conversation. Boris was looking at Brandon from the side and was thinking that he certainly must have been a very attractive woman just months earlier. Boris certainly would have been open to making a play for her. Thoughts of Patricia came momentarily to him, but he quickly dismissed them. He wondered now if Butterworth would classify himself as bisexual, gay or still straight. Or were these labels not an issue for such a figure has Butterworth who had almost become a celebrity poet and literary genius in the last five years for his public stances on popular issues. He was also noted for his ability to combine the accessible world with the clannish environs of academia.

Boris was pondering these things while trying to inconspicuously spy on Brandon. In his mind he was devising a method of approach that would not seem like he was hitting on Brandon. That would come too easily for Boris if he had just left this one to improvisation, so he really felt that he had to plot out a strategy before taking action. He thought that bringing up Butterworth's poetry would be too superficial. He had to find a tactic that was more personal. One that made it seem like he didn't know who Brandon was at all.

On CNN Bo Creeley was being mowed down by federal officials who said that he had been a dangerous man, who headed a dangerous group of people, who had dangerous ideas about the government. Boris again recognized Creeley's photo which they kept showing on the screen. And below on the crawl he read this:

Part of the note that Creeley left behind apparently stated that he had been recently kidnapped by two men dressed in black whom he suspected worked for the CIA and who Creeley said had attempted to brainwash him and his associate. Creeley claimed that he had been bopped on the head by these young men.

Boris' head whirled. Young men. Black clothing. Head bopping. The CNN report went on to say that the group's website had recently been updated to say that a government agent wearing black had been dispatched to reorder people's brains so that they remained in line with the authorities. OneBigLie followers were instructed to prepare for an assault on their liberties.

After the news item was over, he turned his attention back to Brandon who seemed to be laughing it up with the bartender. He got up from his comfortable leather armchair and approached the bar.

"Another bourbon please?"

The bartender nodded but continued to face Brandon.

"And those stupid pamphlets that those clubs put out…"

Brandon was droning on it seemed.

"Bourbon" Boris repeated with more precision.

"Yes, sir."

The bartender turned away from Brandon and began preparing Boris' drink.

Brandon turned to look at Boris. Boris smiled and said that he really had a deep affiliation with the prime mood modifier of Kentucky and asked Brandon what alteration in mood he preferred.

Brandon laughed, obviously already feeling little pain.

"And are you from America, my friend?"

"North America, discovered by the Vikings over a thousand years ago. But they couldn't write down the tales of their time for us to re-experience. No poetic muse seemed to have embodied them. They had no need to convert us it would appear, therefore very little wordy documentation of their moods. Speaking of mood, would you like another of whatever you are drinking?"

"Well, I don't really know you, Mister…"

"It's Boris. Boris Swatcupso. Just call me Boris. I do art here in Montreal."

"Really? And what do you call art?"

"Oh, just reshaping things and ideas."

"Very interesting, indeed."

"So, what is it that you occupy your time with?"

241

"I'm a full-time male impersonator. No just kidding, though that is somewhat true."

Now Boris had not expected such a raw and almost truthful answer. He hesitated before responding.

"Well, you certainly had me fooled."

"And what exactly is it that brings you to the Marriott Hotel on this rainy night in Montreal?"

"This place seemed to be in the way of my getting home today, so I thought instead of dodging the obstacles I would incorporate them into my evening."

"And am I an obstacle to you?"

"That has yet to be determined."

The bartender placed Boris' bourbon on the counter, smiled and then turned to Brandon.

"Another?"

"Sure, why not."

The bartender turned to fix Brandon his drink.

"What do they call a male impersonator these days? Or is that term one for the history books?"

Brandon smiled and skipped answering the question taking it as rhetorical.

"I'm Brandon. I'm a full-time academic assistant to Madison J. Butterworth."

"Well, that is something. Butterworth, that certainly rattles something upstairs. Poet, isn't he?"

"He can be."

"Not a hip-hop artist?"

"Not particularly."

Brandon smiled again barely hiding a sour response to the question.

"You know Brandon I do recall Butterworth. He is on the BBC, isn't he?"

"Yes, that's right."

"So, you are his assistant? Is he here, in Montreal?"

"Right here in this hotel."

"And so, you are presently on the job."

"Well, not exactly. You see we are also lovers, partners. He is a real genuine sweetheart, you know."

Boris almost said that he knew all about it but managed to conceal his reaction under a mumbling and a quick sip of his bourbon.

"And what would he think of you down here in the bar fraternizing."

"He knows and he's happy for me. He doesn't keep me on a leash. I can make my own choices. He likes to go to sleep early. I like staying up at least until midnight."

"It's only ten now. So, we have a couple more hours."

"Have you read any of Butterworth's books?"

"In fact, I have. I really am closeted Butterworth freak."

"Really. And is that a very recent discovery."

"No. I wasn't saying that for your benefit. I know his first book of poems 'Crossing the Channels of A Master'. Then he published a collection of his essays and called it 'Taking the Time to Edit the World' and then…"

"Very good. So, would you like to meet the man himself? Tonight won't work, but tomorrow morning would be okay."

"Will you still respect me by morning?" Boris said wryly. Then he regretted saying it.

Brandon did not seem to take notice of the innuendo and began a conversation about the essays of Butterworth, transgender people and how it could benefit the future. And of course, poetry. Boris ate it all up and really tried to dispel any impression that Brandon may have gotten that he was seriously hitting on him. Brandon was confused about Boris' real motives but he managed to roll with the punches. He was never one for feeling wounded by misdirected affections and never burdened by hubris. They ended the evening with an affectionate kiss and left it there. Boris was pleased that he had gained access to Butterworth. He had been convinced that Butterworth would be safe for the night. But to make sure he booked into the hotel with his credit card on the same floor as Butterworth, after Brandon had gone up to his room.

This adventure was beginning to cost him money that he didn't have he thought to himself. But something told him that in the end it would be all worth it. As he boarded the elevator up to his room he noticed a large presence of police in the lobby. He thought nothing of it. He stalked the Butterworth room for a few minutes then went to bed, sleeping furtively until sunrise.

Frank was the first person, except for the police and the media, to receive the news about the deliberate termination of human life that had taken place at the Marriott Hotel. He had checked into the Lakeside Motel on the Toronto waterfront and risen early, switched on the news and heard that a grisly scene had been discovered overnight in a Montreal hotel. The body of a 25-

244

year-old man was now being taken for an autopsy and the police were looking for a suspect in a brown leisure suit and wearing yellow high top sneakers. They even had surveillance camera footage of the suspect and the quality of the film wasn't that bad. Frank recognized him from somewhere but he could not immediately place where. On a bus or a plane perhaps. But what really captured Frank's attention was the fact that the crime had taken place at the Marriott Hotel where Butterworth had been tracked down by Boris. Frank didn't know that Boris was just getting out of bed at the Marriott when Frank was learning of the crime. Frank immediately called Boris. He wanted to speak directly to him.

It was eleven rings before Boris picked up. His voice sounded like it been recycled from a B-movie, fed copious amounts of hard liquor then asked to recite Shakespeare.

"Frank, zounds and double zounds, why is the dawn ringing in my ear, friend of friends."

"Boris, never mind the poetics, there's been a murder in Montreal."

"A real genuine murder. And how is it that you know this?"

"It's on the news."

"Really, and why is this significant in our lives?"

"It has taken place at the same hotel where our professor Butterworth is staying."

"And where I happen to be staying Frank. Yes, I've been trying to protect him."

"Really Boris. Now that is some impressive initiative but try and not mess this up. They showed the suspect leaving the hotel and I am certain that I have seen him before."

"Certainty is important Frank. Certainty in all things my man. I say that a man who is certain is a man who has an assured destiny."

"Boris, I really don't know the man's name. I am glad that you are there, maybe you could get some inside information."

"That's what I live for Frank, to get inside information, because after all I am inside. Inside because it is in fact raining outside."

"Ok Boris, I get it. You haven't been at the bottle this morning, already?"

"Not yet but soon. But before that I have a job to do."

"And what is that, Boris?"

"I must see that Butterworth and his lover are well. You know rain, Whitman and death does not portent well for them. I have been granted access to their suite. I will be in touch shortly Sherlock, with more clues."

"Boris, try and stay a bit sober."

"That I can only promise you before noon time, but I should have completed my tasks by then. Later."

With that he was off the phone. Frank then searched the net for more information on the killing. He soon found out that the victim had been dressed in black and had been a member of a local indie band called 'Orate This and That'. Frank looked up the band and he found that several of the band's songs had been inspired by Walt Whitman. So now the ones doing the head bopping were becoming victims themselves. But the counterattacks were more than just blows to the head, a person had been terminated. And, by the way, Frank thought that the name of the band was a little pretentious, or maybe audacious, but they did not deserve the ultimate fate because of a little egoism, did they?

But Frank had to get back to Jack White. If that was his name. After a quick breakfast and a shower Frank managed to track down where the darkly dressed Whitman advocate was being held. He had obtained the lawyer's name and used it with the receptionist to confirm White's presence at the Toronto West Psychiatric Hospital. Now the task was to find out who Jack White was and what was his motive?

.

He set out for the hospital with a strategy.

"Professor Butterworth, with all due respect, I have been monitoring these attacks and I must say that I am certain that they are related to some group of people with a fascination around Walt Whitman."

Boris had begun his field work in the Butterworth suite.

"Mr. Swatcupso, I am quite curious about this matter as well. It does not seem too far-fetched of a theory. The fact that I have received a phone from these people and now a murder right above me. But I still would hold out for coincidence in this matter. I am skeptical of and so called ghostly revivals of old poets and scribes. I would venture to say that this is work of a single lunatic and certainly not that of a group resolution."

"Well, Professor even in your own essay, if I may quote it with your permission, you say that there exists a collective consciousness in the artistic community which can be transmitted through time and space. I believe it was in a piece entitled 'Finding the Lost Source of Inspiration'."

"I am flattered that you know the piece, but you must understand that I was not speaking of some mystical telepathic method of communication between generations, but of something perhaps transmitted genetically or by direct conscious or subconscious experience."

"Well, Professor either way it is happening I believe."

"Do you believe that Whitman is actually alive, the same Whitman brought back to life?"

"No, that would be a feat that would defy logic. Yet, somehow this stuff is connected. My friend is in Toronto now investigating another one of these incidents."

"Well, I find that absolutely incredible that you two would be so devoted to this. Why don't you leave it to the police? Why get yourself entangled with what will surely turn out to be a group of pranksters or some deranged mental case who is seeking perverse attention?"

"Professor, I really cannot honestly answer that, but I know now that I am involved and cannot back out, especially with you being a potential victim in this case. I am certain that the guy who was killed was waiting to give you a tap on the noggin."

"Your affinity with my work has no bearing on the matter, sir. Your motivation must come from within you, my good friend. And with that Brandon and I thank you for your concern. Please stay in touch on this matter, but for now I have work to do. So…"

"Right, I'll be leaving Professor."

Brandon got up from where he had been lounging at the back of the room.

"Boris, we can meet later for a drink, call me."

Boris was impressed by Brandon's openly asking him this right in front of the Professor.

"Sure."

Butterworth smiled and walked away toward a stack of papers on a desk. Brandon waved and Boris found his own way out.

thirty-five

"I sing the body electric … they will not let me off till I go with them, respond to them, and discorrupt them, and charge them full with the charge of the soul."

Walt Whitman

On a beachfront on Long Island, New York sat the bearded poet smiling at the ocean with two others. They were in swim wear and engaged in a conversation.

"I know that we have suffered another blow. Another setback and more are to come but remember only the strength that we have gained by our time together. That, no one can take away, even in death. For death is but a moment of doubt and my eternal friends, do not fear doubt, the same as you should not fear death. Live in compassion, live for the awakening of every being that has lost its willingness to strive on, boys. We do not remember at what time or where we lived, but we have lived, are living and will continue to live, forever. Let us feel the Body Electric."

They all shared a laugh as the ocean provided a rhythmic backdrop to their assembly.

thirty-six

"Criminals are not all bad guys,
Police are not all bad guys,
Nobody's all bad guys."

Boris Swatcupso. From his poem 'Good, bad, guys'

Meanwhile Binky and Casey were gathering items for the next issue of 'Conspiremouth.' The last number before the end of the summer would feature several short poems, an article on surviving urban camping issues, some drawings by a local street artist, of people who hung out on St. Amos Avenue and various little sundry items about dealing with police and government agencies. They were working on their laptops in their small office/apartment when they heard a thud on the fire escape at the rear of the building. Binky went to investigate and in the glare of the noon day sun he could barely make out the man in the brown leisure suit waving like he needed assistance.

"Someone's on the fire escape, Casey."

Binky opened the door.

"Listen, do you have a phone. My girlfriend just fell off of the fire escape next door. I need to call an ambulance."

"We'll call one for you."

"Can I just ..."

And with that the brown leisure suit forced his way into the mini-sized dwelling and produced a small metal device for eliminating the life possibilities of things from his upper suit pocket. As he did this a small notebook fell to the floor without him noticing.

"Well, it is time for you boys to meet your destiny."

"Who the fuck, are you?" asked Binky.

"I am the one who is rectifying a gross misconduct on the part of old poet, who should remain dead but is continuously insisting on returning to this world to belabor his metaphysical points. He has no respect for the contemporary writer or for the spirit of our age. And you two know what I am talking about. You are his reincarnated accomplices, but this time we shall put you into the other world without question. You see we know that if you die by violent means, it will require an atonement of perhaps a thousand years, so that me and my colleagues can be free to enjoy words without your wordy boss continuously revising his major works. He can't stop himself and neither can you with your rude attacks on people, deliberately trying to precipitate life awakenings so that Whitman can inhabit their souls and push his continuously updated poetic agenda. Yes, we know the work that has been obsessing you boys for the past few days, but you must understand that we only are being reasonable. We need to find our own voices and for that to happen we cannot have authors always returning to re-edit their volumes. This has been a particularly bad habit of Whitman. He cannot leave his works and their effects on the soul of humanity alone."

Binky and Casey looked on at the armed leisure suit wearing man with some astonishment but they had not exactly been strangers to his motives.

"Who the fuck, are you exactly?"

"I am Theodor, but that is not so important. I work for people who want to let the past be the past. We are here to create a new world for people to live in where all of the old shit will stay old shit. We don't need these souls coming back a telling us how their ideas were right and that they only needed tweaking. That is crap. We have to keep them away. Keep them in the books to be read, but not to be heard from. That is not the new logic my friends. I stand for getting on with the task of making lots of money and creating leisure time not to think about life or contemplate stupidities such as the soul and metaphysical recreations. These things don't really need to exist my little buddies of Whitman. He can keep his versions of beauty and friendship in the past. We want to be free of that hocus pocus. Let's tear back the curtain on these so-called mysteries of life and expose these ancient charlatans for what they were. Frauds. We are simply knocking down one fraud at a time. We cannot wait for the final showdown with Whitman himself. But I can't delay any longer because my brain begins to get really sore when I think too much."

"So, Theodor you get headaches. Have you tried getting better rest and hydrating more often?" Casey attempted to advise generously.

"Listen, let's stay on topic here, boys. I don't need your holistic advice."

"Yeah, but it really fuckin' works, man. Walt has the same problem, except he doesn't go around killing people, so maybe you're a little stressed out."

"Perhaps, that's true, but we're smarter than he was. And when I say 'was' I mean 'was'. He is a 'was' and will remain a 'was', just like his other buddy, that Bucke guy who thought that there was some sort of 'Cosmic Consciousness' working here where these dead guys can come back and change the world. It's all bullshit. And we are here to make sure that it stays bullshit."

"Exactly how many of you fuckers are they're?"

"Oh about 5000, give or take, we're always accepting new CVs"

"That's nice to know in case we decide to change sides."

"Oh, you guys are not going to pull that double agent shit on me, are you?"

"No, definitely not", said Casey.

"No way" added Binky.

"Good, because I don't need the complications. My head's already hurting."

"Are you sure you don't need a glass of water or even a massage?" asked Binky.

"Thanks, boys but I don't have the time, even though a scalp massage does sound like it would be cool right about now."

"Yeah, it goes right along with murdering people."

"That's funny. Look I don't have the time I've got to be in Toronto in five hours."

"Ok no massage, but you don't know what you are missing."

"Listen, don't think that I don't know what you are up to with your metaphysical tricks. First, it's head and neck massage and then next you've got me musings about the heavens and the afterlife. No, I will now terminate you both. Go away to your afterlife and deal with it there, not here."

Casey then reached out with his right arm and with precise accuracy disarmed Theodor. The gun went off and Binky caught a bullet in his left arm. Case was able to hold Theodor down for a time. There was a struggle, Binky grabbed the fallen gun and aimed it at Theodor who immediately stopped resisting.

"Ok guys I give up. I didn't expect you guys to put up such a struggle."

"You think us old souls couldn't fight?" asked Binky.

"Well, I guess you old farts can."

"And now we shall bring you to a new reality, my friend Theodor."

253

Theodor felt a blow to his head. But at the last second, he caught a glimpse of the weapon. It was a tattered volume of 'Leaves of Grass'. In the next instant Theodor was in a semi-dream state and being transformed.

Boris was beginning his almost daily recommended dosage of alcohol intake at DregStore at about the same time. He had gotten information on the victim. He was a university student who had been majoring in English literature. His name was Abdul Rayfidel. His parents were born in Turkey and lived in Providence, Rhode Island. He had been studying in Canada for three years. Boris had tried to find more information on him online and at the university, but only found out that he had done at least four major papers on Walt Whitman. Maybe the cops would find more connection, but Boris did not want to be pressuring the police for information. He would wait for things to develop more and get some direction from Frank. In the meantime, he needed a few to keep the shakes away. Tito was bartending.

"Mr. Boris, how are you?" he greeted Swatcupso.

"I have been touched by a heavenly admirer, not only of the male anatomy, but also of the oceans and the skies. Don't worry Tito, you are safe with me. I only seduce females and I trust that you are of the male persuasion."

"Yes, I am. But there were a couple of hot girls in here just before noon. I think they may have been bi."

"Quite interesting, but I am now semi-retired from the romance business and have gone into the detective business."

"Really, a detective. Yeah, I remember you and Frank talking strangely a couple of days ago. What sort of detectives are you? Isn't that an American thing, the private dick?"

"Well, I don't know yet. It's Frank's idea. But we got a case all right. And I guess if we can get the word out that we cracked a case, and this one is quite a strange one, we might actually get paying clients."

"Don't you need some sort of license for that?"

"I think so. But I'm leaving that all up to Frank. That's his department."

"So, Boris what's this mysterious case that you guys are working on?"

"Can't talk about it."

"I understand. But is it anything that I'll see on the news?"

"Well, maybe, but not entirely."

"What do you mean?"

"Well, there was a murder last night at the Marriott, but it's not exactly the murder that we are trying to figure out."

"Sounds like intrigue."

"It is and it's really beginning to become interesting. But right now, I'd be interested in a large draft."

"Coming right up."

Boris twirled some notions in his head about the murder as he sipped his beer.

"You know, Tito, I don't think that I've really used the portion of my brain that I'm using right now much."

Tito laughed.

"You are a funny man, Boris."

"Right. A funny man. Like Milton Berle funny or Idi Amin funny?"

"Whose Milton Burn … whatever … and Eating Amen?"

Now Boris chuckled and then smiled at Tito.

"Old people, both dead. At least their bodies are gone. But these days I'm not so sure that their souls are still not prowling around the globe besieging people's craniums."

"I like old people."

"You do, do you? Well then, we'll be friends for a long time. Will you join me in a drink?"

"Can't do it. Too early. Boss only let's us do it near the end of the shift."

"Too bad. At least have a sparkling flavored water. Maybe pineapple."

"Why pineapple?"

"Sweet and soft on the inside, but it can be real difficult to negotiate with on the outside. Maybe like Whitman."

"I see, this Whitman guy again. Don't know him. Is he like Burn and Amen."

"Or Burns and Allen" Boris said not addressing the question at all. Then he said,

"Milton Berle. B-E-R-L-E. Berle. He was a comedian in the 50s mostly. And then there is Idi Amin. A-M-I-N. He was an African dictator in the 70s. Big guy who liked to eat humans sometimes and listen to bagpipe music. Both really funny guys."

"Funny guys."

"Yeah, listen give me a minute, I have to call Frank."

As Boris was on his phone trying to reach Frank breaking news came on CNN. Images of police cars and ambulances surrounding a residence in Gary, Indiana. On the screen below it read:

Both federal and local officials have confirmed that at least three people have died in an armed standoff at a Gary, Indiana home that was a makeshift warehouse for a cache of weapons. One of those killed was Bo Creeley, 45 years old. Creeley was believed to be a member of an underground paramilitary organization that had been in dispute with the government for years. Though thanks in part to various right-wing talk show hosts, had not been so much underground of late. Creeley is believed to have been separated recently from his wife and three children.

Then another item came on the crawl. It read:

Frida S. Wharton, an evangelist and suspected cult leader has been formally charged with 23 counts of mail fraud and seven counts of tax evasion by the F.B.I. in Gary, Indiana. Wharton has issued a statement saying that "an entity named Satan had planted circumstantial evidence in order to stop her mission of rescuing people from perishing before the planet gets destroyed." She said that she and her colleagues had done nothing wrong and that all of her followers acted out of their own wills.

Boris' call to Frank was unsuccessful, so he left a text saying that he had gotten the identity of the victim and some additional information. On the next news cycle, Boris watched the crawl about Creeley and Wharton, not knowing the extent of their involvement in the Whitman affair but making a mental note remembering that he had seen this Creeley character in Montreal on the evening of Frank being assaulted. And as for Wharton, he had heard her name uttered somewhere. All of this happening in Gary, Indiana thought Boris to himself. The birth place of the Michael Jackson. He was exercising his brain more and more like a detective.

Frank approached the Toronto West Psychiatric Hospital with a certain plan. He deliberately tried to look a little disoriented and confused in the lobby of the hospital. He even managed signs of distress when he approached the front desk.

"Listen, I'm here to see a brother of mine. I was told that he was here. I'm really worried about his health. You know he really depends on me to keep him on the right track."

"And what is your name, sir?" asked the receptionist.

"George Whitman. My brother's name is Walt Whitman, but he may be using an alias. Last time he called himself Robert Patel, before that it was Louis Meyers, he even used a female name once. So, I am not certain what name he may be under. He does have a tendency to pilfer people's identifications and use them as his own."

"Well, that's all very interesting, Mr. Whitman, but I cannot help you if I don't have a name. Do you have a doctor's name?"

"No, I'm afraid not."

"Well, it would be impossible to find him here then."

Frank paused, put his hand to his chin like he was immersed in strategic thought.

Then he said,

"Listen, he was recently at the house of a friend of ours and the guy told us that he had lost his wallet, id and all. His name was Jack White. Look under Jack White."

"Well, I can look for the name, but I will have to confirm with the patient or the doctor to see whether he is here or not and whether he can receive visitors."

"Fine, whatever, I'll wait here. I'm just really worried that he may think that I've abandoned him, you know how some people can become so insecure."

"Please, Mr. Whitman just sit over there by the big plant."

Frank turned around and noticed the big plant by the plate glass window. He nodded at the receptionist and strolled over to the plastic chairs that lined the wall near the plant. He sat down by the plant touched the leaves with his fingertips and noticed that it was a fake plant. The receptionist noticed him and they exchanged smiles. Then she became engaged in telephoning people, talking at what looked to be rapid speed. She was a fit woman of about 30. Frank considered her good-looking and thought that he might strike up a conversation with her later when he had accomplished what he needed to do with his subterfuge. Frank was feeling a recent surge of self-confidence with his newfound role as detective. He felt like he was living on the edge of something exciting. This fine female specimen at the West Toronto Psychiatric Hospital might be part of the something exciting, but firstly he had to get an objective met. And that was to initialize a conversation with Jack White.

Ten minutes passed. Frank and the nameless female receptionist traded a few smiles, but nothing of significance seemed to be transpiring for Frank. He mused about what tidbits of information regarding patients and doctors this woman might he holding in her head. Probably she had some stories, that she could not tell fully because of confidentiality. He had had very little dealings in his life with psychiatric facilities but had always been intrigued by their portrayal in movies and on television. To Frank they represented a portal into the unseen or mystical aspects of the human mind. He wasn't someone how gave much credence to hard and fast diagnosis of mental illness. In fact, from his limited experience he really thought that people sometimes just had a bad combination of things happen around them and that when stirred in with perhaps bad chemical reactions in the brain prevented them from being fully functional members of society. If that was mental illness, Frank thought, well maybe most of the people here were mentally ill. But he suspected that many of them just were too quirky for the world. He'd leave the theorizing about bad chemicals to the doctors.

After a few more moments the receptionist in a slightly raised voice said,

"Mr. Whitman."

With this she waved Frank over.

He came over maintaining an anxious look.

"Mr. Whitman, you can go down the hall to room 126 and someone will see you there."

"Oh, thanks. Does that mean that my brother is here?"

"Listen" she said with a smile and a glint, which was very unusual for receptionist thought Frank.

"He probably is, but I'm not suppose to give you that information, you know, confidentiality."

She whispered this last word.

"Ok, I understand." Frank whispered back with a little grin.

"Just go to room 126 and wait for someone to come see you."

"Ok" said Frank with a little more assertiveness.

When he found room 126 it was empty except for a small desk and three badly upholstered chairs, which had also been torn slightly on the arms. He sat down and waited, trying to think of what he could remember about Walt Whitman and his brother George. He needed to keep up the agitated state in case a doctor or nurse came in. But if Jack White came in he would act relieved and happy to see him.

As it turned out Jack White came in just ahead of the nurse. At least he had to assume that it was Jack White in order for the charade to work.

"Walter" Frank proclaimed.

Jack White gave Frank a knowing look, like he was a part of the ruse and that the staff or anyone else should not be privy to their exchanges.

"Walter, how are you?"

White shook Frank's outstretched hand.

Frank nodded at the nurse who was in the background, indicating that all was well and that she could leave now. Frank also noticed a hefty man hanging near the door that he assumed was either a police officer or an orderly.

White still didn't say anything, but with his face indicated that he understood that the Whitmanesque spirit was in the room and that all would be well.

"Walter, I know that it has been difficult, but we are all behind you?"

"Yes, they are a brutish and nasty bunch."

Frank assumed that Jack White was referring to the police.

"We will have you out of here in no time."

Frank hoped that he hadn't been too optimistic with that statement, so he followed it with,

"But first I just need you to let me know about this guy Kitchholm. I think that we may have made a mistake with him. Do you remember why we picked Kitchholm? I thought that the writer that we were suppose to hit was a professor named Butterworth."

Jack White, looked anxiously at the nurse, who then quickly left the room.

Jack whispered, "Butterworth was after Kitchholm, don't you remember?"

"Yes, of course. But I just can't remember why Kitchholm. I was afraid that we had made a mistake."

"We don't make mistakes." Then Jack's facial expression changed to concern.

"Hey, I don't remember your face. What's your name?"

"Why it's George, your brother."

With this Frank tried to convey a sense of a secrecy about the whole thing, but he was getting worried that Jack was beginning to mistrust him and his amateurish undercover operation.

"I was never told that George's soul was involved."

Frank came closer to Jack who was now seated in one of the crappy chairs across from Frank.

"You know Jack, I'm only using the name George so that you would consent to see me and the police wouldn't suspect that I'm here to give you your next assignment."

Jack smiled as a sense of community and being loved returned to him.

"What's the assignment?"

Frank had one planned, but first he wanted to obtain as much information as he could about the who and whys of the operation.

"Look, Jack we know that you want to get out of here and you will all in due time, but what you need to do is say to the police that you were just going through a stressful period in your life and that Mr. Kitchholm reminded you of someone that had screwed up one time too many in the past. So, you had a bad involuntary reaction. We need to get you out of this and this is the best way. No more talking about Walt for now."

"That doesn't sound like Walt, he wouldn't be so blatantly dishonest."

"Look he just wants you to get out."

Jack looked like he believed Frank. Why wouldn't he.

Frank had been concerned that he would make the situation worse for Jack, if Jack had truly been ill, but from the direction of the case so far Frank realized that there was some type of group motivation as opposed to the acts being propelled by any individual mental deviation. He felt some strange kinship with Jack and quickly was on his side in this affair, which was a strange feeling, considering that he had been going after this group of darkly dressed Whitman surrogates like they were the criminals. The more had he spent time with the case the more his sympathies changed, especially after one of them had had their life taken from them at the Marriott hotel in Montreal.

Frank slipped Jack White a card with his contact information on it.

thirty-seven

"I dreamed that was the new city of Friends"

Walt Whitman

By that evening Michael Shultzmann was attempting to contact Boris and was having little success. Boris was now on his eleventh drink at the DregStore and had been ignoring his phone. He was engaging Tito and a group of women in philosophical conversation which was now bordering on the improbable and beginning to bore the bartender and incite anger and resentment in the women, whose sexuality seemed ambiguous to Boris.

When the women walked away from him and Tito said that he had to go home, Boris remembered that he was assisting his friend Frank in solving a mystery which now included a murder of one of the perpetrators of the original attacks which had originally provoked them to begin this side project into a world of anarchic investigations. So, he checked his phone and saw that he had seven calls from Schultzmann. As he read the texts he realized that Shultzmann had attempted to become a novice Whitman know-it -all in one afternoon. He was quoting and theorizing like a university degree depended on it. What did this mean to Boris and more importantly what would Frank think of all this. Schultzmann must have talked to or texted Frank, thought Boris. Boris ordered another beer from the new bartender, who looked at him with some consternation like he might not give him more to drink pretty soon. Boris then thought that he might want to get some sleep before getting back on the job. He thought of Brandon. He had said that he would call him. He should call him, tell him that he needed to grab a couple hours sleep and that he would see him later. He also wanted to check on Butterworth to see if he was ok and if any objects had been thrusted into the side of his head.

After calling Brandon he found out that Butterworth had been meeting with some members of the university staff earlier in the day on campus when he needed to relieve himself. On his way out of the men's room at the university he had been smacked on the cranium by a young man wearing a black t-shirt over a brown leisure suit. He had recovered quickly and had a fairly good description of the culprit. Brandon had not been there at the time of the incident but had arrived a few minutes later hoping to meet his Maddi for a drink and some stimulating conversation. He had found a small crowd of students surrounding Maddi outside of the conference room where Maddi and his colleagues had met. Boris had asked if Butterworth needed hospitalization and Brandon said that Maddi had refused it. But Butterworth had been sure of the description of the assailant. This had happened late in the afternoon and the police had yet to be notified. Butterworth did not want any publicity around this. He had had his otherworldly encounter with the soul of Walt Whitman the day before and now this. He thought that he had better spend time reviewing the events before deciding on a course of action. He and Brandon were in their hotel room at the Marriott going over things when Boris called.

Brandon agreed to meet with Boris a bit later that evening. Boris returned to the hotel, where he had booked the room for another night and set his head down on the pillow. He had notified the front desk to wake him up in two hours, which would have been about 9 P.M. A call would come to his room an hour before that.

Schultzmann had finally reached Frank by telephone shortly after 7 P.M.

"Michael, it's good to hear from you. What's up?"

"Frank, I'm cramming for the Whitman final. It's some very esoteric stuff, but he's got me hooked. Boris told me about what happened at the Marriott last night and that the police have one of them in custody in Toronto. This is becoming quite an elaborate web. I want to let you know Frank that all I'm qualified to contribute to this case is some intellectual notes. I don't have the demeanor or the motivation to be involved with criminal elements."

"Relax Michael, just do what you do. Stay with the books. You won't be asked to show your face anywhere."

"That's good."

Frank was almost certain that he was right about this, but he could not be 100% sure, after all it was the first time in his life that he had been so involved in a criminal case. And he had voluntarily put himself in this position to boot. But he felt confident that Schultzmann would not be needed in person. He could not imagine him even having to testify in court since he was not even an English major or Whitman expert. His assistance was purely inspirational.

"Listen, Frank I'm going to send you some notes that I made via email and hope that they help."

"Fire away Michael. I'm all Whitman all the time."

Boris was soon sleeping in his hotel, dreaming of being on a cruise ship with dozens of beautiful women and Walt Whitman. In Boris' dream Whitman was the entertainment director of the cruise and had arranged for an acapella group to sing. There was a trolley car from the 1860s on board the ship giving free rides. It seemed that in the background guests were re-enacting the American Civil War and that some Afro-Americans were singing spiritual songs on the deck. It was a chaotic dream and because Boris had been drinking most of the afternoon he could not clearly remember much of it after he got up to answer the phone call from Brandon Pierce.

"Boris, Professor Butterworth is not doing well and we've decided that we are going to fly back to England as soon as possible so that he can see his personal physician. Don't be alarmed he is not dying. He is just exhibiting signs of dementia. It does scare me a bit, but I would like it if you came and saw him before he left."

"I'll be right over, Brandon. Just let me shake off the cobwebs."

Boris quickly showered, drank some water, fixed his hair, decided to keep the five o'clock shadow in deference to a film noir scene and briskly left his room. Within seconds he was down the hall and knocking on the Butterworth and Brandon's door.

When he entered, he saw Butterworth staring out of at the city longingly from a chair through a window. He seemed to be mumbling something. Brandon looked worried but managed a slight smile when he saw Boris.

"Come in, he just seems to be in his own little world. I don't know what to do and I really don't want to call his colleagues and alarm them unnecessarily. I do have a number of a close friend, but he is in London and is of no use until with get there. I called his doctor and he told me that the only thing to do would be to not leave him alone for more than a few minutes at a time and to come back to London as soon as possible and have him observed."

"How are you, Brandon?"

"Me? Fine. Just need some advice I guess."

Boris paused and gave Brandon a light hug. He was thinking of all that had happened to Butterworth in the last few days, culminating with his being hit on the cranium just that afternoon. He felt a little responsible for not taking better care of the literary master. After all, his poetry and ideas had formed a great deal of what had propelled Boris through his life even up to today. He saw Brandon has an amiable soul with whom he had felt a common bond, perhaps it had been Butterworth, but Boris suspected that there was more.

267

The fact that Butterworth had been solicited by the Whitman entities, one of whom was unceremoniously killed in the room just above him and that he had felt inclined to go to some sordid apartment to meet 'Whitman' himself and just like Boris himself had been drawn into the affair without having any straight forward logical or rational reasons behind doing so, caused Boris to become certain that a metaphysical concept or energy was at work here uniting all of them. He didn't believe in the invisible but had room in his mind for the interchange of ideas, even from the distant past. This curiosity and his being caught up in this series of events was pounding on his brain as he looked at Brandon contemplating what he could do or say that would bring some form of sanity to the scenario. He did not want to appear helpless before anyone, but especially Brandon since it was Brandon that had called him for help. After all, he was now an assistant investigator to Frank and this was beginning to have the markings of a real live case. Boris was taking his role with a little more gravitas now that Butterworth had become directly involved.

"Do you have any coffee, Brandon?"

"Coffee? I think so."

Brandon went to the other room in the two-room suite.

From there he asked, "Milk, cream, sugar?"

"Nothing just coffee."

A moment later Brandon returned with the coffee. Boris was sitting on a comfortable chair and staring at Butterworth staring into the Montreal skyline as its background darken and lights began to light up.

"Professor Butterworth, hello."

There was no response.

"Maddi, you have a guest. Boris is here, the poet and sculptor."

Finally, Butterworth turned his head toward them.

"Boris, it is grand to have you here. My Brandon, excuse me, something has been overwhelming me. A new thought or idea and I have been trying to find the words to communicate it. Maybe that strike to the head is having a latent effect. I seem to have forgotten my basic duties and what it is that I came here to do."

"Maddi, do you know where you are? You obviously remember me and Boris."

"Yes, I recall you two and Montreal. But I just want to search for something else. Something that I don't know. It suddenly feels like I am becoming aware of what I don't know. How can I put it? I have a blank sheet of paper before me and I'm awaiting instructions."

"Maddi, I believe that your being hit by inspiration."

"More than that, my Brandon, much more. I am in flight, my lover."

Theodor, the man who had cause Butterworth transformation, had shed his brown leisure suit and was now dressed fully in black, like the others. Casey and Binky had converted Theodor's brain to Whitman mode. He sat at Coffee Express on University was eating a turkey panini sandwich and drinking a lightly flavored water. His mind had been hit by a powerful jolt of questions for which he could not answer. Suddenly the actions that he had been taking towards achieving a certain goal had been burned into oblivion and now he was being inspired by some spirit that had found its way into his consciousness after the experience with Casey and Binky. Logically his head could not grasp what was happening. Was it brain washing or chemicals, he asked himself? He was so certain just the day before. Was he losing his mind? No, it could not be. There had to be some logical explanation for the fact that he had just hit that professor over the head with a copy of 'Leaves of Grass'. Perhaps it was to assuage his guilt over the killings he had perpetrated recently as part of a mission to let the past be the past. Theodor had recently survived an airplane crash carrying a group of scientists from Geneva to Moscow. He had been part of a team contributing to the search for the 'god

269

particle' by means of colliders, the biggest one being in Switzerland. His mind had been the furthest it could have been from the poetic contemplations of Walt Whitman or any poet or artist for that matter. He had been immersed in linear thinking. He had a deep certainty that humanity was always progressing and gaining more knowledge about the universe. He was convinced that one day we would know all of the basic laws and facts behind the nature of life and be able to determine an exact course for everything. Nothing would be new ever again.

Somehow this mode of thinking had stayed with Theodor after he had recovered from the unfortunate plane crash, even though what motivated him had completely changed. Yet, the doctors that had attended to him were mostly unaware of any transformation in his mind. He passed all of the test and seemed back to normal. They would not have believed that he had been brought to another dimension of reality and now he felt compelled to carry out a series of acts to perpetuate his and many other's theories. His memory had become very selective. He could not find the source of his motivation to act.

But now he was realizing that his flesh, blood and brain were operating on a completely different plane. He knew for sure that he had to consider adopting a whole new logic. After bopping Butterworth, he had been given a whole new set of clothes by Casey and Binky. In the pocket of his new black jacket, he found photos of his wife and two children. He looked at them perplexed at first, taking a sip of his lightly flavored water. Then it began to make sense, new sense. A radically new logic. He had become a double agent to save his life.

I was also in the Coffee Express making sure that Jesse/Jessica was ok and didn't need some comforting words and loving support. But the appearance of Theodor at the Coffee Express as a double agent had been a complete surprise to me. Now I sat back and wondered what Theodor would do with his discovery that he was indeed in some sort of limbo, where much of his concrete memories had faded, but he had garnered a new sense of purpose and meaning. But he had no evidence for anything. I asked myself if this now darkly dressed genius was genuinely trying to curtail his violent acts or was this only part of a ruse to fool the Whitman devotees? I had to wonder if he would continue to take actions that he did not completely understand? This smart brain faced a dilemma as he took another bite out of his turkey panini sandwich and sipped his beverage.

thirty-eight

"I am only drinking to pass the time away, while waiting for the truth to emerge."

Boris Swatcupso. From his poem 'The Politics of Drinking'

Frank was absorbed in the emailed notes that Schultzmann had sent him. To him the theme of Whitman had been really unrequited love. His sexuality had been foiled by the world he lived in, but he had been determined to channel his passion into poetry and underground groups of more liberated souls.

Walt had thrown himself into helping the wounded soldiers of war and wounded souls in general. If, Frank thought, Whitman's soul was indeed somehow at work in the 21st century where would it find its home? At an academic institution? No definitely not. In the military? Well, perhaps, but more than likely amongst some peacekeeping force. Whitman liked the water and nudity. Perhaps in a nudist colony or some cult near a beach in California? No, the most logical place was at 'Conspiremouth', where Boris had told him Butterworth and Brandon had gone. Frank now recalled that Kitchholm had given him a copy of 'Conspirmouth' which had been thrusted on Kitchholm outside L'Hotel Fish Pond. Where had he put it? It was probably lost. They had to have a website. He looked online and found an email address but no physical location. Should he try to communicate via email? Would that bring him closer to Whitman? What about Butterworth could he now find Whitman more easily? Frank finally decided that he would wait for a response from this Jack White. He felt confident that the guy would contact him. Maybe under less strenuous circumstances than a psychiatric hospital he would be able to have a more productive conversation.

In Montreal, Boris and Brandon had been listening to Maddi's newfound inspiration most of the afternoon. They had been able to interject occasional comments but for the most part Maddi's oratorical skills had dominated the hotel room. He had now refused to consider returning to London that day to see his doctor, whom he now called a blatant cog in the bureaucratic machine of medical science. He railed against prescription drugs and useless surgical procedures. He even had critical verbiage for nurses and hospital staff. Alternative medicine was also a capitalistic hoax to take advantage of the public scepticism in doctors. Then he moved on to politics and the cultural world, where his expertise shined. He was far from being shipped out to the backlot of the BBC's radio 4 Extra he said. Now he would steer a new course for the arts by writing about how the creative urge came from an ancient source manifesting itself in objects and souls of the present. At times it was difficult for the two sets of younger ears to follow his logic. When the information entered their brains, it seemed like a string of random ideas and dubious facts, but over more than three hours a thread of logic was developing. It seemed at times that Butterworth was just as perplexed by what was emanating from his mouth as Boris and Brandon were.

Parts of his impromptu lecture were even disturbing, leading to some questions as to whether he might have been exhibiting signs of dementia. But he wasn't. He had been tapped by a soul from the collective consciousness. Truths that had come alive in a human form but were they verifiable. This is what was troubling Boris and Brandon. To Butterworth, he was living this consciousness and needed no further proof, but others would. Or perhaps he could just tap them on the cranium with a book.

Boris was understanding Butterworth better than Brandon was. He knew the underlining motivators, but still was straddling the line with his old perspective of reality. Like Frank he felt driven to solve the mystery and at the same time had accepted its elusive nature. As he listened to Butterworth's diatribe he wondered if any of this could be quantified into equations and values. His limited mathematics caused his brain to seize for a moment when this question appeared on the scene. He wanted to voice it but thought it best to not confuse the situation with problem solving techniques. He would leave that to Frank. Boris was also desirous of a drink.

As Butterworth seemed to be winding down, he suggested drinks. Butterworth shrugged that idea off, but a few moments later said.

"And that is all that one needs for this day. Now I will go and eat my dinner, Brandon order us all steak dinners. Make mine rare."

He then marched into the bathroom and slammed the door. The sounds of shuffling and laughter came from behind the door. Brandon went to the phone and placed the order with room service. Boris went and looked for a bottle. Brandon pointed to his suitcase which was open on the bed. Boris found a full bottle of Irish Whiskey, opened it and poured himself a large drink. Brandon got off the phone and said that he would take a small drink himself. The two of them looked at each other almost shrugging their shoulders at what had just transpired. They were both exhausted from the fiery speech and the thoughts that had been provoked in their brains during the afternoon verbal marathon.

"Well, Brandon it seems Maddi has perhaps found a new muse." Boris finally suggested with a hint of sarcasm.

Brandon did not look pleased with Boris' comment.

"Boris, you don't know him like I do. He has brainstormed like this before. You will see, he will emerge from that bathroom with a clear and logical explanation for all of this even though I must say some of things that he said and implied sounded quite far fetched and that even I would classify as horrific."

"Interesting that you should choose the word 'horrific' to describe what he said. Because I truly believe that we are in a 'horrific' set of circumstances. On one hand is the implication that we are being visited by entities and ideas that have seemingly met their end in the past and on the other is that we know that our five senses and common sense is telling us that this could be all a charade being perpetrated by a very convincing set of actors who have taken the world's stage much too literally. This guy Bucke that wrote that book on Cosmic Consciousness, are you familiar with him?"

"No, but I've heard that he was a good friend of Walt Whitman. He was considered a bit of an anomaly by most academics. A strange but fascinating man who certainly seemed to have found a niche for his ideas, but he was not widely accepted. I don't think that I could honestly comment any further than that on the man."

"Well, my friend Frank mentioned him to me a while back. It seems that he believed in the ability of the human mind to get a grasp on a certain level of consciousness which enable those individuals to perceive the highest level of reality. And I use the word highest relatively."

"I know nothing about that Boris. I just think each person has things that make one tick a certain way and others don't. Everyone sees things differently."

"Oh, come on, that's too easy."

Boris blurted this out and seconds later wished that he hadn't. It was too dismissive. He hoped that Brandon hadn't thought that he was begin disrespectful. Brandon's reaction was silent and unsmiling.

Boris began to attempt to correct his misstep.

"What I mean is that I don't think you can deny that we have many common experiences, sometimes at the same time, but not always. Everything just can't be chucked into the random category. There must be some criteria to begin an investigation or study or we may as well just not pursue anything that involves mental tasks."

There was a silence. Boris took a stiff gulp of his whiskey. Brandon took an exasperated breath.

"Boris, sometimes one has to walk alone on some random path to find truth and beauty for oneself. That is what I was saying."

"Well, that's just great. We agree. And it seems to me that your own life exhibits that premise to a tee."

"Yes, but I don't want to revel in it. I did that when I was younger. Very egotistical of me. To proclaim oneself special and not subject to rules and laws of society or the universe for that matter. I didn't know it at the time, but I really thought that much of what was going on around me, didn't apply to me. It was pathetic where I was back then. I never want to be there again."

"I suppose that you just needed to accept yourself as is and not have any false views."

"Yes, Boris, but I still needed to walk alone for awhile to accept myself."

"Oh, please let's not start babbling out any nonsense about finding ourselves now"

They both laughed aloud.

"Maybe I'll have another drink, Boris. I am not that interested in finding myself quite yet."

"Perhaps we have. Perhaps it isn't that difficult after all."

There was a warm moment between the two.

Strange sounds still emanated from the bathroom. Then Maddi burst forth into the room.

"Gentlemen, we have a task, before us. To re-ignite the spark in a few good people. Just a few, mind you. Don't think that I have completely lost touch with reality."

Here he laughed.

"Oh, imbibing I see. Well, we shall eat and then I intend to compose a statement for general release."

"Very nice", said Brandon.

276

Boris nodded and gulped his beverage.

The three of them had reached some concord.

But Boris' mind still harbored the notion that he and Frank were solving a mystery.

thirty-nine

"Details create the big picture."

Sanford I. Weill

In a prison cell in Chicago Frida S. Wharton sat genuinely praying to a deity that she now was beginning to have wavering faith in. She couldn't understand how her deity had not met her personal demands. In reality, she was desperate and couldn't see that her own thinking had gotten her where she was now, not her deity. Wharton was truly deluded by the idea that her being alive had been a special event in the history of the universe. That idea always preceded any conception of a higher being or supreme force in the universe. So, she was not afraid of what was to come, but was full of expectation that her followers would rescue her from her misfortune. Now there might have been some truth to this, especially in the case of her passive spouse, Jack Bowers but what her devotees could not do was rescue her from her own delusions.

Now she knew that if her own lies were exposed for too long her little queen of the universe gig would be up, so she needed to act quickly. She had gotten a message to her public relations man, Manny Powers to issue a series of statement which explained the events of the past two days. This she believed would bode well for her church. She had arranged that Jack and some of her confidents hide any documentation of her financial records from the government. This was accomplished by throwing all the computers in her offices into the Ohio River and burying paper documents underground at the petting zoo that she operated outside Pittsburgh. Some of those tax records would end up being digested by a goat named Harold. Harold would find the ones from 2014 and 2015 the tastiest. Perhaps the American Internal Revenue Service would have salivated over those years as well, but alas they

278

had their own records and were not too concerned with Harold the goat making a meal out of them.

All of Wharton's business enterprises and her entire staff would be kaput within weeks. She would make a deal with the authorities to give Jack a small allowance for a few years just to keep him off her back. She had also made a deal to keep a modest amount for herself and have all charges dropped. To get this she had to forfeit the rest of her assets and dissolve all of her business ventures And after all that had been finalized Wharton would in a whirlwind of inspiration abandon her husband and move to Canada to become a folk music singer. This had been another one of her passions as a child and now it seemed like the only window of opportunity that she had, at least until the authorities had completely gotten off her back and she could establish a new identity or something. She would smoke some marijuana, wear loose clothing, become a vegan and try and seduce young men. This would all happen she envisioned after all the paper work had been dealt with through her lawyers. After she had paid them, she still had a considerable sum left to live off of for at least a year. One thing that her ego and self-respect would not allow her to do was to go back to her parental home in Pittsburgh. She would invent a cover story for her parents that some of her employees had mishandled her assets and that she was starting a new business outside of the country with a new Canadian lover. There was considerable plausibility in this story. And room for deniability as well. Just the exact tracks where the Wharton choo-choo train liked to operate. But what she didn't know was that her train would be switching engineers and losing a few cars soon.

It was now the second morning following the killing of one of Whitman's advocates. Frank awoke well after the sun had come up in a disheveled state. His mind seemed to have been on some wild jungle pilgrimage while he was sleeping. He could not remember the stops or the personages that he had encountered on his ephemeral, but arduous voyage across the landscape of his subconscious. A barely recognized voice told him that something of significance had occurred during his slumber, but he shook it off. What I don't put value in cannot bother me today, he thought to

279

himself. He decided to wash and dress, check out of the economy motel that he was in with its puke-colored walls and velvet paintings, and go into downtown Toronto. Perhaps Jack White would contact him by then. If not, he then planned to return to Montreal that day and talk directly with Butterworth and Boris. Before he left, he needed to also check in on Warren Kitchholm. He tried to call him. No answer. He left a text. After he had washed and checked out he noticed that Kitchholm had replied:

Out of the hospital, at home writing, got a call from anonymous woman saying that she had info, read about murder of Whitman surrogate

Well, thought Frank, finally someone is offering information. Up to this point Frank was beginning to think that he would have to do all of the work on the case. Now he was learning that waiting was just as important for an investigator as aggressive legwork. So, a mysterious person who happened to be a woman was involved. He could not avoid conjuring up the femme fatale cliché in his mind. Now could this anonymous figure fit into this. He searched his brain for any female connections. He eliminated the women that had been in his life, seeing that they would have no motive or actual knowledge that he had taken up the job of private investigator. And how could they possibly have connected him to Kitchholm? Now wait there was the woman who worked in the coffee shop where Frank and Boris had initially run into each other. Kitchholm had been there and she had witnessed the first attack. Frank wondered what Boris had said to her while Kitchholm had been attending to him. This thread seemed to be lead nowhere. Maybe some witness to Schultzmann being attacked at the lecture hall. But what information could they have?

He needed to find out exactly what Kitchholm had before he left Toronto. He tried Kitchholm's cell number one more time. No answer. He then unceremoniously checked out of the motel and walked out into a hot summer's day still feeling taxed by his dreamed travels, but hopeful now that he had Kitchholm's new information to build on.

He decided to get on a street car and head toward Kitchholm;s home. He would keep calling him as the Toronto Transit Commission carried him through the busy streets of the city that he had been quite familiar with years before. As he moved past certain landmarks he would reminisce on events from his sometimes sordid, sometimes ordinary life, that had unfolded during his years in the city. He had been a student, a husband, and a bum here. He had worked and played here. Did he have more friends than enemies? That he could not readily determine. He had abruptly severed many ties, many times. He felt that he had never particularly crossed anyone here, nor had he been the darling of anyone's affections. Certainly not his ex-wife's.

As the street car approached Union Station his phone rang. It was Kitchholm. Good, he thought.

"Frank, how are you?"

"Good. I'm checking out of the city. But first I need to see you about that text you sent."

"Of course. Listen I don't want to get into it on the phone. We need to meet somewhere. I don't want to do it here at home because of the family. Could be risky now that there's a murder involved. Where are you, now?"

"Union Station."

"Good. Go to Yonge and Bloor, just north of there on Yonge is a restaurant called Mickey's Diner. I'll be there in an hour."

"Okay. Mickey's, one hour."

Frank was feeling anxious anticipation for the first time in years. He could not recall the last time he had been overcome by what was coming just ahead of him like he was now. He stopped at a fast-food place at the station and stuff some proteins and carbohydrate down his gullet to perhaps ward out a dizzy spell. Then he boarded a subway to go to Bloor Station. It was nearly 10 A.M and the train was nearly full. He couldn't find an empty seat. But he decided that he preferred standing anyhow. He tried not to play detective with the passengers, many of whom gave off the aura of wanting to scowl at the first person exhibiting anything near suspicious behaviour. Frank's eyes particularly noticed anyone who wore black. Now he was beginning to have reflexive reactions to his environment. He rather enjoyed this but suspected that it would be tiresome after awhile.

In his just awakening mind, he began equating his subway trip with Whitman's poem 'Crossing Brooklyn Ferry', which he had just been perusing the day before. 'Crowds of men and women attired in the usual costumes, how curious you are to me!' he recalled. He tried not to stare at people. People exited and new ones entered at each stop. A baby in a stroller cried in discomfort, probably from the noise of the train or the fatigue of the trip. An old man coughed violently and reeked of alcohol as he sat on one of the seats near Frank. Some young teenage girls giggled and laughed as they uttered almost incomprehensible words, which apparently only they could understand. A woman ate a large muffin in one of the corner seats. She was overdressed for the weather and seemed to be sweating not just from the heat but from some level of fear. Perhaps her husband had lost his job, perhaps she had lost hers.. Maybe her children were in trouble with the law. It seemed that she was consuming her muffin like it was her only solace. A fat man scratched his left ear and let out an exasperated breath. His face was red and his light blue permanent press shirt had a grease stain on it. Frank still tried not to stare but caught himself a few times being transfixed by details. More and more his mind was seeing details.

Finally, the car arrived at Bloor Station.

He found the restaurant easily.

It was a family type place with a slight nod to a more upscale lunchtime business crowd. Frank asked for a booth near the entrance. He looked around the place for Kitchholm and not finding him sat down. He looked through the menu, decided that it was overpriced and ordered an iced tea telling the female server that he was waiting for someone.

After ten minutes Kitchholm arrived looking quite relaxed, considering that he may have some key information in a case that involved murder. Frank thought he looked too relaxed. Maybe it was just the years of journalistic experience that made Kitchholm look that way, thought Frank.

Kitchholm sat down immediately. He had a light suit jacket on looking the part of a writer.

"Frank, good to see you."

"I'm glad you called."

"Well, I smell a good story. And I really appreciate your investigative nose here. We are in this together whether we like it or not. Remember it was you that got hit on the head first. Hey, that's what started this. Are you eating?"

"Naw, just ate. I'm having an iced tea."

"I'm gonna order some food, if you don't mind."

"Go ahead. So, what do you have?"

"The woman?"

"Yes. This mystery woman that I'm getting so curious about."

"Well, it could be nothing. But we need to check because she seems to know an awful lot about this poetry stuff. She mentioned Walt Whitman and Boris' name."

"Did she mention my name?"

"No, but she wanted to know where Boris was and who he was with. Then she said that when she found him, she would tell us all about the young men in black who knew the poetry of Walt Whitman. I asked her if she believed in life after death. She was silent and then said that Whitman was dead but his soul lived on. I asked her if she knew that he had made appearances in Montreal and that the perpetrators of the assaults seemed to be intimately connected to him. Again, she was silent. This time for at least fifteen seconds. Then she told me tell me the whole truth only after she had found Boris. So, I asked why Boris was so important to her. She was silent again, then said that it was none of my business. Then I asked her how she had found me. She said that an underground paper in Montreal had connected me to Boris, but she had not been able track his whereabouts after L'Hotel Fish Pond. I asked her if she knew of a Professor Butterworth. She said that she had never heard of him. I asked her if that underground paper had been the 'Conspiremouth'. She said yes."

"So, she doesn't know Butterworth, knows the paper. She probably doesn't know that Butterworth met Whitman's soul, so to speak, in Montreal. Now how is it that she knows so much about our friend Whitman yet missed out on his rendez-vous with Butterworth?"

"Now that is a good question."

The female server came by and Kitchholm ordered a club sandwich and a large glass of milk. Frank thought about ordering a beer but changed his mind. It would be a mistake to start down the path that Boris was on. One of them had to be sober. It balanced things out, thought Frank.

"I think your female informant is bluffing. She is getting more information out of you than she may have to give you"

"Could be."

"Your questions tipped her off to the whole thing. What did she give you? Nothing, except that she knows Boris pretty well And that she may have an inside track on what this soul of Whitman is up to."

It was at this time that Boris decided to call Frank and update him on what was transpiring in Montreal.

Frank took the call. He indicated to Kitchholm that Boris was on the phone.

Kitchholm had taken out a notebook and was sketching some ideas while Frank spoke with Boris.

"Boris, good that you called. What's going on up there?"

"Too much, Frank, too much poetry, too much hubris, too much passion."

Boris didn't sound too drunk. It was just shy of eleven o'clock in the morning after all.

"Boris, don't think that I don't appreciate your esoteric sensitivity to the situation, but at this stage I require an inventory of facts and not speculations."

"Well, this whole thing will only be resolved by esoteric speculation my friend. That is what I think."

"Save that theory for later. What's happening with Butterworth?"

"He has tasted the wine of Whitman, Frank. He is raving and crusading. He is getting ready to campaign for the resurrection of 'Leaves of Grass' and is singing songs to himself."

"Great Boris, but what happened?"

"Well, Butterworth got the blow to the head yesterday. He's okay. He's still here in the hotel. We got him to stay another day, but he refuses profession attention."

"We? Whose we?"

"Brandon, his lover, you remember I mentioned him, or did I? Anyway, he's really caring and compassionate."

"Well, that's good to know. What did he say about Whitman? Did he talk about where he might be?"

"Not much about where, but after that blow he seemed to have been converted to some sort of hyper belief in the soul. Inspired, reborn, recharged, motivated. No drugs Frank, I swear. Not even booze."

"So were we Boris. We caught some charge from the blows, but that does not mean we don't have the ability to think. Though I'm not sure your method of thought was aligned with any widely accepted logic."

"Thanks, Frank for the diagnosis. Maybe the blow just returned me back to my normal state."

"Normal, Boris, please don't use that word."

Kitchholm looked on listening with curiosity. He could not hear Boris' end of the conversation nevertheless he marvelled at the banter.

"Listen, Frank I'm going to go to Butterworth's room now. And by the way, I 'm putting all of this on my credit card. I can't afford the hotel, the expenses. When the money starts to roll in I expect to be fully compensated."

"How much are you spending on booze?"

"Just what's needed to get the job done, Frank."

"That's what I thought. Let me know if this Whitman comes back out of hiding. I'm coming back there today or tomorrow and we're going right to this 'Conspiremouth'. Oh, and by the way there is some woman who is quite determined to locate you. She has been baiting us with information that she allegedly has about Whitman. Does that ring any bells?"

"A woman, eh. There's lots of them, Frank."

"I figured that."

"And, ah yes, I will ask Butterworth about that little crew of anarchists. Gotta go."

"Yes, I know the hotel bar is probably just opening. Ciao, Boris."

Kitchholm was smiling when Frank put the phone down.

"Anything new."

"Yes, our Professor Butterworth suffered head injuries and is recovering marvellously by going on self-indulgent tirades. We need to find that woman and tell her that Boris is at a downtown hotel in Montreal. You can meet her somewhere near the hotel, see how severely she is bluffing and then take it from there. I'm also going to investigate this 'Conspiremouth' thing."

"Frank, thanks for letting me in on the story."

"Sure. Why not. But you have to promise me one thing."

"What's that?"

"That you won't break the story before we find out who or what this soul of Whitman really is?"

"Deal."

Kitchholm's club sandwich came. Frank relaxed for a while, closing his eyes, trying to find a place in his mind where this could all make some sort of sense.

forty

By the end of the day Casey and Binky, the main publishers of the 'Conspiremouth', had completed the task necessary for that week's edition. They had everything laid out on a USB key and had transferred the data on to the printers. That week's issue would include a short story about an elite professor of English who suffers a brain aneurysm and is confined to a hospital for over a year. Over that period of time he dictates a seemingly random series of phrases, sentences and paragraphs which are then re-arranged by an associate of his into a book which sweeps the world and makes him rich. The story concludes with him coming out of the coma and denying that he had anything to do with the book. Then he disappears from public view never to be heard of again. The story was credited to a Jack White.

Now Case and Binky were waiting to see if Theodor would return. He had been directed to bring Butterworth on board the Whitman soul train. This would enable the group to have a legitimate voice in the eyes of the general public. But neither Case, Binky nor the new recruit Theodor had reached any conclusion that any larger agenda or purpose was at work here, that would require them to make a larger commitment. They only knew that they were to continue to jolt certain people's brains. Those people then could find clearly buried talents or resources. It really rested upon the recipients of the blows to respond. It did not require any follow up. Life for these people continued on as usual for some, but for others there were radical changes afoot. Jack White, for example, took to being very eccentric and more devoted to the cause. Casey and Binky saw only slight lifestyle changes, while Theodor saw a radical change in his perception on the origins of life and its fundamental meanings. Casey and Binky were not aware of Theodor's connection with the scientific breakthroughs in the field of physics in his earlier life. They did not understand anything to do with how the universe worked in a fundamental way to keep life afloat, which Theodor's mind had tapped into on a much more fundamental level since his plane accident and brain jolt. But Casey and Binky felt validated by the results of their actions.

They sat in their unassuming quarters contemplating what their next action would be, particularly regarding whether to be more proactive with Theodor or wait for their poetic muse to make a soulful reappearance to give them direction. The pair were also staying updated on the events of the day, anticipating that Butterworth would appear either on the BBC or a celebrity gossip website depending on which way his brainwaves shifted. It was amusing to some degree for the pair, but really not in a manner which engendered them with any great sense of power, because after all their little jolts only pointed people in a different direction but did not control their actions after that.

The two were really in the dark about how the taps to the head had affected Frank and Boris. They didn't know how Frank had been inspired to track down the origins of the seemingly random attacks and how Boris, being a close friend of Frank's, had decided to drop his emotional entanglement with his latest female love interest and tag along as his buddy's associate. They also had little clues as to Michael Schultzmann's determined attitude toward doing background research on their muse. Or as to how another associate's redirection of Warren Kitchholm's life in Toronto had added hubris to Kitchholm's life. Unlike Frank and Boris, they had not made the connection between what was happening in Canada with the incidents across the border.

But they did realize that there was a resistance against their vision of pointing people's lives in a more positive direction. This came with the territory of the species. Some individuals desire a greater autonomy then others. But mostly Casey and Binky saw humans as sheep like, needing something to follow. So, in their mind what could be wrong with alerting

289

humanity's brain systems to a more effective and efficient mode of operating. A more direct route to fulfillment as their muse had put it.

In Toronto, at the same time, Frank and Warren were purchasing tickets for the train trip back to Montreal and a rendez-vous with the mystery woman whose messages suggested that she had obsessive inclinations towards a sottish, crazed, artistically inclined, self-centred, but loyal bon vivant and sometimes line cook. They were hoping that she would have some facts or new leads regarding Whitman or the murder of Whitman's surrogate. It had been Warren Kitchholm whom the woman contacted about the information. So, Frank was allowing him to tag along because he felt he was not only an integral part of the mystery, having been a hit on the head himself, but also that he was owed an exclusive 'inside story'. He had been there from the beginning.

Because Kitchholm had some business to attend before leaving they had decided to take the overnight train to Montreal. Frank found himself spending the afternoon and evening visiting some of his old spots in the city. He felt that his present life was so much different than it had been when he had roamed the streets of 'T.O'. He felt asleep in small park by Queen's Quay and soon was in a slumber as the evening fell. Frank went into a pseudo dreamlike state in between rounds of fitful sleep. He would be jarred awake periodically by the sound of a car horn or children shouting nearby. This alternating between a dreamlike state and his immediate material reality created a juxtaposition of thoughts in his brain. This was a revolutionary clarity of mind that his neuro transmitters had assembled whose origins Frank was at a loss to determine.

Some of those brainwaves included a notion that most of humanity is destined to be eternally optimistic. This concept was illustrated in his dream by the constant chasing of people and things. On this particular somatic sojourn Frank was going after some distinguished looking man, whom he assumed was Butterworth, carrying a telescopic contraption and a microphone. He was hoping to get some 'positive' information from the double-breasted suited man, who had a pipe permanently attached to his mouth. Something needed clarification, but in the dream, Frank was unsure of what the questions were that needed to be asked. In the dream Frank's body was also heating up and becoming extremely thirsty, almost to the point of causing him mental anguish. This led to him pursuing any apparent source of cold water. When Frank awoke from this slumber, he was unsure as to whether he had been more inspired by the pursuit of information or the attempt at relieving his thirst. He played with this dilemma for a while then refocussed his mind on the more practical tasks ahead of him.

When Boris had called on Maddi and Brandon earlier there had been no answer. He had concluded that they had just stepped out somewhere. But later when he had inquired at the front desk about them, he was told that a message had been left for him.

It read:

My Friend Boris,

Maddi and I have checked out of the hotel and we are returning to London hopefully, this evening, depending on the flights. We have to depend on standby. Please accept my apology for leaving in such haste. I will be in touch. It is not a habit of mine to text or use iphones, but you can trust that I will be in touch. Maddi has decided to launch a new movement in literature which will emphasize happiness and positivity. He was on about it all morning. He spent four hours typing some sort of manifesto, which he refused to let me see, but claimed that it would inspire many young people to reclaim the planet for life's eternal good. So be it. I must stick with him because I love him, but also because he has over the last three years allowed me the space to become who I am now, while at the same time being fully supportive. I enjoy being with him.

Boris, I found that I had developed some affection for you and we must keep in touch. You have a definite zeal and I like to hoist a few myself. As to these mysterious entities who seem to be provoking all of this. Well, I leave that to you and your partner to solve. I'm not a man who has had many dealings with the metaphysical or the collective consciousness as some people have deemed these ideas. Despite Maddi's recent 're-birth' I am still a man who likes to stay grounded in the basic five senses and the chemical reactions which produce intellectual stimulation. But enough said on that.

Below is our contact information, please do not share this.

Yours, Brandon

And a physical address and email were given.

Boris felt an absence for a moment. He had over the period of a couple days developed a level of endearment toward not just Brandon, but also Maddi. Previous to his getting to meet Butterworth he had only held him up in esteem via his published works and some public appearances. He had almost put Butterworth up on a pedestal, but now he had been humbled by his encounters with Butterworth experiencing him as just another human being. Albeit one with some extraordinary talents and spirit. Through Brandon warmed up to him enough to almost begin calling him Maddi. But Boris did not want to presume anything in his mind about his relationship with the world-famous professor. As far as Brandon, Boris was inspired by the young man's affectionate manners and seeming devotion. So, there was a real emptiness when Boris realized that the couple was intending to leave Montreal immediately. But Boris' well-honed ability to come back to practical reality quickly took hold.

He folded the letter and filed it into his upper jacket pocket. He sat down in the hotel lobby and ran through options. Should he go to the airport to make sure that all was well? Or should he just forget it and wait for Frank to call? He considered doing some digging around himself, like maybe at the 'Conspiremouth'. Finally, he decided to phone Frank himself and tell him that Butterworth had left for the airport. He reached into his right lower jacket pocket, where he normally kept his phone and found it missing.

"Ah, shit" he whispered to himself. Just when he needed his phone it had disappeared. Isn't that just how the universe sets you up sometimes, he asked himself?

He really needed to get a direction from Frank. He quickly got up from the hotel lobby chair and began retracing his steps, back to the front desk, to the hallway and the elevators and back to his room where he had last used it when he had called Frank earlier. No luck. Not another mystery to be solved, he thought as he overturned cushions, bedding and looked under and overtop of things in his room. Where are the things that suddenly just disappear, he mumbled under his breath? After a few more moments of frantically searching, he finally decided to return to the lobby and have a called placed to Frank's phone via an operator since he had no time to buy a phonecard.

There were still two payphones in hotel lobby. He used the one that was closest to the bar entrance. He would get a few belts into him after he had hopefully spoken with Frank and before leaving for wherever he would go next. He hadn't realized how elaborate a task it had become to place a long-distance phone call from a pay phone these days, even with his credit card.

Boris was not by nature a patient man. Plus, he had been without a drink for close to 14 hours. He had not eaten yet that day, lost his phone, had to deal with the departure of Maddi and Brandon and now was having to punch in what was seemingly hundreds of numbers into a pay phone, while listening to a disembodied voice rudely repeating to him that everything he was doing was incorrect or that he wasn't being fast enough with his dialing. This little auditory charade went on for ten minutes. Boris had to start a short pacing sequence in front of the pay phone just to channel his irritability. As he fumbled with his credit card and was placing his wallet back into his

293

pocket, he heard a ringing sound. He sensed success but was not overly optimistic that it was Frank's phone on the other end.

It finally went to voicemail. Frank had recently changed his voice mail message:

You've reached Frank Lee's Inexpensive Investigations. Please leave your contact information in the manner indicated. If you want to leave a voice message do so after the whistling sound. Have a good day.

Then a generic feminine voice indicated the manner in which to leave the contact information.

Maybe Frank had lost his phone too. He did not want to go through a maze of technology attempting another call right away to Frank, so he said:

Frank, its Boris. I lost my phone. Leave a message at the Marriott Hotel lobby. I'll be in the bar. Butterworth and Brandon are fleeing the country tonight. Love and Live

With that he hung up and walked directly into the hotel bar which was almost empty except for a couple of straight-laced looking businessmen in dark blue business suits and a woman of about sixty who was sitting at the bar staring at the television and nursing what looked to be a martini.

Boris sat down at the bar and ordered a beer and a bourbon. The bartender was different from the one that had served Brandon and him a couple of nights earlier. This one was tall and thin with short blond hair. He wore a red vest over a white shirt with black slacks. Boris felt like unloading some of his frustrations on him but after observing the bartender for a few moments decided that this wasn't the guy to do it to. He thought of going to his loft and getting a change of clothes, but that would have to wait until after Frank called back. Damn he lost his phone.

While Boris was sorting out priorities and awaiting a call from Frank, Frida S. Wharton was making her way from Chicago to Pittsburgh to tie up some lose ends in regards to her plea deal with the government. What the authorities didn't know, but suspected was that the Wharton portal to eternity had concealed cash and bonds in several locations, not only in the United States of America, but also on some Caribbean islands. One of those locations was a kale and cucumber farm near Harrisburg, Pennsylvania which was the stare's capital city. Wharton now intended to have some of her most loyal followers return to that farm and dig up the cash. She was intent on saying bon voyage to America and a good portion of her 'shadow cash' was at the farm. After getting a hold of the money she would have three of her closest colleagues travel with her to Montreal separately, each carrying less than ten thousand dollars, so that she could legally bring the money in. This routine she planned to do over and over again until most of her money was in Canada. Wharton still commanded some loyalty from some of her members. So, she had very little concern that any of them would take off with the cash. But if they did, she not only threatened them with expulsion from the heavenly Wharton elevator, but also the possibility that their life here on earth would be made a living hell. She never specified how that would manifest itself, but the message had seemed pretty clear to the employee/followers involved.

Now there were a couple these Whartoneers who were thinking of chucking Frida and her exclusive heaven bound club, but they were silent, waiting for the opportunity for more evidence to appear so that they could sabotage the operation at an opportune time to financially capitalize on the situation. This meant waiting for a time went Frida, herself was out of the way.

Grant Dimietro had taken the Creeley death with a grain of salt, understanding that the guy had a bit of a death wish. He had decided to disassociate himself from Creeley as much as possible after the shooting, really not wanting to have his name placed in connection with his organization or having anything to do with Big Andy Jones. He did begin to talk about having a little more gratitude and appreciation for life after his misfortune though. He was even mulling over leaving a major market city like Chicago and to go work somewhere a little more obscure. Though he resisted this urge because he would be putting his family at a disadvantage financially. He had a wife and a 15- year-old daughter. There was already tension in his home without proposing some major move out of the city and into the country to his family.

No, Dimietro had to find another way to change his life, but what was it? He couldn't severely alter his radio program, that would require wrangling with station management and with his high ratings they would be completely miffed by his desire to change the show. They definitely would not approve. As he was beginning his show, on the same night that Butterworth and Brandon were waiting for a flight to London and the same night that Frank was arriving in Montreal, Dimietro was planning to add an editorial segment at the end of his show regarding the need to revive inspiration in the youth of the day, especially in the arts.

Now this was a major shift in thinking for Dimietro. He had been quite the cynic for most of his time on the planet.

As for Big Andy Jones' and his radio career. He felt the lure of greed as his overnight ratings increased along with an increase in orders for his side products affiliated with the program. Jones was secretly happy when dramatic events like the Creely and friends take down occurred. It boosted his audiences and their outrage. It gave them a thirst for an accompanying conspiratorial narrative which played right into Jones' forte.

Affiliated with that narrative was the 'Big Andy Jones' showdown at the Washington Hilton Ballroom where Jones had invited everyone who subscribed to his twisted vision of the world to assemble and then march to the capitol region. And Jones' bank accounts were positively affected by all of this. But Big Andy Jones had not paid much attention to the series of little assaults that had been happened across the continent, which had resulted in major changes in direction for the lives of those involved. Nor had the murder in the Montreal hotel come into Jones' paranoid purview.

forty-one

"We were just strangers in the fight"

Pink Riot, underground band. From their song 'No Name Sex'

While waiting to board to train to Montreal Frank had recharged his phone, replied to Boris' message then realized that he had called from some strange number so he left a message for Boris at the hotel lobby indicating that he would be arriving the next morning and would come to see him at the hotel before looking into the 'Conspiremouth'. Jack White had called him as well saying that he was awaiting instructions from either him or 'the others'. He said that they were keeping him under observation longer than he expected. He asked Frank to do something about that. Frank said to himself that he would attend to White later. For now, he would be okay in the hands of the doctors, beside Frank had no real legal way of getting him out. Jack White would just have to wait.

When Boris had been given the message from the hotel front desk that Frank would be coming to meet him in the morning, he was feeling no pain and had little sense of the time of evening it was. He had been in the corner of the hotel bar yammering away with a pretty blonde woman from California who was a distant relative of a slightly famous beatnik poet. After reading the message, he seemed to sober a bit.

"Listen, Linda, this is important" he had managed.

And afterwards he had said. "But you are much more important tonight."

And later in his hotel room he had said: "You know, Linda, I think we should get married."

And she had said: "Boris, but we hardly know each other."

And he had said: "What more do we need to know."

"I don't know" she had replied.

"Well, neither do I. So, let's do it as soon as possible, honey."

It was early morning when a loud knock on Boris' hotel room awoke him and his now fiancée, from their slumber. Boris got to his feet with the enthusiasm of a sloth.

"Who's at the door, baby?" said his new bride-to-be.

"Ah, I really don't know. Ah, maybe my business partner."

Now this was the first time that Boris had referred to Frank as his business partner. In fact, it was the first time he had seriously referred to anyone as his business partner. Those words coming out of his mouth had actually surprised him.

While Boris was putting on some clothes he yelled out. "Just a minute."

When he answered the door, it was indeed Frank. And Warren Kitchholm was with him.

"Hey Boris, I hope you can still see this morning."

"Come in, Frank. This is Linda. We're getting married."

"That's nice, Boris."

Both Frank and Kitchholm came into the single room that had a bathroom on the side.

"Linda this is Frank. I guess I work for him now."

Linda turned over, still keeping herself concealed under the sheets.

"Hello Frank" she said.

"Hello Linda" said Frank awkwardly.

"Listen Boris, maybe we'll wait for you down in the lobby" he continued.

Boris then took Frank aside and quietly said to Frank.

"Don't worry Frank I'm on the job. Linda is extremely cool and hip to the whole thing."

"Boris, I'm only concerned that you get your alcohol laden head turned around today so that we can get back to work. As for this Linda, we'll talk later. Whatever you do, don't make your life more complicated than it needs to be, Boris."

"Complicated is not the word, Frank. The word is stimulating. The word is passionate. Not dull, Frank."

"Okay, Boris, okay. Get dressed we'll be downstairs in the lobby."

Boris nodded at Kitchholm, checked his watch. It was just past nine.

Boris still didn't have his phone.

As Frank was leaving the room, he noticed a half bottle of bourbon on the coffee table.

"Boris, no bourbon for breakfast, okay."

"Now Frank, you know that I'm strictly a boiled egg and toast man in the morning."

"About a hundred years ago boiled would have been just the right word for you today, Boris. In fact, I may need to get boiled myself later, but not now."

He turned to Kitchholm who had been waiting by the door and was now smiling at the situation.

After they left Boris made some coffee in the small contraption provided. He quickly showered and dressed. Linda wanted him to stay. She stayed in bed.

"Linda honey, I promise I'll be right back. I'm going to book us in here another night. I just like to take care of business with Frank. And then we'll make plans to go to California."

Now during the night Linda had told him that she had been left a small ranch near San Luis Obiscpo in California by an ex-husband. She had money as well and that her two teenaged children lived there with her aunt and uncle. But it was large enough for everyone. She was 49-years-old. She was not quite convinced of the marriage thing yet but wanted Boris to go to California with her where she hoped that in time, she would have a better feeling about it. She believed that she had really fallen for Boris. Boris was the inspired sort of man that she felt that she needed right now in her life considering that her last husband, who had been a teacher at a small community college had grown into a pedantic bore, disillusioned by where the world was heading. They had been arguing constantly before they broke up. About politics, philosophy, and the arrangement of the furniture and the art work in their home. He soon became an ex-husband.

His name was Woody Fairchild Jr. He had inherited a fortune from his father who was William W. Fairchild, a television host who had given a generation advice on how to live well through diet, exercise and therapeutic activities. Woody had started out well in life with his father as an inspiration, but that adrenaline had dried up after the Fairchild Sr. had passed away. Woody had resigned himself to just meeting his basic responsibilities, of teaching and providing financially for his family. He stopped being sexually interested in his wife and began watching a lot of pornography on the internet. His answers to questions from his family became short and dismissive. So, Woody was not too upset about the divorce settlement. He asked for and got a portion of the cash and stock assets that he figured he needed to live on and left the house and other physical properties to Linda.

Boris was not only bent on marrying Linda for the money. He did feel a deeper connection with her. Whether it was just another of Boris' shots in the dark with women, he wasn't sure, but he really had been thinking that marriage would be a good thing for him since he had been hit on the head and had let go of Patricia. Besides Linda had a connection to an important literary scene in history. She even kept a poetic type journal and a blog of musings.

As for her part, she felt Boris had a good heart, was witty and intelligent, and liked to have a good time. Her kids were 16 and 18 and really didn't need fathering anymore. They had their own lives and would be happy if she was happy. Boris was a tour de force in her heart and soul. And why not jump at the opportunity. It had been quite a while since she had felt real love in her being. But she hesitated on immediately tying the knot, wisely wanting to run it by her friends and family first. She had learned something in her days about consulting others before making hasty decisions.

"I'll be here Boris. I'm going to order some breakfast. Love you."

"Love you" Boris replied back.

And love to them had been that simple. Boris was feeling like a teenager again, about to embark on a new adventure. He went downstairs to meet Frank and Warren Kitchholm.

About that time Butterworth and Brandon were still sitting in the airport restaurant and lounge waiting for the next flight to London to be cleared. An incident of some obvious importance had delayed flights to London. No one could confirm what had happened but something had taken place at the airport.

"Brandy, what do you suppose could be holding up flights to London?"

"Maddi, it's probably some terrorist threat that they are not telling us about."

"Terrorist threat" Butterworth laughed. "Why is it that our society has become so dependent on the negative emotional energy generated by the money crazed media over this 'terrorism' thing. Ever since humans began roaming the planet and developing self-consciousness we have been terrorized. Why is it so special these days? Make a note Brandy: All events and annunciations labelled terrorism are to be recast as simple human frustration at the stupidity and selfishness of world leaders. Nothing has changed because of technology or the advancement of science. More facts have only led to more ammunition for more stupid and selfish decisions. But I am an optimist Brandi and most people are despite lack of vision. Brandi, call up Professor Ambrose Keel for me."

Professor Keel had expected to debate with Butterworth, but after Butterworth's cranium had been targeted, he had cancelled the debate, telling the group of academics in charge of the conference that he had a headache. They hadn't questioned it. How could they have. And it was such a simple excuse that they could not argue with him. But Keel had been disappointed and had attempted to contact Butterworth three times without success in the past couple of days. Butterworth had not deemed it necessary to take his call. But now over a half a grapefruit and a café latte in the airport restaurant and lounge Butterworth had a precipitous desire to have a verbal interchange with his esteemed colleague.

Not saying a word, Brandon left a message with the distinguished academic in charge of the conference saying that Butterworth was keen on hearing from Keel. Then he proceeded to tackle his cereal and toast. The two exchanged smiles but finished eating in silence.

At the other end of the Montreal airport one of the thrice weekly flights from Pittsburgh was dropping off the self labelled heavenly body of Frida S. Wharton, who had managed to swiftly get a hold of $30,000 cash that had been buried on her now forfeited kale and cucumber health farm near the capital city of Pennsylvania and with two of her associates was carrying the cache into Canada.

The threesome had travelled separately to avoid suspicion, taking seats in three different sections of the plane. Wharton had foregone her normal two hour long cosmetic session that morning, preferring to try and remain incognito since her photo may have been disseminated worldwide by now. No one noticed her. That is until after she had gotten through security.

Wharton had followers everywhere and one of them just happened to be at the airport. The adherent to Wharton's afterlife scenario was a homeless woman who had lost her apartment in a fire and was now spending her time between shelters, the streets and the airport. She had a teenage son who had a strong dislike for his mother's involvement in the Wharton parade to the afterlife and had rebelled by running away from home and using alcohol and various narcotic substances to express his displeasure and disappointment with her. She had been in despair and the donations to Wharton and her prayers had not brought her son back home. Then the fire happened and for the last four months she had been living practically homeless with too much pride to rely on friends or to call up her distant family members. She was a single mother who had relied on a small cleaning job and a government check to make ends meet for her and her son. Now she was sitting with her bags in the airport wondering what she should do next.

Then as she was staring off into space, she spotted Wharton. At first, she hadn't recognized her having only seen her on television and in photos, but something looked familiar, so she continued to fix her gaze on the woman until it came to her brain that this was the woman to whom she had sent thousands of dollars to over the years. She still believed in Wharton and had been asking the Wharton spiritual gang to pray extra for her since the fire but had been unable to send much money. She was receiving government assistance and had sent a small portion of that to Wharton. Now her brain lit up when she saw Wharton. This was to be her saving grace. She had refused many of the offers of help from social agencies in the city, but this was different. Wharton, she knew had the keys to happiness. Her brain knew that because it had been repeatedly fed data that indicated that Wharton would lead all her followers to eternal peace. And she had refused to question it, because her fears of anything being different than the stories and visions that Wharton communicated were quite great.

How was she going to approach the Reverend Wharton?

Meanwhile Casey and Binky were leaving their abode to complete their task of bring a Whitmanesque enlightenment back to the world. Little did they know that the son of the woman in the airport had been reading 'Song of Myself' by Whitman, having come across the book at the drop-in centre. He was somehow being inspired by the words of a man who now only existed in soul and spirit and he had begun looking for his mother again. He was finally told by one the woman's shelters that she could be at the airport and that was his destination on this particular morning. He stood on a subway platform waiting to take the subway to a connecting bus that would bring him to the airport. Casey and Binky were about to take the same train. At that moment Whitman was a ghost swimming off of a beach in Long Island.

Whitman had despite fierce and calculated opposition kept a faith that was now manifesting itself again. He knew that there was a type of consciousness in humanity that held the mysteries of poetry, love, the soul, compassion and faith despite some smart skeptics dismissing the ultimate relevance of those concepts. But Whitman did not begrudge his enemies, he was amassing his energies to inspire them. He was laying yet another foundation for coming generations of seekers and those who looked 'elsewhere' for answers.

Jessica/Jesse was just starting his shift at the Coffee Express when he received a call from his brother. It was early afternoon.

305

"Jesse, how are you?"

"Fine. What's up?"

"Listen, I'm going to be busy all day. Are you going to be working all day?"

"Yeah, until nine."

"Look call me tonight. I want to talk with you."

"Okay. Sure. I'll call you"

And that was that.

I overheard Jessica/Jesse on the phone as I sipped an espresso. I was consumed with trying to find out if ghosts could swim.

forty-two

"Each time I take you into my secret place, I lose another room in my mansion"

Boris Swatcupso. From his poem 'Do ghosts have sex?"

Boris joined Frank in a busy hotel lobby. Part of his mind was still upstairs in the hotel room with Linda.

"So Frank, where to, next?"

"Boris, sit down."

Boris took a seat next to Frank, where Warren Kitchholm had been sitting. Kitchholm had obtained contact information on 'Conspiremouth' and Casey and Binky and was busy pursuing leads in another part of the lobby. He was trying to reach the two Whitman surrogates with his phone.

"Frank, what is it, why so serious?"

"Boris, we need to bare down on this case now. Kitchholm is trying to dig up an angle with "Conspiremouth', the paper where Butterworth and Brandon allegedly met Whitman himself."

"Or his stand-in ghost" added Boris with a chuckle.

"Boris, we must take even the rumors of ghosts or such apparitions seriously. Even if it doesn't appeal to your sense of logic or the laws of physics."

"Or reality."

"Right. Now let us assume that these two have some form of connection to at least a Whitman stand-in and by that, I mean someone who

307

has learnt of the poet's tendencies, beliefs, mannerisms and has been able to impersonate not only his soft and compassionate voice but his physical appearance. Who would be fooled by such a ruse?"

"We were, Frank."

"Yes, but not to the degree that these two semi-professional journalists were."

"So, the effect varies."

"Listen, Boris let's summarize. Each person that was hit on the head has had a change in direction happen in their lives. Yet, none of these people has been subject yet to a follow up. Nobody has given them any more directions, specific or non-specific."

"Now look are you suggesting that we have become zombies. Because if that's where you are going, I'm out of here. I will not work for any company that hunts ghosts, zombies or any other Hollywood created fictional entities. That's something that I will not be aligned with, Frank."

"Now come on, Boris, you know me better than that. I'm not about to embark on a wild chase after illusionary beings. But within the facts of the what has happened there lies some sort of cooperative anonymous source of direction which seems to be motivating everyone."

"Something like a cult or conspiracy."

"Some sort of club, Boris. And we are being recruited. Some have gone willingly others with reservation and us who have held out for further questioning."

"And who is at the head of this secret society?"

"Perhaps no one, Boris."

"No one? That's just silly. How can you have a club with no leadership?"

"Well, nominally it is Walt Whitman. At least his poetic outlook on things like the soul, love compassion and the like."

"Well now that is interesting. But how does that explain the fact that these people seem to be continuously obeying orders."

"It only appears that way, Boris. What they are actually doing is following their own particular inclinations, which up to that point they had not been fully conscious of."

"You're losing me, Frank."

"Look at us for example. I came into Montreal with very little direction or agenda. I was here basically to unwind and live free of responsibilities for awhile. We met. You were reeling from the departure of yet another woman from your life. You were despondent, Boris. And overly dramatic about it, until these assaults occurred. I believe they awakened us to things that we needed to do. Or perhaps really had a desire to do but were not sufficiently motivated to start. But we started. All on our own without being prompted."

"Yeah, ok, but what about people like Casey and Binky and the killer of that Whitman surrogate right here in this hotel?"

"Perhaps they had very little desire or ideas in their brains, whether conscious or sub-conscious that filled in the gap after they were hit. Or perhaps they saw just hitting others as being a core value to the world. Even if that was on a subconscious level. And as to Butterworth and Brandon, what has been lit is more of the intellectual variety. Kind of a re-energizer."

"You've been thinking, Frank."

"And you've been drinking, Boris."

"Not enough yet today."

"That will come, Boris. But first I want you to meet with this woman who seems obsessed with you. I suspect that she is a former lover, but maybe not."

"Oh, the one you texted me about. The one who says she has all this information on Whitman."

"Well, Boris maybe she does. Quick, Boris survey your romantic past and see if you can identify any women who may qualify. One who may be inclined to use literary or intellectual information as bait."

"Well, there was Jenny the yoga teacher, but is was too consumed with her body. Michelle was too innocent and good hearted to organize something like this. And Rachelle is here illegally. Why would she have risked being exposed? Helene is a possibility but that goes back way too far. Over ten years, Frank. Even before I met you. Very smart, but not a real game player. Now Patricia, she's angry at me right now I assume, but Frank, she threw me out. Why would she suddenly want me back so badly to do something like this?"

"Are you sure about this Patricia, Boris. She could have had a change of heart."

"I don't think so, not this one. In fact, I think she really had a thing for other women more than men. That's probably who she is with now. Another woman."

"Let's keep her in mind, Boris. Any other ones?"

"Lots, but none who were that serious."

"Ok, Boris try and remember. If not, we will soon find out. I have an email from her. She sent it just this morning."

And Frank showed Boris the email.

It read:

Don't delay – I know what you boys are up to. I want Boris to see me today. I will only tell Boris in person. Sterling Hotel lobby twelve noon. No cops I know that there was a murder. Just Boris.

"Isn't there something, Boris that rings a bell?"

"No. Sterling hotel, eh? I stayed at the Sterling hotel once during a drinking binge last year. I had a week off of work. There was four of us, but I don't remember any of the women."

"Well, there's only one thing to do and that is go there at noon today. I'll stay in the shadows. I don't think she knows me by face, but I don't want to take any chances. She contacted Kitchholm so she must have been near us when he met us at the Le Café Fritz, maybe in disguise. She could have gotten Kitchholm's email from one of the news websites that he writes for."

"Now, I'm getting really curious, Frank."

"So, I'm I."

Boris' drifted back to the Le Café Fritz and the movie posters that hung there. He thought about the movie 'Metropolis'. He recalled its eerie dystopia. He cried a little inside. Frank could see that Boris probably needed a drink and his new love interest, Linda.

"Frank, listen, go upstairs and take care of this new woman, what's her name…"

"Linda."

"Yeah, Linda. Get yourself a couple of drinks. Drink slow, keep it cool and be back here at 11:30. We'll go together to the Sterling. It's not that far

311

away. Meanwhile I'm going to do some internet searching. I may need a drink after this day myself."

"Listen, Frank don't get drunk on my account."

"No, Boris believe me I have enough drinking accounts of my own."

And with a smile Boris got up and left.

Warren Kitchholm and Frank Lee were left in the hotel lobby with a smattering of guests, some of whom were checking out. Frank spent his time observing the guests. He was beginning to get good at doing that. It seemed to be in his blood.

On the metro Casey and Binky were moving towards Lionel-Groulx Station in order to make the connection to the airport. Casey was thinking of why a metro station in this day and age was still named after an overt racist. Binky was noticing what the teenage kid was reading. A copy of Whitman's 'Song of Myself". He nudged Casey, who was sitting beside him. Casey looked and noticed. They smiled at one another.

When they had arrived at the station all three of them boarded the same bus. The two Whitman representatives had both resolved in their minds that this teenage brain consuming 'Song of Myself' did not require any slight brain trauma. They left him alone yet continued to observe him.

At the airport Frida S. Wharton had given her cohorts instruction to meet her at a downtown hotel a couple of hours after the arrival of their flights. She was hungry upon arriving in Montreal having been unable to stomach the discount airliners food on the flight. It didn't have the heavenly stamp of Wharton approval. So, Wharton had found a little deli type restaurant in the airport arrivals lounge and had ordered a sandwich and a juice using some of the nearly $10,000 in cash that she was carrying with her. Most of the money was in American twenty-dollar bills that she had stuffed in a briefcase. As her mouth was watering, preparing for the first mouthful of a light turkey sandwich with tomato and lettuce, a scraggly female voice spoke to her.

"Excuse me, you are Reverend Wharton?"

The Wharton brain had a fury of chemical reactions hit it.

She gave the addresser a dumbfounded stare as she prepared a response, then finally said.

"Yes, I am. And you are?"

"I'm Emily Charters. I'm going to heaven with you when the ship comes to pick us up."

Wharton smiled. Her brain slowed down.

"Of course. You'll have to excuse me Emily Charters, but I'm pressed for time."

Wharton reached into a saddle bag that she had placed on the floor beside her and pulled out a small book. It was entitled 'Where to after the digital world is obsolete?' She handed it to Emily.

"Or perhaps a different one."

Wharton had said this after she had noticed that the women appeared to be dressed in clothes that hadn't been changed in days. Which was true. So, Wharton found another little book entitled 'How we will be rewarded for our sacrifices. And soon.' This she also handed to Emily.

"Thank you, Reverend Wharton. I know you don't know me, but I've been a big supporter of you for years. Now I'm destitute. My son has run away and I'm living on the streets. I really need your prayers. Can you pray for me?"

"Certainly, Mrs... ah.."

"Emily. Emily Charters."

"Emily Charters. May God bless you and bring you rewards for all of the sacrifices that you have made to help fulfill the destiny of the universe. God will shower you with blessings in the future. Emily we will be rescued from this tortuous process that is life. I suffer at this too Emily, just remember I need your support too. So, may God bless us both today."

With that Wharton smiled and gave Emily a five-dollar bill. She wanted to begin her new Canadian enterprises with a certain amount of goodwill. Emily smiled and thanked Frida S. Wharton walking away with her books and a finn. Wharton was glad to be rid of her, because she had many other things on her mind.

Moments later, Wharton had finished as much of her turkey sandwich as she was going to eat. She was collecting her bags and standing up when Emily Charters came by again and said,

"Sorry to bother you again. Could you pray for my fifteen-year-old son, Evan? I don't know where he is. He could be in a lot of danger. He ran away over a month ago. Please help him."

This plea was deep and sincere. Wharton felt it too. And really replied in kind. She sincerely hoped that Emily Charters and her son would be reunited and be happy.

"Yes, I will Emily. And you can be certain that God will answer your prayers. Have a great day and may God bless you."

And with that she walked off.

Emily Charters wasn't completely sure that she felt any better than before she had encountered the Reverend Wharton, but at least she had a little more hope for the future.

Wharton's brain was more focussed on her future with the nearly $30,000 that she and her devoted employees had brought into the country.

All the theorizing about higher beings and universal powers was not occupying much brain space for Maddi and Brandon, who were now informed that they may have to make arrangements to stay in Montreal for another night. An announcement had been made throughout the airport that all flights to London had been delayed at least until 23h00 or eleven that night.

Maddi was very whimsical about the whole thing.

"Well, Keel may yet get to debate me on this Sustainability thing."

Brandon smiled and said,

"Well, Maddi I am now certain that it is foreordained that Ambrose J. Keel's consciousness be interrupted by these Whitman associates."

"You may be trying to be jocular, but I believe that you are on the correct path of thinking Brandi."

Brandi was slowly drinking a coffee.

Butterworth was becoming impatient but chose to not show it. He needed to remain calm.

"Brandi, I think we should get a hotel room here at the airport, even if it is just for the day. I need some private space to work on this address that I want to make when we arrive back in London."

"Sure, I'll go and do that now."

"I'll stay here, Brandi. The hotel may be already full because of all the cancelled flights."

Brandi left. It was now just past eleven o'clock.

At the Sterling Hotel Boris was sitting in a cramped hotel lobby looking suspiciously guilty of something. At least that was how the middle-aged man behind the front desk saw it.

Boris had just come in without addressing the desk or stating his reason for being there and had plopped himself down on a small ornate love seat that seemed to have been left over from the set of an historical movie. The clerk was eyeing Boris periodically. Finally, fifteen minutes passed. Boris looked a little tired and haggard, but had managed to pick up a small bottle of bourbon on his way over to the hotel, so that gave him a somewhat more confident and alive look than he would have had without it. Boris dared not take a nip right in the hotel lobby. He kept his eyes peeled for a woman.

Standing just outside the front entrance to the store front hotel was Frank, who was acting nonchalant in chatting up a panhandler. Frank was dressed in a light suit jacket, jeans and sneakers. He did not want to stand out in any way. He kept his eye on Boris. He had told him not get himself into any jam with the hotel because of his bottle, which he thought was not the greatest idea in the first place.

Then a woman came out of the rickety elevator. She was dressed all in black and had violet hair. She had chopsticks up there and makeup. Her dark outfit was loose fitting so that one could not tell if she was wearing a dress or pants. She walked assertively towards Boris. Boris instantly recognized her.

"Well, there you are. You, big drunken creep" she said in a British accent.

Boris was quiet. He wanted to take a belt from his bottle but resisted the urge.

The woman stood over Boris.

"Let's go up to my room. I have something to show you."

Boris remained quiet but arose obediently. He glanced out of the plate glass front window to see if Frank had noticed what was transpiring. Indeed, he had. Frank nodded slightly. Boris felt reassured. He went with the woman into the elevator.

Now Frank knew that he had to follow quickly. He had to find out which room this woman was in.

"Excuse me, my friend, who was just sitting here in the lobby is visiting with his sister who is staying in the hotel. Now I have some money for him and he forget to tell me what room number that his sister was in. Could you tell me what room the woman who just came down here is in?"

"And who are you, sir?" the front desk man said with a slight Quebecois accent.

"My name is Frank Harmon. I'm a friend of the gentleman who just got on the elevator."

"Oh, the drunk. I saw his bottle. You know, I cannot just give out that information without checking first with the woman."

"Well, you know I want to surprise her. You see I'm an old friend from high school. She doesn't know that I'm here. She was my girlfriend back then. I want it to be like a surprise reunion. Just the three of us."

Frank was not sure that the clerk was buying it.

The man behind the counter smirked a bit.

"She's in thirty-five. Third floor to the left."

Wow, thought Frank that was easy. And he didn't even have to tip him.

Frank intention was not to make his presence known to the woman, but to listen for any unusual sounds coming from the room. He wanted to make sure his partner was okay. He got on the elevator and rode up to the

317

third floor, found the room and pulled out his phone. He would use the device as something to focus on if someone passed by in the hallway, but the hallway was barren and quiet. It smelt of cheap disinfectant and marijuana. Frank found a spot near thirty-five to lean against and kept his ears peeled. Now if Boris had not lost his phone, he could have texted him, thought Frank.

It was close to noon when Casey, Binky and Emily Charter's gangly looking son, Evan arrived at the airport. Casey and Binky were there to reassure Butterworth, whom they had no other way of reaching, while Evan had come to find his mother. Evan had begun to feel badly about leaving her alone. Some of those bad feelings had been brought about by the chemicals released in his brain while reading Walt Whitman. In fact, both good and bad feelings had come from his venturing into that poetic mind field. Evan felt a sense of inspired self-confidence that he could be a good son for his mother, but he also had a slight feeling of guilt for not living up to that. He was determined to find her. He had been looking for two days, before he had received the tip that she may be at the airport.

After checking on flights to London, Casey and Binky realized that Butterworth and his lover, Brandon were probably still at the airport, or in a nearby hotel. They went to the customer information desk to see if they could get Butterworth paged.

Butterworth and Brandon were just exiting the departure level area on their way to the airport hotel when Butterworth heard the announcement in French first and then in English.

"Would a Mr. Madison Butterworth please come to the customer information booth on the arrivals level. A Mr. Madison Butterworth, would you please come to the customer information booth on the arrivals level, please."

"Now Brandi, what is it now?" said Butterworth impatiently.

"Probably some technicality."

"Customer information booth. I doubt that, Brandi. It must be Keel with a message. Now why didn't he just phone you or something."

Butterworth never used a cell phone, but Brandon had one. He rarely used it, but it was convenient to have.

"Now why would Keel bother to come all the way to the airport when he could have just left a message?"

"Well, maybe he is like me and likes to deliver his messages in person. Anyhow let's go and find out what this new mystery is."

The two of them began walking toward the arrivals level when they were approached by Emily Charters.

"Excuse me sir. Is there any chance that you could help me? I'm stranded here at the airport and I need bus fare to get downtown."

Butterworth looked the woman over. She looked in despair. Butterworth was moved. He remembered his days in the Soviet Union. He recalled poverty and wretchedness. He had become a minor intellectual celebrity, but part of him was still with this woman. Especially now with his newfound mental outlook. He smiled at her, put his luggage down and pulled his wallet out.

Just at that moment a crackled youthful voice came from nearby.

"Mom."

The woman turned towards the voice and recognizing her son exclaimed.

"Evan."

"Mom."

Evan strode right up to his mother and embraced her.

She was close to tears.

"Sorry, mom. I screwed up."

"That's okay, son."

Butterworth and Brandon were observing all of this with a certain awe. Especially Butterworth, whose consciousness was firing out signals of warmth and love. He turned to Brandon and wanted to say something profound and intimate to him but could not find the words. Butterworth was speechless for a moment. He stood there dumbfounded, but not without emotion, holding his opened wallet in his right hand.

"Brandon, we have managed to catch one of life's great moments. The reunion of a mother and a son." Butterworth finally was able to say.

Brandon said nothing.

As Evan was hugging his mother, his copy of Whitman's 'Song of Myself' feel out of his jacket pocket and onto the floor. It was quickly spotted by Butterworth who picked it up. His brain chemistry was suddenly charged when he read the title.

"Now, that's more than mere coincidence, Brandon. Look Whitman's 'Song of Myself'"

"Not the whole 'Leaves of Grass'?"

"No, Brandon. Excuse me young man, you dropped this."

Evan turned from his mother.

"Oh, yeah. Awesome book."

"Indeed, it is. I am curious how did you come across it?"

"I just found it."

"Found it?'

"Yeah, just found it."

"That's just extraordinary. So, young man what are your impressions of Mr. Whitman?"

"I think he was a little weird, but in a cool way. He made me want to find my mom."

"Fantastic. Just this little slim volume did that?"

"Well, sort of. Who are you anyway? Do you know this guy, mom?"

Emily Charters turned to look at Butterworth.

"Well, Evan this nice man was just about the help me get downtown. I'm almost broke."

"Sure, that's cool."

With that Butterworth felt the need to introduce himself.

"I'm Madison J. Butterworth and this is my partner, Brandon Pierce. We are kind of stranded here ourselves. You see all of the planes to London have been delayed for the day."

Evan was quiet but seem interested in Butterworth and Brandon.

Butterworth handed Emily two twenty-dollar bills. She took them with some hesitation, first glancing at her son.

Butterworth felt inspired.

"You know, young man, if you want, we can talk some more about this poem. I would really like to know which parts hit you the hardest."

Brandon interrupted.

"Maddi, customer service booth."

321

"Oh, yes. Look you two just go over to that coffee shop area and wait for us. Here, take another ten dollars."

The mother and son looked unsure about the whole unfurling of events. But still feeling good at being reunited they were not inclined to rush out of the airport and so quietly accepted Butterworth's offer to go and wait for him and Brandon in the coffee shop. And they gracefully took his ten dollars.

At the customer service booth Casey and Binky were waiting to see if their summoning of Butterworth was going to yield any results.

"Hey, Casey what is it that we need to say to this guy anyhow?"

"Just that Whitman and we are with him. We have his back. We are big supporters of him now. And the fact that he may need us in the future."

"Right"

When Butterworth spotted the pair as he was approaching the booth, he had another chemical reaction in his cerebral cortex.

"You guys" he blurted out uncharacteristically.

Brandon hung back.

"Professor Butterworth. Don't be scared. We're not here to hit you on the head" Casey said.

"Well, that's a relief. I suppose it's only one attack per person" he joked.

"Yes, that is quite true."

"It is nice to see you again and I've come to some sort of understanding of what it is that you and Whitman's 'ghost' are up to, but I have important things to attend to. What is it that you want?"

"We wanted nothing. Just to reassure you that we will be around if you need us and that Mr. Whitman is also available anytime."

"Well, young men I'm not in the habit of holding séances."

"Don't need to do anything so freaky. Just meditate on his poetry. I'm sure you know how to do that, Professor."

"Very good. And do we ever get to meet the man again?"

"Maybe. He may reappear."

"Well, good. I'm glad you came all this way to tell me this. You two seem to be quite dedicated."

"We do have lives other than this."

"Oh, really. Well one day you will have to tell me all about it."

With that he reached out to shake Casey and Binky's hands.

"Good luck the rest of the way with the cause."

Butterworth turned with Brandon to go back to Emily and her son Evan.

Casey's phone sang. It was Frank's email requesting information on 'Conspiremouth.'

He recognized Frank's name. It was Casey who had hit Frank on the head a few days back.

forty-three

"I only heard the voices of small people wanting big things to happen"

Boris Swatcupso. From his poem 'Marxburg, USA'

At one of the airport restaurants sat two men and a woman around a Formica table with hard backed chairs. They were amiable looking people. Amongst the weary, excited and shuffling travellers they did not stand out. They were looked upon by security or anyone that was interested as just a small group of fliers, like the rest of the people who were at the airport. Even if one looked closely, their smiling faces did not betray any sinister intentions. But if one were to engage them in any type of sober or reflective conversation it would not take long to pick up that their world view was cynical and dark. It postulated a theory that life could be completely explained and that it had an absolute beginning and an absolute end. Therefore, at some point there would be nothing left to learn or strive for. In fact, this trio really thought that that day was near. They had a deep distrust and disgust for anyone who walked about with any great optimism. But they were careful not to show their resentment for these souls that ran toward the mysteries of the universe. In reality, they were 'agent-provocateurs'. These three were now consuming freshly baked croissants with liverwurst and washing it down with herbal tea.

Downtown at the Coffee Express Theodor received a phone call from one of these three.

I was seated only three seats away from Theodor and only heard one side of the dialogue, but it seemed relevant enough to be worthy of eavesdropping. I tried to focus my eyes on the line up for coffee at the counter, while listening to pick up Theodor's end of the phone call. Jesse/Jessica,

Frank's little brother seemed to be in a pleasant working mood behind the counter. They had taken notice of my presence over the past five days but had put me down as just a 'new regular' and had not suspected that I was being included as a minor character in a tale that involved a collection of uncanny characters. They were becoming more of a she each day, but to them this was not something that he suspected as being of any interest to the world. Jesse/Jessica was truly a modest, friendly and reserved soul. I wanted understand them more deeply.

"Well understood. We are to proceed as planned" Theodor said to his cohorts as he sat at the Coffee Express with his latte.

Then there was a pause.

"All of the targets are assembling at the airport."

Another pause.

"I have complete synchronization."

As I listened to this one end of the conversation, I began to sense that events or really serious, dangerous and violent may be unfolding. I thought that things go another way but as I reflected on the tone and content of Theodor's words, I realized that maybe his alliance with Whitman may have been a ruse. I was highly suspicious that Theodor may be a double agent.

"I will be there at 1700 hours."

I was becoming alarmed and I looked at Jesse/Jessica as they prepared an order for a suited man asking myself how will this play out for them?

325

forty-four

"She trampled on the black rose That I was saving for a rainy day."

Boris Swatcupso. From his poem "MoneyLove"

Inside room thirty-five at the Sterling Hotel Boris sat listening to all that he had done wrong in his seven years spent in London, before he had managed to come to Canada and met Helene, the government worker who had been the one to really acclimatize him to life in North America, or at least Canada. The woman who was going through this litany of betrayals and offenses was his only ex-wife. She had hit on hard times financially and came across a small article on the internet about Boris Swatcupso, the poet and sometimes sculptor. If it had not been for Helene, who still had a certain love and loyalty towards Boris, from older days the tiny two paragraph piece would not have been published and this ex-wife of Boris' would not have borrowed money from dubious characters to come to Canada in the hopes of arousing guilt in the man that walked out on supporting her. Also, a part of her still loved Boris. She was a little hopeful of re-uniting with him, so her berating of him at the Sterling Hotel was slowly turning into a seduction of this still virile, mentally stimulating middle-aged man, who for all the money in the world could not recall her name.

Why had he blocked it?

She was still attractive, but she talked too much for Boris' liking. He had never really loved her, he had just liked her company a bit and had really only agreed to marriage based on his immigration status, figuring that she wasn't that bad of a catch. This cavalier and arrogant attitude had soon caught up with him and it had resulted in a divorce after just over a year. From there he had begun planning his escape to Canada at the same time avoiding his financial obligation to her.

326

As she was talking about how she had tracked him down to a series of bars that he hung around in, his brain unblocked the name. Chloe. Must have been the bar references that got his neurons flowing.

"Chloe, what I don't understand is how you came into contact with Walt Whitman?"

"He was a great American poet during the Civil War."

"Yes Chloe, but you told Frank that you knew where he was."

Now that Boris had recalled her name, he would be employing it at every opportunity.

"I was only saying that to get your attention."

"Oh."

Memories began to flood in for Boris.

Boris had asked Chloe to be his wife. He remembered that they had met in a creative writing class in London. Chloe had a stable job with the research department of the BBC. Having dated for close to a year he had married Chloe even though he had not been sure that he loved her. He needed the stability and the advantage of being married to a British citizen. After a while it became apparent that this union was not to be. They had fought through a divorce, before Boris took off for Canada. That was over twelve years ago. Why had she come all this way just to see him? Boris couldn't believe that it was only the money that had motivated her. Maybe she still loved him. The more he gazed at her the stronger he began to feel an empathic wave for her come over him.

"Boris, what you did was nasty. Leaving without any forwarding information. I could have withstood the loneliness, but to completely abandon me with no explanation, Boris that was the worst thing anyone has ever done to me."

Boris began to feel some remorse. After all she hadn't been a bad woman, just too long-winded for his liking. She had taken the reins too many times and despite his dominate nature he never had considered resorting to forceful means to try and control her. Boris listened to Chloe and knew that he probably owed her something.

"Chloe, listen. I don't know why you came all this way. But all that I can offer you is an apology for being such a jerk."

"That's a start, Boris. And a good one. Boris I've run into some financial snags, but nothing that can't be fixed. You were the only one that I could think of that I still believed was capable of helping me and really would. What you did years ago, I willing to forgive and forget, Boris. I still have feelings for you. Then I read where you were a famous artist."

"I'm not exactly famous. I don't make enough to live on it."

"Really, Boris. You're still boozing it up I can see. Maybe that's why you never made it as an artist.'

"I sell a few pieces here and there."

"And what else do you do Boris?"

"I work here and there. I'm working on becoming a private detective. I have a partner."

"Really"

Chloe laughed and said,

"A private detective. Now who's going to believe that you have any business being a private detective. Who are you kidding, Boris?"

"Well, I just sort of stumbled upon it, my friend Frank and me."

"Now who is this Frank? Some drinking buddy you met in a pub?"

"Actually, he is some drinking buddy that I met. But not in a pub. And he is a pretty sharp cookie, Chloe. He is no slouch."

"Another 'ladies' man' I suppose."

"No, not at all."

"Oh, he's gay?"

"Well actually I'm not sure what he is, Chloe. Sex just does not seem to be a factor in his mentality."

"Okay. So, you're going into the detective business."

"Yes. Listen, Chloe. How much money do you have?"

"Enough to stay here a week."

Boris was having a really sympathetic heart for her. Maybe he did love her after all? No way, he thought next.

"Chloe, why don't you stay at my loft. You'll save money and we can catch up. But I will warn you I'm working on a case and I'll be out a lot."

Boris' boasting had risen to the surface again.

"Oh, a case? You mean that Whitman thing? Wasn't he gay, Boris?"

"Probably. That just makes it all the more intriguing, Chloe."

"It certainly does, Boris."

"So, what do you say Chloe. Are you going to come and stay with me for awhile?"

"Boris, I might just do that. In fact, I might just decide to stay in Canada. Get a job."

"So, it wasn't just me that brought you here."

"Mostly you Boris."

Boris and Chloe looked at each other for a moment. Then Boris jotted down his contact information and handed it to her.

"I lost my phone. But my email and address are on there. You'll be here for a couple of days?"

"Yes."

"Well, I don't have time to take you to my place now and besides I don't think you know what you want to do. I'll leave a message here, probably tonight or tomorrow. Take care, Chloe."

Boris said her name like he had been saying it for years. He then walked out of the room. Frank was right behind him.

They both rode down the elevator in silence aware that it might be wise to be out of the range of others before they discussed the matter at hand.

Chloe laid back on the bed in her hotel room at the Sterling and thought about Boris. She really had loved him, and still did.

Theodor arrived at the airport in a cab. He looked dour and determined. He headed straight for the airport bar where the group of three personages dressed in black had assembled. It was close to five o'clock. He found them. He sat down next to them. There was very little acknowledgement among the group of each other's presence. The bar was getting a little busy. It stood out in an opened area of the airport. No doors or exits or entrances were required to visit it. Passersby could see the whole place as they walked by.

"Everything seems to be coming together" said one of the three.

"It is. All we need is Frank, Boris and this Professor Keel to show up. And they will be here by tonight" said another.

330

"How is that possible?"

"I've made arrangements to get them here before midnight."

"What about that translator guy, Shultzmann?"

"He's not important tonight. He may come on his own."

"So, Keel gets it tonight?"

"Yes, and then we execute the plan."

Theodor hadn't said a word.

Boris had convinced Frank that a booth at the DregStore was the ideal spot to discuss what had transpired in room thirty-five of the Sterling Hotel. He still had to call Linda. His thoughts about her come back into focus. His feelings for her had not been trite. Marriage had been proposed. Now, he saw the irrationality of the Linda tryst. A drink would help he thought and then he would call Linda and try and explain that he had only been foolish the night before. He ordered a double. Frank was still holding out on the booze until his first foray into the world of unlicensed private investigation had come to some satisfactory conclusion.

He listened with patience to Boris' litany of an on again off again love and feigned care for this British gal named Chloe. He listened as Boris unfurled his latest twisted path that was to suddenly leave another woman deceived. He would figure out Linda in a short while. He would call her with an excuse for being late.

Boris' storytelling was beginning to weight on Frank level of tolerance after awhile. This Chloe though seemed of greater importance to Boris suddenly considering that Chloe had basically thrown caution to the wind in coming across the Atlantic Ocean to find Boris. She must have some serious intentions toward him. Frank thought this woman was not going to go back to London empty-handed, that is if she had any intention of going back to across the pond at all. Frank decided to remain quiet for awhile about Linda, Chloe and any other woman that Boris was bring into his romantic diatribe. Then Boris became all philosophical.

"So Frank, all of my dilemmas have come to the forefront now. Woman, Wine and Work. Is there a clear choice or path, Frank? Which do I pick, first? Do I pick all three to fix at once? You see my problem, Frank?"

"Boris, just listen to me for a moment. First, I have the funds necessary to sustain us for a few months. I just checked my financial status. I going to sell some small investments that I inherited recently to set us up. So, that's the work issue dealt with for now. Next is what you are holding in your hand. Just keep it periodic, for now. Wait until we have a lull in the action to break out. We'll deal with that as we proceed. Woman are the least of your issues. This Chloe, what can she do?"

"What do you mean 'do'?"

"Skills, talent, background."

"She worked in research at the BBC. She can read, write and has a lot of energy."

"She must have a lot of patience and be a little strange to be in love with you and come all this way, giving up what seems like a good job."

"I don't know the circumstances surrounding her employment. She didn't tell me."

"Maybe Boris, we could use her. Let's keep her on our good side, my friend. She has exhibited dedication, loyalty and determination. I like that."

"I never saw it like that, Frank."

"You are not seeing it at all. One because you had put her on the scrap heap in your mind. And two because of these impulsive 'Linda' decisions that cloud everything. Only an atomic explosion could break through that wall of denial that you've built around you. All of course done for the self-preservation of your own ego, Boris."

"Really, my friend. And where did you pick up all of this amateur psycho babble?"

"You must remember we spent a lot of time together. After all the time we spent together almost anyone would be able to see these things. Except of course the person it applied to. I've learned that a person just never sees themselves like anyone else does."

"That is amateur psychology if I've ever heard it. But, about Chloe, I think you may be right. But she may be too emotional right now to focus on doing a job. She's not even legally allowed to work, Frank. Remember she is only a tourist in the country."

"All that is bureaucracy. Easily overcome, Boris."

As Boris drank another mouthful of draft beer, Frank's phone buzzed. It was Kitchholm.

"Frank, I'm at the 'Conspiremouth' office, talking to the landlord. I found out some interesting facts about the people that operate this paper and pay the rent here."

"Warren, that's great. I hope you haven't attracted the cops."

"I don't think so."

"Good. Meet me at the Montreal International Airport in two hours. Let's say 8 o'clock."

"The airport? Where are we going? Listen I can justify the expense of coming to Montreal, but I'm not flying around the world."

"Relax. We're not leaving Montreal."

Frank put his phone away and looked at Boris.

"You're going to have to get a new phone, Boris."

"Nonsense, Frank. I feel perfectly in touch with the universal. Every fibre of my being is vibrating with the voices of the universe. Words and images are pouring into my consciousness as we sit here, Frank. I am in tune with the cosmos. No apparatus will provide me with anything more of what I need."

With that he downed a double shot of bourbon and gazed off into space.

"Boris, we are going to the airport."

The new bartender at the DregStore was eyeing them as they left.

Professor Ambrose J. Keel had had his phone off all day. He had been in seminars and lectures. The conference had ended around dinner time and Keel was at his hotel room near the university when he checked his phone for messages. The third one in was from Butterworth. Keel opened a bottle of organic soya milk, which he just purchased on his way to the hotel and took a long drink. He re-read the text from his esteemed colleague and focused on an appropriate response.

After jotting down some notes and pacing a bit in his room, he gathered his papers and the small amount of clothing that he had with him, made a phone call to a travel agency and checked out of the hotel.

The sunset was orange, red and purple off the Long Island shore. Children and couples frolicked or just sat looking out at the ocean. Nearby a crew of road construction workers who had worked overtime were shouting proud words and accolades at each other as they finished up for the day. A bearded soft-spoken man walked past these men still periodically looking back at the rainbow-like sunset. He smiled at the workmen and began walking down the road disappearing into the sultry evening air.

Hearty laughter and a shrill voice were the sounds that came out of the rear of the airport coffee shop where an unlikely quartet had gathered.

"Maddi, I haven't seen you laugh like this since I've met you."

"Well, Brandi, Emily and Evan here have just the most amazingly funny and inspiring stories. I am going to sell everything Brandi and we are taking jobs as instructors of street people."

Now Brandi was getting a little worried. Was Butterworth going mad? Was he aping senility? Or was this shift in character genuine?

He had seen Maddi be inspired before, but not with such practical purpose and commitment. And commitment was the operative word for Brandi here.

Emily Charters and her teenage son Evan were engaging in telling Maddi tales of both funny and sad of being without a home and the consequences that came about as a result. Maddi seemed to Brandi to be completely at ease with them. Brandi was not so accommodating, but he had decided that the Professor was gathering data for a penetrating story on desolation in the twenty first century, or something like that.

Finally, there was a quiet moment. Maddi turned to the mother and son combo and expressed his gratitude and pledged to find them an abode within the week. He passed on his contact information and told them he would provide an account for them to use for their living expenses for a year.

Now, Brandi was getting very nervous.

After another silent moment Butterworth said,

"Well, my Brandi, we must go to our hotel room. I need to work on my manifesto. And I am sure that Keel will be here in an hour of so."

"Ambrose J. Keel. Mr. Sustainability."

Brandi echoed Butterworth's tone of enthusiasm when he said this, but really didn't feel it.

With that Butterworth embraced Emily and Evan and walked out of the shop with Brandi in tow.

Now the sinister plotting of the darkly dressed group who had dispersed from the airport bar and were now at various points in the airport was not motivated as much by any apocalyptic vision of the world as much as by a deep frustration at how people didn't behave like this group of people thought they should. This group believed that all ethical and moral behavior should be forced onto people by the discovery not only of natural and physical law but by the implementation of human laws which would compel people to obey its dictates. They were a sad bunch who were without the means to divert themselves from their misdirected good intentions. They were seated just outside of the airport bar where Frank, Boris and Warren Kitchholm were to meet. Ambrose J. Keel had arranged to meet Maddi and Brandi at the airport hotel.

Casey and Binky were also near by, having been instructed by Frank to be on the lookout for him.

As for Frida S. Wharton, she had long departed the airport. She had met up with her associates in an apartment suite around supper time. When she had taken a stroll out onto the balcony of her building she was suddenly hit from behind by some heavy object. As were her two friends. Her assailant had left the money behind.

     Jesse/Jessica and I had fallen into a conversation that afternoon and I had related what I knew of their brother's story up to that point to them and they had been interested enough to come with me to the airport to see its conclusion.

forty-five

"I've never met a dead author that I didn't like."

Max Katz. Comedian and English Literature professor

Keel rapped on Butterworth's hotel room door.

Both were dressed in suit jackets without ties. This was their usual attire. Brandon had shed his jacket in favor of a powder blue dress shirt only. After formalities Butterworth began.

"Now you see Keel I have no fundamental disagreement with you in regards to the idea that we encourage 'Sustainability'. But what a tepid word for keeping life going. I see no strength in it. What are we to learn from it? That we must stay alive. Not brilliant enough, I think. I have written a manifesto on how to tap into the potential of young people. We must not just keep them alive, but nurture inspired thought and dedicated action."

"I would be very interested in reading it. Is it ready for consumption?"

"Consumption, my ass, Keel. People will not consume this like an apple pie, it is something to remotely produce a spark in them. Like me getting hit on the head."

"Yes, what is this about your getting hit on the head, Butterworth?"

Brandon spoke up from his seat just behind Butterworth.

"Maddi got assaulted at the university yesterday and has been reeling with new thoughts since then."

"I see, so Maddi, as you call him, is now prescribing head attacks for everyone. And this Professor is how you see life being saved from peril on this planet?"

Butterworth busted out a strong laugh.

"I don't know Keel. But it may work for a few of us. I don't advocate violence, far from it, but a loving tap never hurt anyone."

"I think you've lost it Butterworth. That would be just like a return to corporeal punishment. It's a complete regression."

"No returning to anything, Keel. Have you read Walt Whitman lately?"

"No why?"

"He may be here tonight?"

"Are you going to lecture me on Whitman now and naturalism, Emerson, Thoreau and the like."

"No. I don't wish to lecture anymore."

"Fine, then let's leave 19th century transcendentalism alone."

"Fine with me. Why talk about someone when you can have the actual person himself make an appearance?"

"Oh, so you have an impersonator of Whitman here with you?"

"No, it's him"

"Very good. Well, where is he?"

"I believe he is en route Keel."

Now Professor Keel was in no way believing that either the body or soul of the real Walt Whitman was scheduled to make an appearance at the Montreal International Airport. He saw Butterworth as conducting an elaborate ruse in order to make his point. It somewhat fit with the far-fetched ideas he had sometimes proposed on his radio programs. But Keel was game and would wait around a while to see what Maddi had up his sleeve.

Casey and Binky sat down at a corner table in the airport where they could easily observe the flow of people moving in front of the wide and open entrance. They had not talked much during their day. Both had ordered fruit juices and were waiting for something to happen. Now Frank had managed to establish contact that day with Casey via his 'Conspiremouth' contact information. The texting had been in a somewhat cryptic style, but it did give Frank the insight that he needed to determine roughly most the events that would transpire that evening at the airport. Casey kept his partner in the loop also. As he sat at the airport, he was now contemplating much of what he and Frank had texted about. Casey was at his core a shy young man who had heartfelt convictions about life. He had believed deeply in the pursuit of his social convictions and really was not very impressed by what the previous generation had done to instill any redeeming social values back into society. He had read all of the literature which encouraged people of all stripes to upset the norms of the older generations and had taken to it with vigor. Frank had texted him that he too had not been able to settle down to a career or life situation that he found satisfying until strangely enough he had been tapped by him outside of the Le Café Fritz just a few days ago. When he read this, it had caused Casey to smile, which had been a rare occurrence in his life.

Later he would feel a kinship with Frank and some others that he had not wanted to feel. He would not be able to openly admit this. Especially to Binky. The two had been part of the struggle against the conspiracy of the machine for years and did not easily admit new people into their circle without some major vetting. This had given Casey a certain sense of

340

exclusivity in his life, as it did his partner. Frank had been the first to get hit on the head and the first to provide an explanation for what had happen to them, even if had been only through a series of abbreviated texts. Casey now fully understood his own experience with Walt Whitman. Casey had first encountered the man while walking through a park. This man had been collecting empty bottles and cans. He had somehow started up a conversation with Casey about how society was in danger of sinking into a simple money obsessed world where all other priorities were shoved aside in favor of the idea that money equalled success. This had impressed him. They had continued the conversation at a nearby café. After a few weeks of talking Casey had been convinced that the gentlemen that he was engaged with was perhaps a surrogate of Whitman. He brought his close friend Binky into the circle that had begun to grow. Now the idea that the man that they were dealing with was actually the resurrected Whitman was formed as a lark originally by the group, who chose to dress in black and began these little sometimes innocent assaults on people based on what they determined to be inspired thought. They had a vague notion that they had tapped into something called a cosmic or collective consciousness. This was encouraged by the reading of people like Bucke, C.G Jung, Bauderlaire, Francis Bacon, Spinoza and even Swedenborg. So, Casey, Binky and several others had drifted away from political change to psychological change, but still compelled to direct action. Some members had begun to believe that perhaps this surrogate of Whitman, might be a type of resurrected entity. Whitman had sat in on dozens of meetings of the group preferring not to lead but only to offer a suggestion here and there. But he had begun to disappear for long periods of time in the past few months.

This information had been elicited by Frank from his phone communications with Casey. Frank had assembled the clues from the 'Conspiremouth' and his cursory knowledge of Whitman, which had been enhanced by Michael Shultzmann's research, and he had drawn a line of logic between all of the events that were in direct relation to his being hit on the head in front of the Le Café Fritz. But he had not taken into account Wharton and Creeley or the any of the incidents on the American side. But from what he had gleaned to date he presumed that there was a covert network of friends who may be considered 'Friends of Whitman'. This term Frank had coined himself even though he did not consider himself to be a part of this society. Now who was this man who seemed to travel freely and appear without notice amongst his followers? This was a question that weighted on Frank's mind and even Casey's at times. Especially on this day where events were transpiring to come to a crescendo. Was he an actual human being or the manifestation of a collective delusion? Frank and Casey could not seriously make any allowance that he was a ghost or spirit. They were not quite that separated from reality. Though was closer to drinking the Kool aid than Frank was.

Casey was holding on to the substance of Frank's text while waiting for him to arrive at the airport. He also wondered about Boris, whom he had texted with as well. He knew him as a close friend of Frank's whom he had personally bopped on the head and a prime candidate for recruitment. Boris had thus become the next in line for a brain readjustment which in this case had been administered by Binky. He didn't know that Boris, despite having a change in direction, continued to just be, for the most part, the same person that he had been before. The one thing that had changed in Boris was that he now had an inspired sense that what he did mattered more than he had previously believed. But Boris didn't know that with any great certitude.

Casey and Binky, even though they had deeply individualistic streaks were waiting for directions. As were Butterworth and Keel. Frank and Boris were for all intents and purposes dependent on the voluntary contributions of the people involved. To Frank, Jack White had proved to this point to be a bad lead who like a stray dog who had lost the scent, but most of the others had been key for him to deduce what he did.

Now there was quite a bit of sadness, anger and resentment which occupied the consciousness of Casey and the others. This had to do with the outright murder of one of their own. But the motivation for revenge was not something that was encouraged in the group. They did not operate on a tit for tat basis. Yet, still an anxiety existed among the members. Who would be next? How do we prevent this type of violence? What do we say to the police? Are they trying to help us or hurt us? Any answers to these questions

342

were unclear. They just assumed that not talking about it would allow it to go away. Maybe it had been only an aberration. Yet, when Theodor had shown up at the residence of Casey and Binky and laid it out that there was a group in direct opposition to not embracing the eye for an eye mentality. Both Casey and Binky had then seen clearly that they needed to either be with the cause one hundred percent or have no affiliation with Whitman at all. Frank and Boris' sudden interest in the matter seemed most fortuitous for Casey and Binky. And it would clarify some things if all of the characters were assembled. At first, he didn't like the idea of the airport as being where all of this would take place because of the heavy police presence. Later he realized that it had been the best place to have everyone put their cards on the table.

forty-six

-

Theodor was bent on causing confusion and disturbing the peace of mind of those around him. His mind was convinced that this would bring him some satisfaction, which it did to some degree. In fact, his loyalties varied because of this. He was now in it for himself only and so could no longer comprehend other people's needs and wants. Now when he had attempted to cut short the time on this earth for Casey and Binky, his brain had been jolted by their little attack, yet in him it had only pushed him into further mistrusting and misunderstanding. His brain could not comprehend, only change in perception. His rationality, in which he had so reveled, had increasingly dismissed certain facts. He had become convinced that his and his colleague's overview of the world was far superior to any other and hence he had taken one further step into self-deception. He was prepared to do some disturbing. He was uncomfortable when those around him were at peace. When it came to beauty, he had failed to see any. He saw his only salvation in some variation of death, because that would end all suffering and misery. In his mind, he included the death of others as part of that relief. He had very little consideration for others welfare, and believed that this life was cold, impassive and without heart. His was a calculating mind. His was a self-justifying mind, powered by some twisted logic that had been programmed into his brain.

The others in his group had similar motivations. And this group of four sat in the airport bar, only focused on the outside world and its lack of law and order and its need to be purged of the disruptive forces that caused pain in the world.

Frank and Boris were riding in the back of a cab on their way to the airport. Frank was warding off a dizzy spell by closing his eyes and attempting some pseudo self-hypnotic procedure. As for Boris, he had procured a small bottle of bourbon on the way out and was attempting to transfer it into a flask as the cab was weaving in and out of traffic along highway 20. It was a bumpy and unsteady ride, what with all of the potholes and closed lanes.

Boris had somewhat arranged his dilemmas with females for the time being. Having been confronted by his past affectations in Chloe and just having succumbed to a new spark with Linda, he had decided that Linda could wait. He phoned explaining that for the next few days he would be tied up in a lot of work and that she should probably carry on and return home. Boris aped a level of consternation that may or may or not have impressed her, but certainly gave Boris justification for telling her that he would keep in touch every day with her despite not being able to come see her in person. In his mind this gave him time. Time to consider the return of Chloe and what that meant.

Frank came out of his little ritual that counteracted his waves of nausea.

"Why don't you just wait until we get there to do that, Boris?" he asked.

"Frank, we are going to the scene of capital importance in this case and I want to be fully prepared upon arrival."

"Well, don't be too prepared, Boris or I may have to retire you from this case."

"Fear not Frank, I am well disciplined in the art of biting my tongue when trouble is afoot."

"Yes, well they may not just be little taps on the skull this time, but a real confrontation. Police, authorities and official kind of people, Boris."

345

"Understood, my friend."

Frank looked at his friend and was satisfied that though he looked fatigued he had enough control of his faculties to at least be there, as long as he kept his mouth shut.

"Just stay quiet, Boris."

As they were pulling into the airport's arrival level Frank had come across the latest issue of 'Conspiremouth' on his phone. Now this was not the issue that Casey and Binky had put a day earlier. It appeared to Frank to be one long editorial by none other than Walt Whitman. Or at least one of his surrogates. Frank scanned it.

He noticed in it a quote from Thomas Paine:

"My country is the world, and my religion is to do good."

Very impressive, thought Frank.

Deeper into the article he saw a paragraph that began:

"Though the soul may seem to have been banished by intelligent men, when irreconcilable impasse occurs in a world that stops listening, its re-emergence will be a welcomed salvation that will remind us of the sources of our lives."

Very thought provoking, mused Frank inwardly.

He concealed the article from Boris, not wanting to provoke an elongated poetically charged rant. At least not at this moment.

Frank paid the fare and he and Boris walked through the revolving doors into the arrivals level.

"You know, Frank, Butterworth and Brandon should still be here. All flights to London have been delayed until tomorrow."

Boris was pointing at a huge screen displaying the latest information on flights.

"I'm going to find them, Frank" he said with an inspired voice.

"That may not be a bad idea. You look for them. I am certain that what is going on here will be of interest to them."

"And Frank call Chloe at the Sterling. Here's the number."

Boris produced a crumpled piece of paper from his jacket pocket.

"What should I tell her?"

"Tell her that I will be at the hotel tomorrow morning. Tell her that I'm okay. Oh, and tell her that I love her."

"Yes, well maybe you'd better save that one for when you see her in person."

"Ok. But I feel like something big is going to go down here tonight. I may not get a chance to see her for a while."

"Don't worry, Boris. Everything is going to be fine here tonight. And you know we may be seeing more of Chloe than you think."

"Oh, and why is that?"

"I'll tell you later. But for now, let her stay safe at the Sterling."

"Frank, such vagueness."

"Don't you think that Linda deserves another update as well."

"I will get to her. I let her know that something came up. She's her own person Frank and she'll know exactly what to do."

Frank smiled slightly and said,

"I hope so for her sake, Boris."

Boris shrugged and then went off to look for Butterworth and Brandon.

Frank made a beeline for the airport bar. He had been there with Boris many times before.

Ambrose J. Keel was seated with Butterworth and Brandon in one of the public restaurants. The three academics had left the hotel room to get a bite to eat. Keel was trying to maintain a semblance of calmness as Butterworth talked about the potential arrival of at least someone who was portraying the persona of Walt Whitman. His intellectual pride and training caused him to be aloof to all of these minor assaults and even the killing that had taken place at the hotel. His perception was that a calm and measured demeanor would get him through what he perceived as Butterworth's moving towards senility, though he was too polite to mention it to either him or Brandon.

"Professor Keel it is only by pushing forward with life do we discover the vibrant soul within us. Not only is sustainability to be aimed for but illumination." Butterworth opined.

Then an eager voice came from the next aisle.

"Brandon."

It was Boris, who had at last found them after some mad scrambling throughout the airport, including inquiring at the airport hotel's front desk.

Butterworth and Brandon looked pleased but were in truth surprised at their recent acquaintance's arrival.

Boris made his way over to the booth the trio of academics were installed in.

"Boris" exclaimed Maddi, "this is Professor Ambrose J. Keel of Hobart University. This Mr. Keel is a recent fellow Whitmanian whom we met at the hotel downtown. He helped us understand and deal with the what transpired down at the university and the horrible happening at the hotel. He is an artist and a mad raconteur. I'm I doing you justice, Boris?"

"Well, professor I think I'll survive those words. And glad to meet you Professor Keel."

Keel was somewhat hesitant to greet Boris but managed a slight salutation.

"Sit down, Boris", said Brandon.

"I don't mean to be rude, but I do have a few words that I would like to say to Brandon in private" Boris asserted.

Brandon seemed to understand and immediately rose from the booth to go with Boris.

"Ah, yes. This must be about Whitman's arrival. Have no fear Boris, our esteemed colleague Prof Keel has been fully updated on the situation and has offered to be a witness to what may transpire here this evening" Butterworth said summarizing to situation.

"And we hope nobody loses their lives tonight" added Professor Keel acerbically.

"Not likely to happen Keel" Butterworth said with assurance.

Brandon decided to reseat himself in the booth and Boris joined him.

Butterworth took the lead.

"Now gentlemen, you do realize that tonight the soul of humankind is on the verge of being relaunched onto a world that has been cynically dissected from the heartbeat of life."

"Isn't that a little dramatic, Professor" interjected Keel.

"And well it should be."

"What is likely to happen is that they put this Whitman in a nice hospital for observation."

"That would be a crime against the cosmic consciousness. The soul of life, Keel."

"Fine, Professor I will suspend my judgement until I have encountered the man himself."

Brandon felt an uneasy at Keel's assumption that Whitman was a man but kept it to himself.

"You know, Keel, Brandi here used to be a woman. That's the way I met him. I fell in love with her and have kept loving him. It's has been an amazingly adventurous three years, hasn't it Brandi?"

"Amazing, Maddi has been amazing. We discovered so much together."

"And more is to come, Brandi."

Keel looked a little surprised and was not sure how to say what he wanted to say. This was quite unusual for him, but he finally managed.

"Well, that comes as a surprise. I had heard that you had some dynamic new partner in your life Butterworth, but this I never excepted. You two do look so happy together."

"Well, I am glad that you said that Keel. Not everyone has such a positive reaction. Some have questioned my motivations in uniting with Brandi, here. They have accused me of only going along with the thing for political reasons. That is bullshit, Keel. Pure contrived and vengeful bullshit. These voices are only old academic enemies of mind who are victims of blind jealousy and other assorted emotions. I wish them all the best now, Keel. I hope that they break free of their pettiness, but you know, I really have come to realize recently that I have no power over them and their assorted opinions. As I was telling Brandi just today. We will not engage in wasteful and idle chatter which does not help anyone."

Keel absorbed the Butterworth declaration for a moment and then said,

"You know Professor I really tend to agree with you on all of this even though I am not familiar with your personal academic battles, I have my own rivals and I have learned to keep my mouth shut at the right times."

"Well put, Keel."

"Professor, you believe that anyone can call themselves male, female or in-between at their own whim and fancy or should we be setting some sort of academic standards for what gender a person is?"

Brandon was about to answer but conceded to Butterworth.

"This question is only for the textbooks, Keel. I propose to you that gender distinctions are matters that require fluidity. Our curriculums will always be separated from the reality. But we can invent new terms to fit new discoveries. Can't we Keel?"

"I suppose."

Brandon decided to add his voice,

"It is time that we all defined ourselves."

Keel was not fully convinced of this last statement.

"There must be some standards."

"Not for the human consciousness, Keel." Butterworth said.

Keel felt that he had a point here. He always thought that if one does not have clearly defined terminology then one cannot properly speak about anything. And he said this to the group. And the conversation continued as the two professors began to cite and reference more and more obscure sources, practically alienating Boris and Brandon. This went on for over forty-five minutes.

Boris and Brandon occasionally eyed each other.

Then an explosion was heard. Loud shouts and screams came from all directions of the airport.

Fear gripped everyone. Bodies ran in all directions.

Butterworth, Boris, Brandon and Keel quickly grabbed their paraphernalia and joined the people who had been in the restaurant as they headed toward the exits.

Some people moved more slowly than others, choosing the path of least resistance.

At the other end of the airport Frank was on the phone with Jesse/Jessica who was working late at the Coffee Express when the blast occurred.

"What was that, Frank?" Jesse/Jessica asked hearing the explosion over the phone.

"I think it's a bomb, Jesse. I have to go. I will call you in a few minutes." And he terminated the call and ran.

Frida S. Wharton, after getting her inspirational head blow had returned to the airport looking for a place of redemption, perhaps looking for the homeless mother and son that she had callously spoken with earlier. When the explosion came, she was thrown clear across a room and into a cement wall. She lay unconscious on the floor of the airport. Her two male assistants, who had waited for her in a vehicle outside, were now in feared anticipation of what had happened. It would be nearly an hour before they would find out that she had been transported to the hospital in a severe coma.

Emily and her son Evan had escaped any harm.

Warren Kitchholm and his laptop were trapped in a washroom underneath a fallen wall.

The mostly academic quartet emerged unscathed as well but frazzled. Boris had gotten Brandon to call Frank's phone and they had managed to meet up with him near the hotel area, which it would appear had been unaffected by the blast.

Casey and Binky were both thrown to the ground by the eruption but had managed to scamper outside to the parking lot. They had a remarkable calmness about themselves. It was almost like they had anticipated that some sort of dramatic event was going to happen.

They huddled behind a shuttle bus with a few others and caught their breath. They both were considering their next move. Should they remain here and try and finger the bombers, whom they suspected would resort to something like this to get attention, or should they stay out of it. Casey had thoughts both ways.

He felt a moral obligation to help society identify the perpetrators of this viciousness that meant only to destroy and spread negativity and cynicism about life, but he also understood the inherent frustration and naïve misunderstanding that the bombers must be full of. After all Casey and Binky might have had some deep unrest in their minds and hearts but their little taps on the head were meant as friendly reminders not as revenge or selfish outpourings of rage.

"Binky, it is time to stick together."

"Casey, I am right here with you."

And the two them went out into the clusters of people, some of whom were still running and screaming, others were crying and many who just stood calmly staring at the airport building or at their phones. Most eventually began calling friends and family.

The pair of fringe journalists and Whitmanites were going in the opposite direction of most people. They were looking for any familiar faces. The ones that had been tapped by them. Soon they reached a small area of greenery near the hotel which seemed unaffected by the blast. They spotted Frank and the others looking askance. As Casey and Binky approached the group an officer began to direct them to move further away from the scene like most of the other people had done. Casey and Binky ran to catch them.

With a furtive glance Boris had noticed Casey and Binky.

"Hey Frank, it's Conspiremouth. They're here."

"Yes, of course Boris."

Butterworth and Brandon clung close to one another as they moved with some urgency across a parking lot. Keel remained in tow.

"Boris, don't lose sight of them."

"I'll try. But they seemed to be following us."

"Good. Very good."

After two more minutes of running Boris and Frank settled on a grassy hill about a quarter of a mile from the airport's main building. Casey and Binky soon followed. Butterworth and Brandon were lying not far off side by side on the greenery. Keel had knelt by an injured little girl who appeared to have a fractured arm yet had managed to get herself away from further harm. But now she had been separated from her parents. She cried loudly and Keel tried to comfort her, but she seemed afraid of everyone and everything. And understandably so.

Frank soon focused his attention on Casey. He approached him.

"So, my friend, where is Walt?"

"Oh, he'll be here very soon."

"Do we know where?"

"No, but he will find us. Our task now is to help, by being the calm in the storm."

"Yes, that is best in this situation. To not perpetuate further fear and panic. I am sure Walt would agree."

"Hey, I know you want to meet him. Don't worry you will. And your friends will too."

With that Casey and Binky went off to attend to some of people who had lain down on the grass, exhausted. Some had minor injuries, others were in tears or perplexed by shock.

Frank thought to call Jesse/Jessica again. It was now close to midnight.

"Frank. Are you okay?"

"Yes, Jesse, sorry Jessica."

"That's alright, Frank. Who did it?"

"I have an idea. Not sure."

"So where are you going to go? Home. Oh, that's right you live in a hotel."

"Not even that, Jess. Is Jess, okay?"

"Don't worry about my name Frank. Jess is okay."

"Listen, Jess. Boris, my friend and I are in this up to our knees. I can't explain it all right now. But don't you worry, it will all be resolved."

"Frank, I'm okay. I'm with a guy who says he knows all about what is going on."

"Really. Is he okay?"

"Seems okay. A little weird, but still cool. He's having an herbal tea with me at the all-night diner across from my ex-girlfriend's apartment."

"Jess, you have an ex-girlfriend?"

"We just broke up yesterday. I'm becoming too much of a woman for her."

"So, who is this guy that says he knows all about what is going on?"

"Some old guy. Calls himself Walt. Cool. Nice guy."

"Jess, stay there. Keep your friend there, too. We're coming down."

As Frank was attempting to obtain the location of the all-night restaurant from Jess, there was the sound of some shuffling on the phone and then Jess' voice said,

"Walt wants to know how you people are? If everyone has survived the explosion? And he says that he will be coming there."

356

Frank hesitated and replied that everyone that he knew was alive but probably shaken up.

"Frank, Walt will be there in a while. He says that anything that needs to be known will be known and nothing happens without a purpose."

"Jess, we have been looking for this guy for a few days. Are you certain that he can be trusted?"

"I believe him, Frank."

"Well, I suppose that's good enough for me. Tell him we will be on the grassy area at the far end of the arrivals parking lot. They may move us. Does he have a phone?"

"I'm coming with him, Frank. I have a phone."

"Good. We'll be waiting."

Now that was quite unusual thought Frank to himself. Casey says we're going to meet him and there he is practically on the other end of the next phone call. But everything about this is weird, he thought. Frank had done, with the help of Michael Schultmann some quick research on the nature of Whitman, but Frank did not have any inkling about how such things as a collective cosmic consciousness worked. I guess most of the human race didn't know either, thought Frank to himself. No one of any scientific creditability had ever explained it and been widely believed, yet there existed some bond or force that seemed to be pulling him and this group of friends and acquaintance together. He dared not speculate on what that might be. He was trying, as a newly self-declared investigator, to be as objective and fact oriented as possible. He knew that his sudden shift in perspective may have been just a psychological twist of mind. Perhaps he did need to see a doctor. But, for now he felt a deep compulsion to see this case through to some satisfactory conclusion, or a least a place where he could pause and say that he had done all he could do to obtain the facts and answers to his question for the time being.

In turning back to Casey, Binky, Boris, the professors and Brandon he began to look at them in somewhat of a different light. Not only because of the tragedy that had unfolded that evening but also because it seemed now that the existence of some living entity named Walt Whitman was making his way to where they were right now. Frank had felt a real reduction in tension between him and Jess as well. Just in the manner and tone of the phone call. He felt that he had a younger sibling again. Brother or sister, it did not seem to matter to Frank. But he was not one to focus on emotion for long. He soon was turning over in his head the facts of the past few days. He decided to not inform anyone else right away that important personage was currently making his way to the scene of the tragedy from an all-night diner. He instead sat down on a small incline at the edge of the parking lot and surveying the scene mulled everything over. Before him, was a lot of smoke, some people running about, dozens of emergency vehicles whizzing around and the crying voices.

Was all of this a conspiracy perpetuated for him? His dizziness returned for a moment. Then he thought to himself that such a notion was far-fetched. Boris would not have allowed himself to be part of anything like that. And these guys running around in black jackets, they seemed motivated by a sincere desire to be helpful, though Frank questioned their methods. Whitman surely would not have advocated for any form of violence, however mild that it may have been. And those little taps on the head to Frank were considered mild, but a violent attack nevertheless. Now maybe this Whitman character was just an imposter, who had inserted his own updated version of how Whitman would operate in the 21st century. Now there, thought Frank, was a very solid possibility.

Frank was now realizing that he was developing an ability to reflect on the larger picture before him. Before the events of the last few days, he had this potential, but it had largely remained untapped. He felt that some doors had suddenly opened for him and that he could at last breath freely. But of more importance was the fact that his brain seemed to now be working at its optimum capacity. He had arrived in Montreal with a very limited and foggy view of what lay ahead for him in life and now he seemed to a have over the course of the last one hundred of so hours to have been placed in a clear place.

As he sat on the small grassy incline his thoughts rebounded between the philosophical and the factual. He could not keep the two separated. And why should he? All he had to do now was to listen to Walt Whitman explain it all. And he was certain that this gentleman would. Frank had a very strong notion on what this explanation would consist of, but he blocked it from fully forming in his consciousness. He distracted himself with small facts about the case, that though relevant, would probably not be of interest to an individual that had not penetrated to the same level of consciousness. These certain details would also interest the skeptic who wanted to see their relevancy.

Whitman certainly had enemies. And Frank thought that many of them could have been responsible for what had just transpired at the airport today. Why had that nameless agent of his been rendered breathless at the hotel? And these seemingly connected attacks south of the border, that appeared to be quite random, what did that say about the question as to whether Whitman had enemies? They may have been unwittingly against him, but nevertheless they were part of the indifference towards any greater appreciation for life. But could there be a solitary figure behind this. No, concluded Frank? Perhaps there was no one at all behind it. No one to blame. But that could not be. All of these type of goings on always have someone to point the finger at, thought Frank.

"Hey, Frank."

It was Boris and he had his flask fully exposed having just taken a good swig. He slipped it back into his jacket pocket and walked up to Frank.

"What are we doing, now Frank?"

"We stay here and help the people, Boris. Here take the phone and call your Chloe. She's probably heard about the bombing and is worried. Call her Boris and be nice."

"Frank, I'm always nice. And you should know that after all these years."

"Sure, Boris always Mr. Nice Guy, here take the phone."

Boris shakily took the apparatus and found the number in the contacts. He began to walk off, to have some privacy.

"And don't forget Linda either" Frank yelled after him.

Butterworth, Keel and Brandon seemed to be trying to console some of the those who were in shock. Casey and Binky were talking to a young woman who seemed to be alone. Some authoritative voices came from vehicles with flashing lights that had assembled near the parking lot. They were directing people to move further back. Where Frank and the others were seemed to be at a safe distance from any harm.

Boris seemed to be engaged in an intense conversation on the phone with Chloe.

As Frank sat back watching and reflecting on everything it occurred to him that he had not seen Warren Kitchholm anywhere. No calls, no sight of him. I hope that he is alive thought Frank. He got up and marched over to where Boris was engaged with Chloe and signaled to him to wrap up the call.

After another minute Boris obliged.

Frank tried Warren's number without success, but the phone sounded like it was still receiving calls. There was no message that the phone was out of service or anything else of that sort. What should I do thought Frank? Would it be worthwhile going back to the airport to search for him? He knew that most likely the authorities would not allow him back in. Could Whitman's arrival shed any light on the situation? No, he would just keep trying to contact Kitchholm. He would leave a couple of messages and that

360

was all that he could do. Or was there more? He could email him. Maybe he could reach him via his laptop.

Boris was laughing with a group of what appeared to be university students or young tourists who had gathered around a small vehicle just at the edge of the parking lot. Frank saw that the connection Boris had made with these young people was wrapped around the fact that they were coping with the emergency by downing beers that appeared to be coming from the back trunk of their car. Good for Boris, though Frank. Frank at this moment had little interest in imbibing until he had at least heard from Whitman. He also wanted to find out for certain who had been the initiators of the crime. It would be best to leave Boris out of it right now, but he would be needed later to interpret Whitman or perhaps engage the man in conversation. Boris was a master at the art of conversation, when he could discipline himself to do it properly.

Warren Kitchholm was just regaining consciousness at the same moment. He could not find his phone. He had his laptop nearby. He could not move. His lower body was trapped. He thought of his girlfriend. He steadied himself a bit. He took a few deep breaths. He thought to himself that he was okay, just trapped. He looked around him and noticed a younger man struggling to free himself from the rubble at the opposite end of the now almost demolished washroom. The man was dressed in black. Kitchholm's fact-based mind immediately connected this man with the group that had been hitting people on the head. But he was a little mistaken about this. He opened his laptop to see if he could contact anyone by Wi-Fi. Amazingly it worked. He emailed Frank.

forty-seven

"I'm waiting for my taxi, but taxis never come"

Ian Dury

I was on a city bus home, when I received the information that Walt Whitman had been dining at the all-night restaurant where Jess/Jessica was. I immediately got off the bus and hailed a cab. Maybe I could still catch Walt and Jess/Jessica before they left for the airport. Or, perhaps they didn't need my help at all. On my way to the dinner, I began to feel a slight nausea coming on. No, I thought, I won't get involved with these characters. I will stay in the background, in the underground. Let the story play itself out. But since I had met Jess/Jessica they had been drawing me in more and more strongly into the stream of events.

Frank soon found Casey and Binky again. They were helping direct the ambulances to the injured. They looked like nurses out there, thought Frank.

"Hey, Casey I need to talk with you a minute."

Casey turned from where he was talking with an elderly man who looked in shock.

"What is it?"

"In private."

Frank waved at Casey to come closer to him. Casey got up and came over.

362

"Casey, don't you feel directly connected to what just happened here? Aren't you a little bit curious as to who did this? I know you know that you could have some responsibility in finding out who did this. Now tending to the sick is great, but shouldn't you be sharing your information with the authorities?"

"Don't you need to ask yourself the same question."

"Sure, of course. But I'm not going to stick my neck out and take all the heat if you guys won't back me up."

"Let's just wait for Walt. How can we be sure it is connected? It could have nothing to do with us at all. Besides there is no need to rush anything. I'm sure the investigators will find out all that they need to know about who did it. We're just incidentals, Frank."

Frank thought about this. He was not so sure that he, Boris, Casey, his friend Binky and the two professors had been just incidentals in what had transpired. After all, one of the agents for Whitman had been eliminated by this Theodor guy. Casey had earlier sent a photo of Theodor by email to Frank and given him some key information about the group he hung with. Frank was certain that he had seen Theodor earlier in the airport but hadn't said anything to Boris or the others. Now he pondered as to whether he could have prevented the big explosion or not. And what should he do now? He was beginning to recognize that these types of considerations were part of involving himself in dangerous matters. He would be faced with such dilemmas again if pursued the life of private investigation. So now what to do? Well, maybe Casey was right. It would be best to wait it out. Have patience. Don't spill the beans until it became necessary to do so. Some of the reticence of his younger years came back to inform him that keeping a closed mouth was sometimes the wisest move. In his mind some of the episodes with his ex-wife were coming back. He quickly blocked them out. Not now, I don't need to mull over the past now. He finally looked straight at Casey and said,

"Your right. Let's just help out for now."

In the distance Boris' voice bellowed out poetic phrases.

Frank walked over to where Boris was and whispered something in his left ear. Boris quickly went and sat down on the grass. A police cruiser drove by. Sirens wailed everywhere. Frank was getting email from Warren Kitchholm.

"You know Brandi I have never felt so exhilarated in my life." said Butterworth.

"Maddi, a lot of people could be dead. Isn't that attitude somewhat insensitive not to mention pompous of you."

"It's the truth, Brandi. The truth. The truth is in the air. I feel it. Let's not let these dark souls be satisfied that their cynicism has prevailed. Because it hasn't and never will, Brandi. I am ready to face it all now."

Keel looked over with deep concern at Butterworth.

The trio had seated themselves on the edge of a parking lot curb thinking about finding a cab. The task seemed nearly impossible. Butterworth was not so anxious to leave, but Keel wanted to get out. He was beginning to have serious doubt about Butterworth's sanity.

"Professor Butterworth," Keel chimed in, "how would you feel about coming back to my colleague's apartment in town for a few days just to recover from this. I suspect that there will not be any flights out of here for at least a couple of days."

"Professor Keel that does sound like the perfect refuge from the storm. We could discuss the entire matter in depth and I could finish writing my next radio address."

"So, let's find a cab."

"Not so easy, Professor."

364

Brandon had gotten up and was attempting to hail down cars that appeared to be exiting.

"Maybe we could team up with some of the others and get a lift?" he said.

The two professors remained quiet. Both were pondering the possibility that the 19th century nature loving, compassionate but divided poet Walt Whitman would be making an appearance. This secretly excited both of them. Inside they were like children revelling in the possibility of a treat coming their way. But their really big brains told them that this was not possible. It defied every law of nature. But still their esoteric sides were hopeful. They both anticipated seeing the poetry of life become life itself. What a tale they could then tell. Keel remained much more skeptical than Butterworth who was almost singing as he spoke.

"Now gentlemen, the circumstances of how we find ourselves here are indeed incredible. But that is why we need to not miss this opportunity to seize this time and this place and deposit it in our hearts and minds in order to carry it on to the next generation. And I do mean to include you my dear Brandi."

Brandon smiled. He was not yet considered academically fully on par with the other two having not even having finished a master's degree, but his voice was listened to by many in the community. So, he presumed that he was fully apart of this time and this place when and where the 'it' was to be carried from.

It was well past the midnight hour as a speeding taxicab barrelled along highway 20 toward the chaos at the airport. The cabbie had told the passengers that he would only be able to bring them close to the place and that he didn't know how close. He had his radio on in the cab and it was blasting news about the tragic events. He wondered why his two customers were heading to the airport. They were both numb on the subject. To the driver they didn't look very much like authority figures or bomb experts. It puzzled him, but he agreed to drop them as close as he could to the scene.

forty-eight

"Whoever you are holding me now in hand, Without one thing all will be useless,

I give you fair warning before you attempt me further, I am not what you supposed,

but far different."

Walt Whitman

Frank I am trapped in a washroom at the far east end of arrivals level. I think one of bombers is here with me – It is a guy all dressed in black. Hope you are ok? As long as there are no more explosions I will survive – I am sure someone will be here soon to rescue us. Trying to get out. W.

Frank answered Warren Kitchholm with a brief reply but made no reference to Theodor. He was now of the opinion that he would let the authorities sort that out, as he was sure that video surveillance and other evidence would quickly lead them to those responsible. Frank did not want to drag all the people involved through the process. He felt some responsibility toward them to not do that. Besides what would Whitman say? Perhaps he had better wait for that to unfold before opening up a Pandora's box.

It was now well past midnight. Frank and Boris sat down side by side, exhausted from the evening's events.

"I am sure this Whitman will get here, Boris. Keep your eyes open and try and not blow any opportunities with your mouth."

"Frank, I am in good form. Chloe and I seem to be back on good terms. She's willing to be open-mined about us. And she has a new project planned that could use my talents."

"Boris, are you not just a little troubled by this bombing. Some people may have died."

"Sure, Frank but you know I think it will all turn out okay in the end."

"You are the eternal optimist, Boris."

"Frank, as long as I have a breath left, I know things will work out."

"Now that can be a good thing or delusional thinking, Boris. I'm not sure which is which today."

"Out on the water, where the sailing men all go, the water's high but all the fish swim low."

"What's that mean, Boris."

"It means stay close to the foundation, Frank and you won't be thrown and tossed around by life."

"Where did you come up with that one?"

"Some song."

"So, Boris are you saying that you want to add stability to your life."

"Maybe. Or maybe I am stable and just want to tell people about it."

"Well, I don't think you've ever had a problem telling people things."

"I've got some new things to say, Frank.'

"Save it for now. Look over there. It looks like my brother and who could that be with him. I can't tell from here."

A short distance away an older slow-moving man with a full beard and ragged clothing calmly walked toward Frank and Boris. Jess/Jessica was at his side looking just as calm and even smiling as they seemed to recognize Frank. The older man displayed a composure amidst the noise that surrounded him. He was about six feet tall and of moderate weight. He had highly arched eyebrows and a round kind face, long fingers and a broad nose. He walked with an elegance and seemed to be disturbed by nothing, yet his ears were large enough to look like they would pick up the slightest sound.

Frank and Boris got up to meet him. As he approached Frank, he seemed to acknowledge him, but only gave him glance. He stopped close to Frank and Boris, who were silent for a moment.

"Mr. Whitman?" Frank said at last.

"And you must be acquaintances of my friends. Indeed, you are now a friend. And your names are?"

"I'm Frank Lee and this is Boris Swatcupso."

"It is a wonderful time to be alive, but for some it is wonderful sometimes to die. I have had the fortune of experiencing both."

Frank was quite skeptical and felt creepy inside. He had concern for Jess/Jessica.

"Now come on, you couldn't have died and be here today. Whitman died in 1892. But I accept your premise whomever you claim to be." Frank said.

"You will see more as your soul progresses through the dimensions of the universe, my good friend."

"Now, just one minute I don't quite put myself into the category of friend quite yet."

"That is fine by me." Whitman said and showed a friendly laugh.

Frank turned to Jess/Jessica.

"Jess, how are you?"

"I'm good, Frank."

Jess/Jessica thought about giving his older brother a hug, but held back and instead just said,

"And you, you seemed to have survived okay."

"I'm good. We're good. Boris and me. And the others are here too. They are quite anxious to meet you Mr. Whitman. I am sure you are aware of this."

"I only follow intuition now my friend. I do not and cannot predict anything. I know so very little, yet I have experienced so much. These friends I may know. Where are they?"

"Just over there."

Frank pointed to a place further along the side of the parking lot.

Meanwhile sirens continued to whale. Whitman displayed a calmness amidst it all. In fact, he seemed to be smiling as he surveyed the scene.

"You know Frank, my radar senses that your life has been turned around. And you too, Boris. And those others. Let's go and see what is up with them."

Now Chloe was back at her hotel room worrying about Boris. She had loved him and it was quite clear to her that she still did. He had told her that things would settle down once they had finished with this little caper of theirs. She did know a lot about the case by now, because of her own research and the details that Boris had supplied her.

Soon she decided that she would go out to the airport herself to see if Boris was alright. Even if he had advised against it. He had told her that she would only be complicating matters. But her intuition told her to go. Boris had also mentioned that she could have an opportunity for employment if this thing that they were doing got off the ground. So, she figured she might as well get started immediately.

Whitman walked toward the trio of Butterworth, Keel and Brandon. He walked with cool, steady steps seeming to mumble some sort of mantra under his lips. As he approached the three, he noticed a haggard looking woman with a young man seated beside her on the grass. He stopped in his path and turned to them.

"Excuse me for being noisy madame, but are you and your male companion in need of assistance?"

The woman looked up. She had a tired look in her eyes, but when she saw the bearded man, she seemed suddenly reassured.

"Don't be frightened," continued Whitman, "all will work out for the best in the end. That is how the universe operates. Just keep persisting and enjoy what you can. All the questions and problems will be answered one by one."

The woman looked dumbfounded by the sudden philosophizing of this strange man. She didn't utter any words but gave out sighs of exasperation

"You two stick together and keep walking, because all will be well" continued Whitman.

Whitman smiled at the mother and son and walked on to the others with Jess/Jessica, Frank and Boris close behind.

As he approached Butterworth immediately recognized the man. Brandon followed next, but Keel's brain was telling him that this was a homeless man who had been caught up in the chaos of the events. Maybe he was living at the airport, thought Keel to himself.

Butterworth took the initiative.

"Mr. Whitman it is an honor to meet you again even under these trying circumstances."

"Yes, isn't it wonderful. You of course have been given the friendly tap, as I like to call it."

"Yes, I believe so. But so has everyone else here. Well apart from our esteemed colleague Professor Keel."

"Well, everyone responses a little differently to it. Each have their own things to work out. And what do you have to work out Mister..."

"Butterworth. Professor Madison Butterworth."

"Ah yes, I recall it now. I am overwhelmed and outmatched by you, Professor. I am just a journeyman printer and who sometimes muses on the world. But the one thing that I have discovered is that it all works toward the best in the end. So, don't worry or be anxious, my friend."

"That is not always easy, well, especially with what has transpired here tonight."

"Professor I have seen war and tragedy, illness and poverty. These are basic stepping stones to freedom of the soul. But you must believe with all your heart and mind in life and in death as well to see it."

Everyone was listening intently. The din of sirens and yelling voices that still pervaded around them had become a backdrop for Whitman's voice.

372

"As I have roamed around recently, I have still been impressed by the ordinary. It is the ordinary not the extraordinary that has preserved me. This little explosion here does not impress me, but you do. And that mother and son back there, these are the things that make me weep and laugh."

Butterworth persisted.

"That is all true and we believe you, but it still doesn't explain who you are and how is it that you are here."

"Minor details that will be worked out over the next few thousands of years, my friend."

Casey and Binky had now joined the group.

"Ah, two more of my friends. Come here and let me hug you both. You have been great workers for humankind. And good publishers." He laughed.

Nearby Frank's phone rang. It was Warren Kitchholm who had managed to call him via his laptop.

"Frank, I'm being taken to the hospital. I haven't been able to find out if they have captured anyone. But I told them that a guy wearing all black was probably one of the bombers."

"I think his name is Theodor. But never mind that, Warren. There's a whole new story here. We have Whitman, right here with us."

"Oh, that's nice" Kitchholm said with a tinge of sarcasm.

"Warren, incredible as it may seem I really think it's him. I mean, in essence."

"Well, that's great. Something inside me does believe you Frank, but I'm going with some from of mental aberration on this Whitman impersonator's part."

"Fine, Warren. Anything broken?"

"No, they just want to examine me. Call you later."

And with that he hung up.

When Frank turned back to join the group, he noticed that Keel was down on the ground and was being attended to by the others. Frank smiled.

He reflected on how he now had all of these people around him, who seemed to have shared in something together, though he wasn't very certain as to it what that was. But he was sure that he would continue down this path. He looked at Boris, who was knelt down beside Keel. I guess he's been a pretty good friend, Frank thought.

Casey and Binky looked like they were sharing a joke. And Butterworth and Whitman were staring intently at one another. Frank found Brandon and spoke to him.

"Your Professor Butterworth's partner, right?"

"Yeah. I'm Brandon Pierce."

"Frank Lee, Boris's friend. And what do you guys have planned from here on?"

"I'm going to go back to London and opening a bookstore and of course still tending to Maddi."

"Oh, you mean Butterworth."

"Yes, Maddi. And you guys?"

"Well, it seems Boris has re-united with an old flame."

"What about the sleuthing business?"

"Well, we will see. I hadn't been expecting that we would have to be dealing with dead people."

"Souls. They are souls."

"Okay, souls. But I don't really think that I want to be in that line of work. Maybe I'll just stick with writing advertising."

"Oh, that would be a disappointment after all of this Mr. Lee."

"Well, we'll see."

Frank really felt he would pursue whatever came next and if that meant stringing words together to sell services and stuff, so be it.

forty-nine

"When we reached the end of the love, we arose from our bed, And shouted a cry that made our lying souls laugh again"

Boris Swatcupso. From his poem 'The love we once hated'

Frank, Boris, Butterworth, Brandon and Jess had ended up sharing a taxi together because of the dearth of them that evening. The professor had decided to wait out the crisis with his partner downtown. They arrived back downtown at 4 A.M. Keel, Casey and Binky had stayed behind with Whitman to be of assistance with the survivors of the explosion.

They all received emailed copies of 'Conspiremouth' which Frank had previously only seem himself.

Even Warren Kitchholm and Michael Schultzmann got a copy. Schultzmann was at his girlfriend's mother's house watching the drama unfold on television.

'Conspiremouth''s lead story began:

What do you see Walt Whitman?

Who are they you salute, and that one after another salute you?

Every living thing on earth, every human being is ready to rise, live and die with through my eyes, through my soul.

So, what Walt Whitman sees everyone can see. Salut au Monde! I salute the world on its cosmic journey.

I shed tears of joy and sadness in its crooked path to leading to wherever it chooses to go. I choose freedom and health and to go where my intuition leads me. I go where I will, so I'll see some of ya on that open road and perhaps we will wave at one another and go our separate ways, but our hearts and minds will be together, going in the same direction even if we are on different routes. Every soul is in me so never worry, guys. And cheers to you all!   Walt

When Frank and Boris arrived back at Boris' hotel room, he realized that he forgotten to call Linda. He was planning to do that and then the bomb had gone off. Oh, shit he thought to himself as they entered the room. He left her a cold, cryptic text message and that would have to do until he could meet her again in person.

"You know, Boris you can really be so insensitive. Where do you think, she went to? I think she's gone forever, Boris. Another broken heart on the Boris train wreck of love." Frank commented.

Boris shrugged. He thought of Chloe.

They sat in Boris' room and watched the sun come up in silence. Frank had deliberately avoided television and media since they had returned from the airport. Butterworth and Brandon rebooked into the same hotel they had been at before. They're was a vibrant but quiet feeling between them that they had come through some sort of battle, survived and now a vague satisfaction was setting in. Yet the exhaustion from the evening's events kept Frank and Boris awake. They both sat wide awake in the hotel room. Boris, had said almost nothing since they had left the airport with the others. Now that was a rare occurrence. A couple of hours passed.

As sunlight poured into the hotel room, they heard a light rap on their room door.

Frank got up. Boris just remained in a large reddish armchair in one corner of the room contemplating the events of the last few days.

Frank opened the door. Casey and Binky stood there looking exhausted but with a glint in their eyes.

"Boris mentioned to me what hotel he was staying at. Is he here?" Casey said, expecting an affirmative answer.

"Come in."

Casey and Binky sat down in the hard-backed chairs along the wall.

"So, where's Walt?" asked Frank.

"We lost him in the shuffle in the parking lot. They have completely evacuated the airport grounds."

"Did they find the bombers, yet?"

"I don't know. But Walt wanted you guys to know one thing."

"And what's that?"

"Embrace the everything, including the evil."

"Very philosophical, but what does that mean?"

"It just means what it says. Message delivered in person. And also, be well guys."

"Well, that's nice. If you see him tell him likewise. I mean, the be well part."

"So, what are you guys up to?"

"We are going to rest on our laurels for awhile and then see about doing this for a living."

"Don't you need a license for that?"

"We'll wing it. I am sure everything will fall into place. That's one thing that we learned from this escapade, right Boris?"

Boris was reflecting quietly in the armchair. He was thinking of Chloe and his loft. He was making plans in his mind for them. He was thinking of getting back to a life of painting and poetry and Chloe. But, in his mind he always encountered the stumbling block of money. This time though he remembered Walt. His brain seemed to have been shaken by the events of the past few days. He thought of a drink. But he would hold off until the afternoon, just so he could absorb what had happened in the recent past. Boris' could not really hear what Frank had just asked him.

"Sorry Frank I just missed what you said."

"I was saying to our guest Casey and Binky that if one persists life has a way of presenting clear paths out of any dilemma."

"That's not what you said, Frank."

"So, you were listening."

"At some sub-conscious level. I just recalled it."

"Very good. So, do you agree?"

"Yes, persist. Brain power. And hard work and all of that. Yes, very good."

Frank turned back to the two guests.

"Casey, I am curious about something. When did you first meet this Mr. Whitman?"

"I don't remember. Maybe a year ago. He was collecting bottles and cans in the park."

"So, why did you believe that he was the actual poet?"

"Do you think that we believe that he is some disembodied soul, like the real guy?"

"Well, you've behaved like you do."

"No, he's probably just some lost poet with a complex."

Frank turned and looked at Boris.

"What?" Boris barked.

"So, my friend how do we explain what has happened to all of the people and what just happened upstairs in this hotel. What happened to us here and who knows who else. We certainly must agree that we have been hit by something strange. And I still aim to find out exactly what it is." Frank said with a raised voice.

"Frank, not today, please. Let's take a break." said Boris.

"Why a break Boris? This is just getting interesting."

"Really. Well, I've had about enough for now."

"That may be. By I am sure that after a good sleep you will be back at the top of your game. And that goes for me as well."

Casey and Binky got up.

"We'll be going." said Casey.

"Don't give up the shop, guys. Oh, and before you leave, what happened to Professor Keel?"

"He has offered to be Whitman's assistant. I guess he got a brain blow as well. And we have a media site to run."

And the pair left.

In the hotel room above Frank and Boris', Butterworth was doing his own interpretations of the events. Brandon had befriended Jess and they were carrying on a conversation about their common experiences and becoming exhausted in the process.

It was nearly 9 A.M when Butterworth broke into Brandon and Jess/Jessica's exchange and offered his conclusions.

"Well, Brandon, Jess, I will tell you what I believe has happened. We have decided amongst ourselves to take a somewhat strange occurrence and make it into a catalyst for change. The blow that happened to me was just an opportunity and nothing more. Professor Keel decided to go his own way, being a more conventional sort, I have chosen of course to not abandon one of the dearest people to have entered my life, Brandon. And I want to put out a stronger message to the world. Who is Whitman really? Well, I don't care. He will carry on in his staid manner, being the compassionate soul that he is, wherever he is, and strange to say whenever he is. I must call those two little amateur detectives and tell them. What are their names again?"

"Frank and Boris." said Brandon.

"Of course, Boris the imbiber, but he certainly can weave a good tale. And this Frank, what's his story? Jess, you're his brother. Or should I say sister. Which is it?" Butterworth said with measured respect.

"Sister" answered Jess/Jessica in a similar tone.

"Jess, was Frank always so curious?"

"No. Well I haven't seen or talked to him in years. I mean before this week."

"But you say he never had much curiosity as a child. Forensics, taking things apart. Secret codes. Detective novels. That type of thing."

"No, just a regular guy. Quiet. He got married. That was a surprise. Then he got divorced.

And that was a surprise. Then I stopped talking with him."

"Well, the path that our brain takes us on is not always premeditated."

Brandon chimed in.

"Maddi, maybe we should get Frank and Boris up here. I would like to say goodbye to Boris before we leave and knowing him, he may skip out of here to go drinking without stopping by."

"Yes, well I want to have a word with Frank as well. Let's check on the airport situation."

With that Butterworth switched on the television. After a few moments he found some news on the bombings. The CBC was reporting that only one person had died and several dozen had suffered varying injuries. The name of the person who had died was not being released pending notification of family. And they had arrested two people and were looking for two others in connection with the tragic event. The CBC reported that the motivation behind the attack was unknown.

Boris was just falling asleep when the phone in his room rang. It was Brandon asking him and Frank to come up to the room for a farewell chat. Boris was reluctant to go, being fatigued, but thought better of it and after agreeing to come up, hung up the phone and yelled out to Frank, who was in the shower.

They both got dressed and went up to Butterworth's room.

Frank was happy to see Jess again, though their relationship was still somewhat cold.

Boris was happy to see Brandon and Maddi had some questions for Frank.

"Frank, what is your conclusion for all of this?"

"Professor, I..."

Here Butterworth interrupted him.

"Call me, Maddi."

"Okay, Maddi. I am certain only of two things here. One is that these bombers take their poetry seriously and two, this Whitman figure has brilliantly portrayed the actual poet, so he must have had some acting background. As for the blows to the head that we all received. I believe that those were all necessary to perpetuate the ruse. But they did have the ultimate effect of motivating us all. They were in essence positive in intention, but a little misdirected perhaps."

"Astonishing, Frank."

"Maddi, I haven't the answer to why we were the ones targeted. Or why some people below the border got it too."

"You know Whitman was a mysterious figure, Frank. Not just because of the probability of his being gay, but also for the fact that he never fully took any strong literary or political positions. Even on slavery of all things. Simply amazing that such a seemingly warm and compassionate man could not step out and be counted."

"Yes, but Maddi you are forgetting that he was much too busy listening to the grass grow to be interested in worldly affairs. All things will work out for the best, provided that we continue to pursue the truth or something to that effect anyhow. That's what he said anyhow."

Maddi chuckled.

Boris was roused by this.

383

"And where do we look for that truth that will free us from this strange affair Frank."

As he said this he smiled at Brandon and then eyed a half bottle of scotch that was on the table.

"Boris, we have to be satisfied with increments of reality. That I'm beginning to see is the crux of this work. Is that not true, Maddi?" said Frank.

"Well, a little humility is always appreciated. And I must say in this day and age there is an almost complete lack of it in my world." Butterworth replied.

"One more thing, Professor. I have this manifesto and these papers."

Frank pulled out the set of papers that he had found at the scene where Michael Schultzmann had been assaulted and handed them to Butterworth.

"Perhaps you may want to examine them. I am sure that they were written by this Whitman impersonator."

Butterworth scanned the papers quickly.

"Well Frank, I thought you being the detective, you might want to find out who this guy really is."

"I have found out. He is Walt Whitman. That is my conclusion. Now it is up to you to say to the world what all of this means."

"Astounding. So, that's it, no alias', no check on escaped mental patients."

"No, this man is of no harm to anyone. That is my conclusion. Let him be."

Brandon broke in.

"Well, my friends, hasn't this been fun anyway. We all have taken away something of value, haven't we?"

"Brandi is right. Let us all keep in touch" Butterworth added.

After a few moments Frank, Boris and Jess/Jessica left the room.

They all returned to Boris room. Jess/Jessica was pleased that they were beginning to warm up to his brother. Boris was refereeing a battle between a drink and sleep in his head. Frank wondered if Professor Keel was doing okay.

Frank's phone rang. It was Michael Schultzmann. Michael's girlfriend Meg was pregnant and he just had just found out. That was nice thought Frank. He told Michael that everyone was okay, even Whitman and that what still needed to be done could be done by the authorities.

Next Chloe called for Boris. She was coming over. Boris had apparently gotten over his fatigue.

Jess/Jessica said that he had to go to work and left.

Frank switched on the news. It was nearly noon.

In a related story a survivor of the bombing at the airport, who had been hospitalized with a coma, has apparently fled the care of the Montreal City Hospital. Frida S. Wharton was seen in the company of two well-built men exiting the hospital. She was described as being of moderate height and weight with blond hair. She was then allegedly seen at a pawn shop near the hospital carrying a guitar. She has been known to propagate the end of the world and can be identified by her offering people free rides to heaven.

385

And this just in. The man who died in the tragedy was Theodor Boone, a rogue scientist who had been discredited by the scientific community. He had been employed at a particle collider site in Europe before being dismissed. He appeared to have had some obsessions regarding theories that would explain everything about everything. He had not been heard from for five years. It is suspected that he could have been one of the perpetrators of the explosion.

Frank switched the channels.

It would seem that the movies of the 1920s are making a moderate comeback on the internet. Producers are adding new and interesting soundtracks to films such as "Metropolis" and re-releasing them. Chicago film critic, Grant Dimietro, who since his release from the hospital after suffering an assault, has decided to champion the films of the twenties, particularly those from Germany. He was quoted as saying that many of the ideas expressed in them mirror exactly what is happening in America today.

Frank switched it off. It seemed to be provoking one of his dizzy spells. He closed his eyes and fell into a fitful sleep. He dreamt of the man he had left behind at the hospital in Toronto, Jack White. He was running madly across the surface of some ocean toward him. On his shoulders were various birds and a monkey. Jack White looked cheerful as he got closer to Frank and then he evaporated into a mist.

The phone rang waking Frank out of his dream. He answered it as if still in his dream. It was Warren Kitchholm. He sleepily exchanged a few words with Kitchholm.

Boris who had been by the window looking down at the foggy morning sky of the city piped up.

"Who is it, Frank?"

"Kitchholm."

"Give me the phone."

After Frank and Warren Kitchholm had exchanged a few more words, Frank passed the phone to Boris.

"Listen, Kitchholm I got that quote that we were trying to remember at the coffee shop a few days ago. I going to text it to you now."

After Frank had taken back the phone and completed the call he turned to Boris.

"And what quote was that, 'you are what you do all day' or something like that."

"No, Johann Wolfgang von Goethe."

"Oh, please no more Boris. Have a drink and get some rest. Chloe will be here in a couple of hours."

"My Chloe, what a wonder, now isn't she the coolest. One more call, my friend."

Boris picked up Frank's phone and texted the quote to Kitchholm.

"You're going to have to get a new phone Boris. As my working partner I insist on it."

"I will, Frank I will."

And with that Boris collapsed on the bed his flask protruding from his jacket. He mumbled something about Chloe to the air and fell into an abyss.

In a hospital bed, across town, Warren Kitchholm read the text he had just received from Boris.

It read:

"The soul that sees beauty may sometimes walk alone."

Frank sat in the hotel room as Boris slumbered and knew that more Whitmans were out there to be encountered. He felt uneasy about that proposition, perhaps even a little madness around it. But beauty sometimes contains madness he thought. How could he explain all this to Jess/Jessica or Chloe and Boris? No, he would keep it to himself, until he was certain of things.

Frank drifted back to sleep and didn't hear Chloe knock moments later. She entered the room, saw Boris passed out on the bed and Frank slumped in an armchair.

She sat down beside Boris on the bed and caressed his head.

A couple of weeks later Jessica and I moved in together. I keep to my affairs and as she does with hers. We may be just good friends who understand the never-ending storylines of people's lives or we may become lovers for awhile. I still have not decided what it is my life needs. All I know is that I must keep an eye and an ear out for any intuitive voice that comes to me regarding affairs that deflect from the robotic world that we are moving into. Meanwhile I will continue to record these events as best I can and try and not despair. Having Jessica around certainly does help. And I still really appreciate a good cup of coffee.

POSTSCRIPT

EXCERPTS FROM FRANK LEE'S NOTEBOOK:

STILL DON'T KNOW WHO REALLY WROTE THAT MANIFESTO,

BUTTERWORTH? TOO MUCH INTEGRITY – MAYBE BRANDON

MUST GET A SUBSCRIPTION TO THE CONSPIREMOUTH –

HAVEN'T DRANK IN ALMOST A WEEK. – I WONDER IF THE COPS

WILL TIE UP THEODOR WITH THE KILLING OF THE GUY IN THIS

HOTEL – THE CURIOUS GUY AT L'HOTEL FISH POND? – DON'T

FORGET TO CALL JESS